JILLIAN BONDARCHUK

THE OATH

THE GREY TOWER CHRONICLES

Hardcover ISBN: 9780578387574
Paperback ISBN: 9780578388687

Edited by:
Patience Voight

Cover art by:
MERWILD
and
Franzi Haase
www.coverdungeonrabbit.com
@coverdungeonrabbit

Formatting by:
Qamar Saleem

The Grey Tower Chronicles

Reading Order

The Shield and the Thistle

The Oath

For Roman and Cannon

There is nothing I wouldn't do for you.

TABLE OF CONTENTS

It is not in the stars to hold our destiny
but in ourselves.

-William Shakespeare

PROLOGUE

MALCOLM
Winter 1658

"Conscience doth make cowards of us all."
-William Shakespeare, Hamlet

In the library of Ghlas Thùr, Malcolm, the laird of Clan MacKinnon, leaned his weight against the mantle and watched a bloody handkerchief burn. Bit by bit, the crackling flames greedily devoured the damp fabric until the weave glowed a brilliant yellow, and within moments reduced it to nothing but ash. Its ghost danced madly in the heat before a chilled draft plucked it from the embers and swept it up the flue.

Please let my brother survive, he prayed and rubbed his thumb over his heart. His fingers tangled in his long, raven-black hair, which lay uncharacteristically wild down his back and over his chest. Malcolm scowled at the flames.

His hair wasn't the only part of him that was out of sorts.

The oath he had sworn to the witch Vanora rumbled like a living, breathing thing just under his sternum. It brushed against his insides, as though it were trying to carve out a home for itself, and caused Malcolm to roll his shoulders when a shiver raced down his spine. The magic he'd witnessed her perform in the bailey only an hour ago planted dread into his thoughts, and his agreement with her now felt more like a curse than the salvation he had hoped for.

Her promise, full of hope and certainty, had overshadowed the fact that she was a witch. He should have known there would be more to his promise than just marriage, for she had neglected to tell him she'd cursed him as well. She had not told him that his oath would feel… alive.

She had not told him his body would no longer be his alone.

Malcolm roughly shoved away from the glow of the fire and traversed the darkened hallways up to the blue room on the third level of the keep. There, he found Maeve knelt beside his brother's sleeping form on the bed. She looked tired, her shoulders drooped as though she held up the weight of the world. Her long blonde curls rested lank and limp down her back. Wringing a cloth over a basin of steaming water, she turned red, swollen eyes his way before she returned to her task.

"Dinnae cry, lass," Malcolm murmured and settled a comforting hand on her shoulder a moment before he lowered his weary bones into the chair by her side. "Next time he wakes—God willing—Colin will be with his wife once again. Ye ken there's no place he'd rather be, so no more tears for him, aye?"

The handmaid nodded in mournful agreement, dashed away the tears that soaked her cheeks, and bit down on her lower lip. In silence, she resumed the cleansing of his brother with scented water until not a speck of blood or fleck of dirt could be seen upon his unnaturally pale skin. The attention she granted the sleeping warrior meant more to Malcolm than a chest of gold, and he had to blink rapidly to keep his own emotions in check. When she'd finished her task, Maeve sniffed delicately before she dipped a curtsy and slipped out of the room to leave him with his thoughts.

Once alone, Malcolm slid out of the chair, knelt beside the bed, and arranged his brother's heavy, limp arms in a more comfortable repose. With Colin's cool, battle-scarred hand clasped between his own, he marveled at the transformation; at all the smooth, healthy skin on his brother's abdomen. The wounds that marred Colin's belly just an hour ago no longer festered with the stink of imminent death. Instead, Malcolm traced the white and pink skin of what looked like year-old scars. Colin's fingers, previously black and decayed from the frozen river's icy grip, were once again a more natural shade.

Malcolm shuddered when he thought of the raw power the witch had wielded to make his brother whole again. He never imagined there were beings capable of such abilities walking the earth alongside ordinary men.

When Colin had summoned Vanora, Malcolm had expected a crone with a hunched back and warts on her face. He had *not* expected a beautiful woman, seemingly normal despite her pale, grey-rimmed irises nor the way they seemed to burrow into his soul like a worm in the dirt. He would never forget the sound of her ethereal voice echoing off the walls while she sang her magic into the bailey. He would never forget the deafening crack of the stone limbs of the oak tree as they broke, or Vanora's last act on earth as she gave her life for Colin's.

The witch had failed to prepare him for that, as well.

A shiver rippled up either side of his ribs when his oath, a living thing, brushed against his insides as it settled, its presence now a constant reminder of what his future held. Of *whom* his future held.

It scared him, this beast that resided within his body. He knew it was a small thing. How could it not be when it fit within the cage of his ribs? But it did not *feel* small. It felt like a mountain, imposing but quiet, that harnessed the inevitable strength of rushing water from its peak. Now, it coiled and slumbered, content to stay within the confines of Malcolm's skin. He couldn't help but fear what would happen if it ever tired of being a prisoner. He tried not to think of the damage something made of magic, teeth, and talons would be capable of.

Malcolm looked at Colin's profile and half expected his brother to look back at him with an arched brow and say, *I'm afraid o' no beast, brother, and ye shouldnae be either.*

But he didn't. There was only the unnatural stillness, the shallow rise and fall of his bare chest, and the faint pulse on his neck. Malcolm's throat grew thick when he realized that's all he would ever see. No more smiles. No more teasing. He'd doomed the one constant presence in his life to sleep the centuries away with no guarantee he would awaken. The finality of it wrenched at his heart.

"Well, brother," Malcolm breathed, his voice hollow in the near-silent chamber, "beast or no', seems I have a bride to collect come the spring."

CHAPTER ONE

MALCOLM

"Cowards die many times before their deaths;
The valiant never taste of death but once."
-William Shakespeare, Julius Caesar

"The marsh violets have budded, my laird."

Malcolm ground his teeth and tried in vain to ignore his guard and focus on the open book in his lap. The late morning sunlight streamed into the library through the wall of mullioned windows and splashed rectangles of gold on the polished wood floor and shaggy hides.

From his chair, he could see the southern hills beyond, painted in the bright brown-greens of spring with new leaf buds. He had days—*days*—until he had to claim his uninformed bride. Each passing second was like a noose cinching tighter around his neck, suffocating him.

The creature that coiled within the cage of his ribs had grown restless of late, urging him to journey east, the compulsion too strong to simply ignore. Since he had sworn the blood oath months ago, Malcolm had prowled the halls of Ghlas Thùr, and fought an internal battle with himself and his decisions.

Never once in his thirty-one years of life had he ever felt so conflicted. One part of his body and mind demanded that he leave *now*, while the other stood firm in its stubbornness.

Malcolm ground his teeth. He'd leave when he was good and ready. Not a moment before.

The winter season, which had lasted weeks longer than the previous years, had taken its time releasing its frozen grasp on the land. But finally, and to his everlasting dismay, the snow had melted and drenched the soil to reveal the plant that would grow the dreaded purple bloom sealing his fate: claim his witch-bride, or die. He could feel the ultimatum in his veins, the steady pulse in every beat of his heart. It kept him up at night, haunted him through the long days, and left him cross and short-tempered.

"My laird?" Farlan cleared his throat as though unsure if he should repeat himself.

Malcolm snapped the book shut with a thump and stood from his chair by the fire. He bit back an angry retort and strode toward the large spread of windows, stopping a handsbreadth away.

Tis no' Farlan's fault I am in this predicament, he reminded himself. Malcolm did not like being cornered. Even if that corner was of his own making, he could not help but fight against the oath's pull until he had no other option.

"I'll leave in the morn," Malcolm said tonelessly as he leaned against the sill and pressed his forehead to the cool glass with a heavy sigh, his breath fogging his view momentarily.

His focus drifted along the horizon to the east. She was *there*. He could feel her in the marrow of his bones, as though his body had become a dowsing rod and she was the water it sought. Always searching, forever drawn like a moth to a flame.

Until a month ago, he had sensed her in the far reaches of the north. But, one morning he awoke and realized she had ventured closer. Every day for over two weeks she grew nearer and the creature beneath his ribs began to thrum with something close to excitement. A yearning. It had nearly driven him mad with the need to go find her.

He had not felt her wander again for over a week.

Farlan stepped farther into the room. "I would claim the honor to escort ye."

Malcolm tore his gaze from the window and met Farlan's steadfast blue eyes. The look on his friend's face was one of worry and determination. A distant cousin and one of his most loyal warriors, Farlan had provided solace to Malcolm in his brother's absence. He was also one of the few not bothered by Malcolm's dark moods of late and continued to show him an abundance of patience and support. But he did not need Farlan's support to collect a bride who knew nothing about him.

Even if she happened to be a witch.

Especially since she happened to be a witch.

"I dinnae need yer protection." Malcolm held his hand up and cut a glare when Farlan opened his mouth to argue his point. "I said *no*. 'Tis no' a situation that needs an audience and will be hard enough to explain on my own."

"But what if she spells ye? We dinnae even ken where she is."

Malcolm turned toward the windows, his back ram-rod straight, hands clasped tight against his spine in agitation. His thumb pressed down on the white, moon-shaped scar on his right palm while Vanora's voice echoed in his mind.

"Laird MacKinnon, as payment for yer brother's life and future happiness, do ye so swear to collect my blooded daughter, Coira, before the marsh violet blooms? Do ye swear to join yer life to hers and keep her safe from all and sundry as long as ye draw breath upon this earth?"

Malcolm frowned at the dread that coiled thick in his stomach. If only he had some proof that his oath had not been sworn in vain. If he could only take a small peek into the future and know his brother had not died… but he feared he would live out the duration of his life without any assurances that his choice had been the right one. That he would live out his whole life bound to a woman he could not love. He felt defeated, as though he was swept up in a current just before a waterfall, the plunge to the rocky ground below inevitable.

"I ken *exactly* where she is," he growled. "And if she forces her witchcraft upon me, then rest assured I will be free from feeling what I do now. That in itself would be a blessing."

Malcolm's eyes snapped open in the darkness of predawn, his pulse thumping erratically in his neck, and sat up to search the corners of his darkened room for some unseen threat. The pull he had been accustomed to feeling these last few months was gentle compared to what it felt like now. It was nearly unbearable and commanded him to *move*, the feeling not unlike tiny bugs that scurried beneath the top layer of his skin. When he swallowed, he imagined he felt the pressure of sharp teeth at his throat.

I delayed too long, he thought, and flung the heavy blankets off his body.

He yanked on his leather breeches and boots, his dirk and short sword already strapped to his belt. He tugged on his shirt and buttoned his vest as he barreled out the door and took the stairs two at a time to the lowest level of the keep. His shoulder bumped almost painfully against the curved stone wall in his haste, but much to his relief, no one was around to witness his blunder in the dark, or when he fell down the last seven steps.

Out in the bailey, the fog was thick and swirled around him as he moved swiftly toward the stable and his black warhorse, Ramsey. Sleepy nickering flowed out of the few stalls, and Malcolm paused when he woke the stable boy, sleeping in a pile of hay. The boy jumped to attention in the darkness and stuttered an apology when he realized who was with him.

"Run to the kitchen, lad, and bring me enough food for several days. Be quick about it," Malcolm snapped and coaxed an irritated Ramsay out of his stall.

The boy nearly fell over himself as he ran to do his laird's bidding and nearly slammed into the torso of one of the night guards who'd come to investigate.

"Do we ride with ye, my laird?" the guard asked.

It was unlike Malcolm to be up at this hour, however, their laird's task was common knowledge to most. Emotions had been high for weeks with the impending arrival of the witch's daughter. The castle residents were just as nervous and apprehensive as he was.

"No. And dinnae think to follow. Yer presence willnae be well received," he warned as he slung a thick wool pad over Ramsay's back and secured it with a length of leather strapping. The bridle came next, settling over his black ears and the bridge of his long, velvety face. Malcolm delayed just long enough to grab some withered apples from a bucket and a bag of grain before heaving himself upon the warhorse's back.

The thrumming in his chest grew more urgent, and with it, the feeling of anxiety intensified. He needed to go. *Now.*

Tapping Ramsay's ribs with his heels, Malcolm fisted the reins and the long black mane tightly when they surged forward, his mount sensing his master's desperation. With barely enough time to duck beneath the frame of the stable door before he lost his head, Malcolm held on with his knees as they tore into the bailey. Several voices raised in alarm, and a particular one snapped through the commotion.

"Wait!" the stable boy shouted. Waving a white sack in his skinny arms, the boy threw it ahead, his aim true.

Catching it neatly in the air, Malcolm nodded a quick thanks to the boy before horse and rider bolted through the gates in a spray of sand and mud and disappeared through the fog-covered field.

A mile or so from the keep, the pressure on his chest lightened enough that he allowed Ramsay to slow from his run and gave the beast a firm pat on his neck. They trotted through the woods toward the sleeping village and the crossroads before heading east through the shallow valley.

The morning sky changed slowly as the fog was forced down to the ground, obscuring the land with a dreamlike appearance. The periwinkle twilight morphed into a bright pink along the horizon before the blinding sun rose over the hills. By the time he lost sight of the village, the last of the fog had burned away and revealed bright green grasses and the spring wildflowers that splashed the fields in purple, blue, and white.

There was not another season Malcolm looked forward to more than spring. He loathed the frigid temperatures of winter and was often found huddled in front of a fire during the day and lingering longer in his bed in the mornings. He dreaded the bite of the chilly floor on his bare feet; hated it when the cold crept into his bones so deeply no amount of hot tea could chase it away.

On the day the first touch of frost crisped the fallen leaves of autumn, he would begin yearning for spring… at least until he had made that blasted blood vow. Although he didn't regret his oath, and would have paid a far greater price to secure his brother's happiness, he wouldn't have been upset in the least if the marsh violets had stayed covered by a few feet of snow for a year or two longer.

As it was, spring was late to arrive and had given him the small reprieve of an extra month. He knew it would make the planting time shorter for the farmers, and he felt guilty for rejoicing, but he was still grateful for the gift of a delay.

While Ramsey followed the rutted road, his gait now lumbered and relaxed as the sun shone down on them both with radiant warmth, he found himself thinking of his letter to Laird Bothan. The one that had broken Malcolm's tentative betrothal to his daughter, Edeen.

He had been invited by Laird Bothan to spend the week at the Chattan castle in hopes of making a marriage alliance through Malcolm and his daughter. Malcolm and his men spent five days in the castle while he courted her. A bonnie lass of sixteen, Edeen had looked at him coyly from under dark lashes and had brushed her arm against his whenever she had the chance. He found himself amused at first, even interested, but whenever he tested her to see if they were an intellectual match, she would become flustered and steer the conversation to the dull, mundane subjects of courtly fashion.

By the end of the fourth day, bored to death of listening to her talk about thread-weight, velvet, and brocade, he felt no attraction between them. At least not on his end. He had verbally agreed to the match with the hope that he would develop a lasting affection toward her once they were married, but he could now admit that it was a lie he had told himself. Malcolm had no doubt Edeen would find a younger, more suitable husband among the Scottish nobility.

His only saving grace was that a more formal agreement had never been signed to Laird Bothan, and because of that, he would not make an enemy of his neighbor. Throughout history, broken betrothal agreements had ignited clan wars that resulted in the loss of many lives, or in some cases, stoked grudges that lasted decades and bled into the next generation. Because of this very real possibility, Malcolm had sent a purse of silver to lighten the blow, as well as renewed sentiments of a respectful alliance between their two clans.

The response he had received, however, had been far less than courteous. There would be no clan war, but Malcolm would need to tread carefully when he next saw Clan Chattan's laird.

If he was being honest with himself, he had felt the strangest sense of relief when Vanora offered him an alternative, and he'd practically jumped at the opportunity. If he was going to be in a loveless marriage, then let his misery not be in vain. His brother's future was worth it, and at least one of them would be happy, God willing. And so, a fortnight after he had agreed to marry Edeen, he swore a blood oath to the witch that was more binding than any signature on parchment.

Malcolm alternated between riding and walking slowly alongside his horse until the sun touched the horizon, and he decided to make camp. That's when he wished he had better prepared himself for the journey. When he dumped out the contents of the sack the stable lad had filled for him, he soundly cursed his bad luck. Besides the half-stale loaf of bread that he devoured around noon, the sack was filled with potatoes, wilted leeks, and turnips. Why the boy thought Malcolm could do without a pot to boil them, he had no idea, and ended up laughing himself to tears at the absurdity of his situation.

Hungry and miserable, Malcolm huddled on Ramsey's saddle pad and glared into the smoky peat fire that did little to warm his bones, and prayed to God nothing else would go wrong.

With the rise of the sun, Malcolm awoke to the same rush in his blood and incessant tug at his chest. Instead of subsiding like it had the day before when he'd raced Ramsey away from the keep, the feeling only intensified to a fever pitch of dread and doom with each mile. Now, as he leaned over Ramsey's sweat-slick neck and demanded the breakneck pace along what he assumed was a well-traveled deer path through a grove of saplings, he was beginning to panic. He was close, so close he could smell the smoke of a cook-fire and see a clearing up ahead.

To his horror, his throat had begun to tighten, and he gasped for breath. His lungs screamed for relief as the young trees whipped at his face with their budding leaves. He cursed the phantom beast that thrashed angrily in his chest as he pushed Ramsey to the limit despite the darkness closing in on his vision. Wrestling with his mind for consciousness, Malcolm felt his body begin to tilt off his mount and the perception of weightlessness was abruptly interrupted when he landed hard on the ground.

White-hot pain bloomed along his right side and the back of his head. The agony of the impact shoved against the darkness for only a moment before his throat closed fully and the creature in his chest sank its talons in deep.

The shadows of oblivion descended swiftly.

CHAPTER TWO

COIRA

Something was coming. I could hear it whispering with the wind. It had felt like a dull ache in my bones since I arrived at my mother's empty cottage a little over a week ago. When it would turn up, I hadn't the faintest idea. I only knew that it would. So, I'd been waiting.

Strolling barefoot out of the cottage, I pressed my toes into the damp earth and breathed the morning air deep into my lungs as I made my way to the garden. It was good to be home.

I had spent the last year with relatives near Inverness teaching the next generation the songs of the earth, the elements, and all living things. I had taught them how to bind wounds and aid in the birthing of babies. I had guided them on how to sing water from the earth when they were thirsty and how to call up a fog when they needed to hide. It was a responsibility I took seriously and cautioned them to keep the secrecy. What we Druid women could do was *never* to be revealed. Our knowledge of the earth, wind, and water had to be defended at all costs, even at the cost of our lives.

My face was proof enough of the consequences if they failed.

The day I had arrived, their fear-filled eyes had laid riveted on the side of my face and neck, and they'd listened without interruption when I told them the story of how my face had become ruined. I had let them look their fill, and even though it had brought a fine layer of sweat to the surface of my skin, I relived that awful day in great detail for them. I had told them, if only so my story might save their lives.

I had admitted what I had done and shared whom I had lost. I told them I was lucky I'd escaped with my life and that there were still days I wished I hadn't. I had told them of the terrible things that could happen to them if they allowed anyone not of Druid descent to see what they were capable of. That they should trust *no one* outside our community and promised they would suffer my fate and worse if they slipped and gave in to their base nature.

I could only hope they took my threats seriously.

When the snow had begun to melt, and the roads became passable once again, I'd bid the young girls and women under my tutelage a tearful goodbye, bought a nag, and made the long two-week journey south alone. It had been a lonely campaign as I kept mostly to the forests and the fields instead of traversing the roads where a lone woman could find herself in danger. Crossing icy streams and a few extra days of travel was worth the inconvenience if it meant I would keep my life and virtue.

I was not entirely surprised to find the cottage I shared with my mother empty when I'd arrived nearly a fortnight past. My mother was a well-known midwife and was frequently called away. Sometimes she was gone for a week, a month at most. Judging by the garden, still dormant from autumn's harvest, and the powdery film of dust that covered everything within the cottage, I guessed she'd been gone a while. There hadn't even been much in the way of food besides a partially moldy sack of flour and late winter's apples.

With all the work that needed to be done since I had arrived, I had expended more energy than I'd ingested, and had begun to notice a difference in the way my homespun frock hung on my body.

I was beginning to starve, and with little coin, I needed to take matters into my own hands. Literally. Mother would disapprove, of course. She would tell me that I should let nature work at its own pace. But I didn't have the luxury of waiting six weeks or more for my garden to mature with any sort of yield. Besides, what my mother didn't know wouldn't hurt her, and I needed to eat.

My stomach cramped and squealed for mercy as I squatted in the freshly turned dirt and burrowed my fingers into the damp soil. I whispered a few lyrical words and directed my energy downwards. The tiny creatures that lived under the surface jolted awake and made the dark soil writhe beneath my palms. I lowered my brows in concentration and focused on the sunlight that warmed my back, projecting it beneath me in pulsing waves. My lips moved with hushed, melodic whispers over the ground as the young seedlings I had planted grew lush, their leaves unfurling, fat and wide to better catch the sun's rays. I pushed my hunger aside and gave them a little more of my energy. After such a long winter, they needed all the help they could get before the rains descended upon Scotland.

"That should do ye." Standing, I brushed the dirt off my skirts and tucked a loose, wavy lock of wheat-pale hair behind my ear.

My stomach rumbled again, a reminder that I had brought too few supplies with me from Inverness, and the scant reserves in the cottage were long gone. Even the snares I had set yesterday were empty this morning. I swallowed the saliva that gathered in my mouth as I thought of fresh meat and huffed a breath. If my snares came up fruitless another day, I'd be forced to journey to the nearest town, a half day's walk away. I may be able to coax the plants to grow, but I couldn't force them to bear fruit.

I tried my best to ignore the strange, persistent unease that lay under my breast and ambled toward the little cottage I had lived in for most of my life.

Tucked firmly at the base of a steep hill, the back wall pressed into the sloped earth to became one with the terrain. Thick mosses covered the thatched roof as well as the stone walls. Bushy ferns hugged close to the foundation, and two tall, drooping pines towered above it on either side. I imagined it looked eerie to an outsider but to me it looked like home, quiet and peaceful. With no one around for miles, it allowed my mother and I to be ourselves. Somewhat.

The daughters descended of the Druid Mug Ruith must *always* assume they were being watched. I was twelve when I'd learned that hard lesson and was reminded of that fact for the last twelve years.

Every time I smiled too wide, and when I dressed each morning, I felt the pull of my skin.

When people talked to me, they didn't always look into my eyes. But I didn't begrudge them. The scars that covered nearly half my body were impossible to ignore. They were a constant reminder to stay guarded and careful. Sadly, it wasn't always that simple. There was always the pull and lure of magic, a seductive and ingrained birthright that was hard to ignore when emotions ran high.

The unexpected pounding of hooves had my hackles rising and I spun toward the sound, my short-bladed dagger already thrust in the air before me. A great black stallion lunged down the narrow path and into the cottage's clearing, no rider upon his back.

"Easy, easy!" I cried as I tucked the dagger away, grabbed the reins, and put a steady hand on the beast's lathered chest.

White froth foamed on the beast's lips and painted his neck. Eyes wild, he tossed his head with agitation as he pawed the ground, and I could feel his strong heartbeat pounding under my fingertips. Words of safety and calm flowed from my mouth as I peered up at the saddle pad and the near-empty sacks tied upon it.

Where is yer master? I wondered.

I looked curiously toward the path leading through the woods and noticed the strange ache I had felt for the last week begin to recede and weaken.

Apprehension pressed down as I realized what I had been feeling was *magic*—and it was dying. Whoever had been on that horse was bound to me… somehow.

"*No*," I breathed, my flesh pebbling with dread as I raced as fast as I could down the path.

The magic of binding souls was old and forbidden. The last time it had been attempted was over four decades ago. But I remembered the stories and the warnings that came with them.

The chill air pulled at my hair as I pushed my exhausted legs faster, heedless of the sharp roots and stones that stabbed at the soft spots of my bare feet as I ran. That dull ache continued to fade, now a fraction of what it was just minutes ago, and panic began to grip me as I feared what it meant.

Then I saw him, sprawled face down in the bracken as I rounded a bend. His arm was twisted at an unnatural angle, and his coal-black hair was a tangled and knotted mess. Falling to my knees beside him, I pulled gently at his considerable weight to get him on his back, mindful of his arm, and winced at the blood that covered his face. Bits of leaves and loose moss stuck to his skin, obscuring his features.

He was so still, his body so loose.

"Please, dinnae be dead," I pleaded.

A snap of energy zapped my hand when I touched his unshaven cheek, and I gasped when his chest expanded with a breath, the sound wet and unhealthy. He let out a pained moan.

Pushing my relief to the side, I speared my fingers through his hair and gently probed his skull, feeling tenderly along his scalp for the source of all the blood, and winced at what I found. Gritting my teeth, I quickly split his thick wool vest with my dagger, sending buttons flying, and yanked up his white shirt. Already, angry red and purple patches covered his right side and wrapped around his ribcage. A quick glance at the ground told that he had probably fallen from his horse right onto the rocks that peeked above the earth's soil and had rolled the rest of the way. With my Druid's sight I could see he had at least two broken ribs, maybe more, and from the sound of his breathing, his lung had been damaged as well. His shoulder had completely dislocated itself and a few of his fingers were bent at odd angles.

A pool of blood slowly spread from under his head and soaked his knotted hair and the ground below. Clenching my jaw, I hardened my resolve and looked around for a tree big enough to save his life, cursing the little saplings that surrounded us. I needed something *big* to undo this kind of damage.

"Just hold on a little while longer," I told the unconscious man.

I quickly scored my thumb with my knife and swiped my blood on the back of his hand as I muttered the Druid word for *sleep,* my voice changing as I used the ancient language. Squatting behind his head, I slid my arms under his body to lift him, wrapped them around him, and wove my fingers together over his chest.

"*Iosa Crìosd,* yer a heavy bastard," I grunted, my legs straining.

Slowly, and with small, lurching backward steps, I tugged his considerable weight off the path toward an old yew tree. His long, booted legs caught on the saplings that pulled at our clothes and plucked my hair further out of its braid. His dark head lolled from one side to the other as I dragged him along and painted the bodice of my brown homespun dress dark with his blood. I stumbled twice on the way to the destined tree, apologizing each time my knees jabbed him in the back, and finally slumped against the trunk.

His head rested against my left shoulder and his forehead met my cheek as I settled him within the cradle of my thighs. His weight nearly crushed me against the trunk of the old yew; the roots dug into the back of my thighs. Drained and exhausted from days without proper nourishment, I heaved in deep gulps of air and fought to calm my nerves. I needed my voice steady enough to form the words to save his life. Even now I felt him slipping, the blood loss too great to recover on his own, his wounds too terrible to heal without my magic. The strange bond I shared with him was as thin as a spider's thread, threatening to snap at any moment. Clutching him close to me, with one hand splayed against his bare chest, I gripped the roots of the tree with the other, closed my eyes, and relinquished my hold on my magic.

The words came easily as I called upon the essence of the yew, my voice becoming ethereal in the way only the descendants of the ancient Druids could sound. Losing myself to the song, I reveled in the immense power that rushed through my veins, and into the warm body I cuddled close to me.

I felt his shoulder pop back into place just as the branches of the yew began to rain down around us. I felt his ribs snap back together with a crunch beneath my hand.

The bond between us strengthened and grew with every passing moment, brilliant and gold in my mind's eye while I chanted life back into his body. With my grip on the root, I could feel the energy begin to wane, the transfer nearly complete. My throat raw and my tongue dry, the last words of my song escaped on a whisper, and I severed the connection with the yew.

Lightheaded, I blinked sluggishly at the stone branches on the forest floor around us. They sparkled faintly in the sunlight, reminding me I would need to come back and break them apart later to hide the evidence of magic.

Much later.

Exhausted and weak, I stared at the sight of the dark haired stranger reclined between my legs, the heavy weight of him pinning me against the now stone trunk of the yew. I listened to the healthy, rhythmic rise and fall of his chest, and it wasn't long before I was lulled into a deep sleep.

The thump of heavily shod hooves in the underbrush pulled me from my slumber and my lashes fluttered open to reveal the black horse gently nosing his master's chest.

"Good horse," I croaked, my throat raw. "I have need o' ye."

It took a few tries, but the beast finally laid down for me and, with great effort, I was able to drape his master's heavy body across its back, allowing me to lead the way to the cottage instead of hefting his large frame there myself. I could have woken him, but I wasn't ready to face him just yet. It was best that he stayed sleeping until I was prepared to have the conversation of *why* he was here.

I left him on a thin pallet of blankets in front of the small hearth fire in the cottage and trudged back to the tree with an old hammer. Beating it with the remaining strength I had, I broke it up until it no longer resembled what it once was. Exhausted, I checked my traps one last time and jumped for joy at the single large hare in the last snare. I hugged the fluffy body against my chest in teary relief. I would not go to bed hungry again after all.

Back at the cottage, I rummaged through my guest's supplies and found a few wrinkled potatoes, carrots, and a bulbous turnip. Not a feast, but it was more than I had. Coupled with the few remaining winter onions from the cellar and the hare, they would make a nice stew. Just the thought of the hot, tender meal had me salivating with anticipation and my stomach cramping with displeasure.

With the stranger still safely under the sleeping spell, I stripped out of my filthy gardening dress and bathed with a bucket of cold, peony-scented water before I slipped on my black gown. It was a bit threadbare at the elbows, but it was clean and warm and concealed most of the damaged parts of my body from sight. Self-conscious, I re-braided my hair and tried my best to arrange the heavy mass to hide the scars on my face and neck that my clothing could not.

From across the room, I frowned at my sleeping guest. His face was still covered with dried blood and debris, and I hesitated to clean it off. I've washed men before, the old and the infirm, but the thought of doing so to *this* particular man seemed foreign and more than a little forbidden. Intimate. Berating myself for feeling even the smallest amount of reluctance to give care to someone in need, I knelt at his side and dipped a cloth into a bowl of clean water. I wiped the dirt, grime, and dried blood from his face and slowly revealed his features.

A few day's worth of dark beard rasped against the cloth as I swiped away the bits of leaves and exposed thick, dark lashes and perfectly formed lips. Dense, slightly arched eyebrows hardened his beautiful face, and I found myself wondering what he looked like when he smiled. His body was not well-defined like that of a warrior, but neither was he exceptionally soft or thin. Long of limb, I guessed the top of my head wouldn't even reach his chin. Biting my lower lip, I felt a ripple of nervousness at waking this hulking stranger that shared a mysterious bond with me. I could feel it now: the connection. Like a warm pebble nestled deep in my chest, it was new and comforting, unlike the yearning ache it had been before. Easily ignored but there if I chose to look for it.

Once he was clean, I broke my stare from his handsome face, reopened the small cut on my thumb, and broke the sleeping spell. When his skin flushed with pink, I retreated to the table to chop the vegetables for the stew and left him to wake at his leisure.

The time for answers had come.

CHAPTER THREE

MALCOLM

"Though she be but little, she is fierce!"
-William Shakespeare, A Midsummer Night's Dream

Consciousness came upon Malcolm slowly. Like pulling himself fully clothed and armored out of the loch, the water weighing down his limbs as he fought to get to shore. Merely lifting his heavy eyelids seemed like a feat, and he blinked slowly and curiously at the flames of a cheerful fire in a hearth. A small cauldron steamed above it, its vapor traveling up the flue. He was in a humble home, neither bright with sunlight nor dark and dreary. The stone-stacked walls on either side of the hearth he faced were windowless, damp, and dusted with spongy moss. Shelving lined the wall of either side, the wooden planks bowed with the weight of jars and vials of all shapes and sizes, each stuffed with dried leaves or filled with clear liquids. A loft stretched above him, spanning half of the ground floor on which he lay.

He felt… *good.* Better than he had in weeks, now that blasted creature was mercifully still and no longer a restless yearning inside him. Only the faintest seed of warmth reminded him it was still there.

Shuffling and the steady *thunk, thunk, thunk* as someone chopped vegetables tore his muddled gaze away from the fire. Memories of his slow suffocation and the dangerous gallop over the narrow path in the woods leaped to his mind. Of his fall and the blinding pain that had followed. Malcolm reached across his chest and clutched his shoulder. He squeezed the rounded contour of muscle that had taken the brunt of his weight, and was surprised to find himself hale and whole. He ran his hand over his knotted hair and grimaced when his fingers came away sticky and smeared with the rusty hue of old blood.

Footsteps startled him from where he stretched on the wood floor. He looked to his left just in time to catch a glimpse of bare feet peeking from beneath the hem of a black dress, and watched a woman dump a bowl of vegetables into the boiling pot.

Her pale-blond hair was plaited and cascaded over her right shoulder, hiding her features from him. Much to his regret, she stirred the contents once and returned to her worktable without casting a glance his way. She kept her back to him, her shoulders and spine stiff as though she were anxious at his presence but not frightened enough to keep him in her sight.

She was a slight thing, her limbs long and slender, nearly waifish. Her hair, thick and long, was the color of winter wheat stalks, and Malcolm found himself wondering if it would feel coarse or silken between his fingers.

He watched quietly from his pallet while her capable hands skinned a hare in one quick pull like he had seen his brother do hundreds of times when they were young lads. Malcolm's gaze traced the line of her slender ankle and heel beneath her too-short hem and willed her to turn around so that he may see more of her.

As though she heard his silent prayer, she looked nervously over her left shoulder for the briefest of moments and teased him with an enchanting profile of luscious lips and high cheekbones kissed pink by the sun. It was when their eyes met, and the soft, beastly purr of his oath thrummed in his chest, that a fissure of alarm snaked up his back.

He knew her. *Coira*. There was not a doubt in his mind. Her mother—the witch he had sworn the blood oath to—once had eyes of the same coloring. Irises, so pale-blue that they were nearly white and rimmed with dark grey, hugged her pupils. They rested upon him for only a moment, but it was long enough to pierce his very soul before she turned back to her task at hand.

So, *this* was the mysterious woman he had sworn his life away to protect. The woman he would bring back with him as the Lady of Ghlas Thùr. How she found him, he hadn't the faintest idea, for he thought he had died when the beast in his chest lashed out.

Sitting up, Malcolm rubbed roughly at the scruff on his cheeks and scowled at the way his hair matted to the back of his head. He hesitated to speak, knowing the conversation they must have was not going to be easy.

She surprised him by speaking first.

"I'd like ye to tell me how it is we are bound to one another."

Her voice was soft and steady, smooth as a lazy river, but he did not miss the undertone of command woven within her words. She kept her attention on the table while she labored to separate meat from bone, one slice of her knife at a time.

Malcolm opened and closed his mouth a few times, feeling like a fish out of water and unsure where to begin. He had not expected her to be aware of their connection, let alone make the gentle demand upon him. No one had demanded anything of him in years, not since his father had died, and he was momentarily taken aback by her forwardness.

"Yer mother—"

"My mother," she interrupted, flashing him a suspicious glance over her shoulder. "Where is she?"

At a loss for words, Malcolm rested his elbows on his knees and studied his hands. He rubbed at the dirt and horse-dust that coated his skin and revealed the scar on his palm. He remembered every moment leading up to receiving it, and every moment after. He recalled the tang of fear on the back of his tongue when Vanora had come at him with her blade, and the sharp bite of pain when she had notched his palm. How their hands had lit from within when their blood joined, illuminating their bones.

Malcolm cleared his throat. "She saved the life o' my brother in December with a strange song," he began, unable to look her in the eye when he told her the story of his brother's demise. The loss of Colin's company was still so fresh, Malcolm's heart ached just thinking about how he'd never talk to him again. "She had demanded payment for saving him—a blood oath—from *me*. I swore to yer mother that I would collect ye by the time the marsh violet bloomed and protect ye with my life. I promised her I would bring ye back… as my wife. It was what she demanded o' me to see my brother survive the centuries… and I paid it."

Coira's strange eyes widened in disbelief.

"Wife." The word slipped from her lips, soft and somber before she squared her shoulders and glared daggers at him. "Ye huvnae answered my question. *Where is my mother?*"

Malcolm took a deep breath and met her piercing stare with regret before he spoke, "I'm sorry lass, but she died that night. I swear to ye, I didnae ken it would—" Quicker than he could track, Coira crossed the floor that separated them. Her fingers speared into his hair, her hand grasping the strands at his crown, and she wrenched his head back, pressing her knife to his throat. She loomed behind him, and he could only twist around enough to see a snarl lift her upper lip. Her strange eyes radiated a mixture of rage, sorrow, and accusation.

"Ye killed her? Ye tried her as a witch even after she helped ye?" she spat and yanked back harder on his hair. Her knife dug into the skin under his jaw.

"No! No… she just… died." Malcolm couldn't tear his eyes away from her, at the wildness and intensity. Her ruthlessness both foreign and somehow familiar. The tip of her blade pricked his skin when he swallowed and continued, "I found her leaning against the tree—the tree she used to save my brother. I swear to ye, I didnae ken it would happen. She said she needed two lives and I thought the second one was mine—" She tightened her grip and glared down at him.

"We shall see about that," she hissed, and pressed the tip of her blade into the vulnerable skin just beneath his jawline. The pain was sharp, and he felt a bead of blood slide down and slip beneath the collar of his shirt. Mesmerized, his focus was locked onto her profile as she brought the steel to her mouth and touched it to her tongue. A moment later her mouth softened, and grief replaced the anger that hardened her eyes.

"I'm sorry," Malcolm said again when she released him and turned away.

She covered her face with her hands, heedless of her stained fingers or the dagger, the fight drained out of her.

"'Tis no' yer fault," she grumbled and wiped at her cheeks with her sleeve. "My mother was always brash in her decisions when it came to me. And because o' that, ye're stuck with an ugly wife. Ye should be feelin' sorry for *yerself*. No' me."

She stood then and returned to the table as though she hadn't just threatened to slit his throat. As though she hadn't just tasted *truth* in his blood. Confused by her statement, Malcolm let his attention wander over the lines of her body, over the shiny blonde hair on her head and the graceful way she moved while she worked.

"I dinnae find ye ugly at all," he admitted as he gathered himself to his feet. In fact, everything he could see was appealing and he hadn't even seen her fully yet; which annoyed him more than he cared to admit. He didn't *want* to be attracted to her.

Coira huffed a cynical laugh, and he tore his gaze away from the dramatic dip at her waist when she spun around and faced him straight-on for the first time.

"And now?" Brazenly, she raked back the hair that had been hiding the right side of her face from him. Her eyes blazed with challenge, daring him to repeat himself so she could call him a liar.

Malcolm could only stare in shock at the sight of her newly exposed skin. Of her burn scars. They started at her right temple and spread down part of her cheek, the sharp angle of her jaw, and then her neck before they disappeared beneath the collar of her dress. He could see more mottled skin on the wrist of the hand that held back her hair. He had never seen such damage from a fire, and the beast in his chest twitched with agitation at the sight, mirroring his response.

Malcolm wanted to tell her that her scars didn't matter to him, that they did not ruin what he considered lovely, but kept his mouth shut. Even though it made him feel like a wretch, he did not want her to know of his attraction to her, lest she expect something from him he could not give.

Her bravado quickly faltered with his silence, and she snaked her braid back over her shoulder to curtain the scars on her neck once more. When she turned her back to him, he could see a hint of further scarring low on the back of her neck, the pale skin tight and textured. He found himself wondering just how much of her skin was marred beneath her clothing. Just the small bits he could see must have been an agony to endure.

Unsure of what to say, Malcolm ran his fingers through his filthy hair, the movement reminding him of his fall from Ramsey.

Ramsey!

Malcolm crossed the creaking floorboards in a few strides and flung the door open. He found the beast hobbled and happily grazing a short ways away in a small field beside a scrawny brown horse that looked so old it seemed he had one hoof in the grave. Ramsey's tack was neatly piled just outside the door.

"How did ye find me?" he wondered aloud as he vividly remembered the searing pain that had ripped down his side when he fell. He rubbed his shoulder again, surprised there wasn't even the slightest ache.

"Yer beast scared me half to death, nearly knocking a decade from my life when he tore through the trees. Ye had fallen no too far away," she said with a shrug.

Malcolm touched the back of his head, his hair damp and ropey. He could smell the metallic scent of blood, but as much as he searched, he failed to discover a wound.

"Did ye… did ye heal me with magic?" He didn't know whether to be grateful or horrified at the thought.

"O' course I did. I felt ye dyin'," she said simply and dumped the meat into the cauldron.

Malcolm's brows hiked up in surprise. "*Felt* me dyin'?"

She rolled her eyes. "Did ye think the bond my mother trapped us into only went one way?" She looked at him as though he were a simpleton. No one had ever looked at him in such a way.

"No, I dinnae suppose it would," he admitted, and felt himself rather curious if she had a wee beastie residing inside her as well. Malcolm offered her a small smile as he extended his hand toward her. "Then it seems I owe ye for my life, Coira."

She looked down hesitantly before placing her fingers lightly against his palm. They radiated warmth like an oven on a cold winter's day, the heat both comforting and foreign.

Maybe this arrangement willnae be so awful after all, he thought.

"I ken that this wasnae yer choice, Coira, and I am truly sorry for that… but would ye come back with me?"

She tugged her hand away and crossed her thin arms over her chest. Regarding him with her glacial eyes, she huffed a breath in defeat and rolled her weight onto her left foot.

"I suppose I'll have to if I dinnae want ye droppin' dead at my feet," she grumbled.

"That is… much appreciated," Malcolm groused, and pinched the bridge of his nose at the concept of dying all over again because she might have said no. "Ghlas Thùr is a two-days ride away if we take our time, which I'm sure we'll have to since ye'll want to bring yer belongings. The sooner we leave, the better."

"*Ghlas Thùr.*" She scanned his body from head to toe with suspicion, and her lip turned up slightly when she demanded, "Who are *ye* that we'll be goin' *there?*"

Malcolm frowned and gave her his Christian name. Her delicate, blonde brows popped high a moment before she burst into maniacal laughter, her features looking both pained, mirthful, and disgusted.

"Och, my mother kenned what she was doin', alright. The conniving snake," Coira wheezed and patted her chest with her bloodstained fingers. "A witch parading as the Lady o' Ghlas Thùr! *Iosa Crìosd,* she had brass balls I tell ye, ropin' ye into a blood oath to marry *me.*"

All at once, her laughter grounded to a halt and her grin melted as she looked down at herself with distaste. Shaking her head and mumbling a colorful string of curses, she rummaged through a chest near the door and thrust a length of linen and a cake of juniper-scented soap into his arms.

"The well is near the garden. Clean yerself and then we can eat."

Malcolm stood naked in the fading light and shivered. He had doused himself with bucket after bucket of water and *still* the chill liquid ran pink down his legs.

How badly did I hit my head? he wondered as he scrubbed his hair for a second time. He had to admit that despite the near frigid water, it felt good to be rid of the travel dust.

Eventually the water ran clear, and he looked forlornly at his soiled shirt. Using the last of the soap to rub out as much of the stains as he could, he hung it on a bush to dry and shoved his damp legs back into his leather breeches. Shirtless and barefoot, with his sword belt in hand, Malcolm trudged back to the cottage and the bossy thing within.

Not since his father had died had he been ordered around so much in one day. *And* she had held a knife to his throat. A dark chuckle escaped from his mouth.

That woman is as mad as they come, he decided. Beautiful, but mad. He witnessed her flit from rage, to tears, to laughter in the span of a minute, and it was enough to make his head spin. The sooner they arrived at Ghlas Thùr, where he could put some distance between them, the better, though he doubted its high walls would keep him safe since she would also reside within them.

Without knocking, he pushed through the door just as Coira placed two bowls of stew on the worn table.

"Smells good. I huvnae eaten this day yet," he said as he gingerly sat down in one of the two hand-carved chairs that groaned beneath his weight. Once he was convinced it wasn't going to splinter, he tucked his long legs beneath the table.

"Yer no' plannin' to eat without a shirt, are ye?" she sputtered as she looked everywhere but at his bare chest.

A witch and a nun. I have all the luck, he griped to himself and breathed deeply of the aromatic steam that wafted from his bowl.

"My shirt was dirty and needed a wash. I dinnae have another and I doubt I'd fit in one o' yers," he explained, and dipped his spoon into the stew. "I'm sorry the sight o' my body repulses ye." He almost cracked a smile when she rolled her eyes at him *again* and plopped into the seat opposite of his.

"Ye traveled here with only the clothing ye wore?" she asked skeptically. "Or is yer clan so poor that ye dinnae have another?"

Malcolm's stomach protested with the promise of food, and he prayed for patience as he stared down the wildcat that would be his wife.

"Hardly. The goddamn curse yer mother plagued me with woke me before dawn, threatenin' my life if I had no' left when I did. Damn near killed myself *and* my bloody horse gettin' to ye," he grumbled and plunged his spoon into the steaming stew, too prideful to admit that he *hadn't* gotten to her in time. That his body would be rotting in the woods if it wasn't for her.

Coira tilted her head and studied him while she fiddled with her spoon, her brows drawn low in thought. "What curse? Ye said ye swore a blood oath."

Of all the things that were holy, would she just let him *eat?*

Malcolm gestured to his chest. "There's a creature livin' within me. 'Tis how I found ye." Shrugging, he shook his head and hoped she'd drop the subject. His stomach was practically in knots with hunger.

Mercifully, she didn't ask another question and they ate in silence. He watched her while she quickly shoveled the stew into her mouth like she hadn't eaten in days. Barely blowing the steam away, she took bite after bite, chewed only a few times before swallowing and immediately shoved another spoonful between her lips.

As he observed her, Malcolm began to think her waifish frame wasn't her natural physique, but more a result of starvation. Upon further scrutiny, he judged the bones of her hands, as well as the delicate line of her clavicle, both too prominent. After she took their empty bowls and filled them again, he openly watched her eat.

"Why do ye stare, MacKinnon?" she asked gruffly. Awkwardly, she tugged at her hair to further cover her scars, as though she expected them to claim his attention.

"When was yer last meal?" he blurted.

Embarrassed, Coira's cheeks reddened, and she set her spoon down in her nearly empty bowl. Not able to meet his eyes, she cleared her throat and said, "The day before last."

Three days. He could not imagine the ache she must have felt for the last hour while she prepared the stew. Being subjected to its mouthwatering fragrance for just a minute or two had been a living hell for him as she had asked her questions.

Without a word, he took her bowl, refilled it for the third time, and set it in front of her, an olive branch between them.

"Eat, Coira. After today, I promise ye'll never go hungry again."

Late afternoon the next day, Malcolm watched Coira look forlornly at her home from Ramsey's back, obviously reluctant to leave.

Truth be told, the cottage looked like it would be swallowed by the steep hill behind it any day now. The rear wall, and a portion of the sides, were completely covered in earth. He could just imagine a landslide breaking off from the main body of the wooded hill and covering the little cottage with Coira trapped inside. The thought made his stomach flip and his mouth turn down with a glower. It was a good thing he had come when he did. One more hard rain and he might not have had a chance to recover her at all. Having seen and felt the power of the vow he had taken, he more than likely would have fallen dead with his face in a book.

There are worse ways to die, he thought ruefully.

Beside him, the nag was burdened with the few possessions Coira refused to part with. They were mostly uprooted plants and carefully wrapped bottles she insisted on bringing, as well as a single book wrapped with waxed linen. When he inquired what was printed inside, she poked him hard in the chest and said, *Ye must* never *open this book. Promise me now.*

Her response told him well enough what was inside.

Malcolm wasn't too keen on bringing a tome of witchcraft back to the stronghold, but he'd been reluctant to force his demands upon her. It was bad enough that he was removing her from her life and home and bringing her to a place where she would be surrounded by strangers. To the place where her mother had died.

Already, he was drowning in guilt over her mother's death. All night he'd been forced to listen to her soft sobs drift down from the loft above as he'd layed on his pallet beside the hearth. The shame of his decision to accept her mother's blood oath had weighed heavy on his heart by the time the sun rose over the hills.

She could keep her spellbook. He refused to give her a reason to resent him further and possibly curse him with warts or worse.

With a dejected sigh and slight drop of her shoulders, Coira turned away from the ramshackle cottage and faced him, the thin skin around her eyes slightly puffy, her lips downturned.

He gave her what he hoped was a reassuring smile and patted Ramsey's rump. "Time to go, lass."

She glared up at him. "I'm no' ridin' behind ye," she snapped. Marching forward, she held her hand up with a defiant glint in her eye and dared him to argue with her.

Malcolm barely refrained from rolling his eyes. It would be a long ride home, he just knew it.

"Fine, demanding woman." He lifted her by the forearm, deposited her between his legs, and ground his teeth when her backside filled the space between his thighs.

She shot him another glare over her shoulder; her flinty stare irked him to no end. "I'm no' happy about this."

"I huvnae forgotten. Ye've told me so at least twenty times," Malcolm growled as he gave Ramsey a tap with his heels and tugged on the nag's lead to follow.

"I dinnae ken why ye bound me to this man." Her words, obviously meant for her mother's ghost, were so faint he wasn't sure if she'd meant for him to hear.

Aggravated with himself and the situation she was in, he ran his tongue over his teeth before he answered her unspoken question the best he could.

"She said ye would be 'free from the fires as the Lady of Ghlas Thùr.' I thought she meant the threat o' witch trials. It wasnae until ye showed me yer scars that I truly understood what she meant." He gave the top of her thigh a sympathetic pat as Ramsey lumbered along. "For what it's worth, I am sorry. It wasnae right o' her to bind ye to me without yer consent, but she must have had a good reason for doin' so, aye?"

Coira swiped at her cheeks and nodded as some of the fight seemed to melt from her body at his revelation.

Meandering off the deer path and through a field, they skirted around a bog to get to the road that would take them west to Ghlas Thùr. Coira leaned to the right and studied the ground past their dangling feet for a few lengths before she chuffed a humorless laugh. She shook her head, sending wisps of her hair to tickle the base of his throat.

Curious, Malcolm looked down to find the charming purple blooms of the marsh violet staring up at him.

"Idiot. Ye waited until the last possible minute." Coira shot an exasperated look over her shoulder. "Ye would have *died* had ye waited any longer or if I had no' found ye. Did ye regret yer oath that much?"

Malcolm breathed deeply of the bog's wet, earthy fragrance and thought of his brother, of the centuries Colin would have to sleep for salvation. If he made it at all.

"I regret a lot, Coira. I regret yer mother's death, and for no' considerin' the changes my oath would make to yer life. But mostly, I regret the future and the dangers that will accompany it. Believe and take comfort when I tell ye that it haunts my every wakin' moment."

～

Most of their journey was spent in silence while they traversed the Lowland countryside. Lost in their own thoughts, neither of them spoke more than they needed to. Taking the longer, less direct route, they were able to stock up on supplies and feed for the horses with what little money Coira had left. With full bellies, they seemed to lose a bit of their irritation toward each other.

It was strange to look at her and know she was destined to be his wife. He didn't know the first thing about her. He didn't want to. It was bad enough his body was drawn to her while his mind fought a useless battle against the pull.

When they crossed the MacKinnon border in the late afternoon of the second day and arrived at the village, he found himself urging Ramsey north instead of taking them straight to Ghlas Thùr. They followed the river until they came to a clearing with fairy pools; smooth, multicolored rocks sparkled jewel-like in the clear depths.

Dismounting, he told Coira to wait for him and quickly climbed the hill along a chain of small waterfalls that fed into the main body of the river. Having climbed the hill dozens of times since that fateful night in December, he bounded over the rocks without a slip, and the caves came into view where the hill flattened. As he approached them, the sight of those black chasms embedded into the hillside set his teeth on edge, but his fear wasn't enough to keep him away. Bright green moss dripped from the mouth of the largest cavern, and their soft fibers caressed the top of his head when he ducked inside.

Every few days he would make the journey here, searching for some small sign that his brother had survived. The time spent collecting Coira was the longest between his visits.

Crossing the sandy throat of the cave, Malcolm scanned the ground as far as the light would reach and thumped the meaty side of his fist against the rocky wall in defeat when he found nothing had changed.

"Where did ye go?" Coira asked when he returned and alighted behind her.

"Nowhere o' consequence, lass," he murmured.

The inaccuracy of his answer weighed on his soul.

Chapter Four

COIRA

In the fading light, I could see the grey stone of Ghlas Thùr through the tops of the trees; the two towers for which it was named, and their shaker roofs, pierced the periwinkle sky above. I tugged at my hair to further cover the scars on my face and checked that the rope of my braid was hiding the mottled skin of my neck. There was little to do about my dress. There was only so much one could do to stay clean on a two-day journey after packing up one's possessions. I attempted to smooth out what wrinkles I could before we broke through the forest and crossed a field dotted with white and blue wildflowers.

Ghlas Thùr was beautiful, yet simple. More of a stronghold than a castle, it still held a regal bearing with its surrounding curtain wall. The massive three-level building spread out from the main body into two wings, one to the north, the other south. A loch spread parallel to the keep, still and silent at the base of the hill on its western side. Most of the windows were lit from within with soft, welcoming candlelight, as though it waited for its master to return home.

As we passed through the field from the east, someone called out an alert in Gaelic. Several men gathered on the lip of the wall and look curiously down on us.

"Ready, lass?" Malcolm's deep voice rumbled behind me.

I wasn't even the tiniest bit ready. I was suddenly very, *very* nervous and wanted nothing more than to flee into the forest, far away from prying eyes. I had never felt more exposed or unsure in my life. The people who resided within this castle knew what I was, had their own ideas of what I was capable of, and it was only a matter of time before one of them betrayed me. I rubbed my sweaty palms on my thighs and tried not to show my fear.

"If I said no, would ye take me back?" I meant to sound challenging, but the insecurity in my voice revealed my lack of conviction. Malcolm was silent for several moments before he answered.

"No. I widnae," he said, a hint of disappointment in his voice.

I released an agitated breath. He *should* be disappointed in being saddled with me. I was a witch, an old maid of twenty-five summers, and covered in scars to boot. Malcolm's hand rested heavily on my waist for the barest moment before he dropped it away.

"Ye have nothin' to fear—"

"O' course I do. They'll hate me. Look at them, they already fear me," I whispered as we rode beneath the wall and the apprehensive faces that peered from above. Malcolm shook his head, and his whiskered chin brushed my crown as we passed through the gatehouse.

"They dinnae hate ye. Yer safe here."

It didn't escape my notice that he hadn't tried to convince me there was no fear. I appreciated that he hadn't lied to me, even though his silent acknowledgement soured my stomach.

I wanted to believe that I was safe, but I knew people, and they were too easily driven by fear. I could see it in their eyes as they stared at me, the wariness and uncertainty. All it would take was a few people who wanted to see me burn, and their prejudices would bleed into the rest.

Once inside the center bailey, Malcolm dropped from Ramsey's back near a small stable. He tugged the bag that held my tome free from the leather ties before helping me down by the waist. Leaving the rest of our supplies and my possessions on the nag, he guided me by the small of my back through the courtyard. At the keep's large double door, a maid dressed in grey held one side open for her laird. I checked that my hair still covered the right side of my face for the fifth time as we edged around a stone tree trunk in the middle of the bailey. My eyes widened in alarm. It was little wonder everyone looked upon me with unease; my mother's recklessness would surely be my death. Why teach me the importance of secrecy and self-restraint if her last act on earth had exposed me more than I had ever exposed myself? Surely, she would not squander the last thirteen years spent keeping me safe. She had literally moved earth and rock to ease my fears, only to unmask me to dozens of strangers mere months before I would arrive to live among them. And worse, the castle residents had had months for their worries to solidify before my arrival.

"Gather everyone in the great hall, I have somethin' that needs to be said," Malcolm barked at the maid when we climbed the steps to the keep.

His brusque command snapped like a whip, demanded the attention of the soldiers in the bailey, and made me stiffen in surprise. No longer still and quiet as when we'd arrived, the bailey walls echoed the whispers and movements of men in a flurry of activity. The maid bobbed a quick curtsy before she disappeared down the south wing corridor at a quick pace.

Stepping over the threshold, I blinked at the enormous, open hall. A large table, long enough to seat twenty people, stood parallel to an enormous fireplace. Stacked trestle tables and benches lined the wall to my right between two smaller hearths; they were easily accessible, as though the MacKinnon clan had frequent gatherings. At the top of the grand staircase straight ahead, a wooden banister split to the north and south wings, with tapestries covering the stone walls above and below. A third-story banister spanned the back wall. More tapestries reached as high as the rafters and depicted hunts and the Scottish countryside; not battle scenes like the ones displayed in the other castles and strongholds I had visited with my mother. Large, white, pillared candles, as well as thin tapers set into candelabras, lit the room with a warm, romantic glow. Swept clean and free of cobwebs, the massive room smelled faintly spicy from the fresh-herb rushes, as well as the mouth-watering aroma of the evening meal.

Ghlas Thùr was not what I expected at all. Instead of a dark, depressing fortress, it proved to be well-organized and welcoming.

A woman with a mass of dark brown hair crossed the balcony above, her arms burdened with a stack of folded linen. Malcolm called up to her, stopping her in her tracks.

"Bredanna, find Maeve and tell her to ready her new lady's room."

"Already done, my laird. These are the linens for her bath," she explained with a quick glance at me before she hurried out of sight.

I followed Malcolm past the dining table and climbed five steps of the staircase before he paused and wrapped his hand around my upper arm. He pulled me close to his side and turned to face the vast room as it filled with the keep's residents and the men of the garrison. When he was satisfied all were in attendance, he spoke to the small crowd, his voice steady and firm.

"This, clan MacKinnon, is yer new lady, Coira. Though we huvnae yet been wed, ken that I am bound to her in life and in death. I expect ye to honor her as ye honor me."

His speech could not have surprised me more had he belched fire. *This* was the voice of the MacKinnon Laird; this was *not* the gentle, indulgent cadence of the man I had traveled with these past days. His expectation filled the hall as wide eyes stared up at me. It was an effort to keep my chin raised, but I suffered their stares even though I wanted nothing more than to hide behind Malcolm's large frame.

He thumped his fist on the thick banister and he said, "Let it be known that any lack o' respect or slights made against her willnae be tolerated and will be dealt with swiftly. We must no' forget what her mother sacrificed for us, and in turn, what Coira has sacrificed. Am. I. Understood?"

I glanced up at Malcolm's profile to find his face resolute with expectation. Those in the room either gave appropriate murmurs of *aye* and *my laird* or stared at me with something more akin to awe rather than fear. It was clear to me that his clan respected him, and it was a relief to know that the MacKinnon Laird didn't rule his people with a heavy hand.

Satisfied with their response, Malcolm guided me away. I nearly sagged with relief that he had not expected me to address them, for I doubted I could have formed a single word. It wasn't until we had disappeared down the south wing of the second floor and up a spiral stairwell that my shoulders relaxed, and I was able to take a full breath.

Following a few feet behind Malcolm, I took in my surroundings and noted that the rest of the castle was just as spotless as the main hall. Tall windows that lined one side of the corridor looked down onto the bailey, while doors and short hallways lined the other. Malcolm stopped in front of the second-to-last door on the third floor and pushed it open to reveal a spacious, fire-lit room decorated in cream, gold, and green. I'd never seen such extravagance.

"If ye're displeased with this chamber, I can show ye to another."

I looked up at him in surprise. "Far from it. I dinnae ken what I expected, but this was no' it," I admitted with a wave at the opulent décor.

"Ye thought I'd make ye sleep with the pigs?"

I opened my mouth, ready to spit out a retort, when I caught a twitch of his lips and couldn't help the grin that tugged at my own. "Maybe. At least until ye said what ye did in the hall."

Malcolm's gaze settled on my mouth a moment before he swallowed, banishing the lightening mood between us. "My chamber is just there," he said awkwardly, gesturing toward the chamber next to mine at the end of the hall with a jerk of his head before he ushered me over the threshold.

A blonde woman, many years younger than I, stood up from her crouch near a copper tub by the fire. She wiped her hands on her white apron before dipping a quick curtsy.

"Hallo," she said softly. Her fingers worried the sturdy fabric of her dress, and I didn't know who was more nervous—she or I.

"Maeve," Malcolm said in greeting as he set my bag of oils and my tome on a chair in front of the fire. "This is yer lady, Coira. Can I count on ye to care for her in all aspects befittin' my wife?"

Maeve worried her top lip with her teeth and nodded quickly. Her expressive grey eyes bounced between us as though unsure of the dynamic between her laird and me, his witch bride.

"Good. I'm puttin' my trust in ye." With a slight bend at his waist and a murmured goodnight, he left me in the strange room under the care of the skittish handmaid. I stared at the door as he pulled it shut with a click, half a mind to race after him.

"May I help ye out o' yer gown?" Maeve asked timidly when the silence became too much for her to bear. Fighting the urge to check that my scars were concealed, I shook my head and took a step backward toward the bed. At a loss of what to do, she gestured at the tub. "The water is still hot. Ye were spotted near the village, so we rushed to have it ready for ye when ye arrived."

I wrapped my arms around myself, feeling a bit defensive. "I'll bathe myself, thank ye," I said curtly and felt slightly guilty when her pretty face fell.

"Would ye like me to wait outside 'til yer ready to dress?"

"No. I willnae be needin' any help. I look after myself."

Her cherubic cheeks heated at my dismissal, but she nodded and skirted past me to open one of several trunks that lined the wall near the door. Removing a soft chemise, she neatly settled it on the bed next to a pine-green velvet dressing gown.

"I'll be back up with yer supper in a short while then."

Once alone, I untied my dagger from where I'd strapped it to my calf and hid it under a pillow on the bed. Once free from my stiff, leather slippers, I stretched my toes and then peeled myself out of my dress, beyond thankful for the privacy to bathe myself properly. The days traveling with Malcolm had left little in the way of cleanliness besides a chilly stream; that hadn't been near as welcoming as the steaming bath in front of the fire. Besides, Laird MacKinnon may be my future husband by my mother's half-cocked decree, but that did not mean it afforded him the right to view my body. Not that he had tried. In fact, Malcolm didn't look at me or touch me any more than he absolutely had to, something that was both an annoyance and a relief.

Blissfully bare, I lowered myself into the tub and sighed as the rose-scented water lapped against my ribs. I hadn't had a proper bath in a month; the effort it would take to fill anything larger than a cauldron was far more trouble than it was worth. But in a castle such as this, with the ability to heat large amounts of water at once… I wouldn't shed a tear over not bathing with a bucket of tepid water again. Peering over the copper lip, I found a cake of peony-scented soap, eagerly lathered my hair, and scrubbed vigorously.

Refreshed and my skin a blushing pink, I stood and rinsed with the last bucket of clean water then wrapped my body in a length of linen. Perched in one of two green-cushioned chairs in front of the fire, I finger-combed my hair and left it loose over my shoulders to dry.

Burying my bare toes deep into a thick, shaggy, sheepskin rug, I visually explored my new bedchamber. It was large, nearly stretching the depth of the building, yet it still maintained an air of coziness. Opposite the door, between two tall windows that looked out onto the moonlit loch, sat a four-poster bed. Thickly woven, cream-colored blankets were piled high on the stuffed mattress, with green velvet pillows and a matching foot blanket stretched over the end.

To the right of the bed, a massive, gilded mirror leaned against the wall between four large trunks. The silver was slightly tarnished with age, the glass spotty along the edges. Despite its flaws, I thought it was beautiful.

To the left, along the wall that separated the laird's chamber from my own, tapestries of highland mountains hung from the raftered ceiling and brushed the polished wood floor. They were beautiful, serene weavings I would have chosen for myself. While I studied them, I caught sight of a soft light that flared beneath the one closest to the window. Padding over on bare feet, I pulled it to the side and found a door that connected the laird's rooms to my own. Frowning, I felt along the seam in the shadows until I found a thick iron latch at the top. As quietly as I could, I worked the bar into place, effectively locking it, and let the tapestry fall back into place to conceal the door once more.

I doubted Malcolm would make a nocturnal visit to my room, but that didn't mean I would welcome one if he did. I snorted a laugh at my own expense. *How disgusted he would be*, I thought, *to discover that my scars covered half my back, as well as my thigh and right arm? He'd take me right back to the cottage and damn the consequences.*

With my hair still hanging in damp waves, I donned the silky chemise Maeve had left out for me and hid my tome under the foot of the mattress. I would have to find a more secure place later, but for right now, it would have to do.

A soft rap on the door announced the maid's return, in her arms a tray laden with a covered dish and a carafe of wine. Setting it on the knee-high table between the two chairs in front of the low burning fire, she removed the cover to reveal a hot, creamy soup and a soft roll.

"I'll be bringin' the seamstress up in the mornin' to take yer measurements so that she may alter yer gowns to better fit," Maeve said while she turned down my bed coverings and fluffed a pillow.

"What is wrong with the ones I brought?"

I only had a few but they fit just fine, even if they were a little faded and tattered at the hem. They only needed a good scrub in the loch.

"Oh nothin', milady. 'Tis for takin' in yer *new* gowns," she explained and opened one of the many trunks to gesture at the colorful fabrics nestled within. A quick glance revealed many fine gowns neatly folded and ready for wear. "They were the laird's late mothers. Now they're yers."

I didn't know what to say. First a hot bath in a lovely room to call my own, and now a wardrobe from a woman who was much more fashionable and noble than I. Instead of commenting, I sat down and tasted a spoonful of soup. My eyes fluttered closed while the flavors of potatoes, leeks, and bacon in a rich cream spread over my tongue. The savory concoction settled in my belly, warm and comforting, and I devoured half of it before I realized the handmaid was watching me.

"What?" I snapped and checked to make sure my scars were hidden. Thankfully, they were.

She flinched and bit her lower lip before speaking.

"I was there that night. I watched from a window while yer mother saved the laird's brother. I thought ye should ken that she saved the most honorable man." When I didn't say anything in response, she backed toward the door. "Leave the tray in the hallway when ye finish. Goodnight, milady." And with a click of the latch, she left me in the quiet.

The soup turned to paste in my mouth with the reminder of my mother's death and her damn meddling that had ultimately brought me here. For years she had pushed me to find a husband. She was the reason I had gone to Inverness. Browbeaten by her constant nagging, I took her suggestion to stay with our relatives in the far north. There were still many Druids in the Highlands who had gone overlooked by the witch hunters, and my mother had hoped I would find a husband within their numbers.

Well, if wishes were gold coins, I'd be a rich woman. Once a man caught a glimpse of my ruined skin, any interest they may have had promptly withered before my eyes and died like a worm in the sun. No man wanted a wife that looked like she had already been burned on the pyre. They feared I would catch the eye of any witch-hunter I may encounter. I didn't blame them. Druids were now a fraction of the number we had once been. No sane man would risk having children with a woman so obviously marked for death.

Snatching up the wine, I ignored the dainty chalice altogether and drank straight from the carafe. I wasn't the laird's wife yet, so I didn't have to pretend to be a lady until then, if ever.

Huddled in the chair, I noted my limbs were relaxed, and lost my thoughts to the low dancing flames in the hearth. Before long, my eyelids began to droop, and the bed beckoned me to climb between the clean sheets.

Setting the tray outside my door, I pursed my lips when I caught sight of the handmaid's skirts around the corner of the stairwell, not quite hidden from view. She obviously took her laird's orders seriously. Feeling a bit guilty for making her job difficult, I closed the door harder than I normally would, letting her know I was finished, then tucked myself into bed. Seconds later, I heard the faint scrape of the tray as she took it away.

Warm and snug in the strange bed, I sank into the pillows and fell asleep thinking of the curious man sleeping in the room beside mine.

CHAPTER FIVE

COIRA

I jolted awake to a sharp banging on my door, and with my next heartbeat, I had my dagger in my hand, ready for whoever was coming to drag me off.

I willnae go down without a fight! My magic flowed through my body, heavy, ready, and waiting for me to unleash it with a word. I flung myself from the bed and landed in a crouch, my blade at the ready.

"Oh!" A feminine voice cried out in alarm.

Blinking the sleep from my eyes, I focused on the two petrified women in the doorway, one familiar, the other a stranger.

"I'm sorry, milady. We knocked three times," Maeve explained, her grey eyes riveted on the dagger pointed at them from across the room.

Her companion, an older woman with fine lines crinkling the corners of her wide eyes, pressed her hand to her ample chest. We stared at one another for a moment longer until I realized I was in no danger. Tucking the dagger back under my pillow, I pulled my hair over my right shoulder and let it drape over the marbled skin of my bare arm.

"I didnae hear," I mumbled and roughly rubbed the last of the sleep from my face. "I thought I locked the door." Pressing my fingertips over my eyes, I willed my body to relax, afraid my heart would beat right out of my chest. I couldn't believe I had slept so soundly.

"I have a key," Maeve explained, her face flushed with embarrassment as she ushered the other woman into my chamber. "I promise I willnae enter yer chamber again until ye give me leave." They tugged a wooden dais over the threshold, and the corner of the box banged against the door. "This is Caitrin. She'll be altering yer wardrobe."

Once our introduction was complete, Maeve left us alone and promised to return with tea.

The seamstress was in her middle years, her gaze assessing and frank, but wary as she cleared her throat and looked me up and down. She seemed to shrug off the fright I had given her and, with a deep breath, began opening the many trunks that lined the wall. One by one, she emptied them and spread the many gowns, skirting, shirts, and cloaks out on my bed in some semblance of order.

"Please, stand up there, milady." Caitrin motioned to the dais and opened a little box that contained pins, ribbons, and other such things.

I nearly declined but did as she asked and nervously wrapped my arms around myself while I waited in the thin sleeveless shift I had worn to bed. The seamstress held open a gown of deep blue wool, her brow quirked up in question as though asking, *Do ye like it?* Smiling faintly, I nodded and stepped into the skirting. She moved behind me to fasten the little, silk-covered buttons lining the back.

While she placed pins at the hem, I inspected the fine weave of the wool. Warm but lightweight, it lacked the scratchy heaviness of my tired gowns, and I breathed a sigh of relief that the sleeves were long enough to cover my wrists. I wondered how to broach the subject of leaving them as they were instead of cutting them to the more fashionable three-quarters length. Engrossed in the fine stitching and weave, I nearly jumped out of my skin when Caitrin brushed my hair off my neck and her fingertips grazed my damaged skin. Spinning around, I clumsily toppled off the dais to face the seamstress.

"Dinnae touch me," I hissed, and fought to suppress the hot tears that threatened to blur my sight.

"Forgive me, I didnae ken," she whispered, her hands held up in surrender as she stared at the side of my face and hesitated. "Would ye like me to go?"

Part of me wanted her to. A small part of me wanted to scream my frustrations until my throat was raw and she was far, far away and I only had myself for company. But my mother had given her life so I could be here, and I would not squander her sacrifice by making enemies of the people I would live with. They were already uneasy with my presence, I didn't need to make it harder.

"No. I just… dinnae touch me, please."

I turned and gave her my back, and with shaky hands I lifted my hair off my neck and bore my shame to a stranger for the second time. I hated the sharp silence and the time it took to compose herself before she began her work anew

Her fingers didn't wander past the fabric line again.

In time, she relaxed enough to ask me my opinion of the gowns, of which I had none. Being a midwife and healer, fashions had never interested me. I was used to practical cuts and shapes with easily cleaned, durable fabrics. However, the seamstress didn't seem deterred and slipped yard after yard of silk, wool, and fine linen over my head and around my hips. I had never had such delicate fabrics touch my skin; it felt decadent and a little forbidden.

"How would ye like it if I raised the collars?" she queried after I stepped into a gown of gold and cream silk.

"Ye could do that?" I asked hopefully.

Caitrin flashed me an assuring smile that dripped with confidence just as Maeve entered with a tray of tea and biscuits. "I can do anythin' with a needle and thread," she chirped. "Leave it to me, and I'll see that it's done."

After two cups of the most glorious tea I've ever tasted, and countless fittings later, Caitrin declared she was done. Gathering the pinned gowns, she left with her arms heaped so high I worried she wouldn't be able to see where she was going and tumble down the stairs.

"The light grey wool fits well enough for now," she said to Maeve as she breezed out the door.

Alone with my handmaid, I noticed she looked uncomfortable.

"Would ye like another to attend ye?" she asked gently as she twisted her fingers together and focused on the floor.

Damn, this guilt! I thought as I paced in front of the bed and shook my head. "This is all verra new to me, Maeve. I dinnae want ye to think yer unappreciated—I just—I have…"

"I saw them," she murmured, her voice full of understanding. She looked at me from beneath her lashes. "I willnae tell anyone, milady."

Relief that I wouldn't have to explain myself overwhelmed me. Swallowing my emotions down, I pulled back my shoulders and nodded once. "Then ye may dress me. I dinnae think I'd be able to manage without ye anyhow." I shrugged. "They all close in the back."

Maeve's lips tugged up in a small smile as she held out a dove-grey gown. Her nimble fingers were quick and capable as she tied the corset and fished out stockings and soft leather slippers that were only just a little big. I even allowed her to plait my hair and was pleased with how she wove and draped the pale lengths to hide all of my imperfections.

"Thank ye, Maeve." I said, truly appreciative of her special consideration, even as I wrestled with my self-consciousness.

Some time later, I found the laird by accident while I wandered the hallways. The second-floor library was inviting and cozy, brightly lit by the floor-to-ceiling windows, with padded chairs and thick, woolly cowhides covering most of the floor. With his back to me, Malcolm lounged comfortably before a cold hearth, his legs stretched out in front of him.

"I trust ye slept well?" Without taking focus from the book in his hands, he gestured to the chair beside him like a king would offer his subject a seat.

I rolled my eyes and crossed the room to sit on the edge of the chair separated from his by a low tea table. Like most of the common rooms, this one was also well kept. No dust haunted the shelving or the bindings of what was possibly hundreds of books that dominated the wall on either side of the hearth.

Above the fireplace, the painting of a man and a woman caught my attention, the likeness of the man resembling the laird beside me. The woman sitting before him was beautiful. Blonde curls caressed her face and an angelic smile curved her lips.

"My father and his second wife, the woman who raised me," Malcolm said when he noticed my study of the painting. He closed his book. "Have ye need of somethin', Coira?"

This man was straight and to the point, a quality I could appreciate. I tried hard to ignore the fact that he was even more handsome with a fresh shave. His raven hair was smooth and secured at his nape with a leather tie. I blinked at him like an idiot and scrambled to reorder my thoughts.

Why could he no' be ugly? I cursed. Tearing my stare away from his warm brown eyes, I addressed my needs. "I need a garden—for the herbs I brought with me as well as privacy and space for my work."

"And what, exactly, is yer work?" he drawled and twisted in his chair to fully look at me.

I held his heavy stare for a moment. I knew what he was thinking, it was what all men feared in a witch's presence. So typical. I decided to have a bit of fun and leaned my weight on my elbow closest to him. Bending slightly over the armrest, I peered behind me and down the hall to make sure we were truly alone, then turned toward him with a feral grin.

"I found a way to enslave the minds o' men by boiling toad skin and newt eyes." Licking my lips, I pinched my thumb and pointer finger together. "Just a tiny drop in their mead is all it would take and they widnae ken they'd fallen under my spell until it was too late. They'd have no choice but to bend to my will."

I nearly lost my nerve when his eyes flared in shock. I was confident he wouldn't hurt me, my mother's blood oath assured that much, but the thrill of teasing him was too tempting, too easy. Something in my face must have given me away because his dark brows lowered, and he leaned over the small table until mere inches separated his face from mine. My bravado melted away when his juniper and parchment scent settled over me and teased my senses; I had to grip the armrest to keep myself still.

His lips curved into the barest of smiles, disarming me. "Are ye pickin' on me, lass?"

With a grunt, I shrugged and slid my focus away from him, suddenly finding the racks of antlers displayed high on the far wall more interesting.

"Maybe I am." Reclining in the chair, I crossed my arms over my chest. "The need for a garden is self-explanatory. As for my other work, I make medicinal oils as well as teas and tinctures. 'Tis messy work and cannae be done in my bedchamber."

Malcolm nodded sharply and stood, his book forgotten on the table. "Ye may use the south tower above our chambers to do yer 'messy work' as well as the garden just outside the west wall. If that is no' suitable, we can find another area for ye. Sufficient?"

I nodded eagerly and followed him out of the library up to the third floor. Bypassing both of our chambers, he led me along the steep spiral stairwell that wound within the turret wall and opened into a circular space with high rafters. My spirits lifted when I immediately began to imagine the potential of the cluttered space. Diffused light seeped in through the four grimy windows facing each direction: north, south, east, and west. Old armor, chairs, and chests covered in a thick layer of dust were spread and piled throughout, all connected by decades of chalky cobwebs. It was perfect, except for one thing.

"There's no door. I'll need a chest with a lock and possess the only key. I cannae have anyone snoopin' in my book."

"I can do that," he said softly from behind me. I turned to find his stare fixed upon the lower half of my dress, then he looked away and cleared his throat. "I'll have it cleared for ye this day. Enlist whatever help ye need to make it to yer satisfaction. Is there anythin' else?"

I hesitated a moment, then nodded, my throat thick as I forced myself to speak. "My mother's grave. Where does she rest?"

Malcolm's lips tightened with regret and apology as he motioned for me to join him at the western window. After wiping a pane clear of dust and soot, he pointed down to the pebbly shore of the glass-smooth loch.

"She's there."

I followed his viewpoint south to a small grouping of young birch trees, their spring-green leaves stark against the white, velvety bark. Malcolm stood at my back, and his deep voice rumbled in my ear.

"I didnae think she would have been content buried within the church grounds, or even the clan graveyard, surrounded by strangers. I did my best to give her the respect she deserved, and ye will find her there when ye're ready."

I nodded and blinked away the hot tears that threatened to escape as I stared down at her resting place. Just knowing she was so close gave me comfort. "Thank ye for that, and for this space."

Malcolm's sleeve brushed against mine when he headed for the stairwell and descended a few steps before looking back with a mix of annoyance and guilt. "Here, at Ghlas Thùr, we open the gates to the clan every other Sunday for supper. I ken that it is sudden, but tomorrow we will wed. Ye will be presented to the clan as my wife during the evenin' meal in the hall."

What small happiness I had felt for the gift of a workspace, and the honor of the beautiful resting place he had given my mother, wilted like a plucked honeysuckle bloom.

I knew we would marry eventually, but *tomorrow?*

"So soon?"

"I am sorry Coira, but yer mother's magic is no' subtle. To be honest, I'm havin' a hard time keepin' myself from draggin' ye to the church this verra moment."

I frowned at the thought of the blood oath causing him pain and shifted on my feet. "Do ye want—"

"No, Coira. 'Tis kind of ye to offer but I can wait another day. 'Tis bad enough I've forced ye into this marriage. I willnae deny ye a proper wedding."

But I didn't need a proper wedding. This union was not born of love or even lust, but I didn't tell him that. Forcing a tight lipped smile, I feigned an affinity I did not feel, and turned back to the window once he was out of sight. My spirit plummeted while I listened to his footfalls recede. This whole thing was a sham, loveless and depressing. Just a small taste of what the rest of my life would be like, and I didn't need to be surrounded by strangers in a church to make it feel any less so.

The rest of the day went by quickly. A team of the garrison's men had arrived shortly after the laird left me and wordlessly hauled away everything but a sturdy chair and an old dining table, its thick top worn smooth from decades of use. On a large, faded, red and blue, woven rug, borrowed from an unused space on the lower floor, sat the many linen sacks and the two small chests my horse had borne from the cottage. Maeve, being the only woman I was somewhat friendly with— and who wasn't terrified to be alone with me—helped clean the rafters of cobwebbing with a rag-wrapped pole. Now she rubbed beeswax into the thick table legs in an attempt to polish some life back into the drab wood. Two tall shelves were also procured for me and stood along the curved wall close to the landing. Light spilled through the windows. Cleaned of soot and grime, they eliminated the need for lanterns. It was nearly perfect. All that was missing was a secure spot to store my tome.

Striking her hands on her filthy apron, Maeve peered over my shoulder and into the chests when I opened them. Interest and curiosity gleamed in her eyes, but I hesitated, unsure if I should divulge the contents and, most importantly, if I could trust her not to make more out of my work than it was.

I must start trusting her at some point, I thought to myself and decided a full accounting would reveal that I was not a danger. Reaching for a stoppered vial adorned with a painted purple blossom, I handed it to her.

She hesitated for a moment before accepting it. "What is it?"

"Essence of lavender. Mix a drop or two with water or oil, then rub it on yer neck and chest for a good night's sleep." I watched as she delicately sniffed the bottle and failed miserably to withhold her smile. I held up another vial. "Peppermint for bloating and nausea, a godsend for pregnant women."

I listed the use of each vial and placed them on the shelves. When she set the lavender oil down, I gave it back to her and closed her fingers around it. "A gift. For being so kind to me."

I spent the remaining hours leading up to the evening meal outside the west wall, transplanting the herbs and roots I had brought. The garden that Malcolm had gifted for my use was surprisingly well-stocked, with a few herbs I had left at the cottage. Although I had seeds stored, the established wild garlic and self-heal at my disposal was an unexpected boon.

Late into the afternoon, I worked the soil with a sharp rock. Black earth darkened the whites of my nails and marked my grey dress with streaks of damp earth. With each new bed completed without the gardening tools I had left at the cottage, I felt more like myself.

I was not meant to be kept as a noblewoman, clean and tidy in the safety of a solar with a needle and thread. No, thank you. I wanted my hands in the dirt. I was meant to cultivate life from the soil. To watch it grow and blossom, then make it into something else entirely, whether it be a meal or medicine. It was one of my great joys and I was glad Malcolm hadn't expected me to give it all up because of some oath my mother imposed on him. He would have been sorely disappointed if he insisted I be anything other than myself, anyway.

In fact, so far he hadn't expected anything besides my presence and a hasty wedding tomorrow.

I pressed a dusty hand to my chest, directly over the seed of warmth that slept deep within me. He had mentioned a curse and a creature of teeth and talon that dwelled within him. The creature that had driven him to find me and carry out the rest of his oath. I frowned at the thought of being compelled to do something I didn't want to do, with the threat of death looming over me should I refuse or fail. *I* at least had a choice. I could have refused him, let him die on the path, or, at the very least, sent him away. The opportunity had been there… but I couldn't. My mother *had known* I'd never choose my own inhibitions over the life of another, even if they were a stranger to me. She'd known I'd make the choice to come here.

Malcolm had had no choice once he offered my mother his blood. It was either fulfill his oath… or die.

When the belly of the sun touched the hills, two of the garrison's men appeared from the direction of the main gatehouse and leaned against the towering wall at the end of a row of blackberry canes. They watched over me while I watered the last of my transplanted herbs and pointedly looked away each time I tried to catch their stare. There was also a man above me on the wall with his bow half drawn and his focus intent on the forest not far away. What trouble they thought I could get into while working in a garden, I couldn't guess. When the purple twilight stretched above the castle, I trudged on exhausted legs back up the hill and made my way inside the walls with Malcolm's men silently following some distance behind.

Back in my chamber, I found Maeve rummaging through one of the trunks.

"There ye are, milady. May I help ye dress for supper?" she asked with a sweet smile. At some point throughout the day, my handmaid had abandoned most, if not all, of her fear of me, and morphed into a bubbly girl with a carefree attitude.

I hesitated, still not completely comfortable with the idea of undressing before her, but she had seen my scarred body this morning and had not ridiculed me for it. Oblivious of my uncertainty, she didn't wait for my answer and skipped behind me and began freeing one button at a time while she yammered on.

"Caitrin already finished three o' yer gowns. I thought ye could wear one tonight."

Impressed with the speed in which the seamstress had worked, I scrubbed off all remnants of my gardening in a basin filled with scented water. I chose a gown of dark blue wool and allowed Maeve to re-braid my hair before I ventured down to the deserted great hall.

Someone had set the table for two, and since I was the first to arrive, I sat next to the head of the table and waited with my back to the fire. Faint sounds of female laughter drifted up a stairwell to the left of the grand staircase where I assumed the cookery was. Heavy footsteps alerted me to the laird's arrival as he blundered down the stairs and sat heavily to my left.

He is quite possibly the loudest person in Scotland, I thought and watched him fill both of our chalices to the rim with dark red wine instead of the ale I had expected.

"How was yer first day at Ghlas Thùr?" he asked after a stretch of uncomfortable silence.

I studied him from the corner of my eye. Unsure if I should mention his hovering guards since he was most likely the one who ordered their spying, I decided to hold my tongue when the kitchen maids appeared. One after the other, they set their platters and bowls down before making a hasty retreat. Two of the three maids made a subtle sign of the cross. The third hooked her fingers in a blatant ward against evil, her hand hidden from Malcolm's view.

My face reddened. I had seen several people throughout the day make one sign of protection or another when I traversed the castle halls. I hated to admit it, but each motion cut me a little deeper. They all spoke the same, silent words: *Ye're no' welcome here, witch.*

"It was busy… and enlightening," I replied vaguely and placed some roasted root vegetables onto my plate. Famished, I tucked into the delicious fare, never having tasted chicken cooked so tender and juicy in my life.

Malcolm pushed his food around on his plate, seemingly more interested in his wine. "About tomorrow—" He cleared his throat and rubbed his chest, a pained look on his face.

I raised my eyebrows and looked pointedly at the hand pressed against the space over his heart. "What's wrong?"

"The blasted curse is what's wrong," he grumbled. Draining his cup, he refilled it as he explained. "'Tis a restless thing when ye're so near."

"This doesnae surprise me. Most o' my mother's more inventive magics were untamed, violent, and compulsive, often taking on a life of their own. We took oaths when we were young never to do harm and to only use our abilities for the good o' the earth and mankind," I shrugged, "but some slip. They bend or even break oaths when they feel they must, when they choose to, or when emotions override their good sense." *And it seemed my mother had felt the need to bend hers before she died.* My unspoken thought made my throat heat with shame, and I traced the scarring on my right wrist with my thumb. I was the last person who should pass judgement on broken vows. The day the fire had licked hungrily at my face and caught my dress in a painful blaze was the day I had forsaken my oath. I had planned to use it in the worst possible way; to destroy life. After that day, I vowed to never give in to the pull of that terrible side of my power again. I knew if I did, the dark magic would cleave who I was in half and change me forever into something I did not want to be. I had felt it. Touched it. There was a wild, vengeful creature lurking deep within my mortal soul, capable of incredible and savage magic.

The elements had raged alongside me that day, and I am thankful that I had only been thirteen, my knowledge incomplete, not a full Druid in my prime like I was now. If I had been, I would have succeeded in destroying everyone in my path and most certainly myself in the process. I was not the first Druid to be seduced by the earth's power, many in the past centuries had succumbed to its lure. And they had become something inhuman, without conscience or morals.

There was a legend of a Druid who gave in to the pull in a fit of rage and heartbreak. Betrayed by her lover, she had cursed him with a fate worse than death: to walk the earth for all eternity, forgotten and alone. Never known. Never loved. Never remembered. Her body had weakened and was unable to control the amount of energy she had called forth after she cursed her lover and she'd ultimately been consumed, painfully and horribly. The patch of earth upon which she had died was still scarred and sterile, incapable of supporting the life of even the most resilient weed.

I cast another glance at my future husband—a man not of my choice—and the frustration he tried to hide while he brooded beside me. My mother should have never bound the MacKinnon Laird to me. It was cruel. She should have just healed his brother and gone home, where she'd be alive, and I would not be here, where I was unwanted.

"I would release ye if I could," I breathed, even though the thought of doing so made me feel uncomfortable for a reason I could not name. Malcolm shrugged a broad shoulder. Poking at his food some more, his next words stunned me speechless.

"Yer mother saved my life the day I was born. She told me that she took the last bit of energy from my mother at her request to see that I survived. Before I swore that blood vow, she told me I had been her first… and my brother would be her last. I didnae understand what she meant by that until I found her dead."

The fine hairs on the left side of my body raised as I stared at him with new understanding. Mother had told me the story of the first life she had saved using the essence of a dying mother many, many years ago. A sweet babe only minutes in this world and the firstborn son of a great laird. She had told me she felt something in him when she held his tiny body, fresh from the womb. A kinship she had never been able to explain and had disturbed her for years after. And now, here he was, grown and strong, twice affected by my mother's magic. Once blessed. Later condemned.

I was never one to believe in fate—not with the things I had seen and endured—but as I walked the darkened hallways to my chamber that night, I began to wonder if such a thing might exist.

CHAPTER SIX

MALCOLM

"All is the fear, and nothing is the love, as little is the wisdom,
where the flight so runs against all reason."
-William Shakespeare, Macbeth

The church had always been a place of peace for Malcolm. He loved the scent of wood polish in the air, and the way the late afternoon light blazed through the massive stained-glass window behind the altar. It was not the Word of God spoken from the pulpit, but more the feeling of peace that swelled in his chest while he was within the church walls. Most services, Malcolm would close his eyes and just *feel*. Feel the stillness of the air and the subtle tremors through the bench he sat upon as he emptied his mind. That was all he needed to feel close to God. Sadly, he had not felt God since he had made his blood oath.

Today was no different.

Standing before the priest, two steps above them, Malcolm cast a side-glance at his witch-bride while the priest spoke the ancient words of marriage in Latin. Her cream and gold gown glowed softly in the warm light. Her head bent and lashes lowered; her gaze was on the floor. The mass of her pale blonde hair was wavy and loose over her shoulders, framing her face, and draped like a cape that reached the small of her back. Her face a mask of serene calm, she looked to be a dutiful bride soaking up God's word; the picture of a humble, pious woman.

Malcolm knew better.

He had felt Coira's demeanor change the moment she'd entered the walls of the church. As they walked down the aisle toward Father Blount, new to this parish from England last autumn, she had turned within herself. Her shoulders had curved inward the closer they got to the altar; her skin seemed to lose its luster, and even the pale white-gold of her hair had dulled.

Fear. Fear and dread did that.

Malcolm knew she would not have chosen him for a husband. But to *fear* the prospect of becoming his wife was enough to make Malcolm seethe, only he was unsure who exactly he was mad at. It was *his* fault she was in this predicament, not hers. Even so, he'd done everything in his power to make her transition within the MacKinnon clan comfortable and welcoming. He'd given her new gowns to replace the rags she'd arrived in, and a chamber to call her own. He'd gifted her a garden to grow her herbs, and space to make her tinctures and potions. He had not given her reason to fear him.

Annoyed with himself for not doing more to ease her dread of their marriage, Malcolm glared at the priest and nearly growled in frustration when the man droned on and on. *I just want this to be over*, he thought.

"Do hurry up, Father." The words tumbled out of his mouth before he could check himself. "I'm an impatient man."

Shocked and amused whispers hissed through the small cathedral. The priest balked at Malcolm's words, his loose jowls pulling down in a hard frown. Malcolm could tell the priest wanted to berate him for interrupting but refrained. *Wise choice, auld man,* Malcolm thought as he stared him down from his superior height. Even with the gradation, Malcolm still had an inch or two on the short Englishman.

"The r-rings?" the priest sputtered. His arthritic fingers gripped his Bible as he glared daggers at the worn pages.

Interesting. This priest did not like being given orders, not that Malcolm cared. He almost wished Father Blount would speak up, if only to give Malcolm a target to direct his anger.

When the priest wisely kept his mouth shut, Malcolm produced a ring with amethysts inlaid into the silver band. He placed it upon Coira's slim, trembling finger and spoke the words that bound her to him as his wife—until death. When she pushed a thick band of gold upon his own finger, the creature within his chest purred, hungry and proud, the thrum within him so deafening he wondered how no one else could hear it.

"I now pronounce you man and wife," the priest mumbled and gave him permission to kiss his bride.

Instead of taking the liberty, Malcolm took Coira's hand, marched her down the aisle, and out of the church without a backward glance. Pushing through the doors and into the sun-drenched courtyard, he tugged her along, ignoring the talk and laughter they left behind.

"I'm sorry to cause ye so much grief, Coira," Malcolm grumbled as he wrapped his hands around her too-small waist and swiftly raised her onto Ramsey's back. Mounted behind her, the golden silk of her gown draped over his kilted leg. She looked up at him from over her shoulder and searched his face, her pale eyes boring into him.

"Ye huvnae caused me grief," she said, but her protest was weak.

Malcolm snorted his disagreement as he turned Ramsey sharply and urged him back toward the keep, annoyed that the first thing she would say as his wife would be a lie. "And yet lately, all yer sorrows begin and end with me."

When they trotted through the gates of the church grounds, he felt her body give a little shiver as she replied, "No' all o' them."

⁓

"I worry the seedlings willnae be strong enough when the wet season arrives, my laird," a farmer said from where he sat on Malcolm's left.

"I dinnae mean to be bringin' it up on yer weddin' day, but 'tis a worry we all have after such a long winter."

Malcolm's vision was a little unfocused, but he rested a hand on the farmer's shoulder with a reassuring squeeze. "I willnae let ye starve, James. That I promise ye. Put yer faith in God and all will be right in the end, ye'll see."

Bowing his head, the grisly man nodded with a small smile. "Yer right. I forget myself sometimes."

James was not the first farmer to approach him with similar concerns. Coira said little throughout dinner, only speaking when spoken to and smiling very little, as they took a closer look at his new wife, now their lady. Her features looked haunted, her focus mostly down at her lap if she wasn't looking nervously at the door each time someone new arrived. Her meekness was beginning to wear on him. What had happened to the fierce woman he'd met at the cabin in the wood? The one who held a knife to his throat and tasted his blood for truth. Tonight, he could not find a trace of her.

The evening wore on and the dancing was far more subdued than the last wedding celebration that had graced his hall. There were no demands for the groom to kiss his bride. No calls for speeches or toasts—although most of the garrison's men pressed a tankard of scotch-fortified ale in his hand when they stopped to give well-wishes to their laird and lady. All in all, it was a rather dreary affair masquerading as a joyful one, and as the hours dragged by, Malcolm got well and truly drunk.

A rough hand shook him from a dizzying slumber, and he cracked his eyes open to find not one but *two* Farlans smirking at him. Much too close, his friends seemed to be trying their best to keep from laughing.

"My laird, if ye dinnae wish to be accompanied, I suggest ye take yer bride to bed."

Malcolm blinked twice as haze, from what must have been a whole blasted barrel of scotch, pressed down on him. He scanned the room and the expectant faces of the clan until he found the beauty beside him, her face a scorching red from embarrassment.

Ah. The bedding. The moment all grooms look forward to, he thought miserably. *All grooms but this one.*

Clumsily pushing away from the table, he teetered slightly on his feet and reached for Coira's hand only to miss it entirely, his fingertips jarring the table. Furrowing his brow, he tried again only to find it had moved once more, but he could swear she was sitting still. Blast it, her hand wouldn't stay in one spot! Nervous laughter echoed in the hall, and he rubbed his face in frustration, silently commanding his mind to take back control of his body. Frowning unhappily at the crowd, Coira stood and took Malcolm's arm in a surprisingly firm grip and tugged him gently toward the stairs.

"I believe ye'll be disappointed tonight, lass!" someone yelled.

The hall fell quiet, like the moment after someone shatters glass, before everyone erupted in awkward laughter. Their jovial heckling chased them as Malcolm climbed unsteadily after Coira and continued long after they disappeared from view.

Feeling slightly proud that he had only bumped into half the walls on their way up and not all of them—although he did knock over a candelabra and a portrait of some long-dead relative—Malcolm fumbled with the latch of his chamber and pushed through with a crash. The door banged loudly as it swung on oiled hinges, and he crossed the room to plop gracelessly onto the bed. Tearing at the buckles of his boots with numb fingers, he had nearly forgotten he wasn't alone until he caught sight of his wife hesitating over the threshold. Her form danced erratically as she closed the door and leaned back against it.

"Dinnae look so petrified," he slurred gruffly. "I'm no' goin' to pounce on ye." What kind of man did she think he was that he would force himself upon her? *One that took her from her life and made her marry ye, all in the name o' someone else's happiness?* Scowling at the truth of his own thoughts, Malcolm abandoned his battle with the buckles and fell back, only to immediately grip the blankets when the world tilted alarmingly fast.

"Och, if I ever recover from this night, I'll make them all suffer," he groaned.

Prone, with the rafters swirling above him, Malcolm imagined all the perverse forms of revenge he could use to repay his men for pressing the endless amount of scotch-spiked ale upon him. He could task them to dig a moat with their bare hands or scrub the garderobe shafts. Perhaps he'd slip a handful of salt—or five—into their morning porridge.

Malcolm's vengeful thoughts were interrupted when a slight pull on his leg brought his mind back into focus. He lifted his heavy head to look wearily down the plane of his chest and found Coira kneeling on the floor. Her beautiful face was full of empathy as she removed his boots one at a time. After a drunken struggle, Malcolm heaved himself up on his elbows so he could watch her, and a strange warmth invaded his chest as she undressed him. Her fingers were steady and light as they grazed his calf and freed him from his boot. Her slight touch sent faint pulses of desire through the scotch-induced fog that wrapped around him.

"I didnae kiss ye in the church," he blurted and winced, instantly wishing he had kept his thoughts to himself. Her glacial eyes snapped up, wide with surprise, and her cheeks heated as she clambered to her feet. Oh, how he longed to make other, more intimate parts of her blush.

"Do ye want to kiss me now?" She looked nervous at the prospect as she hugged herself.

"No. Aye… no." Och, he was so confused. He wanted nothing more than to tear Coira's dress from her body and bury himself within her warmth. Everything in his being was demanding that he claim her. *Ordering* him to do so.

Heaving his heavy body upright, she squeaked delightfully when he grasped her hips and spun them around until her back was pressed into the soft bedding. The thick pad of blankets embraced her when he half-covered her with his body.

"Weddings," he crooned as he traced her smooth cheek with his nose. "mean lovemakin', lass. No' just chaste kisses."

The smell of her drove him wild as he shifted his weight and settled his hips in the space between her thighs; the fabric of her gown rustled in the quiet, candle-lit room. Her wheat-blonde waves fanned out around her, beckoning his hands to delve in their softness. As drunk as he was, he was not so bashed that he failed to notice how rigid she was beneath him. Breathing heavily, her breasts strained beneath her bodice, and her fingers dug hard into the muscles of his shoulders as she held him back. With a scowl, he eased off and fell to her right to give her some space and his muddled mind room to breathe.

"Be assured there willnae be any o' that between us, Coira. Dinnae think I failed to notice yer *misgivings* when ye stood beside me at the altar. Although for the life o' me I dinnae ken what I have done to make ye fear me so."

Coira turned her face away and lifted her hand between them. Her pointer finger traced the line of demarcation that crept along part of her cheekbone and the side of her neck, the line that separated the marbled skin from the smooth. This close to her, he could see her scars quite clearly, even through his drunken haze. For the first time he noticed her ear wasn't whole, the shell eaten away at the edges by the fire that had marked her. The mottled river of skin and scars flowed down her neck to adorn her collarbone, then disappeared down her back, leaving her chest unblemished. Tracing the ruined flesh, her lower lip trembled in such a way that he wanted to rip out his own heart.

He was not prepared for what she said next. "The priest that married us… he gave me these scars."

CHAPTER SEVEN

———

COIRA

Norwich, England
Twelve Years Ago

"**C**an we go faster Da?" I squealed when I glimpsed the great Norwich Cathedral looming above the city in the distance.

With a shake of his head, my father chuckled and reached into the back of the wagon to ruffle my hair, his light blue eyes twinkling.

"No, Coira, my love. Practice yer patience, we'll get there soon enough." He smiled and settled his arm back around my mother's shoulders.

Ness squirmed beside me and grasped my hand like she always did when she could barely contain her excitement. My cousin and my mother's ward since she was but six months old, Ness was my sister in every corner of my heart. Three years younger than my thirteen summers, it was just the two of us growing up, our bond unbreakable and full of love. We slept together, back-to-back and heel-to-heel. We played and learned the way of the Druid life side-by-side. She was my champion, and I was hers, and we promised one another it would be like that always.

Since before I could remember, my parents would make the trek north to the Druid village near Inverness each year in autumn. We'd stay for a month, then journey back to our cottage before the snows smothered the highland roads. I vaguely remember the year we returned home with Ness.

Her mother had died on the birthing bed, with no father nor family to claim her. My mother took one look at Ness's bright green eyes and took her as her own. *"She's strong, her blood as pure as my own,"* my mother declared. The strongest Druid in all of Scotia, she insisted Ness come home with us where she would get the proper training. No one objected.

The English breeze blew a stray copper curl into Ness's face, and she giggled while we looked toward the city with bubbling enthusiasm. "What do ye think the city will be like, Coira?"

I tucked her hair behind her ear and smiled. "I dinnae have the faintest idea, but I feel a thrill in my bones like I've never felt before."

We'd never been to England, nor to a city anywhere half as large as Norwich. Mother rarely brought us to the surrounding villages, let alone a city. She said it was safer that we stay behind at our cottage deep in the woods until just this past year.

"Yer old enough now," she'd said the day she had revealed that we would be making the journey to England with her. *"And I trust that ye willnae expose us, for ye ken the consequences."*

There weren't many Druids among the population of England. Our people mostly preferred the wide-open spaces of Scotland and Ireland, where the earth's magic was thickest and easily called upon. But we had distant relatives in Norwich and my mother was invited as guest of honor to teach their younglings the Druid ways. My chest puffed with pride at being a descendant of the purest bloodlines of Mug Ruith's bloodlines, and I looked forward to following in my mother's footsteps someday. In the past generations, none of the women in my family had strayed from the Druid lineage, ensuring their daughters were born with potent abilities.

As one of the most powerful of our people, Mother often took responsibility for instructing the young when it came their time; but she had a rigid, violent approach to her teachings that regularly shocked and disturbed me. All her lessons were designed to leave an impact so great, they stuck with the novice forever. I'll never forget the day she taught me the importance of the Druid word for *sleep*. That day would be forever fused into my memory.

I was eight.

"Coira!" my mother called out from the woods while Ness and I practiced our runes in the sand where they were harmless. Brushing the dirt from my knees, I ran toward my mother's voice and my father caught me by the arm as I rushed by.

As he crouched before me so we were eye-to-eye, he had a strange look about him when he said firmly, "No matter what happens, lassie, ken that yer mother and I love ye." And with a kiss on my forehead, he walked in the opposite direction, his shoulders heavy with some unknown burden.

With less enthusiasm, I entered the forest and pushed past the low-hanging pine branches. Thick, bristly ferns grasped my bare ankles as though they knew something I did not and wanted to spare me from finding out.

"There ye are," Mother said, her voice throaty, her face void of emotion.

Apprehension began to creep up my spine when I recognized her teacher's mask. She always became distant when she taught me the harsher, more disturbing magic.

Before I could ask her any questions, she stepped to the side, and her skirts revealed the furry orange body of my cat writhing in the bracken. I cried out in horror.

"Alistair!" I screamed. My heart lurched at her betrayal, and I rushed forward to crouch beside him, my hands hovering over the dagger that protruded from his belly.

"Call upon the earth, Coira," Mother said over my tears, her voice urgent.

"What?" All I could think about was the pain Alistair was in as his struggles grew sluggish. Why would she do this? She was mad!

"Call upon the earth and heal him, daughter. He's dying. Ye can save him," she barked, instigating even more anxiety.

Choking down my sobs, I did the first thing that came to my mind and yanked the dagger out of Alistair's belly. His agonized yowl permanently ingrained itself into my soul as I pressed my palm hard against his bloody wound and reached out for the prickly bramble beside me. Then I closed my eyes and began to sing the ancient words of healing life and transference that willed the energy from one living thing into the other through my body. Tears streamed down my face while Alistair howled and scratched my arms and hands and wrist to bloody ribbons. The bush turned to dust within moments and I panicked. Too small. I needed something bigger. With my beloved cat's pain-filled cries in my ears, I tucked him to my chest and lunged the few yards to a young pine and continued my song.

The power that galloped within my blood sang its own anthem, beckoning me to lose myself. To become power.

It frightened me.

Slowly, Alistair stopped struggling in my iron grip. His little chest heaved under my fingers, and his green eyes were so wide I could see the whites of the orbs. With his healing complete, I severed the connection to the pine and dropped the cat; my fingers numb and limbs like jelly. Hissing and spitting, Alistair fled deeper into the woods, his tail puffed up three times its normal size. I feared I'd never see him again.

Dropping down to my knees on the forest floor, I pressed my face into a soft mound of damp moss and sobbed, cradling my bloody forearm against my chest. When I fell quiet, Mother came to stand beside me and crouched down, her head tilted to the side as she looked me over, her teacher's mask still in place.

"Why did ye no' make him sleep before ye healed him?"

I gasped and sat up, her question shocking me to my core. Dismay coiled within my belly like an oily serpent. Why didn't I execute the sleeping spell? I had done it dozens of times before.

"I—I forgot," I whispered, feeling ten times the wretched girl I was. I looked down at my arm. Alistair's claws had dug deep, and as my blood pulsed from the wounds, I realized the horror of my actions. By not putting him to sleep, I had forced him to endure the worst kind of agony while his flesh knit back together. While the dagger had gone in smooth and quick, severing flesh and piercing organs, the reverse was slow. I had been told it was akin to molten metal racing through your veins, knitting muscle and sinew together at a sluggish pace. My stupidity and carelessness had forced Alistair to endure every terrible moment of it.

"Well," Mother's voice was soft with what I thought was understanding until she grasped my bloody arm in an iron grip with one hand and the half dead pine with the other, "I ken just the way to make it so ye never forget again."

I begged and pleaded with her, but my screams for mercy went unanswered while we watched my flesh knit back together inch by agonizing inch. When she was done I ran deep into the woods, ashamed and full of self-loathing. My father found me hours later and carried me home, his strong arms wrapped around my back and beneath my knees.

"I dinnae understand, Da." I sniffled against the warm skin of his neck, and uselessly rubbed my tears away just for them to be replaced by another. "Why does she teach me that way?"

Da was quiet for a time and mulled over his answer as he picked his way around the moss-covered stones in the grey light of twilight. It was one of the many things I loved about him and could always count on. Where my mother was brash and rigid, he was composed, thoughtful, and sympathetic. I knew whatever he would say would be a balm to the phantom pain in my arm.

"Druid women, especially yer mother's line, are exceptionally special, Coira. The unique ability to harness the force o' the earth, wind, and water is no small thing. Anyone would be a fool to teach a youngling how to wield that sort o' power without making them feel—and understand—the ramifications o' that influence. Aye, she did a horrible thing and it will take ye a while to forgive her." He set me down on my feet and took my face between his rough palms. Crouching down to my level, his blue eyes held me captive. "But do try to understand the why, *my daughter. She taught ye two verra important lessons today in a way ye'll* never *forget. A week, a year, or a decade from now, ye'll never heal another without thinkin' back on this day. For all her cruel ways, ye'll grow stronger for it."*

I scratched lightly at the inside of my forearm when we entered the city and pulled myself out of my memories to stare with my mouth agape at the largest buildings I'd ever seen. Ness looked similarly in awe at my side. Mother had told us the Druids in England were weaker, their abilities a mere drop in the ocean compared to ours. They could perform small magics worth learning, but they were incapable of executing the complicated songs that came so easy to us; that was why we had made the journey here.

Colorful banners and triangular flags stretched between white-washed and grey stone buildings. Da told us there would be a summer festival later in the week making Ness and me squirm with excitement. Norwich was known for its cloth and invited weavers of linen, wool, and lace from near and far to display and sell their goods each year. Ness giggled incessantly, and by the time we arrived at the large two-story home jammed between many others on a busy street, our cheeks ached from smiling. Like most other buildings around it, the second story, with large windows across the front, faced the street and was built out, sheltering those walking below from rain.

The week went by quickly. Mother taught the few young Druids in her care to light candles with a whisper and direct the flow of water, things I had learned to do when I was four. Lighting cook fires and controlling the garden's watering had been mastered by the time I was five. The girls here were my age and just barely grasping the thread of magic that tied them to all things, their blood diluted from generations of breeding with common men. They'd never be able to command the weather like Ness and I could. Never heal a mortal wound, tame a wildfire, or call lightning from the sky. It saddened me to know that their great-grandchildren would barely have enough power to command a gentle breeze.

With enthusiasm, we coached alongside Mother, eager to show our skills. We made candle flames twist and wave madly in the air and raced water droplets from one end of a table to the other, enchanting our audience. It was liberating to be our true selves among others just like us, not hiding or repressing our nature. It was the best time of my life. Surrounded by girls our own age, we were content to stay in the large townhouse teaching until the day of the festival finally arrived.

First to wake, Ness and I eagerly ate our porridge and squirmed in our seats at the opportunity to explore the city. Clothed in the most beautiful sky-blue dresses, gifted to us by the lady of the house, we twirled and skipped around the kitchen in our finery. My father took pity and escorted us through the crowded cobbled streets ahead of the others in the household.

To our delight, not only was all manner of cloth displayed and sold, but there were trinkets and exotic foodstuffs as well. Da treated us to a cup of freshly-pressed juice from a sweet and tangy orange that made the back of my tongue sing with pleasure, and a small cinnamon pastry that left sticky sweetness on our fingers. It was while Ness and I strolled along, licking our fingers clean, that a window opened above us. With barely a call of warning, dirty water splashed down to the street and directly onto Ness, soaking her copper curls and staining her lovely, new dress.

"Bloody idiot!" Da yelled up at the window as it slammed shut. He ushered us under the awning of the house like a mother goose with her wings out as he bellowed his irritation. "Tossin' soiled water out like there's no' a hundred people down here!" He frowned at Ness's ruined dress and wet hair as she wiped her face and shook her hands miserably. "Och, my poor Nessie. Wait here and dinnae move, I'll be right back with somethin' to clean ye up."

I wrapped a protective arm around Ness, and as we watched him hurry away, I found myself wishing Druids could cast hex's like the fabled witch people feared we were. I'd hex the woman who threw the water with the pox, I would! At the very least, conjure a black wart to grow on the tip of her nose. A hairy one! While I imagined all the truly terrible things one could wish upon the stranger, I felt the barest brush of magic against my skin and all my senses heightened. Looking around fearfully, it took me a moment to realize the magic was coming from beside me.

"What are ye doin'?" I hissed and watched in horror. The filthy water beaded up to drip out of Ness's hair and ran down the fabric of her dress like rain off the back of a duck. It landed in a circle around her slippered feet, turning the cobbled stones a dark, muddy grey.

Ness gave a little shiver and looked up at me defiantly. "No one saw, Coira. I only *just* got this dress, and I didnae want Da to make us leave. We've been stuck inside all week."

Fear and sharp pricks of heat tingled along my lower back, behind my knees, and under my arms. I looked around once more, convinced someone had seen and we would be exposed. Grasping her hand, I dragged her along the row of houses, away from the damning circle of damp stone.

"Ye should no' have done that. Mother will have yer hide when she finds out."

That made her pause, and her spring-green eyes widened with distress. Mother dealt out punishments swiftly and justly. As the more reckless of us, Ness knew exactly what was in store for her.

"Ye willnae tell her, will ye?"

"I dinnae want to, but Da will ken what ye did as soon as he sees ye." Pulling her into my arms, I searched frantically through the crowd for my father's golden-brown hair and spotted him a few minutes later with a yard of rough, white linen in his hands. His triumphant smile melted when he neared.

"Nessie, what have ye done?" he whispered harshly when he found her dry and clean. Taking her by the arms he shook her tersely, his face anxious. "Were ye seen?"

"No, Da." Her bottom lip began to quiver, and her eyes brimmed with tears at his disappointment.

He scanned the faces of the crowd warily. "Let's go. I dinnae ken what Vanora will do with ye, Ness, but—och, dinnae cry sweet Nessie. No one saw ye, right?"

I'd seen Ness take a walloping from my mother more times than I could count and walk away with her nose in the air and a smirk on her lips. But to see my father's face tighten with displeasure was her complete undoing. If only she had thought of *him* before she pulled that little stunt for anyone to see.

I watched as he wiped the tears from her freckled cheeks and wanted nothing more than to run back to our relative's home and lock myself inside until it was time to go back to Scotland. My blood hummed with worry, and the faintest breeze agitated my skin. Something was telling me to hide, although no one was looking at us and I could find no threat in the mass of people that passed by.

"Come, now. We've a long way to go." Taking us by the hand, he led the way, his mouth drawn in a grim line. I'd never seen my father look so worried, and I wondered if he possibly felt the same unpleasant hollow in his belly that I did.

The uneasiness that raced in my veins failed to abate as we navigated the city streets away from the festival. I'd almost begun to think I was overreacting from my cousin's reckless use of magic when a shout rang out just behind us.

"You there!" an English voice called out.

"Dinnae slow, daughters." My father's hand tightened around mine as he walked faster, towing Ness and I along. "No matter what happens, ye stay by my side."

The thumping of several pairs of boots raced closer and we were quickly surrounded: there were four men, a boy no older than I, and a priest, his plain black robes menacing in the bright sunshine. At the sight of the clergyman, my bowels knotted up. Every Druid knew a priest's presence meant that tragedy was not far behind.

"That's them two girls, Papa, I seen em' wit' me own eyes!" Pointing an accusatory finger toward us, the boy's brows were drawn low, his pimply face spiteful as he glared at Ness. "She's a witch, I tell you!"

"*Witches*. In *my* parish?" the priest gasped. He made the sign of the cross in the air before Ness and then me, his features full of abhorrence, fear, and anger. Two decades or so older than my father, he was short and soft, with thinning hair and the beginnings of arthritis in his clenched hands.

"*No*." My father wrapped his arms around us both protectively, his grip like iron. Facing the boy's father, he pressed me against his side so hard my neck popped. "No witches here. Yer lad is mistaken."

"He told me the red haired girl shimmered in the shadows! Called to him like a siren in the ocean, she did." The boy's father turned his wary gaze from Ness to me. "And *she* threatened to bewitch him!"

The blatant lie was told so earnestly I could only blink, dumbfounded. *This* was what my mother had warned us about. She had told us the fear of men would twist our power, given to us by the earth herself, into something dirty, wanton, and evil.

My father sputtered a response while a small crowd collected around us and watched with interest and excitement. Panic seized my limbs, and I began to shake in terror when the priest narrowed his sight on Ness and gestured toward us both.

"It seems as though your daughters may have been conversing with the Devil, good sir. Fear not. I will get to the bottom of their sins."

The priest stepped back and jerked his chin at the men beside him. "Take them to the church."

"No!" My father bellowed as the four men moved in and tried to tear Ness from his grip. "Ye willnae take them from me!"

He pushed me away roughly, yelling at me to run, but fear gripped me like a rabbit caught in a snare, choking my reasoning. Within seconds, someone lifted me off the cobbled street and slung me over a meaty shoulder like a sack of flour. The sticky pastry I had eaten, now wedged thick in my throat, threatened to purge itself from my body. From between the strands of blonde hair draped over my face, I watched in horror as Ness fought like a thing possessed, biting and scratching like a feral cat at the arms that restrained her.

It was the sight of my father getting hit on his head from behind while fighting to get to me that snapped me out of my shocked stupor. I watched in horror when his body crumpled and stayed motionless on the ground. Anger like I had never felt before raced like wildfire through my limbs—my soul—at the sight of my father's motionless form in the filthy street. I raged against the man that detained me and beat my fists against his back as he carted me away. And in my fury, I began to chant.

My voice morphed into something not of this world, snaking through the people that gawked at me as I was carried past them. I could feel the pricks of energy in my fingertips as I spoke, and knew the sky was rapidly darkening by the cries of the people around us. Thunder vibrated through the clouds above, but immersed in the pull of my magic, I was only half aware. Ness's face whipped toward mine, her tear-streaked face slack when she realized what I was doing. I could only think of my father, prone and swallowed by the crowd as we were hauled farther away from him. The thunder grew closer, louder, the rumble building up strength and charging the air.

"Stop her!" I heard someone bellow.

I'd drown them all. I would call the sea to flood the streets and fill their homes for what they were doing to us!

The strength beneath my skin was like nothing I had ever felt. Love and hate, victory and defeat, it tasted like sweet nectar in my mouth as I sang and sang.

The man's grip loosened, and I abruptly dropped to the ground; he pressed his dirty hand against my mouth. I bit down hard, grinning madly at the painful cry and blood that coated my tongue.

I continued my song.

I would make them all pay.

"Cease your spell, witch!" the priest hissed. Someone shoved a bit of cloth into my mouth, muffling my song and effectively halting my vengeance. "Bring them straight away, no trial necessary. I've seen her evil with my own eyes."

Leather strapping was wound tight around my wrists, and I looked over to find Ness trussed in the same fashion: a gag in her mouth, her hands bound behind her back. She looked at me with a mix of fury and panic. I'm sorry, Nessie. I tried my best to convey my thoughts to her while I struggled to escape my bonds and my shoulders screamed in pain when I jerked against them.

The crowd followed us to the church, spitting and jeering the entire way. It was so terrible that I actually felt a moment of relief when we were shoved through the open doors of a church, past the pews, and down some stairs to the basement. No one followed but the priest.

"Separate them," the priest snapped, and opened a thick wooden door.

No! I had to be with Ness! I kicked and howled through the wad of fabric in my mouth, trying to get to her as she was shoved into the room and locked inside.

"This one is trouble, Father Blount," a gruff voice snarled in my ear.

"Indeed. Bind her further. She cannot be allowed to speak."

They wrapped thicker bindings around my wrists and ankles, and a sash was firmly fastened over my face before I felt blinding pain on the back of my head. Intense, white light took over my vision, and I felt myself falling to the floor a moment before everything went dark.

"I have been searching for another for years, Father."

An Englishman's rough-spoken, muffled words, followed by a wet cough, flowed from the other side of the door, rousing me from my stupor. Light crept in from under the thick crack near the floor, barely illuminating the dark room I'd been locked inside. My vision swam, and I fought against rolling nausea as my memories resurfaced. Memories of being dragged to the church.

Ness!

My confusion chased away, I tried to focus on the conversation in the hallway.

"You must let me take the younger girl. I doubt I could control the elder."

Low, disembodied murmurs responded, and I inched myself closer to the door on my belly so I could hear better. A fit of coughing drowned out the soft voice.

"I know, I know, you have your society. But I have mine, and I want her."

Unease lifted the hair on my arms and neck as I peered under the space at the bottom of the door and saw a pair of fine, black shoes, polished to a high shine. Beside them, the hem of the priests long black robes brushed the floor.

"Yes, I've heard what you do up there. It's a sin, you know," Father Blount sniped.

"Perhaps. Or, could I possibly be doing God's work by punishing sinners?"

Father Blount scoffed at the owner of the strange voice.

"I didn't think you'd agree. No matter. Before I take my leave, I could not help but notice that your church is in need of repair. Allow me to make a... donation, *if you will, to your humble parish."*

The heavy pause pounded in my ears, and a whimper crawled up my throat. He wouldn't! *Sell* Ness? For the price of what? A donation to the Christian God?

"A generous one, I think, would be satisfactory," the priest intoned greedily and turned on his heel. The owner of the polished shoes followed him down the hall toward the room where Ness was kept.

My breath came out in rapid pants through my gag at Ness's fearful cries, her terror fueling my own, and I was forced to listen helplessly as the stranger wrestled her into submission. I railed against my bonds, flopping uselessly on the floor. I watched through the crack under the door as her small feet kicked and pounded on the slate tiles as she was dragged away. Then she was gone, and I was left alone with her screams echoing in my head.

Lost in sorrow, I wailed at the injustice done to us and squirmed on the floor attempting to loosen my bonds. I needed to break free! I had to chase after her! Frantic to escape, I rubbed my face on the floor in an effort to dislodge my gag, leaving my cheeks chafed and the soft skin of my wrists raw. I had succeeded in loosening my ankle wrappings and had just kicked the bindings off when a tall, balding man opened the door. He glared down at me, his thin lips twisted with disgust.

"Don't look at me, witch," the Englishman spat. He stood me up with a harsh jerk on my elbow and pushed me out into the hallway.

I bolted, hoping against all hope that I could outrun him while I searched for a way out of the church, realizing too late that I was headed the opposite way Ness had been taken. With no other option but to continue, I raced down the hallway with my hands tied behind my back. I stumbled up a short stairwell, jamming my toes on each narrow step, and whimpered when I saw a door half-cracked, daylight spearing across the slate floor. I didn't think twice about the low hum of voices on the other side; all I knew was the tall man's footsteps were closing in on me and I had one chance to escape.

With a grunt, I slammed my shoulder against the door and found myself in a courtyard… where several dozen had people gathered around a pyre.

"Never thought a witch would be so eager for judgement," the tall man snickered from behind and gripped my upper arm with his boney fingers, propelling me forward.

Jeers and sneers were maliciously hurled at me by the agitated crowd. Moldy fruits and vegetables peppered my face and clothing, their rotting odor clinging to everything they touched. I moved past them in a blur, their faces dull and insignificant through my fear, as we approached a platform, and the priest who stood waiting for me. The look in his beady eyes dripped with loathing and satisfaction as I was forced toward my demise.

While the priest listed my crimes, the tall man pushed down hard on my shoulders with a grunted order to "*sit*". He tied my hands to a heavy metal ring in the floor of the platform before he brandished a single-edged dagger. My blood drained from my face when he roughly grabbed a fistful of my hair. I expected him to slice open my throat, and nearly sobbed with displaced relief when he began sawing through the pale-gold locks along my scalp. They fell in lifeless clumps on the wood planks around me; all my hair Da had lovingly told me looked more beautiful than a winter sunrise. At the thought of him, hot tears ran in rivers down my cheeks and absorbed into my gag. I wished for nothing more than his arms around me one last time. I did not want to die without feeling that comfort and safety again.

"She is gagged because her very voice is polluted, and she intends to ensnare the souls of men. You can see now the way the Devil beckons you forward through her eyes!" the priest shouted at the crowd below while he circled me, his voice echoing off the tall walls of the church. "Thou shalt not suffer a witch to live!"

I closed my eyes at those damning words, unwilling to watch the men and women below cheer for my death. I did not want to die. I had barely begun living. I had only experienced the faintest taste of what life had to offer me. Surely I was born for more than this!

The priest continued preaching as he paced the platform. "I release the Fire of the Holy Spirit to consume this witch working against my destiny…"

I scarcely felt my body as I was lifted to my feet and pushed off the platform onto the pyre. My arms circled behind me and were affixed to a thick beam that jutted out of the center of the piled firewood. I don't know if I fought against them, or if I complied, but the seconds blurred from one to the next, like the time I rode a feral highland pony. One moment I was on, my legs gripping its rib cage, racing fast as the wind, and the next I was flat on my back staring up at the clouds.

"I declare that I am immune to the enchantments and divinations of witches…"

I choked on my sobs and gazed numbly over the heads of the people gathered to watch me die. I couldn't look at their excitement or listen to their curses or taunts. Instead, I did my best to focus on the wall that circled the courtyard and the flowering vines that climbed it. A pair of doves took off in a flurry of grey feathers, and as I watched them climb high in the sky, I found myself envious of their freedom.

"We have a witch in our midst, and her powers are real. But the power of God is even more real and powerful!" Blount raised his Bible in the air and bellowed at the awestruck crowd. "But no devil or his children can match the power of God…"

My magic whipped through my veins, my fear bolstering it to a wave within my body, power that would condemn them to death. But the gag kept the words from forming, and my magic was locked within with no way of escape. Muted, I was forced to wait while the priest paced the platform behind me. Father Blount continued to recount my crimes and beseeched God to rid me of my demons.

It was subtle at first. If I hadn't been watching the doves, I would have missed the darkening sky above the surrounding buildings. The white cloud puffs grew thicker and thicker, until they muted the bright, summer sun. Then the wind picked up. A quick gust tickled my neck and nearly-bare scalp like an old friend. I swore I felt my mother's finger trace my cheek like she'd done all my life.

Movement drew my focus to the right, where a hooded man dressed all in black cracked a flint to light the end of a torch with orange flames. Close to the pyre, he stood patiently, awaiting the order to burn me alive. My knees began to shake so badly that, if I wasn't tied to the post, I surely would have crumpled among the kindling.

"But the cowardly, the unbelieving, the vile, the murderers, the sexually immoral, those who practice magic arts, the idolaters and all liars—they will be consigned to the fiery lake of burning sulfur. This is the second death…"

Thunder rumbled in the distance while the priest continued his pretty speech, the grumble rolling closer and closer until the clouds blocked the sun completely. A few women in the crowd cried out with the first crack of lightning. Sharp branches of white light skittered along the bellies of the dark clouds, the thunder that followed deafening. Gooseflesh pebbled my bare arms, my stockinged legs, and the flesh of my back. *Mother is here*, I realized. Hope bloomed in my chest and I looked around wildly, straining for a glimpse of where she had hidden herself. She had come to save me.

"See here?" the priest howled as he pointed his Bible accusingly at me. He turned and nodded to the man holding the torch. "Witness how she invites the Devil! She calls her wrath upon the God-fearing and the true!"

No, no, no! I watched in horror and tried to kick out when the masked man shoved the torch into the kindling on my right. The flames reached for the dry twigs and straw and ate them greedily. I wailed through my gag; my cries ripped painfully at my throat as I watched the fire flourish and grow ever closer while my executioner moved around to the other side of the pyre.

A flash of blinding light and a deafening crack so loud my ears rang, singed the air to my left, and struck the man in black. A woman screamed, high and shrill, when his lifeless body collapsed to the ground, and the torch rolled harmlessly away to be snuffed out on the grass.

The crowd had barely enough time to react before a preternatural roar filled the courtyard, the otherworldly tone more beast than man, and my father appeared beneath the arched gate across the courtyard.

Shocked by his strange appearance, I almost forgot the heat of the fire as I beheld him. His body had grown nearly twice its normal size and height, and twin orbs of glowing white light replaced the blue irises that I knew so well. His face was a vicious mask that promised violence as he shouldered through the throng, shoving men and women alike to the ground as though they weighed little more than wheat stalks. He surged forward, unhindered and determined, just as the flames reached the hem of my dress.

I didn't have more than a moment to wonder how my father acquired his newfound body before the heat of the fire took its first taste of my skin. The bite of pain didn't start at my feet like I had expected, but my thigh. The flames burned an agonizing trail over my hip and waist, greedily devouring the fabric of my clothing, crawling like a gluttonous demon up my right arm just above my wrist. Mother's wind pushed at me from my left, but the damage was done. My dress was a bright flame, and I screamed, the agony indescribable as it quickly spread. I could smell the damage it was doing to my body, tasted the flavor of my charring flesh, and for a maddening moment, I was thankful they'd shorn my head.

I could hear my father's roar of fury past my own screams when the fabric on my shoulder caught, and the flames began to reach—up, up, up—for the gag wrapped around my face. Fear seized me with obsidian claws of embers and ash, and I lost consciousness.

It couldn't have been more than a few moments before awareness returned to me, and someone ripped the gag off my face where it had weakened by the fire. I looked up to find my father standing in the flames with me, a look of purpose and rage twisting his face. His clothing, tight and shredded at the seams from his transformation, had caught fire while he fumbled with my bound hands. Indifferent to his own pain, he tore at my bindings until they were nothing but shreds.

All the while, the sky above continued to pulse with lightning, and tearful cries melded with the frightened and confused shouts of the crowd as they scattered.

My dress hung off the right side of my burned body in sooty ribbons, and my father clutched me against his too-large chest. Holding me in his arms, he leaped off the pyre to the ground… only to come face to face with three armed men I vaguely recognized as the ones who took me in the street.

The first drop of rain landed on my scalp when they pointed their rapiers at us, their expressions full of fear, not sure if they should flee or fight. I knew Da looked like a monster, unnatural and formidable with his glowing eyes and immense size. But he didn't frighten me. With great care not to cause me more pain, he pushed my shaking, half-naked body behind him, leaving me to beat the dying embers still smoking on my dress.

Rain fell in a thick, grey sheet the moment my father unleashed himself upon the men. His movements were quick and measured, faster than I had ever seen. The glow of his eyes illuminated the faces of each man as he slaughtered them one by one with his bare hands, and I watched them fall dead to the ground with broken necks, missing limbs, and shattered bones.

A small part of me rejoiced at their stillness.

The rain drenched everything in the courtyard in a matter of moments, the water a soothing balm to my ruined, tender flesh. Da picked me up and carried me swiftly across the now empty courtyard and approached the flower-shrouded wall.

"Where's Nessie?" he barked over the crackle of thunder. My tears came harder.

"Gone," I barely managed to whisper over the rawness of my throat. I couldn't bear the sorrow that passed over his face. His eyes, still illuminated in an unworldly glow, glared through the downpour.

"Give her to me." My mother's voice drew my attention to an open gate tucked into the vine-covered walls. My heart leaped into my throat when she stepped out of the shadows on the other side. Anger and devastation twisted her features as she looked over my wounds.

Heavy, booted footsteps echoed off the walls of the church behind us. I cast a worried glance over my father's shoulder and trembled at the sight of nearly twenty men as they marched out of the church. They wore the red coats of the guard, each armed with swords and flintlock rifles, and they headed straight for us.

"Go." My father's chest rumbled against my cheek before he set me down and urged me through the gate to my mother's side. Standing beside her, I caught a look pass between them. I had never seen my mother look that way, so full of love, understanding, and complete and utter misery.

"*Bidh mi thu a-rithist,*" she moaned. He traced her cheek with his thumb, and fresh tears spilled down my own at the broken sound of her voice.

The white glow of his eyes illuminated the tracks of her tears and tremble of her bottom lip. From his towering height, he bent at the waist to press his mouth against hers in a searing kiss. Too soon, he stepped back into the courtyard and pushed the gate shut between them, the metal bars separating us with a grotesque finality. A small smile passed over his lips, a silent goodbye, and then he turned to greet the guards with a father's fury.

And a husband's devotion.

It was then I realized… when my mother had told him in Gaelic that she would see him again, she meant in the next life.

I whimpered while she dragged me away, the ache in my heart overpowering the pain that lashed at my body as we ran through the shadowed alleyways. The sound of screaming, gunfire, and metal clashing chased after us like shadow demons nipping at our heels.

It was the sound of my father's death dance as he held them off long enough to secure our escape.

"I understand it hurts, but ye must keep movin', Coira," she said, her grip on my left wrist like a vice as I stumbled behind her. But she didn't understand. This was all my fault, and even as my body screamed in agony, my heart suffered a hundred times worse. A thousand. I knew I would never overcome this torturous guilt that clawed at me from the inside. First, the loss of my sister. Second, my father.

We arrived at our relative's home, out of breath and exhausted. The rain lessened, and the clouds began to break up to reveal the descending sun as my mother released her hold on the elements. She pounded on the door.

It opened a crack, and our cousin's face appeared, but she refused us entry. "You can't come in. I hear there's a witch hunt—"

"Ye *will* let me in, cousin, or I will raze this city and all within to its foundations… starting *here*," Mother hissed, and wrapped her arm around my shaking form, her face set in hard determination.

With the knowledge that she would rip into the very earth below the city for me… guilt clogged my throat like a lump of partially-chewed bread, heavy with repentance. I did not deserve such fierceness or unwavering loyalty from her.

My body, spent and exhausted from all it had endured, sagged against her side. What energy I had left I'd used to keep my cries at bay while I fought against the throbbing agony that rippled up and down my back and arm. The door opened, however reluctantly, and we were allowed entry. The clack of several bolts sliding into place faintly registered through the chattering of my teeth as we shuffled through to the back of the house.

"Where are the others?" our cousin asked as she quickly bolted the door.

At the mention of Ness and my father, Mother's eyes grew dark, but she waved away the inquiry. "I need to heal her," she snapped when we reached the door to the rear courtyard that divided the stable from the townhouse.

"But my husband took the animals for slaughter with your wagon. They left hours ago."

Mother whipped around, staring daggers at our cousin, and spoke through her teeth, "Have ye no goat? A dog? Look at what they've done to her!"

I could feel her rage in the air and on my tongue like the acrid grit of charcoal. And the lady of the house could as well. I saw the fear plainly in her eyes as she beheld my mother's rage and swallowed thickly as she wrung her hands.

"We have two chickens," she whispered with nervous apology.

"*Two*," Mother hissed in disbelief, then blinked down at me with regret. "Bring them to me."

She guided me down to the cellar and bid me to lay down on the cool, dirt floor. I curled on my left side, and my tears flowed freely while she cut away the tattered fabric that did little to hide my body. My hand held to my mouth, I failed to muffle the sobs that broke through my failing restraint and flinched at the gentle touch to the short hair on my scalp.

"Sweet daughter. Sleep now." Blissful darkness enveloped me in its welcoming embrace, and I fell willingly into a dreamless slumber the pain of my wounds could not reach.

When I opened my eyes, I found myself prone in the back of our unmoving wagon. My mother's face, full of sadness, hovered above me, the clear, blue sky beyond. Around us I could hear the breeze through the trees and the noisy blare of waterfowl in a nearby pond.

My first thought was that I no longer felt any pain; only a residual tightness lingered on my skin. My second thought was of my father as I stared at the thick streak of white hair that now grew out of my mother's part. The colorless locks framed her face, the tell-tale sign of a bonded Druid deep in mourning. At the sight of them, I knew he was truly dead, and it would only ever be the two of us from then on.

"I'm sorry, Mother," I sobbed and sat up, blinking away my tears and reaching for her. "'Tis my fault Da and Ness are gone."

We sat in the back of the wagon for a time, my cheek on her shoulder as she rubbed my back and rocked us both in silence. Someone had dressed me in a strange grey frock, the sleeves too short and the waist loose, but it was clean. Other than the strange lack of hair on my head and the pain in my heart, I felt fine. When she released me, I caught her looking remorsefully at the side of my face as she gripped my right hand, her shoulders slumped in defeat, a posture I had never seen her display before.

"What is it?" I asked.

She shook her head and sucked her trembling lips between her teeth. Her forefinger swept an arc along my wrist, the sensation felt unfamiliar. Muted.

"The damage was too great for what I had available. Just a pair o' hens. No' nearly enough. Ye only healed partially, and by the time I got ye out o' the city yer body thought it was hale and whole. I failed to smooth the fire's damage beyond this," she said sadly, almost as though she were chastising herself.

I shook my head, wanting to tell her that none of this was her fault, when I caught a glimpse of the back of my hand and my scars for the first time.

Marbled, slightly shiny webbing covered my wrist, and I yanked up the short sleeve to find them spread over most of my forearm. Horrified, my hands flew to my face. I grazed the pads of my fingers over the ridges and bumps along my ear, down my neck, and over my shoulder.

For a moment, I thought this was one of her lessons—to leave me scarred this way as a reminder—but her eyes were hollow as she watched me, and I knew. She had not left me this way in punishment, although I would have understood if she had. I almost wished she had, for my remorse and self-hatred was nearly overwhelming.

My loving father was gone from this world and Nessie had been taken to places unknown. I did not harbor delusions that she was alive and well. My heart broke with the knowledge that I would never see her again.

Side-by-side, we drove our wagon north to Scotland. Mother and I barely spoke, both deep in the darkness of our grief. But at night, when we settled down on our blankets beneath the stars, she wrapped her arms around me and told me it would be alright in the end.

I didn't have the heart to tell her I didn't believe her.

Chapter Eight

COIRA

Self-sequestered in the south tower of Ghlas Thùr, I packed fresh lavender buds into the cloudy alcohol that simmered over an oil lamp. All day, I isolated myself, as I had nearly every day for the last month, since my wedding to the MacKinnon Laird.

The healing supplies in this castle were deplorable, and I labored night and day to replenish my stores of oils infused with lavender, garlic, oregano, and ginger. I shuddered to think what the people would do if another plague struck this part of Scotland. Without the medicinals I created, the loss of life would be devastating.

Mostly, I spent my days in solitude, either here in my tower or my garden outside the curtain wall, where the ever-present rain soaked through my cloak. One of Malcolm's cousins or soldiers was always present, watching over me and the surrounding area from a short distance from the garden. Within a few days, I grew accustomed to them and soon barely registered their silent company. If they wanted to watch me push around dirt and rock all day, they were welcome to.

The rainy season had arrived with a vengeance, making up for the time it had lost with the long winter. Since my garden dominated the space at the top of the hill before the ground sloped down to the loch, the drainage was exceptional. But still, I spent one exceedingly muddy day shoring up the herb beds so that they wouldn't wash away. If I hadn't turned heads before, the sight of me, exhausted and covered in mud and bracken from head to toe as I trudged into the keep that evening, surely did.

"Milady, may I come up?" Maeve's bell-like voice drifted up from below, probably bringing the noon meal.

I had not yet met the cook or many other residents besides the serving girls who avoided looking me in the eye, as well as Malcolm's soldiers who barely spoke to me. It was clear, even after a month, that Malcolm's people were still uncomfortable with my presence. The hours were long between my morning tea and supper with my husband and his kin, but I vastly preferred the pains of an empty stomach over being subjected to the wariness in their eyes. Thankfully, Maeve had begun showing up with a repast when the sun was at its zenith, and I hadn't been hungry since.

I filled my days to the brink with my work so each night I would fall exhausted into bed, alone. Not once had my husband joined me. *'Tis because he doesnae want ye*, I told myself, and recalled the look on Malcolm's handsome face when I had told him of my history with the priest.

His thick, black brows had drawn low while he listened to my story, had barely moved, barely breathed as he lay beside me. When I had finished my tale, he'd simply pulled my back tight against his front, his breath soft and warm on the back of my head.

"Yer safe now, just as she wanted ye to be. Sleep."

I'd nearly wept at the comforting feel of his arm around me, had reveled in the strength and size of his chest pressed close against my back. It had been so long since I'd been touched in such a way; the last time when my mother and I had cuddled for the sake of warmth under the blankets one particularly cold night two winters ago. Far longer than most people, I would think.

The weight of Malcolm's arm over my ribcage, and the way his hand barely brushed my stomach, was so unlike the awkward, brief touches we'd shared on our journey from my cottage. It sparked something within me, and I found I didn't want that feeling to end.

When his soft snores started, I dutifully closed my eyes and found myself hoping that things would look brighter come the dawn. But the next morning, I found myself cold and alone in my husband's bed, that budding hope shriveled like a forgotten berry at the bottom of a basket.

It did not make an appearance again.

For days after that, I hadn't joined him for supper, too embarrassed by his obvious rejection, although I should have known better than to expect anything more. After all, we barely knew one another. I should be content with his civility and the space he gave me. I should be grateful for it, shouldn't I?

It was rare we saw one another before the evening meal and even rarer to exchange words beyond a hasty greeting. I never ran into him in the corridors, or out in the baileys, but I caught sight of him a few times while he trained with his warriors in the rain below the eastern window of my tower. I remembered one particularly rare day just last week, when the sun had decided to show itself. I'd nearly dropped the fragile bottle in my hands when I had spied him sparring, shirtless, against a seasoned man with blazing red hair. Even from the tower's height, I had plainly seen the way Malcolm's powerful thighs bunched beneath his dark kilt as he prowled over the packed dirt, sword in hand. The power in his strikes and movements in the sparring ring had been breathtaking, as beautiful as the sun that beat down upon his bronzed back, slicked with sweat.

I may have watched for longer than necessary that day.

"Milady?"

Maeve's second call roused me from the covetous thoughts of my husband's body, and I blushed as though I had been caught doing something indecent. I bade her entry and double checked that my tome was locked in the shallow strongbox bolted to the table. Four strips of steel interlaced over the lid of the box, ensuring no simple thief could easily break into it and steal its precious contents.

"Well, well! Ye've been busy today. Never thought the tower could smell so lovely on a day so dreary," Maeve remarked. She beheld the mounds of sorted flowers and herbs on the table as she stepped onto the landing with a tray in her arms.

Bushels of mint, oregano, and tight-budded lavender, as well as the soft, furry petals of a sage plant, awaited their turn to simmer. Along the curved wall to the right, between the table and some shelving, four earthenware bowls steeped on the floor, each containing a different herb or flower. They would soak there for the next three days, at which time I would discard the wilted leaves within and add new ones. The fragrance of the alcohol they sat in would grow stronger and stronger with each new addition of fresh leaves and petals. After eight rounds and nearly three weeks of patience and effort, there would be enough oil to skim off the surface to store. Easily blended with carrier oils for medicinal use, they would also be used to make lotions, or soaps. The remaining liquid would be either discarded, used in my bath, or sent for use in the laundry.

With every inch of the table covered in blossoms and leaves, Maeve placed her tray on the red and blue rug and sat down to pour our tea and arranged a picnic.

"What's in the basket?" she asked. I turned to find her pointing curiously at a basket filled with bark.

"Cedar bark and berries, to make cedar oil for the Gathering next month," I explained as I snuffed the oil lamp I had been using to heat the lavender infusion.

"What is it used for?"

"Applied topically, it will relieve sore muscles. I ken the men will need it, and I've had the time." I plopped down beside her and took a healthy bite out of a stuffed roll. The savory and sweet flavor of chicken, berries, and honey rushed over my tongue. Without contest, the talented cook's concoctions were my favorite part of living in Ghlas Thùr.

During one evening meal last week, Malcolm's identical twin cousins, Bram and Finlay, complained over muscle ache from their training. Then they'd proceeded to debate over which competitions at the Gathering would inflict more damage to their bodies. The very next day, I had stripped the husky bark off a few cedar trees in the woods close by, as well as asked Maeve to bring me cloves from the kitchen.

Maeve stared at me for a moment before she arched a delicate blonde brow and her pretty face split into a playful, taunting grin.

"Could it be that ye've warmed to us, milady?"

While I could appreciate the teasing nature she had begun to show me, I found I couldn't return her smile. I reached for my tea and reflected on all the times I had come across someone on my way to dinner or my garden. They had practically fallen over themselves to get out of my way, sometimes even took an abrupt turn through the nearest door or hallway. At the very least, they had pressed themselves against a wall until I was out of sight, their stare resolutely on the ground as though I did not exist.

"How could I warm to those who cross themselves as I walk by?" I asked sadly.

Maeve's face fell, her cheeks mottled with embarrassment. "I dinnae ken why they do so. 'Tis true I feared ye at first, but no' anymore. I've tried to tell them that ye're no' what they think."

I shrugged in an effort to hide my disappointment and sipped my tea before saying, "Thank ye for that, but I doubt I'll ever be anything other than evil to them."

She didn't bother to convince me otherwise. We both knew what I said to be true.

It took the rest of the week, but I was able to develop a sufficient store of medicinal oils. My fingers were chapped from being constantly wet, and raw from tending my garden with my bare hands. In my chamber that evening, Maeve rubbed lanolin onto my fingertips while she chatted on about the evening's events. It was Sunday, after all, the day Malcolm opened the gates and invited his tenants to dine with him in the great hall.

"What will ye wear tonight? Ye huvnae worn the rose silk yet."

She spoke of the new style the seamstress, Caitrin, had made for me. True to her word, she had fashioned it with a half-collar that came up high on the back of my neck, to better conceal my scars. It was the most beautiful gown I could ever imagine wearing, the color a pale, soft rose-grey with a cream underskirt.

I shook my head. "I dinnae think I'll attend."

The thought of being on display at another clan gathering made my skin crawl. No one spoke to me, and they quickly averted their eyes if I caught their stare. I could hear their faint whispers, could see the blatant gestures warding against evil. I'd be a liar if I said it didn't eat at me.

My only joy would be in listening to my husband's rowdy cousins and their tales. Some were so outlandish I had to hide my smiles behind my napkin, but what I enjoyed the most were the moments Malcolm would laugh. I swore my heart had stopped beating the first time I saw him truly smile, devastated as I was to see it. I wanted him to smile at *me* that way. As it was, he rarely looked in my direction, except to refill my chalice. Somehow, the man always knew when it was nearly empty.

"Och, but ye must!" she tittered as she brushed my hair. "Ye barely made an appearance at the last one."

I frowned and nearly pressed my aversion to enduring another evening as the fool, but she was right. I couldn't hide up here forever, and I could suffer a crowded dinner twice a month.

"Verra well. The pink gown then," I agreed and jumped slightly when she squealed with delight behind me.

To say Maeve didn't make a fuss would be an outright lie. An hour later, I nervously picked my way down the darkened stairwell toward the great hall. My skin practically glowed and smelled faintly of heather blossoms from my bath. She'd elaborately interwoven my mass of hair with a string of seed pearls. They twined through the braided rope of my hair and complimented its luster. The dusky-pale silk of my gown hugged my waist like a lover's embrace and, to my eternal mortification, pushed the tops of my breasts high. I balked when I saw them in the mirror, on display like creamy pillows, and panicked at the shameless expanse of exposed skin.

My body had changed in the last weeks. The regular meals, the result of the cook's delicious recipes, had filled my body out in the most shocking of ways and given me sloping curves and softened the sharp angles of my face. When I made to take the gown off, Maeve promised me I looked *"absolutely perfect"* before she practically shoved me out the door. Lightheartedly, she chastised me that I was going to be late, shut the door in my face to tidy my chamber, and left me standing in the hallway like a nervous doe in the middle of an open field. I almost bolted up to my tower to wait out the evening but couldn't bear to sit alone in the dark.

On the middle level of the keep, from my shadowy hiding spot just off the balcony that ringed the hall in a sharp U shape, I watched the tables fill. No one had seen me yet, too interested in greeting one another to lift their eyes and spy me tucked just around the corner.

"Do ye plan to watch from above like a wee fledgling scared to test her wings, or may I have the honor of escortin' ye down the stairs?"

I spun toward the voice and came face to face with one of the twins, his seafoam-green eyes bright even in the shadows of the candlelit hallway. Mischievous brows rose high when he took in my new gown, and he gave me a dazzling smile. The brothers looked completely identical, both with curling brown hair cut shorter in the back and left long and wild on top. But it was the devilish grin that gave this particular twin's identity away.

"Finlay, I—I was just goin' back to my chamber," I lied. Panicked, I made to sidestep him and rush to the safety of my tower.

Before I took even a step, he caught my arm and tucked my hand into the crook of his elbow, holding me firmly in place. I knew he would have relented if I had insisted, but after listening to his stories most nights while I ate, I found I liked him too much to risk offending him. Besides, this was the first time anyone besides my husband, the seamstress, or my handmaid had purposefully touched me. I stared, speechless, where my fingers gripped the crook of Finlay's arm and he patted their tips.

"Och, ye cannae leave now. Supper is nearly served and 'tis best when eaten hot, ye ken." He gestured down at the tables piled high with fresh rolls and cauldrons of brown stew. Tugging me along gently, I had no choice but to follow, even though my guts tightened with unease. Halfway down the grand staircase, the merry murmur of conversation faltered to a low hum. Even though I stared pointedly at the floor, I could feel the scrutiny of all as we neared the laird's table.

"Look who I found, my laird. A wee butterfly fresh from her cocoon," Finlay chirped as we rounded Malcolm's massive chair from behind.

The Laird MacKinnon looked up curiously from his wine and froze; his jaw tightened, and his earthy-brown eyes blazed with fury. I quickly averted my gaze and settled into my chair to his right, my cheeks aflame with embarrassment.

If I could just die right now, I inwardly groaned. As I cursed Maeve to the ends of the earth and beyond, Malcolm's gaze traced the angles of my face and neck, then lingered on the stretch of soft skin just above the low bodice of my gown. I positively *itched* to cover myself with my linen napkin and nearly snatched one up to tie around my neck. Mortified, I quickly picked up my chalice, determined to ignore everyone around me the best I could until the meal was over and I could finally escape to my chamber. With Malcolm's focus still riveted upon me, I chanced a glance at him to find his expression near murderous before he looked away and closed his eyes as if in pain.

"Sit, Finlay," Malcolm snapped with agitation.

Nonplussed, Finlay stopped his lingering and swaggered to his seat where he launched into an animated story about the time he found his twin in bed with a pig.

"Only cause ye put it there, *a 'dèanamh bòidheach*!" Bram griped accusingly.

I bit my lower lip to keep from laughing. Poor Bram, ever the recipient of some antic by his twin. The latest gimmick being the pig. Finlay had dressed it in a woman's shift and placed it in bed with his brother after a night of gambling and many, many pints of ale. While the table laughed at Bram's expense, I filled my trencher with steaming stew and said a silent prayer that I would not spill any on my gown.

I ate the tender meat in silence and spoke to no one while I listened to the minstrel's lute and the whispers that floated my way from the castles workers and villagers while they dined. Throughout the meal, Malcolm held court with several villagers and listened to their woes and fears of a bad harvest. He gave them what advice he could and assured them they would not starve. Each farmer or shepherd bowed deeply before leaving, but not before they subtly hooked their middle and forefingers in my direction, always out of direct sight of their laird.

Malcolm may have made his decree my first night here, but the villagers and castle workers obviously feared a witch's presence far more than the ire of the laird they loved. By the time the trenchers were cleared, and the trestle tables pushed against the wall with the benches, I felt depressed and well and truly defeated. I did not belong here, masquerading as a fine lady in this beautiful dress, hated and rejected by not only the people but my husband, too.

When the minstrel took up a frenzied beat with the pounding of a drum and the villagers began to dance, my resolve solidified, and no one objected when I excused myself to my chamber.

Smiling and breathless, Maeve rushed through my door shortly after to help me out of my gown and didn't think twice when I dismissed her back to the revelry.

"Have sweet dreams, milady. I'll see ye in the morn," she promised, and pulled the door firmly shut behind her, leaving me in silent reflection.

Reaching beneath my pillows, my hand closed upon my hidden dagger.

"No," I sighed. "Ye willnae."

CHAPTER NINE

MALCOLM

"And since you know you cannot see yourself,
so well as by reflection, I, your Glass,
will modestly discover to yourself,
that of yourself which you yet know not of."
-William Shakespeare, Julius Caesar

Malcolm seethed as he watched Coira lean over her trencher of stew for the tenth time. Her breasts, barely contained, strained against the silk of her bodice.

That gown will be the death o' me, he inwardly groaned.

Searching the hall, he locked eyes with Maeve when she passed by. He wanted to roar his frustrations at that goddamn, knowing grin on her face and tightened his grip on his chalice when she turned her back on him and took her seat. Damn meddling woman. He should have never requested that harpy serve his wife, for Malcolm was under no delusions who had chosen that audacious, pink ensemble. Oh no, that had Maeve written all over it, and he wasn't entirely sure if he wanted to throttle the handmaid within an inch of her life or throw himself at her feet in gratitude.

It vexed him to admit that it was probably an equal mixture of both.

The beast within his chest purred in Coira's presence, brushed against his insides, and stirred his blood into a frenzy each time she leaned forward. He was so fixated on the seductive creature by his side and distracted by her movements he could barely follow what his tenants said to him. He only hoped he'd responded to their worries appropriately and that no one had requested anything he shouldn't have granted.

She's a siren, he realized, and at some point, he'd become the unsuspecting fisherman. Her body, her face, the scent of her skin, lured him into murky depths even though she did not sing.

Coira had *not* looked that way when he'd collected her a month ago, close to starvation and dressed in tattered, threadbare frocks. If he had thought Coira easy on the eyes then, she was devastating to look upon now, all rosy cheeks and soft curves… and those goddamn breasts. Idly, he wondered if they would overflow his hands or if they would fit perfectly against his palms. Clenching his teeth, Malcolm settled deeper into his chair to brood into his chalice and failed miserably to ignore her. Tonight, like most nights, her pale, enchanting eyes remained downcast even though he knew she listened to the stories told around her. Twice, he'd caught the lift of her lips, quickly hidden with a sip of wine or a dab of her napkin, before she schooled her face into that cool mask of indifference he'd begun to despise.

When she had arrived on Finlay's arm, a ravishing sight in that daring gown, he'd barely restrained the compulsion to rip his cousin's offending appendage off his body just for touching her. Since he brought Coira to the stronghold, Malcolm found his emotions to be wild, unpredictable, and unpleasant. These last weeks he had only been able to keep a firm grip on them by sheer will alone. He trained with the garrison more than ever, pushing his body to exhaustion. When he wasn't sparring with his men, he kept to the corners of the keep he knew his wife never explored and would quickly flee when he felt her nearby through the bond. The only time he could not escape her presence was during supper. He looked forward to those short hours each evening when he could watch her while she studiously ignored him.

Malcolm caught a rare glimpse of the shiny, puckered skin on her neck when she looked longingly toward the staircase. The rage he'd felt when she had told him about the priest on their wedding night came back full force at the sight of her scars. He had listened through his drunken haze, stretched alongside her; she in her golden wedding gown, and he in his black shirt and kilt. It amazed him how a lass so young could endure something so terrible and still grow to be kind.

The horror of her story had haunted him for days. His oath had lashed at his nerves as though it demanded vengeance for past slights. Because of the beast's murderous intentions, Malcolm could only feel relief that the priest rarely ventured far from his church. Where Malcolm had once seen the priest's absence during Sunday suppers as a slight, he now saw them as a blessing. Father Blount was still new to the parish, only having arrived this past autumn following the passing of their previous priest, Father Gentry. From what Malcolm could gather, Father Blount was not very well liked by the villagers. It was said he spent most of his time in the tavern and rarely left before sundown.

Malcolm had sent a request for a replacement the day after his wedding, but those things could take months—sometimes years, if they were granted at all. Until then, Malcolm had devised a way for Coira to stay hidden in plain sight. As much as he preferred she stay far away from the priest, he knew the people would think it odd if their lady was not present for church services.

It had taken some convincing, but Coira had finally relented to a veil. Lace held in place by a circlet of hammered silver hid her face and most of her back by a webbing of dark blue. Matching gloves hid the scars on her wrists.

During the first service after their wedding, Coira had dutifully sat at his side, panicked to the bone. She'd barely breathed or moved a muscle, as though she feared the priest would see through their trickery and demand her immediate death. Back tense and fists clenched, as soon as they had exited the church she'd practically bit Malcolm's head off for putting her through the stress.

Malcolm stabbed aimlessly at a turnip and listened to the merry conversations around him. Perhaps Blount would find the people here lacking and move on to a new flock on his own. *Or perhaps he could fall and break his neck and put an end to my wife's nightmares,* Malcolm thought wryly, not the least bit ashamed at his dark thoughts. He took a deep swallow of his wine, focused on the unblemished side of Coira's neck, and found he could live with either of those options. Until then, besides when they attended service, he planned to keep his wife very, *very* far away from Father Blount.

"I'll retire now," Coira said softly and pushed her plate away, her voice a balm to his raw nerves and dark thoughts.

After nodding his permission, he fought the urge to turn in his chair and watch her ascend the stairs—unlike his cousins and favored guards that dined at his table. Ten pairs of eyes peered over his shoulder at what he knew to be the hourglass curves of his wife's waist and the enticing sway of her hips as she climbed each step. Teeth set, Malcolm slammed his fist on the table. Horn cups and pewter chalices danced slightly from the force, the only warning he would give to his men to cease their gawking

"*Iosa Crìosd,* can he blame us?" someone muttered from down the row of men. Finlay probably, damn the man.

Malcolm rubbed his face and sunk deeper into his chair. His nerves settled slightly with the distance Coira put between them, and he tried his best to enjoy the rest of the evening.

Nearly an hour later, he became disturbed and restless, as though he had forgotten something but couldn't quite figure out what it was. Rolling his stiff shoulders, he distracted himself by walking the room and sought out the villagers who hadn't greeted him yet. While he toured the hall, he became more and more concerned with the farmers' and the villagers' worries. They were all the same: the long winter had made for a late planting season, which meant the seedlings had barely popped above the earth's surface before the time the rains came. Half of the crops had been lost to drowning and insufficient sun, the tiny shoots scarcely mature enough to withstand the amount of rain that fell on them before they withered and rotted. The rest were in danger of following the same fate if the hard rains did not abate.

"My laird." Farlan brushed against his shoulder just as the minstrel's melody faded and the crowd began to disperse. His face was close as he whispered, "Yer lady has gone. One o' the men saw her sneak out the south gate and make haste to the east on foot—"

A low, animalistic rumble broke loose from Malcolm's chest, giving Farlan pause.

"And they didnae think to stop her?" Malcolm growled, his hands curled into fists.

Farlan cleared his throat and looked at his laird with regret, shaking his head. "Some o' the men are convinced she'll curse them or set their bollocks on fire if they even look in her direction, let alone touch her. The few who dinnae fear her supped within the keep this night."

"Set their bollocks… but that's absurd," Malcolm sputtered. His friend raised a brow and looked at him pointedly. With a heavy sigh, Malcolm realized Farlan was right. As much as he brushed off the collective superstition, he still knew it was there and he had failed Coira by not putting an end to it. The truth was, he didn't have the faintest idea how. He couldn't *order* his people to stop thinking a certain way, and Coira certainly didn't help matters by hiding up in her tower day after day.

Malcolm pinched the bridge of his nose and prayed for restraint. "I'll go fetch her."

"I dinnae ken how ye'll find her in the storm. There's no torch nor lantern that will stay lit in that mess," Farlan said as he scratched the stubble under his chin. But Malcolm was already striding away in grim determination because he knew something his wayward witch did not.

With the blood oath restless and yearning in his chest, Malcolm could find her anywhere.

Three miles away from the warm, dry interior of the keep, Malcolm's mood plummeted from determined to downright surly. Soaked to the bone and irritable, he was closer to catching a chill before he would his wife.

"She's probably runnin' as fast as her legs can carry her," he grumbled to himself while he climbed yet another hill and stumbled over hidden rocks in the underbrush, half-blinded by the relentless, pounding downpour. "Or perhaps she coaxed a wild horse down from the moors and gave it wings. Better yet, grew wings *herself* and called upon this twice-damned wind to spirit her away."

His musings grew more fantastical the higher he climbed toward the craggy crest in the darkness. The wind battered him from all angles, whipping his hair into his eyes and freezing his ears. His ascent was slow, with quick pulses of lightning the only illumination to guide him, and he felt his anger grow with each step.

When Malcolm reached the hill's crest, he shielded his eyes from the driving rain to scan the open field below and the black edge of forest beyond. She was out there, he could feel her like a pulsing echo in his blood. Peering into the darkness, he waited for the next flash of lightning. *There.* Malcolm's mouth twisted into a humorless smirk when he spied her running with impressive speed through the field; her black cloak billowed behind her, and a white sack bounced against her back.

His descent was much faster than his climb, the eastern face of the hill blessedly free of stones as his long strides devoured the lead she had on him. When he reached the forest, he felt elated, the pounding of his heart having as much to do with the chase as it did with his mad dash across the open grassland.

In this corner of the woodland the trees were old and unfamiliar, their trunks thick and canopies high. Dense moss covered the ground, roots, and fallen trees and hung from branches, offering her the perfect place to hide.

But no' from me, he thought with determination. *Never from me.* He could feel her and sense the part of her soul that Vanora had tied to his. She was so close.

With purpose, Malcolm stepped boldly into the gloom, eager to be done with this pursuit and return to the keep and the heat of a fire, his wife in tow.

Ahead, the snap of a branch excited him, and he prowled deeper into the forest. The treetops swirled a mad dance with a wind that grew stronger by the second. Heedless of the gale that battered his face and ripped at his sodden shirt, he pushed on.

Trusting his instincts, he loosened the fragile tether he kept on the creature within… and allowed it to hunt. He fancied he could smell her perfumed hair on the wind as he rounded tree after tree in near silence. The moss under his boots and the storm raging above muffled his movements.

The attack came swiftly and without warning. He didn't have time to protect himself from the thick branch that whipped out from behind a tree to land squarely on the soft spot beneath his ribs. His breath left his lungs in a whoosh just as a female figure darted away. Reaching out with a speed he hadn't known he possessed, he snagged the thick fabric of Coira's cloak and wrenched her against him as he fought for air.

She let out a fearful shriek and she lost her footing, landing on her back with a whimper. Then, with a quickness he could barely follow in the heavy shadows, she pulled a dagger from beneath her tattered black gown. She swiped it through the air, narrowly missing his knees by mere inches.

"Touch me and I'll kill ye!" she spat, her teeth bared. Between flashes of lightning, Malcolm gaped as she pointed her short-blade directly at him, her face hard and unforgiving.

She was beautiful—and deadly.

He pushed away the confusing sense of betrayal at her feral response and bared his teeth right back. "What's the difference, wife? If ye leave, I'll die anyway," he bristled. His words were met with her sharp intake of breath.

"Malcolm?" she blurted in surprise.

"Who else would it feckin' be? Henry the Eighth?" he snapped as he wiped the rainfall from his eyes.

"I—I didnae ken it was ye, I swear."

Malcolm scoffed. "Ye lie. I ken where ye are every moment o' the bloody day, and ye expect me to believe ye cannae feel the same?" He narrowed his eyes at her confusion. "Ye told me yerself ye felt our connection when I came to get ye—"

"Ye mean the day ye nearly died if it weren't for me?" she mumbled. Malcolm blinked at her. Would she never let him live that down?

He laughed bitterly. "Aye, I barely made it to ye before my oath took my life for payment. Now, answer my question."

She stared up at him through the rain. "I feel the part o' me that's connected to ye… but no. I dinnae ken when yer near…" Her eyes grew wide a moment before hurt passed over her features and vanished just as quickly. She cleared her throat and wiped the rain from her face. "If I had realized it was ye followin' me, I widnae have attacked."

Malcolm's anger thawed at her revelation, and he reached down to help her up. "Alright then. Let's get out o' this blasted rain, aye?"

Coira nodded and grasped his hand. Gathering her feet beneath her body, she stood tall and whisper-sang a few words under her breath. By the time she released his hand, the treetops had ceased their violent rhythm, and the wind had died down to a gentle breeze. Malcolm gaped at her in shock, as well as something akin to awe, when the rain disappeared entirely, and silvery moonlight filtered through the canopy above.

"Did *ye* call that storm?" he asked accusingly as he gazed up at the few stars he could see through the leaves, amazed at how quickly the weather dissipated. She stayed quiet a moment before she lifted a shoulder in surrender.

"Aye. I didnae want to be followed, but I can see now that yer a special sort o' stubborn," she murmured, her lips pinched.

"Yer no' the first to call me such," Malcolm admitted with a frustrated shake of his head. He raised his arms, only to let them fall to his sides in a sodden slap of defeat. "Are ye so miserable that ye felt the need to run? Have I no' given ye every comfort? Given ye everythin' ye asked for?"

Even in the gloom, he could see her bottom lashes brim with fat tears that threatened to spill over. The sight of them blew the wind out of his sails as though he'd been slapped.

"Yer clan fears me, Malcolm!" she snapped miserably and wrapped her arms around herself as she took a step back. "They think my presence is to blame for their failing crops or any ache o' the body they've had since I arrived. They believe I've set a curse upon their lands, their children, their livestock—"

"No—"

She rocked forward on her toes. "They do! Ye think I cannae hear their whispers? They hate me."

"They dinnae hate ye, Coira," he sighed and closed the space between them to clasp her arms just above her elbows. "'Tis true they may fear ye—"

She waved a pointed finger in his face. "Exactly my point! 'Tis only a matter o' time before they'll call for the witch hunters." Her voice became shrill, and she snatched her finger away to curl a fist over her heart. "They'll try to burn me again, and next time they'll succeed." Averting her eyes, her body began to tremble, and tears spread over her already wet cheeks.

In that moment, he wanted nothing more than to kiss her tears away, to promise her safety. The need to comfort her was overwhelming. Instead, he tilted his head to the side and bent at the waist. Lowering his face to the same level as hers, he touched the underside of her chin and willed her to look at him.

"They willnae do that, Coira. Aye, they fear ye, but they ken yer mother gave her life to save my brother. Colin was beloved and respected by *everyone*. And they willnae slight yer mother's gift to the clan by betrayin' me."

Her brows furrowed in confusion. "Betray *ye*?"

"O' course. Yer my wife, and even if ye dinnae want to be, yer a MacKinnon now." He found himself stroking her arms while he spoke, and his large hands nearly engulfed her limbs as he attempted to soothe her stiff frame.

"That doesnae change the fact that they think I'm a walkin' curse, Malcolm. They cross themselves when they're near, warding themselves like I'm some—some *devil.*"

Realizing his touch was getting nowhere, he braced himself over his knees and met her grave stare with one of his own. "Aye, so what if they do. What are ye goin' to do to change their minds?" he challenged and nearly laughed when her ice-colored eyes popped wide and her plump lips parted, appalled at his question.

"Wh—what?" she sputtered. "I cannae change their minds, are ye daft?"

God help me, I'm gonna choke her, he prayed.

"Ye infuriatin' woman," he growled. "Let's have it out, shall we? Ye'll be comin' back with me since I'm no' too keen on findin' myself dead, although ye may put me in an early grave yet. But *aye*, ye *can* change their minds." To drive his point home, Malcolm poked her chest just under the clasp of her cloak and waved his other hand madly at the clear sky now full of stars. "If ye can change the bloody weather with a whisper, Coira, surely ye can sway their opinions with a smile or two."

They glared at one another in the shadows of the forest, and when Malcolm could no longer suffer their unyielding silence, he bowed his head in defeat. He could almost hear Colin's voice in his head say, *Ye've met yer match, ye stubborn bastard.* Malcolm chuckled darkly at the very real possibility.

Without asking permission, he tugged the sack off her shoulders to carry himself and slung the tell-tale shape of a book against his back. Had she truly left the castle with naught but her spellbook and the clothes she wore? The thought that she felt the need to flee the keep, knowing that she would travel hungry and without protection, saddened him.

What an unhappy pair we make, he thought miserably, and ran a hand along his waterlogged shirt.

"Have ye at least a spell in this wee book to dry our clothes?" he asked doubtfully as he turned on his heel to pick his way west, confidant she would follow since he held her book hostage.

He took five steps before he heard her song, the words entirely foreign, soft, smooth, and *alive*. But they felt *familiar*. As familiar as spring grass between his bare toes or the sound paper made when he turned the page of a book.

To his amazement, his clothes lifted from his body, followed by the peculiar sense of water rolling down his skin like cool glass beads from his head to his shins. It took mere moments, and the water droplets fled the fabric of his shirt and breeks as though he wore oiled leather and left everything from his knees up dry and warm. Amazed, he turned to find Coira looking at him shyly, dry as well.

"I cannae lift the water out o' yer boots. The buckles are too tight," she explained with a shrug.

Malcolm blinked at her. His witch-bride, who could call the elements to heel, had apologized for leaving his feet wet. He nearly laughed, the situation so impossible.

"No one's perfect, lass," he teased.

As they left the forest together, side by side, Malcolm wondered if maybe she really could grow wings and fly.

~

Two days later, Malcolm stretched his stiff limbs and set his book down on the small table beside his chair, his vision blurred from reading *Hamlet* by candlelight. *Even Shakespeare must have slept sometimes,* he mused as he splashed his face with cool water from the basin in the corner of his chamber.

A soft knock and the sharp voice of his cousin Gavin filtered through the door. "My laird, 'tis urgent."

Alarmed, Malcolm crossed the room in moments and ripped his door open wide. "What is it?"

"She's crossed the wall again. Finlay's with her," he whispered and explained how Coira had walked boldly through the southern gatehouse only minutes ago, flatly refusing to go back inside but had allowed Gavin to send for him. "It was luck he was on duty. Besides Maeve, he seems to be one o' the few here she trusts."

Malcolm tried not to let Gavin's comment sting as he rushed down the winding stairwells and into the south bailey, where the air was misty and thick with impending rain. *What the hell is she doin' outside the wall after midnight*, he raged, more upset with himself than with her. If she had trusted him, surely she would have told him where she was going. His only speculation was that she was attempting to leave him again. Malcolm felt a bit of animosity at the creature within him that it had decided not to forewarn him as it had before.

On the other side of the gate, Finlay nodded when he saw Malcolm stride through the heavy mist, then returned to his post, revealing Coira in the warm glow of lantern light. Dressed in black, she'd pulled the cowl of her cloak low over her face, obscuring her eyes and nose in shadow.

"Leavin' again so soon? Ye ken I would find ye, so why try?" he snarled. Gavin's words and the unspoken indication that she didn't trust *him* repeated in his head.

Unmoved by his outburst, Coira scoffed and turned on her heel. "Come with me."

Malcolm ground his teeth at her order but grabbed a lantern from its hook on the wall and stalked after her. Beyond the barn, they crossed the south pasture, and she stopped at the edge of a tilled spread of soggy, waterlogged soil that served as the keep's main garden. Malcolm could barely make out the tiny sprouts that poked out of the black earth. Falling to a crouch, he gently nudged a ruined seedling, pale and limp with no hope of survival.

"So many have rotted. This has happened before but no' to this extent," he said sadly, and realized his tenant's worries were indeed valid. He felt terrible for brushing off their worries with the promise of taking care of them. At the sight of these pitiful sprouts, Malcolm knew he wouldn't be able to feed the whole clan, no matter how much he wanted to. He lifted the lantern and gazed out at the sad spread of decay. "We're gonna starve."

With a soft squelch, Coira knelt in the mud and plunged her hands up to her wrists in the soft, oversaturated earth.

"No, we willnae," she said gruffly.

Malcolm's breath caught in his throat, and his flesh tingled, raising the hair on his arms when the first wave of energy washed over him.

"What are ye doin'?"

"Shhhh…" A slight smile graced what he could see of her lips, then she bowed her head… and began to sing.

It wasn't loud. Nothing like the powerful incantation he had felt deep in his soul the day her mother turned the great oak in the bailey to stone. It was a whisper, a hum, both deep and resonating, and it trilled high like a tiny bell. The layered harmonics permeated every corner of his mind while he watched, utterly captivated, as her lips moved in the warm glow of the lantern. He didn't recognize the words, but he listened as she drew each completely foreign and lilting syllable out. It was a language made to be sung, painfully beautiful and overwhelmingly majestic.

It was the movement below that tore his rapt attention away from what little he could see of her face, and he gasped at what he beheld. Fat, plump leaves unfurled before his eyes, like a babe stretching out of its swaddling clothes. They trembled as they reached up, up, up— and stopped nearly eight inches from the ground when her song drifted to an end. Malcolm looked around in silent amazement. Every seedling in a twenty-foot radius had grown into tidy mounds or strong stalks.

Coira humbly knelt in the mud and drizzling rain within the circle of green that should have taken weeks to grow, not a few moments. Without a word, she avoided his stare, stood, and picked her way down the neat rows of healthy vegetation before settling on her knees once more in a barren area. She repeated her previous hymn with her hands deep in the soggy soil. This time, Malcolm watched the seedlings closely, witnessed them fill out and twirl like floppy corkscrews out of the earth, leaves quickly sprouting from the main stem.

Over and over, he wordlessly watched her encourage life out of the saturated soil. Hour after dark hour, Coira migrated around the spread of land and continued long after the mist and drizzle moved on with the clouds. Malcolm's lantern had long since run out of oil, and he could see the faintest hint of dawn in the clear sky above the eastern treetops.

It had taken her all night, but the field was filled with promise.

Breathing heavily, her voice hoarse and strained, the last notes of her song floated away on the wind. She lifted her body up over the mud, her cloak filthy, her hood limp on her head. She stood on shaky legs and met Malcolm's stare with a mix of pride and exhaustion. Stunned at her pallid complexion and the dark smudges beneath her eyes, he had only a moment to react before she swayed on her feet and fell unconscious into his arms.

With Coira's warm body tucked against his chest, Malcolm picked his way through the field of green and back to the keep just as the sky turned periwinkle and grey, not a cloud to be seen in the sky. The beast hummed beneath his ribs while he studied her face. For once, relaxed and peaceful with sleep, it was not pinched and guarded as it had been since the day he met her.

I did that to her, he berated himself. *I took her from all she had and surrounded her with superstitious fools. 'Tis no wonder she's so unhappy.*

"Sleep, beauty," he murmured, and tightened his hold. "Ye've earned it."

After a few orders to the guards as he crossed the bailey, Maeve was summoned from her bed. With her arms loaded with fresh linens, she skidded to a halt just inside Coira's chamber, her blonde curls chaotic and eyes wide with jubilation as she took in the muddy mess in Malcolm's arms.

"Is it true?" Maeve whispered excitedly as she ripped the blankets off the bed. She hurried to unfastened Coira's cloak and tugged off her muddy slippers. "Did she truly make the crops grow overnight?"

"Aye, she did. She's exhausted herself," he answered, his voice laced with prideful admiration as he let her cloak fall to the floor with a wet slap and gently laid her down on the sheets. In sleep's deep embrace, Coira did not stir when Maeve began untying the front laces of her bodice.

"Go on now, my laird. I'll care for her from here," Maeve trilled over her shoulder with a haughty raise of her brow. "She may be yer wife, but I ken ye huvnae seen any more o' her than the rest o' the clan has."

"Yer a pest, Maeve," he said with a half-hearted snarl and took one last look at his wife before he made to leave the room. He chuckled at Maeve's pert *"ugh huh"* as he pulled the door quietly shut behind him.

Every evening meal for the next twelve days, Coira ate enough to cause his men to raise their brows. Late at night, when there was less chance of being spotted, Malcolm escorted her to the fields and gardens of his tenants and returned early each morning upon Ramsey's back with her asleep in his arms. Some nights, depending on the size of the plot, she was able to sing her song in several locations and left behind lush, healthy vegetation.

On the night before the Sunday supper, Malcolm brought her to the last farm under the light of a full moon. While she worked her magic, Malcolm caught his tenant's pale face in the window from where he stood over her. The old man watched as his garden flourished before his eyes, and he pressed his hand flush on the glass in thanks before wiping away tears of relief.

While Malcolm carried Coira home that final time, he hated to admit that he would miss hefting her slight weight back into the keep. He'd miss her breath puffing against his neck, her earthy scent of lavender and soil, and how her body heat pervaded his bones. At some point, it had become the best part of his day.

Once back at the keep, Malcolm left an exhausted Coira in the capable hands of her maid. Bleary-eyed, Malcolm returned to Ramsey and rode north with the rising of the sun. He had not inspected the caves in two weeks, too tired from keeping the midnight hours, as well as his daily routines, to make the journey. The guilt of it burdened his heart.

Please let there be something, he prayed when he ducked into its shadows with a lantern to light his way. But just like all the times before, he returned to the keep hours later, empty-handed, aggravated, and depressed. Was it too much to ask for some small sign of success to soothe the part of Malcolm's heart that festered with regret? As he passed the door to Coira's chamber and slipped into his own, he clung weakly to the hope that proof was possible.

CHAPTER TEN

COIRA

Sometime in the last month, Maeve had become more companion than handmaid. I believed it had started when I'd insisted that, if she continued to serve my noon meal in my tower, she should at least enjoy it with me. The invitation quickly morphed into frequent interruptions of my work to share with me all the latest gossip. I didn't mind. Lonely and starved for companionship, I gladly listened to anything she felt the need to speak about. She seemed to know what everyone was doing as well as what they thought, whether they worked in the laundry, kitchen, or garrison. Having all that information packed inside my head would drive me insane, so it made perfect sense that she couldn't seem to keep it to herself. It all fell right out like an overflowing bucket.

"I'm thrilled to be attendin' ye at the Gatherin' next week. Last year, my sister was heavy with bairn and I had to stay behind, but no' this year!" Sprawled on her back atop the red and blue woven rug, she clapped with glee, the remnants of our picnic lunch spread out around her. I couldn't help but smile at her enthusiasm.

"My mother and I would run a stand selling healing herbs and oils, as well as the ones that have no use other than to smell nice." My heart squeezed at her memory. Those days were long gone.

I had never enjoyed the Gathering, but I wasn't about to tell Maeve that. It was the crowds. They had overwhelmed me, but I would listen to the gaming fields from afar. I would imagine what was happening in my mind while I stayed near the relative safety of our stand on the far side of the bazaar. To think I had been in the same valley as Malcolm each year, the crowds the only rift between us, boggled my mind. As I stuffed dried herbs into a glass vial, I wondered what would have happened if I had braved the mass of people and met him without my mother's meddlesome blood vow.

Nothin', o' course! He's a laird, and I'm naught but a witch with a ruined face, I griped to myself. The dark thought spoiled my good mood. Pressing a cork to seal the dried St. John's Wort, I set the vial down harder than had I intended. Oblivious to my silent tantrum, Maeve chatted on and gathered the dishes together.

"O' course, it takes five long days to get there, and we have to bathe in the streams and piss in the woods." She paused with a full body shudder and hefted the tray into her arms. She talked the whole way down as she descended the stairwell. "But it's all so romantic. All those half-naked warriors strutting around is enough to make a lass swoon dead away. I cannae wait!"

I frowned with envy at Maeve's particular lust for life. Opening my tome, I added a subscript in the margins about what I had learned when I had sung life into that last garden yesterday. I wrote that if I altered the incantation for *grow* to a lower octave, the roots would stretch deeper into the soil. It was good information that could be adapted to the words that governed water and fire.

Alarmed, I spun in my chair when heavy footsteps announced a male presence, for only Maeve had visited my tower since the garrison's men had emptied it of clutter. To my surprise, Malcolm peeked over the lip of the steep stairwell and paused his climb.

"May I come up?" His deep voice caused my belly to flutter.

"Aye. Though I dinnae ken why ye feel the need to ask. 'Tis yer castle."

I allowed myself to take stock of him while he made a slow perusal of my tower and inspected the hanging flowers and plants that dried from the rafters. His body had changed in the months since I had arrived, the soft body of a scholar shed to reveal the definition of a warrior. Where he was always tall and broad, the muscles under his shirt had grown larger; his leather trews hugged the thick muscles of his legs and backside tighter as well. I knew I wasn't the only woman who had noticed *that* change. Maeve hadn't shut up about it for the last week.

At least all those long hours he spends in the bailey avoidin' me isn't for naught, I thought wistfully and wondered why he sought me out when he never had before. His revelation in his oath-given ability to sense my whereabouts still stung, but now I knew why I had never run into him those first couple weeks. He hadn't wanted to see me.

I let my attention roam over the lines of his body while he moved around, inspecting glass vials of oil, or the dried herbs I stored in the small drawstring sacks Maeve had brought from the village.

"Why did ye insist I no' open yer wee book here when 'tis naught but filled with whorls and runes?"

Tearing my gaze away from the sinful leather he wore, I realized he had begun flipping through my tome and the sacred Druid writing within. Frustrated for not being more careful and allowing him that glimpse, I slapped the book closed and pushed against him gently to tuck it back in its strongbox. With an irritated glare, I slipped the key into my bodice.

"Ye shouldnae have seen that," I snapped. Malcolm only shrugged and rested one of his thighs on the table, and his booted foot brushed my skirt. Blushing from that innocent touch, I looked away and began to tidy up my already neat workstation when he continued speaking.

"It doesnae matter much if it's no' in English or Gaelic. I cannae read any other languages, so ye have one on me there."

I blinked at him in confusion. "One on ye?"

"Languages, lass. Ye can read three, one more than I."

I shook my head. "I can only read this one." Brushing off the remnants of dried peppermint onto the floor, I faced him and found his thick, dark brows lowered with concern.

"If ye cannae read English, lass, that's easily remedied. I'll teach ye myself."

"No," I said stubbornly and crossed my arms over my chest. "No Druid woman is taught to read or write naught but the Druid language until their later years, if at all. 'Tis too dangerous for the ancient knowledge to fall into the wrong hands." Malcolm didn't look convinced. I pursed my lips as I tried to think of a way to explain the devastation that would occur. "Alright, imagine a king that doesnae die because he found a forbidden spell in the common tongue and had a witch in his possession that could speak it. We've been held captive before for far less than eternal life. Think about how terrible that would be. How disastrous. We dinnae teach our girls to read or write in the common tongues for that verra reason. 'Tis true some learn when they are older and wise, my mother being one o' them after my father died, but I've never had need of it."

"Eternal life?" Malcolm asked, his voice awestruck.

I looked him square in the eye. "Eternal life is a curse, Malcolm. It tarnishes the soul in its quest for power while the mind goes mad with the need for rest. Only misery comes with eternity," I promised.

He looked like he had a thousand questions on the tip of his tongue before he heaved a breath. "I yield to yer better judgement on the subject. However, when it comes to reading, please tell me if ye change yer mind. It would be my pleasure to teach ye," he said sadly, as though my being unable to read English was something to mourn.

My lack of ability to read had never affected my way of life, living mostly secluded in the woods as I had. All I'd ever needed to read were the runes in the tome that had been in my family for generations. Mother took care of the rest.

"As for the reason o' my visit," he continued, "I thought ye should ken ye were the talk o' the village these past few days." Dread coiled in my stomach, and I hung my head at his words, wondering what offense I could have possibly committed. Malcolm pushed away from the table and headed toward the stairs. "They say an angel comes down from the heavens at night to save their crops."

I huffed a humorless laugh at that. Angels were divine, flawless creatures, beautiful and devout. None of which I was.

"Then they definitely have no illusion it was me," I said to his back.

Malcolm cast a glance at me over his shoulder. "No' yet, Angel."

His response warmed my heart.

~

"No. Absolutely no and never again," I hissed vehemently when Maeve pulled out another one of Caitrin's more provocative garments to wear to the Sunday supper, this one an emerald green. "I still huvnae gotten my dignity back from the last time ye stuffed my... my..." I just knew the ends of my hair had turned ruby-red along with my face while I waved my hands over my breasts. "Well they nearly popped out last time!"

"A shame," she admonished, but aired out one of my favorite dresses instead. A demure dove-grey, the fabric was light and soft. Best of all, it covered *everything*. "The laird will be most disappointed."

"What?" I squawked. "Malcolm *hated* that gown, Maeve, ye didnae see his face."

I had, and it would be forever carved in my memory. Never again would I wear that rose-grey dress. Burn it, cut it for scraps, I didn't care, as long it never touched my skin again.

Maeve shook her head and laughed, bell-like and full of mirth. "Och, he was mad as a badger, alright. Nearly murdered me with a look, he did." Pleased with herself for some ungodly reason, she bid me to step into the skirting before she fit the pearl buttons up the back.

"Then why *ever* would ye want to provoke him again?"

Her grin was positively wicked when she said, "Because as angry as he was, he couldnae take his eyes off ye... *just* as I predicted, I might add." I held onto the bed poster in disbelief while she talked. "*And* he nearly took the heads off the men who stared after ye when ye left."

I tried to imagine Malcolm behaving that way and failed. All I could see was the way he glared at me from under his brows when I sat beside him, how he squirmed in his chair while I ate my stew.

"Oh, Maeve, that's just no' true."

Giving me a pointed look from over my shoulder, she snorted and began to fuss with my hair. "Whatever ye say, milady."

Seated next to Malcolm at supper, the atmosphere in the great hall was different, and I tried to figure out what it was without looking at too many people. The stares from the villagers were still there, as well as their whispers, but the cadence of them had changed. I didn't feel their usual malice or unease while they talked amongst themselves and glanced my way. A few women even *smiled* at me from across the room.

"What's goin' on?" I whispered over the rim of my chalice.

Malcolm looked at me questioningly and then waved an unconcerned hand toward the packed tables in the hall.

"Thanks to ye, I see nothin' but the members o' my clan supping without the worries that have plagued them these last months."

"Oh." My cheeks grew red and my stomach dipped when it occurred to me that he might have told them I was responsible for the flourishing crops. "Ye didnae tell them it was me, did ye?"

"I didnae have to. A farmer witnessed yer wee magic and spread the word before I had the chance."

My tongue felt as though it had dropped down to my knees, and I nervously tugged at the hair that draped over my scars. It was one thing for Malcolm's garrison to witness from afar but quite another for a commoner to see from his bedroom window.

"Malcolm, this… I… och, I should never have done that." Panicked tears welled in my eyes as I thought of the witch hunters descending upon me and tying me to a pyre. It was different for the people to suspect, but to *know* what I had done or that I was able to wield such power would be catastrophic. I was better off with their prejudice and fear.

Malcolm slipped out of his chair to crouch beside mine and took my face between his hands. The contact between us was so unexpected I could only stare at him.

"Yer safe here, Angel. No one is goin' to harm ye, and I willnae allow any to take ye, I promise." His voice washed over me in low, even tones, and he pressed his thumbs lightly against my lashes to sweep the moisture away. As upset as I was that I had exposed myself, his kind words and gentle touch made my pulse flutter, and I tried my best to hear the truth he spoke.

"Ye set out to show them ye're no' the evil they assumed ye were. Well, just *look* at them, Coira. Ye saved their children from hunger and their families from poverty, and had asked nothin' from them in return. Let them talk about ye this night. Within a month, they'll love ye."

But will ye? I wondered as I searched his warm brown eyes and spread my fingertips along the backs of his hands. "I want to believe ye."

Malcolm tracked the movement and swallowed before he said, "Then stop wantin' and just do it." Releasing me, he fell back into his chair just as Finlay called out from the far end of the table.

"My Lady!" All conversation in the hall fell to a hushed murmur when every soul focused on the more devilish twin. Finlay's mouth twisted into a wicked grin when I peered down the table and he locked eyes with me. "I have to ken… do ye think yer magic can grow Bram here a bigger cock?"

My mouth fell open, rendering me speechless as the hall fell completely silent a moment before every man and woman erupted with roaring laughter.

Through the hilarity, Bram stood from his chair on the opposite side of the table, his face a furious puce.

He bellowed at his mirror image, "We're *twins* ye feckin' idiot!"

The look of pure confusion that passed over Finlay's face did me in, and true laughter bubbled up from within me for the first time since my arrival as Ghlas Thùr. For the first time in *months*.

I didn't bother to hide it. I laughed until my tears blinded me, my cheeks cramped, and I lost the ability to breathe. And in that moment, I felt good. I felt free. Relief crested over my head in waves, pummeling me, and I willfully submitted to my euphoric hysteria. When I finally regained my composure, I blotted my eyes with the sleeve of my gown and glanced at where Malcolm openly watched me, a half-smile upon his face.

An undignified giggle-hiccup escaped me. "What is it?" I asked.

"I dinnae believe I've ever heard ye truly laugh. At least no' like that." His smile faltered, as though he didn't much like the truth of his words.

I was unwilling to let the black cloud of honesty sour my mood, so I held out my chalice for him to refill and let my happiness shine. "Maybe ye'll hear it again sometime," I quipped.

Malcolm stared at me for a moment, his heavy focus on my mouth, before he nodded and lifted his drink to his lips. I barely heard his mumbled response, but I thought it sounded a lot like *I hope so*.

With the sun shining on me, I sat on the back of a well-tempered sorrel mare named Una and looked down upon the valley below.

The Gathering.

We had finally arrived. It had taken us five days of rugged travel northeast to get here, just like Maeve had said. And there it was in all its glory under the afternoon sun. A burbling brook ran south down the length of the valley until it split to head both east and west. It gave the Gathering's people some semblance of order and split the land into three sections with the rushing water creating areas for specific uses: camps, market, and gaming fields.

West of the burn, and the largest section, the clan camps spread out. Crowded, but not uncomfortably so, each clan had claimed their own area. With defined borders of either open space, stones, or trees, it was easy to distinguish one clan territory from the next.

To the east sat the market. A mix of tents and more permanent rough structures, the stands were set up in messy rows where people sold anything the heart could desire. In the distance, I could barely make out the small space my mother and I had always claimed for our small camp nestled along the trees on the far northeast side of the valley. With her absence, I wondered how long it would take for someone to claim that spot as their own.

Lastly were the gaming fields, south and below where the water forked. By far the smallest divided section of the valley, it was still almost a mile across and free of trees and rock. It was ideal for holding competitions in archery, horse racing, and bare-knuckle boxing, among other sports of endurance and skill.

"Och, there it is," Maeve sighed with wonder when she reined in her mount beside mine. She had been my constant companion on our journey here, even sleeping with me in my small tent when we camped along the road each night. Her smile was infectious as she beamed at me, her blonde curls blowing unbound in the wind. She pointed to the valley. "We're early yet. The fun willnae start until the day after next."

Our party picked its way down the hill and navigated the rough wagon paths through the camps just as the sun disappeared over the western ridge and cast the valley into shadow. Maeve openly waved to a few people in yellow and blue tartans when we passed them by.

"My mother's people," she explained. "She met my father one Gathering twenty years ago and hand-fasted with him on the last day, forsaking her name and the McNeely colors for the MacKinnon's. There was some bad blood for a few years, my mother being the favored daughter and all, but it all turned out well in the end. I'll visit them while yer at the meeting with the chieftains tomorrow."

I grumbled at that, less than thrilled at being reminded that I was expected to sit through a long day of self-important men bickering amongst themselves. I imagined they would strut around, fluffing their feathers while they argued over territory and the like, their wives' mere decoration beside them. Thankfully, I would only be subjected to that for one day and would be playing nurse the remainder of the week.

After a small argument with my husband to allow me to act as the clan's healer, I replaced Tavin's wife, Crissy, who was newly with child and sick more hours of the day than not. I had left her with my full store of ginger root and peppermint tea the morning we set off. Both gifts were accepted gratefully from where she knelt over a bucket in her chamber.

Ready for anything, all my supplies were safely packed into the wagon the cook handled, stored among the many, *many* waxed bricks that were, according to her, *"the most heavenly thing ye'll ever put into yer mouth."* I hadn't believed her until she had given me a taste, and suspected that maybe a little magic was practiced in the kitchens as well.

We arrived later in the day than planned, the muddy roads having made quick travel impossible, and reached our camp with only an hour of light left to pitch the tents while Mrs. Cook readied a meal. To my relief, the MacKinnon camp was one of the more secluded, with a grove of birch trees, forbidden to be used for firewood, and large boulders that provided privacy from neighboring clans. With no other clan between our camp and the burn, we had an unhindered view of the gaming fields and easy access of the stone bridge that led to the market. I couldn't have chosen a better spot myself.

Raven-haired Bredanna, the laundress and wife of the warrior Farlan, helped me erect the tents along the edge of the birch grove. While she had been shy and timid around me at first, she had warmed up during our five days of travel, as did the other women who traveled with us. All of them married to the guards in our group, they held positions in the laundry or the kitchen. All had apologized one night around our campfire on the side of the road and asked forgiveness for their less than warm welcome. Graciously, I told them there was nothing to forgive.

I felt as though a heavy weight had been lifted off my shoulders with each smile and kind word they'd given me, though I was sure much of their affection came from the lack of rain during our trek. I hadn't had anything to do with it, but if the idea had put me in their good graces, I didn't see the harm in letting them believe it.

"What I wouldnae give for a bath," Bredanna groaned as she pushed sweaty strands of hair off her brow. We had finished with the last tent just as the final rays of sunlight slipped beneath the horizon, so I was of the same thought. I'd worn the same traveling gown for the last five days and could feel nine layers of dust clinging to my skin.

"Grab yer husbands so we can cleanse ourselves in the forest. Ye ken the spot," Maeve said as she wiped her face with her sleeve.

I shuddered at the thought of a group-bath in the burn, but the opportunity to get clean overwhelmed my shyness enough that I rummaged through my belongings for a fat cake of pine soap.

Within minutes, all seven women, besides Mrs. Cook, who still labored over her stew pot, marched out of the camp in the gloaming and along the water's edge with guards consisting of Malcolm and Farlan. The burn snaked into the woods between the hills where a large pool, formed by man, sat in a small clearing. It was just dark enough to provide privacy. The moon, only a crescent in the sky, cast the forest in shades of grey and drab browns. Maeve happily stripped out of her dress as soon as the men had turned their backs to keep watch for prying eyes. I could feel my face and chest flush the deepest crimson while I unplaited my hair and slowly untied the front laces of my traveling costume. No one besides my mother and Maeve had seen my naked body. To be exposed before so many made my fingers shake, and I couldn't help but cast a nervous glance at my husband's back.

"Come in, milady. I promise we willnae bite," a woman called from the pool, her nude body submerged to her waist. She scrubbed herself vigorously, and the flawless skin of her shoulders and arms glowed faintly in the soft moonlight.

Gritting my teeth, I shook my hair from its thick plait, slipped out of my clothing at Maeve's encouraging smile, and arranged my long hair to cover my back and most of my right arm. Terrified and bare, I plunged into the chilled water without an ounce of grace to preserve my dignity, splashing the others as they scrubbed their hair. Playful laughter and squeals filled the forest as the other women splashed one another, looking like a bunch of wood nymphs. At the first swipe of soap on my skin, the spicy scent of rosemary invaded my senses. Partially hidden by the dark water, I blissfully scrubbed the road from my body and hair, and relished in the sensation of the day's heat sloughing off my skin with the cool water.

"Allow me to wash yer back." Bredanna giggled from behind me and pushed my hair over my shoulder before I could protest.

Her sharp intake of breath let me know that she had seen—that she now knew what had been done to me. Without thinking, I spun away from her and wrapped my arms around myself. I inched toward the shore, and seven pairs of eyes looked up at me from the depths of the pool. No, I realized. Not at *me*, but something behind me. My teeth chattered, and I peered over my shoulder to find Malcolm staring at me in the moonlight. His gaze took in the scars that covered half my back, from my ribs to my thigh, and nearly every inch of my right arm. I hated the look of despair on his face. The regret. His teeth were clenched tight, his jaw a sharp, hard line as he stared openly at the damage done to my body.

"Milady," Maeve murmured soothingly from the pool. "Let us finish and then retire for the night. 'Tis been a long day."

Ashamed and near tears, I turned away from Malcolm and reluctantly rejoined her. All merriment ruined, the rest of the women stayed silent while we finished our bath and washed our soiled traveling gowns. Only Maeve spoke to me or looked my way, her grey eyes full of pity.

I wanted to scream from the humiliation.

Wrapped snug from head to toe within a clean cloth for our walk back to camp, I kept my eyes on the ground, too afraid to look at my husband again. Once back at the camp, I fled to my tent and collapsed onto the pallet I would share with Maeve in a heap of disgrace and wrapped the damp linen tightly around me. I brought my knees to my chest and brooded, abashed and completely mortified.

Maeve dressed and left me alone, frowning at my refusal to eat. How could I possibly eat when my stomach was in knots? I don't know why I thought I could hide my scars from Malcolm. I had told him how they happened, and it was inevitable that he would see them at some point, but nothing prepared me for the look on his face.

On everyone's face.

Hours later, my tent flap pulled aside as the camp grew quiet and everyone found their beds. I scooted over to make room for Maeve and jumped when a distinctly masculine touch traveled down the fabric covering my naked back. Alarm raced through my body, and I twisted around to find Malcolm staring down at the curve of my uncovered shoulder. My heart hammered in my chest at the sight of him.

The firelight that crept between the loose opening of the tent illuminated one side of his unshaven face, leaving the other engulfed in shadow. I couldn't read his features, but allowed him to gently push me back down and tug on my wrapping to reveal my ruined flesh. Cool air whispered across me, and my blood rushed through my veins with anticipation, and more than a little fear, at what he would do next.

The first press of his lips to my marbled shoulder tore at my heart; the second shattered any resistance I had left against him. I burned with an unfamiliar heat low in my belly when his breath softly tickled my neck, and the short, rough hairs on his chin rasped against my sensitive flesh. He loomed over me for a moment, his mouth just inches from my ear, his hand splayed heavily on the dip of my waist. I let out a soft whimper when his lips grazed my lobe, and his fingers tightened on the bone of my hip. I inched my arm out of its binding, eager to touch him, but he pulled away before I could and left without a word. The fabric doors of my canvas shelter fell closed with a sigh, and I stared after him with my heart in my throat.

Maeve joined me a short time later, her presence announced by a giggle and a provocative murmur to whoever escorted her. I feigned sleep as she cuddled up beside me, and focused on the phantom caress of Malcolm's lips on my skin until it was branded into my memory.

Against all odds, I fell asleep that night with a smile upon my lips.

Bredanna met me outside my tent the next morning with an embarrassed look on her face. "I didnae ken, milady. If I had… well, I want to say I'm sorry for what was done to ye."

Stunned, I could only nod as my throat closed on the tears that threatened to form. No one had ever said they regretted what had been done to me, as though they held some blame. Within the Druid community, my scars had been used to teach the importance of secrecy, to instill fear in the young girls who were inclined to believe themselves invincible. It was a necessary thing that I had braved year after year for the greater good. One look at me and they had seen they were not immune to the fears of man.

Bredanna timidly met my tearful gaze. "None of us will speak on it again."

As promised, and to my relief, when the clan gathered around the campfire to break their fast with bowls of hot porridge, all had returned to normal. Perched on a log, I listened to the excited conversations around me and watched as Mrs. Cook hustled toward the market with the largest man I'd ever seen in tow. As they passed, he grumbled about how unfair it was to watch over a woman's stand in the bazaar.

"Ye willnae be grumblin' when ye taste what we're sellin', Wallace," Mrs. Cook chirped and waved at him to hurry up.

With my belly full, I tipped my chin toward the morning sun where it crested the hill, and let the rays chase the chill from my body. At a soft brush against my thigh, I looked to my right and found Malcolm settling back against the log on which I sat. He rubbed his face vigorously, his features still soft with sleep. He wore the MacKinnon tartan today, not his leather breeks, as well as a black shirt and wool vest. I longed to run my fingers through his silky, coal-dark hair and pull it from the binding low at his nape.

"'Tis my least favorite day," he bemoaned. "Hour after hour filled with men quarreling like auld crones until near dusk is no' how I want to spend my time. I am sorry ye'll have to be privy to it, Angel. I truly am."

"Do all the wives go?" I asked as I gave my empty bowl to one of the women cleaning up the morning meal and tried my best to hide the elation I felt at the endearment he'd used twice now.

"Aye. Although I dinnae expect ye to speak with any o' them unless ye wish to."

"Will I be sittin' with ye?" *Please say I will,* I pleaded silently. I didn't know how I would survive an hour, let alone a whole day, surrounded by noblewomen. They'd know I was different within moments and tear me apart.

"O' course ye will." Malcolm turned toward me and licked his dry lips. "Coira, there's a sayin' I wish to share with ye. One that I want ye to emulate before we enter the pavilion and find ourselves surrounded by braggarts."

"What is it?"

"*'Look like the innocent flower, but be the serpent under it.'* 'Tis a quote from my favorite playwright."

I grinned and leaned closer to him to whisper, "Ye mean ye wish me to be a serpent in a room full o' serpents?"

Malcolm's gaze dipped to my lips as I spoke before turning away, his eyes troubled, and brushed some dust off his boot.

"Aye. That's exactly what I mean."

CHAPTER ELEVEN

COIRA

I walked toward the pavilion in the center of the camp which was surrounded by the colors of each clan fluttering in the breeze. With Malcolm by my side, and both Farlan and Gunn looking menacing as they prowled behind us, I felt as though I marched to war dressed in armor of my own. Where the men were clad in leather strapping, steel, and the MacKinnon colors of black, green, and blue, *I* was draped in the daring emerald silk gown that Maeve had packed away for this very occasion.

When she'd held it up for me earlier with a challenging look in her eye, I had blanched but allowed her to tie me within its folds. She'd then dressed my hair in an elaborate braid to fall over my right shoulder and had woven a thin silver rope of citrines within my white-gold locks. Upon my chest she'd laid a pendant of gold, inlaid with tiny gems the color of spring leaves.

"Ye look like a spring goddess," Maeve had said, bolstering my courage a moment before I revealed myself in the silken armor that would shield me against the shrewd stares of the other clan leaders and their wives. When I had emerged from my tent wearing the low-cut gown— my scars hidden by long sleeves and the high half-collar—I'd squared my shoulders and stared with confidence at the MacKinnon laird.

He inspected me with a heated look, his eyes growing dark, and cleared his throat before nodding once.

They will take measure o' me today, I counseled myself as I crossed the field at Malcolm's side, *and they will either find me worthy, or they will find me vicious and something to fear.*

"'Tis just one day," Malcolm murmured low enough for only me to hear. "If they vex ye too much, who am I to stop ye from sendin' all manner of wee beasties to plague their shelters tonight?"

Smothering a laugh, I looked around just to be sure we weren't heard. "I cannae do that. Though I would much like to, now that ye've mentioned it."

The side of Malcolm's mouth lifted in a wry grin as he swept aside the entrance to the pavilion and bade me to enter, our guard of two following close on our heels. The large shelter was warm and stuffy with little ventilation, and I immediately wished someone would tie back the east and west openings to allow the breeze to carry away the heat. I could already feel the backs of my legs begin to sweat, and it wasn't even midday.

A cold firepit dominated the middle of the pavilion with dozens of wooden chairs and stools surrounding it, each supplied by the laird who would occupy them. I noticed each chieftain had an attending guard as well, fearsome men who glowered at anyone who dared get too close to their laird with ill will. With a quick peek up at the two men behind me, I could see they had the same threatening expression plastered on their faces—death. Death was their promise, and they vibrated with it.

"MacKinnon!" A shout came from the far side and drew my attention toward a man in his middle years. A sad half-smile upon his face, he strode up to us and rested his palms familiarly on Malcolm's shoulders. "I heard the news about yer brother, may God rest his soul. He was a good man, and will be sorely missed this year and all the years to follow," he said as he tugged my husband into his embrace and clapped him once on the back. Pulling away, Malcolm nodded his thanks and reached out for me.

"Laird McRoberts, please allow me to present my wife, Coira." With my husband's hand resting against the small of my back, I met the McRoberts' stare and smiled politely.

"Well, well. She's a beauty, Malcolm." His rough hand grasped my fingers and brought them up to his lips for the briefest of kisses. He studied my face and how my cheeks flushed at his compliment. "I dinnae at all blame ye—"

"Would ye mind makin' the introduction to Lady McRoberts?" Malcolm interrupted with an odd cadence to his voice. "Coira could use a friendly face today."

The Laird McRoberts' dark brows popped up at the mention of his wife and released me. "O' Course. It would be Aurilia's pleasure to take the new Lady MacKinnon under her wing."

At the mention of her name, a woman floated through the growing crowd and came to stand beside him. No more than ten years older than myself, she had a kind face with deep brown eyes and hair the color of rich honey.

"Lady MacKinnon. I believe we will be fast friends by the end o' this dreadful day," she cooed, and slipped her arm through mine to pull me away from Malcolm's side. She patted my hand when I hesitated. "Och, I willnae take ye far, just a turn around the room. 'Tis stifling in here and I mean to demand a breeze let through."

She had a frank way of speaking, something I instantly liked about her. With a few sugary words and a light touch upon the forearms of the men posted at the pavilion openings, Aurilia had the breeze she so demanded and the first few gusts drove away the pressing heat.

"That one there," she whispered in my ear, motioning to a woman in a rust-colored dress. "Dinnae trust a word to come out o' her mouth, for ye will find only sugared lies and stories that never fully make sense. And the woman she is always with? That's her sister. They are two peas in a pod."

She guided me at a leisurely pace around the outskirts of the pavilion, introduced me to those she deemed worthy of her own friendship, and simply nodded to the rest.

"I'm grateful for yer council and yer company this morn."

"Och, we need to stick together. These noblewomen can be cruel to those like us."

"Like us?"

"Aye. Common folk." She grinned. "Redd was the son o' my father's laird. When I was sixteen, I accompanied my father to the castle, he was a stone smith ye see. Redd took one look at me, and I at him, and I felt as though I'd found something I'd been searching for. I didnae care that there was fourteen years between us, it was instant, ye ken." Aurilia looked over at her husband, quietly arguing with a fat man wearing a green and red tartan whose round belly folded over his belt like dough. "We met in secret for over a month, and by then, well, we were so in love, our fathers could no' rightfully deny us. So here I am, a commoner trussed up as a fine lady."

I grinned. "What a lovely story. No wonder Malcolm put me in yer capable hands."

"And how did *ye* wrangle a wedding vow out o' the MacKinnon? He's been much sought after for many years."

"Oh, um… my mother is the healer who tried to save his brother." I shrugged and prayed she wouldn't ask any more questions.

"'Tis a pity she didnae succeed. Colin was a legend in Scotia. Are ye also a healer?" Her genuine interest filled my chest with pride.

"Aye, and a good one. I'm a midwife too, and never lost a babe."

"Yer extraordinary, Coira. I'll have ye beside my next birthing bed if I can."

"Milady," Gunn's gruff voice rumbled from beside me, "my laird requests ye sit with him."

I smiled apologetically at Aurilia and followed Gunn to Malcolm's side where a padded chair awaited me.

"Enjoy yourself?" Malcolm asked curiously.

"I did. Thank ye for that," I whispered.

The pavilion drew quiet when a pompous-looking man with grey hair and a hooked nose stood to welcome the room and read off a list of subjects that needed attention or debate. His nasally voice droned on, territory lines being the most frequented subject, as well as marriage alliances and how *they* changed the territory lines. It was boring, to say the least, and his words began to blur together. To keep myself from dozing in my seat, I scanned the room and noticed a group of four women who stood in the far side of the pavilion from where I sat, whispering to one another. A tall, thin woman with silver-streaked brown hair glared at me with malice and unprovoked anger that raised the fine hairs on the left side of my neck. I met her glare with one of my own, emulating the serpent in the garden. I envisioned her as a mouse, tiny and trembling beneath my gaze until she looked away, and I released the breath I'd been holding. Encounter over, I settled back into my chair and dismissed her from my thoughts.

Two hours later, my eyes dry and scratchy and my legs long since gone to sleep, a break for the noon meal was ordered.

"Thank God," Farlan groaned from where he stood behind me.

"Ye look like ye could use a nap," Malcolm said when he helped me to my feet. I suppressed the need to rub life back into my backside and gave him a lame smile.

"Ye weren't jesting. 'Tis an awful way to spend the day," I agreed.

I spent the next hour with Aurilia nibbling on cold chicken, hard cheese, and grainy bread.

"Who is she?" I asked in a low voice and gestured at the woman who had looked at me so bitterly earlier.

Aurilia looked over and rolled her eyes slightly, a mocking smile on her lips. "*She* is Robena Bothan, and I'd stay clear away from her if I were ye."

"Why? Is her husband no' allied with my own? I didnae think there have been any clan quarrels in decades."

She gave me a peculiar look before saying, "No, 'tis because yer husband spurned her only daughter to marry *ye*." My face must have shown complete and utter shock because her eyes grew wide and apologetic. "Ye truly didnae ken?"

I shook my head, not trusting myself to speak lest I burst into tears, embarrassed to hear that Malcolm had been betrothed to another when he swore the blood vow to my mother. Oh, how angry he must have been to know the only way to save his brother's life was to give up the woman he loved. Then, to find himself bonded to someone far more plain and common than the fine-bred woman he had chosen of his own heart… it was little wonder he avoided me every day. With that dismal thought, the snake Malcolm had wanted me to embody became a worm, and my confidence deflated.

Aware of my inner turmoil, Aurilia quickly changed the subject to that of her children and I tried my best to smile and nod when expected. But on the inside… on the inside I was miserable. When the meal ended, I shuffled back to my seat as though I walked to the gallows. Now that I knew the truth, I felt even more the sham inside the fine dress I wore.

"Now, onto the subject of the clan Murray and their holdings at Bàs Dhubh," the speaker called out to his audience. "With Struan Murray's murder and his direct heir missin' since December's first snow, the clan has assumed the worst and a distant cousin has taken up the mantle of laird."

Excited murmurs filled the pavilion with that information, and several men rushed away after a softly spoken order from their chieftain. I lifted a brow and watched them dash away. *That* was interesting.

"An untested new laird with no grooming. I smell a war coming," Farlan murmured from his station at my back, answering my unspoken question.

Malcolm's jaw worked a moment before he shrugged. "'Tis no business o' Clan MacKinnon. Let it burn," he grumbled, to which he received grunts of agreement from the two warriors standing behind us.

By the time the sun had shifted past the hills that cradled the valley, I was well and truly exhausted. For the last couple hours, I had struggled between staying awake and mulling over what Aurilia had told me. Finally, when all subjects had been hashed over, and the bickering slowed to grumbling agreements and truces, I nearly jumped out of my seat in my haste to leave.

"MacKinnon." A gruff voice pulled me out of my reverie of a hot meal and my bed, and I turned to find the short, rotund man Redd

McRoberts had argued with earlier. He stared up at my husband with annoyance, his meaty hands flexed with irritation at his sides.

Robena Bothan stood just behind him. She glowered at me, her cold eyes pressed into angry slits. Her presence hinted that this man was her husband, Laird Bothan, and the father of the woman whom Malcolm had broken his betrothal.

From his staggering height, Malcolm looked down upon the man who would have been his father-in-law and bent at the waist in respect, his face almost repentant.

The older man frowned, clearly surprised at the deference Malcolm was showing him. His jowls became more defined for a moment before he said gruffly, "Dinnae get me wrong, MacKinnon, I'm angry that ye broke my sweet Edeen's heart. Were ye a younger man, I'd box yer ears bloody, but I dinnae want there to be bad blood between us."

"Nor I," Malcolm agreed.

Robena stared daggers at the back of her husband's head, as though she had expected him to say something much different, and was disappointed with the change of heart.

Malcolm clasped Bothan's forearm with a firm grip. "I would still want ye for an ally, that hasnae changed. Our alliance just cannae be through marriage."

Laird Bothan nodded dismally, opened his mouth like he would say more, and then waddled away. His sour-faced wife followed without a word spoken to either of us. For that, I was relieved, because I hadn't a clue what I would have said in response. I felt embarrassed and ashamed standing beside the MacKinnon laird when we both knew it should have been her daughter. I couldn't even look at him when he blew out a heavy breath and muttered something about needing a whole cask of wine to himself as he led me out of the pavilion into the cool, fresh evening air.

When we arrived, my husband's people had already gathered around the fire, their plates loaded with roasted meat and potatoes with brown mushroom gravy. Gunn and Farlan immediately collapsed upon the closest bench, rested their forearms on their knees, and with their backs bowed, attempted to stretch their sore muscles. The strain of standing sentinel all day, on uneven ground and the added weight of their armor, had taken its toll on their bodies. I had to admit their day had been even more taxing than mine. I ducked into my tent and searched for the clove and cedarwood oil I'd mixed before searching out Bredanna and found her easily enough. Both she and Gunn's wife were cooing over their warrior husbands, who moaned and groaned like babes at an empty breast.

"Here." I pressed a small bottle into each woman's hand. "Rub a small amount onto whatever hurts and press down with yer thumbs in a circular motion. Be sure to wash yer hands after. 'Tis a poison to the gut and no' to be ingested," I stressed as both women nodded eagerly.

"Here ye are, milady," Mrs. Cook said kindly as she handed me a wooden plate of food. Looking around, I pursed my lips to find the only empty space to sit was next to the laird. Had I been dressed in anything but the beautiful green gown, I would have sat in the dirt; since that was not the case, I plunked down on the smooth log at his side and dug into the meal. Mindful that no grease would spill on the silk, I turned my shoulder away from him, hoping he wouldn't speak to me.

I was not so lucky.

"So, ye survived yer first clan assembly," Malcolm noted wearily, oblivious to my foul mood. "Did Aurilia coach ye on the finer points o' Scottish court life?"

"Oh, aye, she did," I said sardonically and shoveled more buttered potatoes into my mouth. "Probably more so than ye would have wished." From the corner of my eye, I saw his horn cup pause in midair, and he glanced at me cautiously.

"How so?"

Setting my barely touched plate aside, I stood and smoothed my skirting and said brusquely, "She told me what I wish *ye* would have *months ago*. Ye broke yer betrothal to Laird Bothan's daughter?"

Malcolm's features smoothed into a mask of indifference. "What does it matter?"

"What does it—" I sputtered and slapped my hand against my chest. "Did ye no' think I should have been told? I've been paradin' around in these fine clothes meant for someone else!"

Conversations around us grew hushed or ceased altogether while I glared down upon the laird. I didn't care one bit that I was making a scene. I was hurt, embarrassed, and confused by the betrayal I felt. A betrayal I shouldn't feel. I may be married to the MacKinnon laird, but he wasn't *mine*. Not really. I didn't have any right to feel betrayed, but he should have prepared me.

I bit down hard on my lip before I could say anything further and turned on my heel for the relative privacy of my tent before I broke into a dozen pieces. Ignoring Maeve's astonished expression, I did my best to hold myself together and quickened my pace.

Unaware that Malcolm chased after me, I gasped when his strong hand wrapped firmly around my arm and propelled me past the row of tents.

"As ye were!" Malcolm snapped at the people we left around the fire. He led me into the deep shadows of the birch grove and pressed my back against a towering boulder.

"I dinnae appreciate being spoken to that way," he growled as he loomed over me.

The nerve of this man! My anger boiled, and I squared my shoulders. "Then maybe—" His hand covered my mouth and stifled the words I railed against his palm.

"Please, Angel. Cease yer rage against me and allow me to explain," he began. His deep voice rumbled between us, and he bowed his head, resting his forehead against mine. "We've had a hard courtship, ye and I, and I dinnae wish to argue with ye."

The gentleness of his supplication, so contradictory to the pressure of his hand on my lips, disarmed me. Falling silent, I relaxed against the stone at my back and let him talk.

"I brought ye here, married ye, and have kept ye when it was so obvious ye want to leave." His hand slid from my mouth and braced his arm against the stone above my head. "I thought it would be only I who would atone for my brother's happiness and future. At the time, I wasnae thinkin' about how yer mother's blood vow would affect ye. How it *still* effects ye. I was selfish and I'm sorry for it." I stayed silent, shocked by his admission. "There was no formal betrothal agreement between me and Edeen Bothan, Angel. We only had a four-day courtship, and we didnae ken one another well."

Oh. Part of me jumped with glee at that revelation; the other part was still troubled by the mention of his self-imposed atonement.

"Why cannae ye be happy?" I whispered. I itched to reach out and touch his chest, to soothe him in some way, but kept my arms crossed loosely over my belly.

"'Tis no' that I dinnae want to be." One of his fingers sketched a line from my temple down my neck and grazed the soft flesh displayed above the low neckline of my gown. That small, feather-light touch left a trail of fire in its wake. "The guilt o' my betrayal is what eats at me. Colin didnae want me to… but I did anyway. How will I ken if he—" Malcolm's throat bobbed, and he shifted on his feet. "What if he doesnae make it, Coira? What if I doomed him to half a life and stole ye from yers all for naught?"

His voice dripped with shame, and I couldn't help but feel saddened at his confession. "He'll make it," I promised and gave in to the impulse to reach for him, to give him whatever comfort he would allow. "And I specifically remember ye *askin'* me to go with ye."

My fingers sifted through air when he stepped away, and I let my hands fall awkwardly to my sides. Malcolm cleared his throat and smoothed back the dark strands of hair that had escaped from their binding.

"Come," he said gruffly and offered me his hand to soften the sting of his rejection. "Let us have a drink together. 'Tis been a long day, and I am more than ready to see it come to an end."

We rejoined our merry group around the fire and sat side-by-side, content to watch the dancing and revelry instead of partaking in it. Accepting a goblet of wine from Malcolm's personal cask, I made myself set aside the day's quarrels and enjoyed the remainder of the evening. All around us, song and dance filled the valley underneath the starlit canopy. The fast-paced melodies of fiddles and lutes and the pounding of countless drums in neighboring camps wormed their way into my blood, heightening the effects of the wine. I absorbed the energy around me and watched the people around us grow a little more sensual and wild as they drank and danced. I closed my eyes and swayed with the music from my perch on the bench, letting it wrap itself around me and soak into my soul… and then I felt myself *become* the music.

The beat purred in my throat and thumped in my pulse as I sung a soft, wordless tune and my skin tingled with wave after wave of hot and cold. Like a breeze over a still pond, the ripples flitted from my shoulders to my fingertips and tingled the soles of my feet.

A feminine cry snapped at my attention, and I opened my eyes to find a ten-foot flame twirling toward the heavens as though caught in the wind. The orange peaks reached higher and higher, pulsing and quivering to the beat of the music. Mesmerized, we watched the flames morph into the shape of a woman, her provocative curves eerily similar to my own while her white-hot hair blew wild above her.

Then she took a step out of the fire toward the man beside me, her bare foot singeing the dewy grass with a hiss.

I snapped my mouth shut and cut off the flow of magic, effectively halting the spell I had been singing. Any hint of my magic vanished, and the flames folded and melted in on themselves until they burned like any ordinary fire. Everyone turned toward me, stock-still and silent, their features a mix of astonishment, excitement, and worry. I cast a nervous side-glance at Malcolm, expecting a berating, only to find his dark brows hiked high, his wicked mouth curved in a half-smile of surprise.

He plucked my half-empty cup from my hand and poured its contents into his own, then said, "'Tis probably best ye give up the wine now, lass, before yer fire sprite seduces every man for miles around with her nakedness."

Even though his open acceptance of my unintended spell eased tensions in the camp, my cheeks flushed with mortification. I had hoped the nudity would have been overlooked.

"What a shame." Finlay laughed from the other side of the firepit. "I wouldnae have minded being seduced by a naked fire sprite."

Finlay barely shielded himself in time before my empty cup sailed out of Malcolm's hand, aimed straight for his head.

Chapter Twelve

MALCOLM

"Some are born great, others achieve greatness."
-William Shakespeare, Twelfth Night

"Move out o' my way!" his wife bellowed and shouldered her way past men twice her size who surrounded Bram sprawled stone-still on the trampled grass. She knelt beside him, yanked up his shirt without any preamble, and pressed gentle, nimble fingers to his skin to assess the damage to his ribs.

"How bad?" Finlay demanded while he fretted beside his twin. "He's no' wakin' up."

Coira did not answer as she ran her fingers through Bram's sweaty curls, her eyes closed and brows pinched with concentration. Malcolm rested a heavy hand on Finlay's shoulder in a silent command to calm himself while Coira pulled a small tin from the pocket of her dress and cracked it open under Bram's nose. Instantly, his bright, sea-green eyes snapped open with a sharp inhale and a snort, and Finlay sagged with relief.

"Just knocked out cold. He'll be fine in a few hours," Coira said with a grunt, and helped Bram sit up before she turned his face toward her with a firm grip on his chin. "No more horse racin', Bram. In fact, ye get to sit with Mrs. Cook for the rest o' the day."

Malcolm shook his head when Bram looked up at him for support. "Ye heard my Lady. Finlay, take him back to camp."

After the little crowd dispersed, Malcolm picked up Coira's cedar healers-box. She'd had him tote it to each competition his men had entered for the last five days when he was not in the pavilion with the other chieftains. Even if it made him feel like a pack mule, it was a task he looked forward to, for he could see her work closely for the first time.

So far, she had bound several broken ribs, a few jammed fingers, and pushed Caelen's shoulder back in its socket after the MacKinnon's won the tug-o-war for the third year in a row. The worst injury resulted when a brawl had broken out near Mrs. Cook's stand in the market the previous day. For whatever reason, Wallace, who had volunteered to watch over her each day, had been in the thick of it. He'd earned himself a particularly gruesome gash on his calf which Coira stitched up after dousing it with scotch to cleanse the wound. Malcolm had never heard such a large man scream so shrill in his life and hoped Finlay would remember that particular detail to recount later.

Coira forged ahead of him, past the area where men threw hatchets at wooden bulls-eyes and toward the roped area for bare-knuckle boxing. While she marched from one area to the next, Malcolm's focus adhered to the curves of her waist and the swagger of her hips.

She had grown confident in the past week and had shed the shyness and reserved state she had wrapped around herself like a thick winter cloak. *This* was the fierce, strong woman who'd boldly pressed her dagger to his throat in that little cottage in the wood. He vastly preferred this side of her to the meek, uncertain creature she had been when she thought the world was against her.

He'd nearly choked on his wine when she had hummed along with the music the night she'd made the fire dance, the sight forever etched in his memory. His kilt had lifted at the sight of her naked reflection in the fire. The roaring inferno had invitingly opened its shapely legs and ran ethereal hands along womanly curves, beckoning all to join her in the flames. There was not a doubt in his mind that it was Coira's body that danced and writhed to the music while she swayed beside him to the beat of the drum. She had unknowingly shown him the sensual, wanton side of herself. Damn him to hell, but he hungered to experience it in the flesh, to taste her upon his tongue.

He had felt more than a little disappointment when the vision faded to nothing but heat and smoke.

Malcolm had kept careful tabs on her wine after that night and had allowed himself to fill her cup only twice before she would retire to the tent she shared with Maeve. Never once had she looked to him for an invitation to sleep in his. He wasn't even sure what he would have said if she had.

"Stupid, stupid, stupid," Coira muttered when she caught sight of Gavin the moment he spit an impossibly large amount of thickened blood onto the packed dirt near the boxing arena. At the sight of his laird, Gavin shot him a satisfied smile and raised his arms in triumph, his bare chest covered in sweat and dust, his teeth stained red.

"Third place my laird!" he boasted. "I was doin' well until I got my face beaten in by the Sinclair."

Malcolm laughed as he set down Coira's box and peered closer at Gavin's crooked nose and blackened eyes. "Och, just a few more years and ye may beat them all, cousin."

Coira pushed him away. "Sit over there," she said with a huff and pointed to an old stump, unimpressed.

Gavin sat down as though the half-rotten wood were a throne, filled to the brim with gratification, and openly winked at her.

"Yer vanity is certainly somethin' to behold, young Gavin MacKinnon," she mocked as she stationed her thumbs on either side of the twisted, swollen mess in the middle of his face. Gavin only grinned wider. With a tilt of her head, she returned his smile with one of her own and crooned, "But this is still gonna hurt."

And then she pressed her thumbs together. Malcolm cringed inwardly at the wet, violent crack that emitted from Gavin's nose as his bones realigned. Gavin wrenched his face out of her hands so hard he toppled backwards onto the grass behind him.

"Feckin' hell!" he cried and then inspected his face gingerly. "I thought ye'd taken it right off! Healers are supposed to be gentle creatures, ye ken."

"Mmm. Let me see yer fingers." Indifferent to his outburst, she grabbed his wrist and rotated each finger in turn. "At least ye kept the force to yer knuckles and ye didnae lose any teeth." She unlatched her box, fished out a bottle of clear liquid, then splashed it onto the open wounds of his hands. Her grip was locked tight on his hand as she rubbed it into the open areas where his skin was split. "Be still, ye beetroot! Ye need to let me clean yer hand or infection will set, and I'll have to cut it off at the wrist when it grows foul and green." Worried, Gavin stopped struggling and stared at her while she wrapped his hand with a strip of linen over a thick pad of elder moss.

"Can that happen?" he asked in disbelief.

In answer, Coira slapped her box closed and arched a haughty brow at him as though to say, *isn't that what I just said?* Without further comment, she went off in search of another clan member in need of aid. Malcolm could only laugh at the terrified look on Gavin's face.

When the sun descended on the final day of the Gathering, and the competitions had ended, Malcolm escorted Coira back to their camp one last time. Assembled around the fire, his people feasted on good fortune and joy while they shared stories of their many triumphs and a few failures achieved throughout the week. They toasted each speaker and gave a lengthy cheer for a proud Mrs. Cook and the two scullery maids who had sold their sweets all week long in the market—all seven hundred pounds of it. The money they had made filled an entire chest with coin and would go far in the way of maintenance, improvements, and the overall longevity of the keep.

Sitting at his side, Coira grinned and listened to everyone who spoke, and Malcolm wondered when she had stopped fretting over her scars. Her pale hair, usually pulled over her right shoulder, was knotted at the back of her head to battle the day's heat. Her ear was still concealed, but the back of her neck was exposed for the first time.

"We've forgotten someone," Malcolm called out and felt Coira go still beside him. *Aye, my Angel. Dinnae think ye went unnoticed,* he thought as he ran his hand lightly down her back and lifted his horn-cup high. "To my wife, whose presence has been a balm to sore muscles and broken bones. I have watched her tend to most o' ye this week. She did so tirelessly and without complaint. A true Lady o' Ghlas Thùr." Malcolm held her shy, tender stare while the camp cheered their agreement.

The evening wore on until Malcolm's casks of ale were emptied and the music in the valley fell hushed.

"Goodnight," Coira said with a yawn and smiled shyly at him before she headed for the tent she shared with Maeve. He watched her leave the dim circle of light cast by the dying fire until she stopped dead in her tracks a few lengths from her tent and her hand flew to her mouth. Within moments he was by her side, ready to jump in front of whatever had caused her alarm.

"What is it?" he asked, only to hear Maeve's muffled, breathy giggle drift from their tent as bodies brushed against the canvas.

Coira stifled a laugh at the sound of frenzied lovemaking and awkwardly backed toward the fire to wait it out. "I think I'll be out here for a while longer after all."

Without conscious thought, Malcolm grasped her slim fingers and blurted, "Stay with me."

Coira's blonde brows raised in surprise before she nodded and allowed him to lead her to his tent.

"Ye did good work today," he said nervously to break their silence and said a prayer of thanks that she could not see the blush that mottled his cheeks.

"I enjoyed it. Thank ye for allowing me to continue the calling. 'Tis all I ken, and it would sadden me if I were no' allowed. I dinnae think I could stand aside and watch the sufferin' if I could help."

"Nor would I want ye to. I want ye to do what makes ye happy, and if it pleases ye to set bones and make tinctures, then so be it," he said when they arrived in front of his tent.

The darkness was his enemy as he drew her inside, the creature within him awakened and waiting. She stood close, her shadowed face upturned and expectant.

Malcolm swallowed thickly before he said, "Let's get ye out o' this… unless ye plan to sleep fully clothed?"

Her shadowy figure nodded once, and with deliberate slowness, Malcolm untied the laces of her bodice and listened to her shallow breathing. Once loosened, he pushed her gown off her shoulders to let it fall in a pile at her feet. She looked like a ghost, stark in the gloom with only a white shift to veil her body. With a swift tug, Malcolm shucked his shirt and guided her down onto the pad of blankets and furs that made his bed. He bit back a groan when her softer body pressed flush against his harder one.

What am I doing? he thought as he allowed his hand to wander along her ribs, over her hip, and back up again to tease the soft curls at the nape of her neck.

He hadn't expected her to agree to his suggested sleeping arrangement. Now she was here beside him with her scent in his nose, the heat of her body pressed against him, and that goddamn oath writhing in his chest. Malcolm realized what a terrible mistake he had made when she rested her hands upon his bare chest in clear invitation. With the last of his self-control, he grasped her hand tightly and pressed her palm to his mouth before firmly arranging her back against his front, lest her wandering touch break the fragile tether he held over himself.

"Dinnae think yer no' wanted, Angel." His lips brushed against her marbled skin, and he wrapped his arms around her. *It's that I cannae allow myself to have ye*, he finished in thought.

Though her voice held hints of sadness, she said, "I understand, Malcolm; I truly do. I have dealt with my guilt over Ness's disappearance. Had I no' shown my magic to the priest… I cannae pretend to ken what would have happened. Maybe Ness would have burned by my side on the pyre, or my father could have gotten us out before a trial ever took place. I'll never… I'll never ken what could have been if I had no' done what I did." Coira turned in his arms and firmly placed her hand over his heart, the heat of her skin like a balm to his nerves. "We make our choices in life, Malcolm. We cannae change them, but we can live with them. We only have to accept them. Ye're no' ready to accept the choice ye made yet… but I want ye to ken that I think ye were verra brave that night. I believe that if I were separated from my love and Ness had taken an oath to ensure I had a second chance with that love, even against my wishes… I would be grateful."

Malcolm's eyes burned, and his chest felt like it would cave in on itself as he listened to her words. "I want to believe that."

Coira smiled sadly and patted his chest. "But ye dinnae. No' really."

He shook his head and hated himself when her smile melted. "No. I dinnae believe it at all."

Malcolm expected her to argue her point, but she kept silent and turned around to snuggle her back firmly against his chest. With her head pillowed comfortably on his bicep, she traced the muscles of his forearm with her fingernails.

Tugging a thick woven blanket over them, he tried to relax while he focused on her even breathing and thought on her wise words.

He didn't know the order in which they fell asleep, but he knew which of them had woken first when he found himself alone with the breaking of the dawn, cold and bereft.

Ghlas Thùr had been a welcome sight after their long, uneventful journey back, the heat of full summer blazing down upon the fields. In the morning, five days after their return, Malcolm sparred with Magnus in the south bailey. Their blunted practice swords gleamed in a silver blur as they traded blow for blow until they were breathless, and their muscles begged for mercy.

The weapons-master pushed his unruly, red hair out of his face and crowed with laughter. "Ye would give yer brother a hell of a challenge, my laird. I only wish he could see ye now," Magnus said with pride.

Malcolm's heart twinged with sadness as it always did at the mention of his brother. *Will it ever get easier to speak o' him as though he were no' here?* he wondered. *As though he was truly dead and no' resting in an endless sleep in the keep?*

"I miss him," he mumbled and rotated his sword at the wrist, enjoying the sound it made when it whooshed past his ear.

"We all do," Magnus agreed, his ruddy features regretful as he looked up at the clear blue sky and his breath caught. "Every damn day. I loved that lad like he was my own—and ye too."

Malcolm nodded, and kicked at a few pebbles, his focus on the ground. "I keep wonderin' if I made the right decision," he admitted.

"No, ye cannae think that way," the weapons-master said firmly, and pointed the tip of his sword at Malcolm's chest. "He is *exactly* where he's meant to be. I feel it in my gut, and my gut's never wrong. O' course, it pains me every day he's no' down here in the dirt beatin' the shite out o' the lot o' us… but he's no' supposed to be *here*. He's supposed to be with *her*. With Meggie. Colin just needed a little push is all. He'd never admit it, but he's just as stubborn as ye, ye ken."

Malcolm chuffed a laugh and blinked the moisture from his eyes. "I hope yer right, auld man," he said and gripped his sword with both hands and grounded himself. "Another round?"

"Aye, I'll make a warrior out o' ye yet," Magnus taunted and then rained down blow after blow on his laird with his blunted practice sword.

An hour later, exhausted and famished, Malcolm pushed through one last round with Farlan when the weapons-master broke away from the young man he was sparring and bellowed, "What the blazin' hell is that goddamn noise?"

The steady *tink-tink-tink* Malcolm had been hearing for the last half hour stopped abruptly. Bram, stationed above them on the eastern wall, chuckled to himself.

"What is it?" Malcolm demanded as he wiped the sweat from his brow. But Bram only shrugged his shoulders with a smirk and went back to looking out over the fields.

"'Tis gone now, my laird," he called over his shoulder, unrepentant for revealing nothing.

Several occasions throughout the week, rain or shine, the sound of chipping stone could be heard while he sparred with the men, always from the wall Bram was manning. The noise would stop abruptly when it drew attention, the culprit nowhere to be found. Neither was there any evidence that anyone had damaged the wall. Bram was naturally tight-lipped and flatly refused to speak on it.

One morning, while Malcolm relaxed in his chamber and broke his fast with a delicious fried bread with honey and berries, the nerve-rending *tink-tink-tink* drifted through his open window, set his teeth on edge, and soured his mood. "Enough is enough," he growled, and looked down on the rear bailey below where Bram surveyed the loch, his bow at the ready beside him.

Before the mystery stone smith could be warned, Malcolm swiftly navigated the halls and stairwells, crossed the center bailey, and ran through the main gatehouse where Bram could not spot him. Hugging his body close to the wall, he crept toward the sound of chiseled stone that had been driving him mad and caught sight of the offender.

He did not expect to find his wife.

Her back bowed, she knelt in the grass, a small hammer and chisel in her hands, laboring to carve something into the base of the wall. Malcolm's mouth pulled down in confusion and he backed away to inspect the foundation of the wall. It took some time, but he found what he sought. Every ten feet, a line of runes was expertly carved— so small, if they didn't know where or what to look for, no one would know they were there. After a few moments of internal debate and without her knowledge of his presence, Malcolm returned to the keep and let his wife have her secrecy. She would tell him what she was up to soon enough.

"The stable boy is dead, my laird," Farlan said when he rushed through the open library doors. "He was found floatin' in the loch by the children as they played just now."

"Damn," Malcolm swore as he set his book down and rushed with Farlan to the front gate. "He sleeps in the stable, where are his kin?"

"The village. He's the eldest o' seven."

Malcolm swore again as they left out of the main gate and met two of his guards carrying the boy up the hill. His thin, pale limbs swung freely, his smooth cheeks the light grey of death.

"What do ye want us to do?" one of the men asked.

"Give him to me," Malcolm said sadly and wiped the boy's wet hair away from his face with regret. "Farlan, make haste to the lad's mother. She needs to be prepared for when I bring her son home to rest."

Hours and a lifetime later, during the evening meal, Malcolm pinched the bridge of his nose and struggled with his inner turmoil. He was unable to get the sound of the mother's mournful wails out of his head. He'd heard them long before he had reached the village as he guided Ramsey, who'd pulled the wagon with the boy's wrapped body in the back. Coira had insisted on personally bathing his little body in lavender water before she wrapped him with a white sheet. At the very least, she hoped her care would give his mother some comfort, knowing her son had been provided the utmost respect.

Malcolm hated every moment of this day. He didn't know which was worse: bringing a mother the lifeless body of her firstborn or watching the grief on the father's face when he had settled his eldest son into the coffin.

"*Some responsibilities come with great heartache,*" his father had said many years ago, but knowing that didn't make days like this any easier.

"Can I do anything for ye?" Coira asked softly from her place beside him.

"No, Angel," he sighed. "Some burdens just lay heavier on my soul. This is one o' them."

Farlan cleared his throat before he spoke from his place at Malcolm's left. "I ken this is a raw subject, but I found a temporary replacement to tend the stable. He's a bit old for the position, but he's in need of coin before he travels on to the highlands, and has already built something of a rapport with some of the men while in the tavern the past week."

"Alright, I'll give him two weeks, but ask around for a more permanent replacement within the clan. Fair?"

"Aye, my laird."

"Then have someone fetch him in the morn."

Chapter Thirteen

COIRA

Scarcely an hour after we arrived back at Ghlas Thùr from the Gathering, I watched from my tower window while my husband rode his great black beast through the gatehouse. He headed north like I had seen him do so many other times before, somber and alone.

Curious, I had asked Bram the reason while I tended my garden later that afternoon and got my answer.

"He's hopin' to receive some sign that Colin survived the centuries." Bram had said. "The uncertainty gnaws at him."

That's when I'd known what I had to do, and asked Bram to escort me to the village where I commissioned the smallest chisel possible to be made by the blacksmith. Days later, chisel in hand, I had begun fortifying the keep's walls with simple, powerful runes. Etched in vertical lines to keep their strength, I'd carved them into the base of the wall. Hidden from those who didn't know what they were looking for, they would protect all who resided inside the walls from damaging wind, water, fire, and earth.

The runes ensured the wind would not topple its towers and no amount of rain would flood its foundations. The earth's movements would not damage the grounds within, nor would fire escape the hearths or candle wicks. I'd whispered my strength into each rune, all one hundred columns of them, and had nearly drained my body of stamina and power, causing me to collapse into my bed at the end of each day.

Without my asking, Bram kept my secret and had even warned me when someone came to investigate the telling sounds of my hammer against the steel chisel. Eventually, I wizened up and wrapped them both in cloth. That fine idea hadn't come to me until I was halfway around the wall and battled a snarled patch of blackberry vines. They had torn my arms bloody, and by the end of the day, the sight of the scratches reminded me of my cat, Alistair, and my mother's harsh lessons.

On the last day of backbreaking work bowed close to the ground, the rhythm of pounding hoofbeats caught my attention. I watched as a man raced through the main gatehouse, a look of sheer panic on his face. Abandoning my tools in the shade of the wall, I hurried to follow him into the bailey and toward the alarmed male voices shouting within.

"She's gonna die!" the young man raged, his face streaked with tears, and his eyes bloodshot. "I need her help. She can save them, I ken she can."

I stood behind the guards holding the man firmly in place as he pleaded with them, and another ran inside the keep to summon the laird. The distraught man grabbed Gunn's jerkin and shook him with a strength I wouldn't have assumed he had, being that Gunn was a head taller and three stone heavier.

"My wife! She's been on the birthin' bed for too long—"

"How long?" I demanded.

The man twisted around, and his haunted eyes snapped to mine a moment before he lunged for me. Breaking past the surprised guards, he dropped to his knees at my feet and beseechingly held his hands out before he gripped the hem of my dress. I had never seen such a look of misery and anguish.

"Please help me," he cried. "I cannae lose her. I'll pay any price."

Resting my hands upon his shoulders, I shook my head and said, "There is no price."

No time for my own mount to be readied, I allowed the man, whose name was Cam, to hoist me up behind him. I demanded my healer's box be delivered to me, as well as clean linen and scotch, and we raced out of the bailey, my arms wrapped tightly around his lean waist. I looked back through the open gates to see Malcolm striding out of the keep's thick main door as he roared my name, and his face twisted with a furious scowl.

"Dinnae stop," I urged. The MacKinnon would survive his anger, but Cam's wife needed me.

At a breakneck pace, we thundered through the woods that divided the village from the stronghold, Cam's fear pushing the poor beast to its limits while I held on for dear life. Minutes later, we crossed the open field and entered the small hamlet.

Outside a modest cottage, Cam sharply reigned in his exhausted beast, and pulled me down to the ground into the middle of a large gathering of villagers listening to Father Blount as he read from his Bible. The sight of the priest sent a jolt of fear down my spine, and I pleaded to whatever gods were in the heavens that he would not look my way.

"Precious in the sight of the Lord is the death of his faithful servants," Blount intoned to those who stood around him, his gaze resolutely on his Bible. The villagers' heads were bowed in prayer, their hands clutched to their chests while they listened.

"No!" Cam cried at the mention of death. Distressed, he left me beside the agitated horse and shouldered through the crowd toward the small cottage.

I followed behind, prepared to console the grieving husband, and firmly closed the door between me and the priest. Cam's whimpers from the far side of the single, darkened room plucked at my heart. I crossed the floor to pay my respects and found the laboring mother's weary, agonized brown eyes staring up at me.

"She's no' dead, milady," Cam sniffed. He held his wife's pale hand and kissed it reverently. "Father Blount said… I thought…"

I let him talk to himself and rushed to the other side of the bed, the young woman's listless stare tracking me all the way.

"May I touch ye, mother? I'm here to help," I said gently when her body clenched up tight.

At the faint nod of her head, I peeled away the heavy blanket to reveal her belly. Sweat bathed her body, soaking the thin shift she wore to near transparency. Her legs were spread and bent in agony while the birthing surge ran its course, her belly tight and oddly shaped. When she sagged against the pillows, I placed my hands on her and closed my eyes. Palpitating her torso, I reached out with the senses that made Druid women the very best midwives.

"Is this yer first babe?" I asked, the cadence of my voice calming and sure. She gave a slight mewl of ascent, and I continued my exploration, feeling along the small being under the mother's tight skin before lifting the limp hem of her shift. "No blood. That's a verra good sign. Let's have a closer feel to what's goin' on, alright? Where is yer midwife?" I asked Cam as I washed my hands of dust in a basin of fresh water on the table.

"Attendin' another. Fiona's time arrived hours after she was called away. That was two days ago."

A sharp knock preceded Farlan with my box of supplies, and Maeve followed close behind him, her arms full of clean linen.

"Maeve, yer stayin'," I said and ordered her to boil more water.

"The laird is outside, my lady," Farlan murmured.

"And there he can stay while I save this babe. Go."

Banishing Farlan, as well as my disgruntled husband from my mind, I rolled up my sleeves and crawled onto the bed between Fiona's limp legs. A minute later I knew what had to be done and looked adamantly at Cam from where he knelt beside the bed. His eyes were glassy as he glanced up at me with worry.

"Time for ye to go now," I said sternly. "Ye did all ye could by comin' to fetch me, but I'll handle things from here."

He looked between me and his wife, unsure of what to do until Fiona lay her pale hand upon her husband's cheek and nodded. Her pallor had grown waxy since I'd arrived, the smudges beneath her eyes darker and her lips drawn and bloodless. I needed to act fast or risk losing both mother and babe. Once he was gone, I gripped Fiona's bent knees tightly, and willed some of my energy and strength into her. She gasped, her eyes flared wide, and her skin broke out in tiny chill bumps.

It was a risk, using my magic so blatantly in front of a villager, but it was a risk I was willing to take.

"Fiona. Yer babe is turned and cannae be born without help. What I need to do is goin' to hurt, and I'm verra sorry for that, but ye *will* survive this, do ye hear me? I willnae lose either ye *or* the bairn."

Her eyes filled with unshed tears as she mouthed a silent *thank ye* with trembling lips, and with her consent, I began a labor of my own. In between each violent surge of Fiona's body, I turned the fading life inside her belly inch by inch while she cried and pleaded. Finally— mercifully—there was a distinct settling of her abdomen and we both expelled a sigh with relief.

"The rest is up to ye now," I said with a smile. "Ye can do it."

Even after witnessing dozens upon dozens of births, I still found myself in awe of the process. I praised and encouraged Fiona as she found the inner strength all women possess when they've brought forth new life into the world. She panted—she screamed—she gritted her teeth, and all the while, her eyes were locked with mine.

When the babe slipped into my outstretched hands, I wept with joy at the sight of his little, pink face. Angry and pinched from his long wait, he squalled with fury. We cooed over his perfection as Maeve announced the healthy birth to the villagers, and from the sheer volume of the ovation outside, I estimated every villager was out there waiting for that good news. Cam rushed through the door, Father Blount in tow, and nearly knocked Maeve over in his haste.

I flung a blanket over Fiona's legs to preserve her modesty and hurried to gather the soiled linen from the floor. My pulse hammered in my ears, and I kept my gaze averted from the priest. He had not seen my face since the day he married me to the laird, and I had no shield, no veil my to hide my features.

"Come, pray over this new soul," Blount called out to Maeve and me, busy with cleaning.

Maeve dutifully knelt beside Fiona's bed and I followed suit, clasping my hands together. I pressed my thumbs against my forehead to hide my face from his sight and discreetly wiped at the beads of nervous sweat on my brow.

"She did it! Oh, my sweet Lord, she did it," Cam moaned. Slumped next to his wife, he wept, his forehead pressed to her shoulder.

Father Blount's voice filled the cottage as he prayed over the thriving baby in Fiona's arms, each word from his tongue like a nail in my skin. I watched from under my brows at the way Fiona looked up at the priest, her gaze full of adoration and gratitude as he blessed her child. I could not begrudge her. She did not know him as I did.

At the closing of his prayer, Father Blount circled the bed and prayed over Maeve, his hand on the back of her head as he bestowed God's love up on her.

Then he moved behind me.

The rush of a thousand ghostly ants made my skin itch when I felt his touch on my crown, and I squeezed my hands tighter. They crawled through my hair, into the crevices behind my ears, and marched on sharp feet down the back of my sweat-dampened gown.

"Blessed be the Lord who guides this woman in His work. Who becomes His hands…" Father Blount continued his prayer, oblivious to the fact that only thirteen years prior he had called on God to take my life. He had demanded it and had nearly succeeded.

"She's sent from God, she is." Fiona's tired voice drew my gaze, and I found only appreciation in her gaze. "An angel sent to me from heaven, for we widnae have made it without her."

Tears prickled my eyes at her kind words, and when the priest excused himself, I let out a relieved breath that another day had passed without his recognition.

I could only wonder on how long it would last.

Maeve departed a short time later with a little wave and I sat down beside Fiona. I ran my fingers lightly down the baby's small, naked back, and then smoothed Fiona's hair from her face. Cam snored softly, sprawled out beside her.

"Ye should sleep now," I chided. "The hard work's only just begun."

"Another few moments," she sighed and grasped my hand, squeezing me tightly, her focus never leaving the little being on her chest. "I'll never be able to repay ye for what ye did."

"Och, I think a wee cuddle with this sweet one is payment enough, dinnae ye think?" I asked, unwilling to admit that I knew of which she spoke. If I didn't acknowledge the fact that I had pushed my energy into her body, then maybe she would think it was a figment of her imagination.

I stayed with them for an hour longer until mother and babe were completely clean, settled, and fast asleep. Exhausted, I left to find my husband reclined against the stone just outside the door, and the sky dark with the coming of the new moon. With only the stars to see by, it made reading his facial features nearly impossible as I awaited his wrath. I looked up at him expectantly, completely drained from the hours I spent warding curtain wall, gifting Fiona my energy, and the stress of Father Blount's presence. His wrath did not come.

"Today, I realized I ken nearly nothin' about ye." His voice was soft and contemplative as he held his arm out and guided me toward a patient Ramsey. Grasping my waist, his hand rested like anvils on my hips, and he tugged me slightly forward. "And I learned that yer no' just an angel to my people, but a warrior, too."

I ran my lower lip between my teeth and shook my head. "I'm no warrior."

"Ye are. Maeve told me what ye did. That woman would have certainly died if ye had no' fought for her to live."

I looked up at his shadowed face. "Yer no' mad at me?"

"Furious," he admitted and lifted me upon Ramsey's back before he settled with ease behind me. The muscles of his thighs pressed against the backs of my own. "I understand why ye left so quickly. I just… I dinnae like surprises, Angel. Next time, I need ye to at least tell me where yer goin'."

"But there was no time." I twisted around to look at him. "I cannae spend precious moments to await yer permission. I willnae do that when it comes to life and death. They were minutes from dying, Malcolm. *Minutes*. I cannae promise what ye ask."

He was silent for a long while as Ramsey carried us through the twists and turns of the cottages and buildings of the sleepy town.

"Alright," he said with a relenting sigh. "Just promise me ye'll be careful. I need ye safe. I dinnae ken what would happen if ye were ever in danger."

What an odd thing to say, I thought, but nodded in agreement. I leaned back against his chest, enjoying the way my body rubbed against his to the movements of Ramsey's gait.

"Father Blount still hasnae recognized me," I murmured.

Malcolm grunted. "Let us hope he stays ignorant. When Cam ushered him into the cottage to pray over the bairn, I nearly followed after him. Thankfully, Farlan stopped me, or I widnae have been able to explain my actions."

"Such a knightly thing to do. I must admit I would have been relieved to have ye by my side." A yawn forced its way through my words, and I rubbed my tired eyes.

Malcolm's arm snaked across my chest, and drew my body tight against his. I savored his strength, settled further between his thighs, and allowed myself to doze with the knowledge that he would not let me fall.

Since those nights we'd spent together while I aided the growth of his people's gardens and fields, I had noticed the laird had started to warm to me. He had sought me out more and more these past weeks, always with an excuse to touch me; the brush of his hand on the small of my back, the tuck of a stray hair behind my ear, or the gentle press of his foot against mine underneath the table while we ate our evening meal. Each small, seemingly innocent and unnecessary contact ignited something in my blood that overrode my composure, but it was the one-sidedness that burned and frustrated me the most. It had taken me a while, but I'd learned to keep my reactions to myself, for if I reached for him, he would back away like a skittish spring colt and I wouldn't see him for hours after. Sometimes a full day.

So there I sat and feigned sleep, my hands resolutely in my lap while he lazily rubbed my arm with his thumb, and I didn't want him to stop. I *never* wanted him to stop. I'd become dependent on his touch, craved it every hour of the day and every minute I spend alone in my bed at night.

But now I knew why he shied away from me. It was why I'd spent countless hours warding the curtain wall, with the hope that those runes would keep his brother safe. Then maybe, just maybe, Malcolm would forgive his deception and allow himself some happiness. Until then, I could be patient. Even if it ripped me apart.

Chapter Fourteen

COIRA

Tragically, two weeks after I finished warding the wall, the stable boy drowned. I hadn't known him well—barely caught a glimpse of him while he tended the horses or ran menial errands to the village. But his death caught me off guard. The guards had called it a bathing accident, even though he was found fully clothed.

Among my people, the cleaning of the dead fell on the midwives, and we, who seemed to always have one foot braced against death's door, took the responsibility seriously. I had tended to the elderly, the unfortunate, and the children whose lives had been snuffed too soon. Each one had been a heavy loss. No matter how much time had passed, I still remembered each of their faces as though it was yesterday. And I will always remember the stable boy. I'd remember the softness of his cheeks when I wiped away the remnants of the loch's murky water; the fan of his thick lashes; his pale, calloused hands. Like those before him, I would carry him through my life in memory. I considered it my duty to remember him.

Malcolm, I could tell, did not feel the same way. He felt great responsibility for the boy's death and spent most of the following day down at the loch where the boy had been found. It pained me to know

I had the power and knowledge to heal the body of almost any wound, yet I could not heal my husband's heart of his sorrow.

"Are ye goin' riding, Angel?" Malcolm called after me from the balcony above as I crossed the great hall three days after that unfortunate day. Twisting around, I looked up and gave him an enticing smile.

"'Tis a fine day, and I've the need to get out for some air. Would ye like to join me?"

The weight of his warm brown eyes settled on me a moment before he nodded. Once in the bailey, Malcolm ran his hand along the tall, stone trunk of what was once an ancient oak. Perhaps someday, I would carve runes of protection along its grey cylinder.

Mucking out a stall in the shadows of the stable, the new groom greeted us with a raised hand. "Ready the lady's mount," Malcolm ordered brusquely and disappeared into Ramsey's stall.

I raised my eyebrows at Malcolm's unnecessary gruffness toward the young man and flashed him an apologetic smile. Shrugging good naturedly, he guided Una out to strap her saddle pad to her back, all the while looking at me curiously. He was a handsome lad, maybe five years younger than I, with dark blond hair that fell over his brow and slightly turned up brown eyes. Lean and nimble, his corded arms, revealed by his rolled sleeves, hinted a great hidden strength. Catching my stare, he winked at me just as Malcolm guided his black war-horse out of the stall. Embarrassed to be caught studying another man, even as innocent as it was, I took Una's lead and tugged her out to the sunny bailey as though the stable were on fire.

As I checked the saddle pad straps, strong hands wrapped around my lower ribs, and I straightened in alarm.

"Up ye go," Malcolm's deep voice purred close to my ear.

Relieved he was not the stable hand, I allowed him to lift me up and deposit me upon Una's back. Chancing a glance toward the stable doors while Malcolm mounted Ramsey, I found the dark eyes of the groom riveted upon me, a crooked smile upon his lips. Damning myself twice over for giving him reason to think I had been staring for any other reason than simple curiosity, I sat rigid in my seat and urged Una through the gate, leaving Malcolm to catch up.

"I dinnae care for that lad. He's too bold," Malcolm said bluntly a few moments later when he'd guided Ramsey beside my mount.

That I could agree with, and then idly wondered if he would still have a position within the keep walls if Malcolm should discover the way he had looked at me.

"Farlan will have a replacement soon enough," I reminded him. "So, unless ye plan to have one o' the garrison men muck out the dung, we're stuck with him until that day comes."

"Och, I'd have myself a mutiny if I dared suggest it." Malcolm chuckled and lifted his face to the sun. I could almost see the stress bleed away from the harsh lines that had taken up residence around his mouth. "I just… I dinnae care for strangers in my keep, is all. There was once a time when they would be welcome, but those days are gone."

"Yer afraid they would discover yer brother?"

"Aye." His mouth wrenched down in a scowl at the mere mention of possible discovery. "That's exactly what I fear."

"Then be rid o' him and I'll wield the pitchfork." I grinned at his bark of laughter just as we entered the southern forest.

"Dinnae tempt me." He cast a heated glance at my leg, hidden beneath my skirt, and shook his head. "No, I doubt I would survive it if ye paraded around in breeks, even smeared with dung and covered in horse stink."

"Well, now that I ken how to get yer attention…"

I felt his focus settle heavily on the side of my face.

"Ye always have my attention, Angel."

The thrill of his confession had me sitting up a little straighter. Malcolm had never talked so openly during the few rides we had taken together in the past weeks. We usually rode in companionable silence, our conversations safely centered around our surroundings. I would point out the plants as we traversed the land, teaching him of their healing properties, and in return, he would show me the places where his clan had fought battles in the generations before.

Emboldened by his statement, I turned to face him and admit that he had my attention as well. But the words stalled on my tongue at the sight of the frown that soured his face—as though he found his admission distasteful. My stomach dipped uneasily, and I faced forward to hide my disappointment.

"'Tis only the nature o' the blood vow. Ye dinnae have a choice but to feel that way with the oath binding us," I said before he could. "We both ken this to be true." *But I wish it wasnae the case*, I thought miserably.

I kept Una ten paces ahead for the rest of the ride to hide my flaming cheeks, and we returned to the keep just as the sky was darkening with grey clouds. From the courtyard and through the keep's open doors, I could see the first of the villagers had already arrived for the Sunday supper. Eyes downcast, I released Una into the groom's care and fled from his intense stare to the safety of the keep. I felt his gaze on my back, an uncomfortable nudge between my shoulder blades, until I entered the great hall and dashed down the hall for my room.

"Coira."

At the sound of my name, I stilled on the spiral stairs leading to the third floor and found Malcolm prowling up from below. Wholly unprepared, my breath caught in my throat when he urged me firmly against the curved wall. This close and in such a confined space, he was enormous, dominating, and very distinctly male. Towering over me with his chest pressed against mine, heat bloomed low in my belly when his lips brushed along my temple, and his hands swept from my wrists to my elbows and back again. To keep myself from touching him, I bunched my hands into the fabric of my riding costume and closed my eyes to savor the feeling of his caress.

It was agony. I wanted nothing more than to lift my lips and catch his, to experience what it would be like to be kissed.

"'Tis no' just the blood vow, Angel," he murmured into my hair.

Elated by his words, I tilted my head to the side to give him better access to my neck and fully submitted to him with an inviting sigh.

Kiss me. Taste me, I cried inside. I was so close to begging him aloud when he dipped his head and pressed his mouth against the pulse just under the line of my jaw. My lashes fluttered closed, and the back of my throat ticked with anticipation. I could die from wanting him, I realized, and for the first time since he pulled away from me in that birch grove at the Gathering, I reached for him.

He stiffened at the first brush of my fingers along his lower ribs, and I nearly pulled away when he sank further against me. His mouth burned a wicked line of fire to my ear, and his hands delved into my hair, his fingertips not nearly as gentle as mine. I let out a breathy moan at his touch, panting at the sensation of his body pressing me against the unforgiving stone. My emotions crested like the tip of a wave and threatened to sweep me away. I felt light, as though the earth's hold upon me would snap at any moment, and I would float away with the current of lust that raced through my veins.

Malcolm brushed his lips in the direction of my mouth. It was the barest of touches, hardly more than a whisper of skin against skin while his callused hands held my face, and he tilted my mouth up to receive him.

Yes, yes, yes! Finally!

The soft rasp of leather against stone barely registered in my mind until an amused voice cracked the silence of the stairwell, and Malcolm tensed with a predator's stillness in my arms.

"Och, how many times have ye told me *'the stairwell is no' the place for that kind o' thing?'*"

An inhuman growl vibrated low in Malcolm's chest, and the laird turned slowly to glare at the twins who'd stumbled upon us on their way to the hall. I assumed it was Finlay who had spoken and stared at us so devilishly, unconcerned with the wide-eyed glare of his twin.

"Do ye have a death wish, man?" Bram hissed, and dragged his brother back up the stairs, far away from the reach of their angry laird.

I nearly whimpered when Malcolm released my face. Alone again, his throat bobbed as he searched my eyes, his jaw locked hard.

"I'll see ye at supper," he finally said, his voice hoarse, and descended the stairs.

Left feeling a strange mixture of hot and cold, I continued to my chamber on weak legs and wished Malcolm had elaborated when he said it was not just the blood vow.

~

I scanned the great hall as the remnants of the meal were cleared and listened with only half an ear to the minstrel while he told the story of *The Bear and the Hare* to the children who sat around him near the massive hearth. Through the open doors, thunder rumbled in the distance and muted pulses of lightning flared. I felt strange—some small niggling flutter low in my gut that I couldn't explain. Sipping on my wine, I restlessly jiggled my leg and tried to shake off the sense of… what? What was it? There was no danger here. No monsters lurked in the shadows. I was surrounded by nothing but happy people who listened to the minstrel's tale with smiles upon their faces.

"What vexes ye?" Malcolm asked me. "And dinnae tell me 'nothin'.' Yer shakin' the whole damn table." I stilled my leg immediately and shrugged when he shifted in his chair, leaning toward me. "Is it about what happened between us?"

"No." I placed my hand upon his and gave him a small smile when he did not pull away. "Never that. I think I'm just tired."

His brown eyes bounced between mine for a heartbeat. "As ye say." He didn't look convinced but did not ask me again and instead, turned toward a villager who had asked for a word.

The villagers and farmers all greeted me now, and included me in their conversations and complaints, too. I did not have much to contribute unless it involved an illness or some malady, but I listened to each one in turn and tried my best to shake free of my nerves.

Hours later and alone in bed, I listened to the rolling thunder that seemed to be directly above the stronghold. *He's no' comin'*, I pouted as my eyes began to droop. It had been an hour since I'd heard Malcolm's heavy footsteps pass by my door. Surely it would not take him so long if he had meant to make a nocturnal visit to my room? Disappointed,

I got up just long enough to lock my door and blow out the lone candle burning in front of the window, before snuggling on my side under the blankets. Sleep enveloped me in its warm embrace within minutes.

Wake up.

    Wake up.

    WAKE UP.

My eyes snapped open in the darkness at my mother's ghostly voice. A slight scraping sound drifted from the other side of my bed, raising every inch of my unscarred skin with gooseflesh. My heart hammered wildly in my chest and my throat.

I was not alone.

Casting my Druid senses out like a net into the near pitch black, I felt it… the other being in my room. With deliberate slowness, I slipped my hand under my pillow and searched blindly for the dagger I kept hidden beneath it. My fingers connected with nothing but crisp linen, and dread coiled around my guts like a slippery eel when I realized it was gone.

"Ye willnae find it," an unfamiliar male voice taunted me, menacing and dripping with the promise of pain.

My heart leaped into my throat, and before I could call out for help, a heavy weight landed upon my bed and a fist connected with my belly just below the protection of my ribs. My breath raced violently from my lungs, and I gasped, my mouth open as my body screamed for air that would not come.

The dark figure, lean and hard, straddled my thighs and caught my wrists in an iron grip above my head. With my legs trapped beneath the blankets, I struggled to break free and suck down the life-giving air my body demanded. I still couldn't see him. The stormy, moonless night and the cold hearth did nothing to brighten the room, and I had no voice to call upon a flame. The first touch of a blade under my chin halted my struggles and I let out a whimper.

"Ah ah ah… that's a good lass." The sharp tip traveled along the line of my neck and paused at the hollow of my throat.

"Wh—who are ye?" I panted and vaguely registered a light *pat, pat, pat* to my left. The window was open, and the rain came through to beat a soft, measured staccato on the floor.

"I'm wounded ye dinnae recognize me, considerin' the moment we shared earlier today. It was a long wait for this hour. The storm was a boon, though. No one bothers lookin' up when it rains, ye ken. It made my climb too easy."

Realization dawned on me just before a pulse of lightning illuminated the face of the stablehand bent over me, a dangerous leer upon his mouth. As water dripped from his wet hair onto my cheeks and between the flashes of lightning, my eyes better adjusted to the gloom. I watched in horror as he dragged the tip of the dagger across the soft skin of my throat, then down my sternum. Little pricks of pain followed in its wake when the blade snagged at my skin.

"I think ye ken by now that I'm here to kill ye," he crooned as he cut the small buttons off the bodice of my night rail one by one with a flick of his wrist. "And I must say—" *Pop* "—I'll enjoy it more than I did killin' that lad at the loch. I didnae enjoy endin' his life—" *pop* "–but it was necessary." *pop* "I needed a way in the keep." *Pop* "And now that I'm here, I'd like to have a little fun—"

A deafening roar rattled the windowpanes and the sound of something massive slammed against the wall that divided my chamber from my husband's… on the door I had bolted shut my first night I arrived.

Choking on my tears and the overwhelming feeling of helplessness, I fought back my nausea and begged for my life.

Boom!

Boom!

Boom!

The man lifted one side of his lip and scowled at the wall of tapestries before he returned his attention to me.

"How in the bloody hell does he ken I'm in here?" the man hissed and then continued to slash at my shift while I struggled.

Boom!

"That door is as thick as my arm," he panted, and the feral gleam in his eye turned lustful when he bared my breast. His eyes locked on the tiny beads of blood that rose up from my skin. "Too bad for ye, he'll never get through in time, and I'll be out that window like a ghost in the night while yer blood is still warm on the sheets."

Boom!

"This is no' what I had planned. I wanted to take my time with ye," he growled, and flipped the dagger in his fist so the blade pointed down. "But I dinnae want to get caught."

Boom!

He cast a nervous glance at the tapestry-covered door before he said, "I'll make it quick." He raised the dagger above his head, its tip aimed straight for my heart.

Tears of fear and anger streamed into my hair as I struggled anew and bucked my hips in a last-ditch effort to win control of my arms. With a curse, he lost his balance and leaned heavily on top of me; with so much of his weight on my wrists, I thought my bones would splinter. I did not want to die, but neither was I going to go quietly into the everlasting night and just allow this man to end my life without a fight.

Boom!

With a thunderous crackling of splitting wood, the door was nearly blown off its hinges, the thick slab impossibly split down the middle. The twisted pieces ripped away the tapestry and revealed the most menacing sight I had ever beheld. My breath caught in my throat and my sight wavered as I wept with relief at the sight in the threshold of the ruined door.

He was vengeance, justice, and honor.

He was life and death.

Savior.

Husband.

Nearly twice his natural size and naked as the day he was born, Malcolm's pupilless eyes glowed with some otherworldly brilliance. He glared dangerously at the man who held me captive before he let out a resounding animalistic bellow of rage and violence. I nearly smiled at the power that resonated off him in waves. The very air in the room trembled, and I closed my eyes to soak in the sheer glory of his fearless presence.

I had always wondered why my father had looked the way he did the day he saved me from the witch's pyre. I asked my mother once and she had refused to tell me, forbidding me from ever asking again. Now, I knew.

He had sworn a blood oath to protect me.

CHAPTER FIFTEEN

MALCOLM

"Come not within the measure of my wrath."
-William Shakespeare, The Two Gentlemen of Verona

Malcolm hauled his fatigued body up to his bedchamber. Eager for the day to be over and to start anew, he cast only a cursory glance at Coira's chamber door before entering his own. She would be asleep by now, having departed the great hall long ago.

Rubbing the muscles of his shoulders, sore from the previous day's training, he tried his best to ignore the ache in his balls from his encounter with Coira's delectable curves in the stairwell. He was losing his mind, would swear his sanity was being chiseled away bit by bit with every sway of her hips and coy smile she flashed in his direction.

"I should stop fightin' it," he grumbled to himself as he shed his clothes and blew out a heavy breath. Once naked, he flopped onto his bed and glowered at the door that would allow him access to Coira's chamber. A door he'd never attempted to open.

It was becoming an old, nightly argument with himself. To consummate their marriage… or not. It would be so easy to pass through that door and cover his wife's body with his own in the span of a few moments. She would not deny him either. Oh, no. He'd seen her face soften to that of a welcoming lover in the stairwell, and he'd adored and savored her soft panting and the brush of her nails at his waist. That slight touch had nearly shredded his self-control. That is, until that little shite Finlay had interrupted them.

Shame had been quick to douse his lust and had smothered it into an oily sheen of guilt. As soon as she was out of his sight, he'd berated himself for behaving so… so like *Finlay*. No doubt the sly devil had had lasses in every corner of the keep, their skirts thrown over their shoulders, out in the open for anyone to discover.

Malcolm refused to treat Coira as such.

Angry and frustrated with himself, he snuffed out the candles and tried his best to sleep while the creature in his chest stirred and purred like it always did with Coira's nearness. Eventually, between that droning hum, his exhaustion, and the rain that tapped against the windows, he was lulled into that strange plane between reality and dreamland. He could feel his body upon the bed, his skin cool from the lack of coverings. When he reached blindly for a blanket to pull over himself, his body shuddered with a rush of energy so violent he gasped and clutched his chest. His breathing heavy and fast, Malcolm sucked in great amounts of air as the beast inside him writhed and thrashed like a clawed serpent in water. A burning sensation raced through his veins and radiated through every muscle, pore, and hair. His skin was on fire! Panicked, he furiously rubbed his limbs to smother the flames, only to find there were none.

What is happening to me? he wondered with alarm and more than a little fear.

A small whimper, soft and muffled, drifted from under the door that led to Coira's chamber, and some primal instinct rose from within him. A low growl resonated in his chest as the beast within him writhed with rage, and something savage and ancient overrode his senses and logic.

Everything inside his body screamed, *Protect, Protect, Protect.*

Surging to his feet, the top of his head brushed the rafters. He did not have time to consider the fact he seemed to have grown ten inches or that the room was illuminated with soft, white light. There was no time to explore the different way his teeth settled together to accommodate the larger incisors that pushed from his gums. A cursory brush of his tongue told him he had indeed grown something akin to fangs. He took two long strides toward the door, prepared to shove his way through, and wasn't entirely surprised to find it locked from the other side.

Another fearful whimper whispered from beneath the space under the door, and the distinct low tone of a male had Malcolm baring his new teeth. With a furious roar, Malcolm threw his body into the stout wooden barricade that separated him from his wife.

Relentless, Malcolm battered the door, the force of impact shaking the dust from the rafters and weakening the frame in which it stood. His mind was crazed, nearly mad with the need to break through, and the oath ripped at him with phantom claws. When the door finally surrendered to his strength and splintered into several pieces, it fell to pieces with a crash, and pulled a tapestry down with it. Icey-cold air flowed over his back, even as the fire in his blood burned hotter with the illuminated scene before him: the stable hand atop his wife, a dagger poised at her exposed breast. Coira released a garbled cry of relief at the sight of him.

Terrified, the younger man looked up at him in shock and swore. Malcolm caught sight of himself in the large gilded mirror propped up on the far wall. He looked menacing. Feral. Just his appearance promised pain and death.

Without warning, Malcolm launched himself toward them, heedless of his own safely. Only Coira's mattered.

Fingers curled like claws, Malcolm tackled Coira's tormentor with a crushing grip around the ribs and they both landed in a puddle of water on the other side of her bed. The dagger the stablehand had held clattered uselessly to the floor and slid behind the mirror. He screamed in panicked terror when Malcolm rose above him, teeth bared.

Malcolm slammed his fist down upon his enemy's face with a meaty crunch before he wrapped his hands around his throat, severing the cries.

The stablehand's face began to turn a deep plum, his lips silently moving in some sort of prayer for release while he scratched uselessly at Malcolm's hands and pounded his feet upon the floor.

Malcolm relished the feeling of the life that weakened under his fingertips, but through the frenzy and the violence, he felt no satisfaction. The rain fell upon his bare back from the open window as though calling for his attention, then his lips twisted in a feral grin.

Bloodshot eyes stared up at his new, sharp teeth.

"Ye snuck in here like a rat to do unspeakable things to what is *mine* to protect," Malcolm said softly and loosened his hold to allow his prey to take a relieved breath, much like a cat playing with the mouse would, claws sheathed but ready and waiting. "As much as I would like to see ye gutted, I willnae allow ye to die in here for yer ghost to haunt my halls, so allow me to show ye the way out."

Malcolm switched his hold on the man's throat and jerked him up as easily as he would a kitten by the scruff, heedless of the struggling. Before the stablehand realized what he had planned, Malcolm tossed him out the window where he disappeared into the black night. A scream echoed in the western courtyard for only a moment before it was cut short with a muffled thump. Appeased, Malcolm ignored the surprised shouts of his men on watch and turned to find Coira staring at him from where she knelt on the bed.

Illuminated in the soft, white glow, she clutched her ruined night rail closed, her pale blonde hair unbound and silvery in the strange light emitted from his eyes. Thin, drying rivulets of blood ran down her neck, and the sight of them elicited a rumble of anger to escape his throat. Chest heaving, he rested a knee on the bed and took her face into his hands. He tilted her chin to the left and right so he could inspect the shallow wounds that were nearly dry. Her body trembled under his touch, her pale gaze riveted on his own.

"I willnae hurt ye, Angel," he promised in a guttural voice, reminding him he must look like a monster. Malcolm let his hands fall and he rose from the bed to give her space.

"I dinnae fear ye," she whispered through fresh tears and reached for him, her shift falling open. "Dinnae leave me alone, Malcolm."

Seeing her like that, scared, disheveled, and still seeking the comfort of his touch even after what she had just endured and witnessed—the prideful creature in him swelled and overrode all thought. Malcolm's focus, primal and a bit feral, locked onto the creamy swells of her breasts and the way they moved with each breath beneath the torn fabric. Head lowered, he inched closer, and a low, predatory snarl crept up his throat as though he were a beast intent on a mate.

Startled by the foreign urgency, he wrested control of his mind and opened his mouth, fully intent on apologizing until she walked the pads of her smooth, warm fingertips along his shoulders. Coira urged him closer with gentle pressure on his back, and his muscles rose beneath her touch. Enchanted, he closed his eyes and allowed her to guide him closer. She smoothed her hands over his face and pushed his tangled hair over his shoulders.

"Yer magnificent," she breathed and leaned forward to kiss his cheek, his temple, and then the sensitive spot below his ear. "Thank ye for saving me."

Malcolm groaned at her tender touch and the vibrations her lips made against his ear as she soothed him. He wrapped his fists within the blankets to keep from touching her, afraid he would bruise her skin if he attempted to hold her. His body still felt more beast than man as the preternatural strength of the oath continued to hammer through his limbs, his breath still ragged, his thoughts not completely his own. But he could enjoy this, this special attention she gifted him. He could feel his body rising with her touch as she unknowingly coaxed his lust to the surface. With the absence of clothing, his cock thickened, reaching for her, and the beast roared with need for the woman before him.

The need to claim.

"My laird!" Sharp rapping on Coira's chamber door and heavy footfalls of several men in the corridor snapped him out of his desirous state into one of defensive rage. Baring his sharp teeth, he whipped his attention to the door with a savage hiss, ready to fight, ready to kill—

"Dinnae come in here!" Coira's voice rang out. She grasped his face between her small hands and forced him to look at her while she yelled in the direction of the door. "We're fine! Give us a moment!"

"I must hear his voice, my lady."

Through the receding rage, Malcolm recognized a familiar voice and fought to steady the all-consuming need to protect the woman before him. *There is no more threat—she is safe,* he repeated to himself several times before he called out.

"All is well, Gavin. Stay there." His words sounded like broken gravel, and he relaxed when his cousin gave his promise to stand watch outside the door until Malcolm was ready to come out.

"Dinnae pay attention to them," Coira murmured as she reclined on the bed and coaxed him down alongside her.

Coira wrapped her arms around him, twisting to hike her right leg over his waist, and settled his cheek between her breasts. Her warm hands made gentle but firm sweeping motions over his bare back and into his hair. She rubbed small circles against the base of his skull and ran her palm up and down the arm he draped over her stomach, kneading his muscles along the way. It was the most soothing touch he had ever experienced, and within a few minutes, the tension left his body and his breathing returned to normal. With his cheek nuzzled against her bare skin, he pulled her closer against him, spread his hand over her ribs, and slowly melted against her body.

The calmer he became, the bright glow in the room softened and eventually left them in near darkness, except for the momentary flickers of lightning as the storm moved farther away. Focused on her heart's steady beat, Malcolm breathed a heavy sigh of relief when his teeth returned to normal.

Her body was warm, feverishly so, and the heat radiated into his bones, her touch all the more irresistible. Coira continued her gentle exploration and rubbed the tight muscles of his neck, scratching lightly at the two day's growth on his face. The soft rasping of the short hairs was a strange music to his ears that he never wanted to stop.

"What happened to me?" Malcolm asked, breaking the silence.

"I've seen magic like that only once," she whispered in the dark as her thumb traced his eyebrow and then stilled. "I dinnae ken how it happens. My mother never taught me, which is good because the dark side of our culture should be forgotten… she was wrong to have done that to ye."

Malcolm thought on her words and wondered if he would have entered into the bargain with Vanora if she had told him he'd turn into a crazed beast when Coira's life was in danger. Maybe Coira was right, that their dark magic should have been forgotten long ago, but he found himself grateful for it tonight. Without the extra strength he needed to break down the door, he never would have gotten to her in time, and he'd be dead right alongside her. The thought soured his gut.

"It doesnae matter. What's done is done." He nudged his cheek against her breast in a silent request for her to continue and nearly purred when she traced the shell of his ear with her fingertip.

"He killed the stable boy. He confessed it to me just before ye broke down the door." Malcolm popped his head up and looked into her sad, ice-pale eyes in the moonlight that had begun to creep through the windows. Guilt hardened her mouth, "He said he did it to open up a place for him within the keep, but I dinnae understand why he would want to harm me. I'd never even seen him before today."

"I should no' have killed him so quickly," Malcolm said gruffly and berated himself as he left her side and stepped over the splintered door into his chamber.

After shoving his legs into his leather breeks, he opened the door to find ten of his men in various stages of dress, and a frightened Maeve pressed against Finlay's side. Her blonde hair and white ankle-length shift and robe stood out starkly in the gloomy corridor with the light of the candle she held. Malcolm pushed the door open wide.

"See to yer lady, Maeve." Without a word, the handmaid ducked under his arm before he let the door close with a thud, and turned a thunderous expression on the men in the hallway. "The man who flew from yer lady's window—is he dead?" Malcolm asked his men.

"Unless he figured out how to breathe through his arsehole, I dinnae believe he survived the flight."

Malcolm's focus fixed on Finlay, and he was pleased to find his cousin's face a mask of seriousness despite his comment. The rest of the men wore similar expressions, all of them concerned and disturbed that Ghlas Thùr had been breached, and by someone many of them had vouched for.

Malcolm thumped the meat of his fist on the door, drawing the focus of all of his men.

"Let me be clear. Things are goin' change around here indefinitely. Our stable boy was murdered by the verra man who scaled our walls with the premeditated plan to murder my wife." His skin raised and prickled, and he fought down the beast that stirred anew at the thought of Coira in danger again. "From this day forth, *no one* that is no' Clan MacKinnon will be employed within these walls. Remember, 'tis no' just yer lady who was exposed this night. Ye all ken who else lays vulnerable and reliant upon us to defend him. Because o' that, no one who is no' in residence will be permitted past the great hall—*no excuses.*" The men voiced their agreement. "I also want a guard stationed outside the blue room in four-hour shifts day and night."

"My laird." Farlan's voice rang out with a slight tremor as he pushed his way through the other men to stand before his laird. "I take full responsibility for what happened tonight. I was the one who suggested him for the position and I will submit to any punishment ye require."

Malcolm ground his teeth a moment before he settled his hand upon the side of Farlan's neck. "A mistake any man here could have made. I willnae punish ye for it, though I believe ye will execute my new orders to the letter, aye?"

Farlan nodded. "With my life."

Similar oaths were promised in hushed voices and pride filled Malcolm's heart as he nodded his acceptance. Loyalty was not a thing that could be purchased, and when he looked upon the men outside his chamber, he felt richer than the King of England.

"Burn the body and never speak o' what happened this night. I willnae allow us to be seen as weak, welcoming every vagrant north o' the English boarder to scale our walls."

An hour later, Malcolm stood in the window of his chamber and watched the flames of the pyre reach high with the lightening dawn. In his hand, he gripped the red-handled dagger he had recovered from behind Coira's mirror. Rubbing the thick pad of muscle over his heart, he marveled at the creature that slumbered within its boney cage and for the first time was grateful of its presence.

Exhaustion pulled at the edges of his mind, and he cast a glance through the open passage to his wife's chamber. The remnants of the door had been carted away, no doubt to be used as kindling for the fire that raged by the loch. In the faint light of pre-dawn, Malcolm stared at the two women huddled close together, pale faces peeking out from under the woolen covers.

My men are no' the only loyal servants in this house, he noted.

Maeve was curled against Coira's back, her arm thrown over her mistress in a protective embrace. Studying the thick spread of Coira's lashes against her cheek, he longed to be the one who lay behind her. He wanted it to be *his* body that sheltered her.

Mind made up, Malcolm stowed the intruder's dagger and crossed into Coira's chamber to gently lift his wife from her bed. Startled, Maeve opened her mouth to protest until she saw who had disturbed their slumber and settled back into the pillows with a tender smile.

With Coira's body tucked against his chest, he brought her into his chamber and settled her in his bed. Her bright eyes fluttered open when her body touched the cool sheets and she blinked in surprise when he joined her.

"Ye'll sleep in here from now on where I ken yer safe."

Curled on her side, she pressed her palms together and rested her cheek upon the back of her hand.

"Is that the only reason?" she whispered, catching her bottom lip between her teeth.

Malcolm's chest tightened at the way she looked at him, full of innocence and hopeful invitation. The beast stirred and then settled again with a soft, content purr.

"No. That's no' the only reason," he admitted, and tore his gaze away from the welcoming sight of her enchanting face and pleasing form in his bed. Caught between his internal turmoil and the newfound bud of appreciation and longing for his wife, Malcolm closed his eyes and willed himself to sleep.

Chapter Sixteen

COIRA

Summer relinquished its hold upon Scotland during the weeks that followed that terrible night in my chamber and gilded the leaves with orange and gold.

Chisel in hand, I worked my way along the west side of the castle as the sun rose. My palms were still raw from the endless days etching the curtain walls, but I powered through, unwilling to rest for even a day longer.

I blew an errant lock of hair out of my face and ran my thumb down a finished line of Druid script. In addition to the runes of protection that adorned the curtain wall, I had added two more that warded against thievery and harm that I hadn't carved into the wall.

The day after the attack, while I'd watched the garrison's men spread the ashes of a dying bonfire on the shores the loch, I had realized the castle itself needed defense. Curtain walls were fast becoming a thing of the past, their stones dismantled or at the very least lowered in height. I had been naive to think that the walls surrounding Ghlas Thùr would still be here in the next twenty years, and decided it was the stronghold's *foundations* that needed protection, for a foundation couldn't be removed without first removing the structure above.

Alone along the quiet west wall of the keep, I etched my protection into the base of the cookery window, lost in thoughts of the day I had decided to trust the MacKinnon laird with what I truly was.

It was on the morning after my attack while I had openly hammered away on the base of the keep's main doorway. I hadn't even finished the second line of runes when Malcolm's shadow had fallen upon me.

"What are ye doin', lass?" he asked as he crouched on the steps and ran his fingers over the ancient words I etched into the grey stone.

Pursing my lips, I weighed the merit of an explanation and decided to take a leap of faith. Looking into his warm, brown eyes, I picked myself up from the ground, slipped the chisel into the pocket of my apron, and said, "Walk with me to a place we cannae be overheard. I have somethin' I'd like to share with ye."

Interest sparked in his eyes, and I led him to the loch and onto a long, flat rock that jutted out into the water. A chill breeze tangled my unbound hair as I settled onto to the small, stone peninsula and told him to sit down in front of me. After casting a wary look around, and only when I was sure we were well and truly alone, I began to speak.

"All things in nature, whether they are dead or alive, have a true name," I began softly as I cupped his hands together and lowered them until his knuckles rested on the cold stone.

Satisfied he wouldn't move, I sung the words for water and motion and allowed the cadence of my voice to guide a thin stream of liquid to break away from the loch and snake into his waiting palm. At his sharp intake of breath, I looked up to find him enthralled by the dancing water he held, mesmerized when I asked it to swirl over his fingers and in between like a caterpillar on a leaf.

Then I turned it into mist and told the wind to carry the vapor across his cheek and away.

"How is that possible?" he asked breathlessly. His fingertips lingered on his unshaven cheek where the mist had kissed him. There was no fear in his eyes, only wonder, when he leaned forward like a child eager for the rest of a story.

"I have been called a witch, but that is no' what I am," I said and tucked a lock of hair behind my ear. "I cannae curse anyone with a pox or cause two people to fall in love. Nor can I turn straw into gold or control the minds o' men."

Malcolm's lips twitched, and I knew he was thinking of the potion I told him I planned to slip into the clan's drink my first day here.

"Newt eyes and toad brains?"

"Toad skin." I giggled, and my smile faltered when he grinned broadly at me.

My soul ached at how beautiful he was, his skin golden from the sun and lit from within with boyish mischief. It was a side of him I had seen only a few times, but I wanted to know all his facets. And all his faults, too.

"We are healers and midwives. Some o' my kin have… special abilities, like Sight."

"Sight?"

I nodded. "'Tis rare, but they can see another's future. They dinnae ken when these visions will come about, only that they will. Women with Sight often keep the ability to themselves, for it isn't likely any good comes out o' sharin' their visions."

"Why?"

"Well, I cannae imagine it would be verra enjoyable to ken disaster will befall another, but no' be able to tell them when. *Besides, I hear there's nothin' one can do to stop it. What a Seer sees is fate."*

But what I would have given to have that ability when I was thirteen. Maybe my life would have taken a very different path, *I thought, and instantly regretted the unspoken fantasy.*

If I had changed my path, I wouldn't be here, *with him.*

Malcolm picked up a pebble and tossed it into the water. "I remember ye mentioned Druids. Is that what ye are? A sorceress?"

"We are the descendants of the Irish Druid Mug Ruith's daughter. Her name was Tlachtga, and she was one o' the last immortal Druids to walk the earth. She was as powerful as she was beautiful and learned her father's magical secrets while she followed him around the world. Sorrow befell Tlachtga when she was raped by the three sons o' her father's mentor. She fell pregnant and abandoned her father to return to Ireland. There, she gave birth to three sons, each sired by one o' the brothers who raped her." I picked up one of the many dried leaves that riddled the stone we sat upon and tore it along its veins while I shared with him the history of my people.

"As much as Tlachtga loved her children, she could no' forgive the men who sired them and in turn could no' permit her sons to use the power than ran through her veins. So, she bound their magic, and effectively cleaved any they would have wielded from their grasp. She raised them in the Irish moors, where they eventually

married and had children o' their own. It was after the birth o' the first girl child that Tlachtga learned that there were two flaws in her binding spell. Her female descendants were no' bound like the men were, they were free to speak the Druid words and draw upon the earth's magic."

"None o' the men can?" Malcolm asked, and I tilted my head from head side to side as I considered his words.

"That would be second flaw in Tlachtga's binding spell. Generations later it was realized her male descendants could wield magic, but only when their emotions ran high. It wasnae somethin' they could control, ye see. The ability was always rooted in despair and only appeared during matters o' heartbreak or when emotions became overwhelming. I've never seen it firsthand but there are some auld women in Inverness that witnessed the anomaly when they were young. I have heard them tell the stories. It is a magic that is raw and unfettered. They need no words to control it and their power has an intensity much akin to… to the darker side o' my power. Power I have only felt once before and never wish to experience again."

Malcolm thoughtfully gazed out at the foggy loch over my shoulder before he stretched his legs out beside me. Leaning back onto his hands, he cocked his head in that lairdly way he does as though to say "continue".

Bossy bastard.

I bit back a smile.

"Tlachtga shared with her granddaughters the true names o' all things: fire, wind, water, earth, blood, and bone. These elements can be manipulated by those with the same blood that runs through her veins. O' course, there are thousands with her blood across Ireland and Scotland—even England. Most familial lines have been watered down and they have naught but a mere wisp o' her power. They canna do much beyond coaxing a soft breeze or lighting a candle."

"But ye… ye can do so much more." Malcolm fingered the spot on his head I had healed all those months ago and looked up at the south tower of Ghlas Thùr. I knew his brother was at the forefront of his mind.

"Aye. My mother's line—my line—is verra powerful. She had married my father, the only son from another undiluted line, at my grandmother's urging. She was lucky that they grew into a love match. They—" I cleared my throat and moved away from the subject of Druid mating. "Mother was the strongest among us, but she didnae share all her knowledge with me. Because o' that, some o' the lore will be

lost forever." I shrugged and looked meaningfully at his chest. "I cannae say that I would want to ken how she managed the bit o' magic that bound ye to me, anyhow."

Malcolm snorted. "We can agree on that, lass."

With a nod, I leaned close to the surface of the loch and whispered upon it. Ice crystals crackled and collected at the edge of the water where it gently lapped at the stone we sat upon. Fingers of parchment-thin ice speared out over the depths like the branches of a tree.

"Although Tlachtga stayed young and beautiful with each passing decade, she couldnae bear to watch another o' her grandchildren's children die and made the choice to pass on from this world. It is said that because she is immortal, she couldnae take her own life. Because o' this, she bound her soul to her descendants before she allowed her magic to obliterate her body."

I bowed my head and thought of all the heartache Tlachtga had endured. "In her honor, we teach our daughters the sacred words, how to blend them together with their song, and bend the elements to their whims, much like I did the day I tried to escape ye."

Malcolm grunted with remembrance and shot me a look filled with promise should I ever try again. I rolled my eyes before continuing. "We can call upon a rain to ease a drought, deny a raging fire the air it breathes, and rearrange the landscape. We can heal the body, taste the tang o' truth or the bitterness o' lies, and even send a powerful gale from east to west for a short time. Since my bloodline is strong, I hold the ability to ward against harm, which is what I'm doin' to the stones o' the keep, to protect it and all within."

If Malcolm and I had children, and was blessed with a daughter, her power would be inferior to what ran through my veins. I chewed on my lip, unsure if the thought upset me or not, and decided I wouldn't fret over the what-ifs that may never happen. It was naïve to think that just because we had grown more comfortable with one another, we would grow to something more. And then there was his ever-present guilt that still stood between us.

"Tell me about yer brother," I blurted and earned a startled look, catching him off-guard. I had never pressed into his personal life before now, but I figured, an eye for an eye, and I was hungry for more of this man.

Malcolm cast a wary glance up at the keep before returning his gaze to me. "Ye've never asked me about him before."

"I've always been curious, but ye keep information about him so secret. I ken what others have told me—that he was brave and true and honorable. But everyone talks as though he's dead, no' sleepin' up there under guard."

Malcolm frowned, deep-set lines hardening his face. "We talk about him that way, no' because we wish it to be so, but because his survival depends on it. Only those who witnessed yer mother's magic kens the truth and I have forbidden them to speak about it. None o' the villagers have been told anythin' more than that yer mother tried to save him and that she failed."

I gawked at him. "How did ye keep his absence a secret from the rest o' the clan?"

Malcolm let out a heavy sigh, and his shoulders drooped when he said, "In the winter, the bodies o' the dead are usually stored until the spring thaw when the soil is soft enough to dig the graves, but I couldnae allow the chance o' someone discoverin' our deceit. It took ten men all day to break through the frozen earth so that we could bury a coffin filled with stones wrapped in wool."

I clenched my fingers in the folds of my gown to keep from reaching for his hand and said, "That must have been hard, to say goodbye to someone ye can still see every day."

"No. The hardest part has been living with my own shame," Malcolm murmured with a sad shake of his head. "Colin refused yer mother when she told him she could enchant him to sleep long enough to see his wife again because he didnae believe I would find love with a witch. Ye see, Colin was in love with his wife—so in love with her he risked his life for hers. He said he wanted me to find the same love he had with his Meggie, even if it meant he'd never see her again."

"Oh." My throat felt tight, and I blinked away the threat of hot tears. No words had never flayed me so completely.

"And in return, I betrayed his wishes and swore the oath to Vanora the first chance I could. Against my promise to him, I bound myself to ye and then made him drink the valerian root I had mixed into his scotch." Malcolm looked at his open palms, eyes haunted and a thousand miles away. "The look on his face when he realized what I had done... it haunts me still. I took his choice away from him, because I believed I knew better than he.

"Even though I took up the mantle verra young after my father's sudden death, they call me a great laird. I've brought my people wealth, prosperity, and peace. I have earned their loyalty and love. But I betrayed my most devoted brother even *though I believed at the time I was doing it for his own good. I shouldnae have done it. Every day I fear somethin' will happen to him while he sleeps the centuries away. He has three hundred more years to wait after I die. What if my descendants forget to pass on the story? What if the castle burns to the ground? The worry gnaws at my gut every wakin' moment. It's convinced me I made a terrible mistake, and I'll never... I just wish—"*

"He'll make it, Malcolm," I said fiercely and grasped his chilled hands within my warm ones to give him comfort. "Is that why ye go to the caves in the north? What do ye search for? Proof?"

"Aye." He stared at our joined hands a moment. When his jaw flexed, I knew he was going to pull away. My pride told me to sever the contact first, to salvage and protect what was left of my heart, but I just couldn't. When your heart has made up its mind on whom to love, you just don't have a choice any longer.

Malcolm turned up his haunted eyes to mine.

"How can I allow myself any thread o' happiness with ye, when I've sentenced my own brother to death?" he asked, his voice barely a breath on the wind before he shook his head. "I'm sorry, Coira. Ye deserve better that this. Better than me."

He then untangled his hand from mine and left me strangely numb while I tried desperately to piece my heart back together.

I chiseled away at the grey stone, lost deep in thought on what Malcolm had said to me that day. When the sun was high in the sky, I stretched my back, the muscles sore from my stooped position. I thought two more weeks and I would be done. Nearly every threshold, window lip, wall, and stairwell needed my runes protection for Colin to have any chance of surviving.

⌒

Autumn was a busy time for all. Between the long hours I spent carving runes, I harvested and dried my stock of herbs from my garden outside the west wall. I saved the seeds in little sleeves of velum, the plant sketched upon it, to be used come spring. I taught Maeve the method of drawing oils from herbs and flowers, and after a couple of weeks of instruction, I gave her unrestricted access to my tower. Efficient with her time, she quickly took charge of ten small bowls, each with a different herb or petal, and collected an impressive stock of oils within three weeks.

"Are ye sure yer have no witch in yer veins, Maeve?" I teased as I sniffed the small vial of peppermint oil she handed me. Not a drop of water to be seen, the oil was so potent it cleared my sinuses and opened my lungs with a punch. The corners of her mouth pulled up in a wry smile.

"Yer no' the first person to have accused me o' that," she mused.

On the evening I finished the warding, my fingers blistered and bruised from the countless times my hammer missed the chisel, I crawled into the bed I shared with Malcolm after dinner. Maeve had just finished greasing my hands in lanolin before wrapping them in linen, indifferent to my weak protests that she not fuss over me.

"Ye'll thank me in the mornin', milady," she tutted as she tugged the blankets up to my chin. Moving around the room, she shuttered the windows and banked the fire before sashaying out the door. My belly full to bursting from the evening meal, and exhausted from a full day of warding, it wasn't long before my lids grew heavy, and I let my mind drift into sleep.

Save for the red-orange embers that pulsed in the hearth, the large bedchamber was in total darkness when I felt the bed dip beside me and was roused from my dreams. Malcolm always made a point to wait until I was asleep before joining me in bed, although I didn't understand why he bothered. The lumbering hulk was far from subtle when he slipped between the blankets.

Feigning sleep, I kept my eyes closed and bit my lip to keep myself from smiling while he inched his way closer to me. It was a nightly game we played. He'd sidle closer and I would move just enough to open my body to his advances until I was tucked up against him, my leg draped over his thigh. My head cradled on the muscle between his shoulder and chest, I could faintly hear the curious purr of the beast inside him, pleased with my presence. I was careful not to move the rest of the night, lest he realize I was awake and bolt from the room.

It was there, wrapped up in his arms and listening to his soft snores, that I heard a crack of lightning in the distance, followed by a slight trembling of the windowpanes a few moments later. Gooseflesh pebbled the skin of my cheek and raced down my arm and back as I stared into the dying embers in the hearth.

My instincts told me that it was not an impending storm that shook the earth, but something else entirely.

I spent the early part of the next day with Malcolm in the library while he read to me the story of *Romeo and Juliet*. It was something he stood firm on; since I was not interested in learning to read English, he insisted on reading it to me. Three times a week, before the noon meal, and when he wasn't training in the yard with his men, I sat with him in the library for nearly an hour. Curled up in the padded highbacked chair beside his that faced the windows, I basked in the sunlight that filtered through the glass and the sound of his deep voice while he smoothly read from his book. Judging by its appearance, I gathered it was his favorite, for the leather binding was as worn as my tome and the pages yellowed and worm-eaten at the edges.

"'Sin from thy lips? O trespass sweetly urged! Give me my sin again…' Are ye listenin', Angel?" Malcolm reached over to tug playfully on the plaited rope of my hair.

"Aye." I sighed and hid my smile. If he only knew how well I listened to him, he'd be shocked.

One of his dark brows arched in challenge. "And what have ye gathered from what I've read today?"

I grunted. "That Juliet's been kissed more than I have."

Relaxed from the cozy fire and the late autumn sun streaming in through the tall windows, the words had tumbled out of my mouth before I could stop them. My heart stalled, and I swallowed nervously and peeked at Malcolm.

Stock-still except for the rhythmic rise and fall of his chest, he cleared his throat and asked in a gravelly voice, "Have ye never been kissed, Coira?"

A heavy silence settled between us, and my cheeks flushed when Malcolm's focus landed intently on my mouth. I didn't have to answer him—he *knew*. He'd kissed my neck in the stairwell, dragged his lips along my marred skin the first evening at The Gathering, but never had he touched his mouth to mine.

Self-consciously, I touched the puckered skin on the side of my face. I barely thought about my scars anymore, rarely gave them a second glance in the mirror or checked a dozen times an hour to be sure they were hidden beneath the veil of my hair. But now, they were in the forefront of my mind, the very reason no man had ever wanted to kiss me.

Malcolm let the book fall haphazardly to the floor when he slipped from his chair and settled on his knees in front of me. Boldly, he grasped my calves, unfolding and arranging them so he could push his much larger body into the space between my knees. Alarmed, I sat up straighter. This was new—*exciting*. My pulse hammered in my throat, and I blinked at him. With his body in line with mine, he palmed my neck and, with his thumbs, drew a line of fire from my cheek to my jaw and back again. Then he pulled me closer.

"What are ye doin'?" I breathed, scared he would stop… petrified he wouldn't. This close, I could smell the juniper in his soap and see his pupils dilate as he looked intently at my mouth.

"I'm goin' to kiss ye. Would love nothin' more than to teach ye how it's done."

Yes, yes, yes! With delicious anticipation, I inwardly sighed when he lowered his mouth and hovered a moment before his lips molded to mine. Drawing my upper lip slightly into his mouth, his teeth lightly grazed the bottom edge. The unexpected friction caused my body to come alive with an unfamiliar surge of energy that started at the back of my throat and jolted down to my navel.

"Ye taste heavenly, Coira." Malcolm's guttural words against my lips caused my knees to clench around his hips. "I need more, Angel. Give me more."

The moment his lips pressed firmly to mine, his hands delved into my hair, then everywhere at once. They swept up and down the curves of my waist and the buttons that lined my spine; his touch left behind a burning inferno that I felt low in my belly.

For the first time since I had received my scars, I experienced a moment where I felt truly free from them.

 I felt desired.

It was liberating. Intoxicating.

In that instant, I knew I'd give him anything to continue feeling this way: all that I was and all I could be. I was starved for touch—*his touch*—and I never wanted it to end.

At the first brush of his tongue along the seam of my lips, I eagerly opened my mouth and rejoiced when he groaned. It seemed he was as hungry for me as I was for him, and I couldn't help feeling a small victory in his response. Our tongues danced with one another, mine timid, his sure and bold while he tasted me and branded my skin with a scrape of the short, black whiskers on his chin.

I would never be the same again.

It was the firm press of his cock against my core, demanding yet harmless behind the leather of his trews, that dragged a moan from my throat. Panting, he pulled away from me, his dark, lust-filled eyes fixated on my lips, his shoulders tight and tense beneath my palms.

No. I curled my fingers into his shirt.

"Dinnae stop, please," I pleaded and tried to pull him back to me. I nearly cried out in protest when he gathered my hands in his own, kissed my knuckles, and set them firmly in my lap.

Disappointment, frustration, and anger doused the fire that had raced through my veins only moments before, and heat collected behind my eyes, threatening tears. I rapidly blinked them away.

"Why do ye punish me?" I hissed and curled my hands into fists.

Malcolm sat back on his heels and ran both hands roughly over his face. "I'm no' punishing ye, Angel. I—"

A dark, humorless laugh escaped me. "That's right. Ye seek only to torture yerself, and oh-bloody-well if it affects anyone else," I seethed, and shoved him away to stand on trembling legs.

Marching toward the open doors, the joy and desire he had awakened within me dragged behind like a beaten dog, pathetic and unwanted. I bit down on my kiss-swollen lip and turned back to find him looking just as devastated as I felt, an unspoken apology plain as day on his face. But his regret wasn't enough. I wanted to tell him I couldn't do this, that if I couldn't have *all* of him, then I didn't want *any* of him… but that just wasn't true. I'd take any scrap he would give me and covet it as though it were a precious gemstone, even if I hated myself in the process.

My heart sank into a bleak pool of shadow and misery and realized Malcolm was right, I *did* deserve better.

Defeated, I raised my hands and let them fall against my thighs before I murmured, "I want to *love* ye, Malcolm. I dinnae understand why ye willnae let me."

With my pride in tatters from his rejection and my lips still tingling from his kisses, I fled to my tower, wishing it had a thick door I could slam behind me. Sullen and a bit bitter, I leaned my elbows on the lip of the east window and looked down on the central courtyard just in time to see Malcolm storm across the yard and disappear into the stable. He reemerged moments later atop his black warhorse and thundered through the gatehouse, dirt and sand kicking up in a spray from heavy hooves.

"Ye can run, Laird MacKinnon," I mumbled as I dragged my finger in a sharp line through the fog my breath had created on the window. "But yer still stuck with me."

Envious of Malcolm's freedom, I wandered the grounds that afternoon with half a mind to sneak through the south gate and disappear into the wilds just to spite him. Of course, he would come after me and drag me back to the keep by my hair if he had to. A small part of me found the opportunity to make Malcolm chase me through another storm a bit thrilling, and I wondered just how far I would get before he caught me again.

Then I wondered what he would *do* when he caught me.

"I ken that look," Maeve chirped when she found me standing in my garden just as the sun set behind the loch. She bumped her hip against mine. "'Tis the same look all women get when they cannae make up their mind between lovin' a man or stranglin' him with her bare hands."

"Am I that transparent?" I frowned at being so easily read and crossed my arms over my chest as I studied the blaze of golds and pinks of the sunset.

Maeve shrugged and hiked her thumb over her shoulder. "'Tis the same look I get when Finlay frays my last nerve—which is daily, o' course. Man's as daft as they come, but I adore every curl on his perfect head."

A quick peek up revealed that Finlay was indeed on the wall standing guard over us, his bow strung and keen eyes sweeping the land around us. When he caught my stare, the corner of his lips curved into a roguish grin, and he winked before he resumed his watch on the forest. I raised a brow at Maeve.

"Ye and Finlay?" Of all the gossip she'd shared with me in the last months, she'd never shared any of her own.

She blushed. "Aye. I've loved him since I was a wee lass and did everythin' I could to catch his attention. He finally noticed me the year before last when I stopped bein' all knees and elbows," Maeve said with a little chuckle. "'Tis our hope to marry in the spring. That is if he doesnae get me with child before then, but I'm happy to wait."

"Truly?" I must have looked skeptical because she laughed and grinned broadly.

"Some things are worth waitin' for. Like yer braw laird," Maeve whispered mischievously and drew my arm through hers. We walked back to the keep just as the last sliver of sun dipped below the horizon. She bowed her head close to mine. "'It has been interestin' to watch the laird become this… this *mess*. He's always been so cocksure with never a hair out o' place. He would be aware o' everythin' anyone did on any given hour o' the day; nothin' would get past him. And then *ye* showed up and turned his whole bloody world upside down. 'Tis been a joy to see."

~

After my bath, Maeve dressed me in dark grey wool and cinched thick white stockings high on my thighs to ward off the evening chill. From the pocket of her apron, she pulled out a small vile of purple liquid and crouched down in front of me to dab at my lower lip.

"Beet juice," she explained with a wink and a giggle, then nudged me toward the mirror. "Let us see if we cannae unravel yer husband just a wee bit more, hmm? He's bound to break at some point."

Huffing a laugh at Maeve's conspiracy against my poor husband, I realized this was not her first attempt to rankle Malcolm's self-control. There was the day she stuffed me into the ash-pink gown and failed to convince me it had drawn his rapt attention instead of his ire, and again at the Gathering when she'd transformed me into the goddess of spring. I opened my mouth to thank her for her efforts when I caught sight of the alluring reflection in the gilded mirror.

The woman that stared back had my eyes, my nose, but she was a stranger in every other sense. I took in the reddened lips and the smudge of kohl Maeve had artfully applied to darken my lashes. With my silver-gold hair arranged over my shoulder in a thick plait, my pale-colored eyes large on my face, and my lips pouty, I looked both innocent and seductive.

With a nervous glance over my shoulder, I took in Maeve's excited smile and hoped she knew what the hell she was doing, because I surely did not.

CHAPTER SEVENTEEN

MALCOLM

-William Shakespeare, As You Like It

Malcolm lunged up the steep path he'd climbed dozens of times as though in a daze. Pushing past rust-colored bushes, crushing brown and golden leaves under his boots, the caves came into view at the crest of the hill. He knew how their magic worked; Colin had told him while he lay dying in his bed before Coira's mother had saved him.

Striding up to the largest cave's gaping mouth, he ducked inside. Once his eyes adjusted to the gloom, he moved deeper and listened to the way his labored breaths echoed strangely in the cavern. The equinox had been two days prior, now safely dormant. He had always been careful to avoid the caves when they were awake and hungry since he had no desire to be taken away, either by accident or on purpose.

He studied the wet sand that shifted under his feet and found nothing but the tracks of small woodland animals, but no sign of another human having passed through since his last visit.

Malcolm chewed on the inside of his cheek and glowered in the darkness, irritated with himself that he had come all this way, only to leave frustrated yet again. He slapped the damp cave wall and turned, about to leave, when his eye caught something that seemed to glow in the shadows. His heart leaped into his throat, and he practically pounced upon a white envelope wrapped in some sort of clear, flexible vellum. With shaking hands, he hurried out of the cave into the late afternoon sun and cracked open the smooth pouch.

Inside was an impossibly crisp sheath made of folded paper, the cleanest and most pure white he had ever seen. His name was written neatly in Colin's handwriting next to a smear of dried blood, dark and rusty. After tearing the seal, he pulled out the single-page letter nestled within.

Malcolm's legs gave out, and he collapsed heavily against the trunk of a fallen tree next to the burbling water. He smoothed the creases of the page and, with the hunger of a starving man, absorbed his brother's words.

My Laird, My Brother,

We hope Meggie's blood will bring you this letter and finds you in good health. Words cannot express how grateful I am for having such a stubborn bastard for a brother, for I am the most blessed of men to be reunited with my Meggie.

Life is different here, loud and fast. I spend time with yer descendant, Morrison, who reminds me of you in more ways than one. His friendship eases some of the aches in my heart, but I fear I will always mourn yer absence even though I am grateful for it.

I am happy, fulfilled beyond measure, and only wish for ye to find some semblance of the same happiness with yer witch.

With love,

Colin, Meggie, and Malcolm

Confused by the signature, Malcolm folded the letter to slip it back into its sheath only to find resistance. The paper caught on something. With a frown, he reached in with two fingers and pulled out a thin painting on glossy paper.

The painting was done so masterfully Malcolm could make out every strand of hair and every eyelash of the artist's subjects. Sitting on the front steps of an unfamiliar house, Colin and Meggie sat close together, their smiles radiant while they looked down on a young boy sitting in Meggie's lap. Brown hair the color of Meggie's flopped over his forehead, while eyes of piercing sapphire-blue looked directly at the artist.

Their son—his nephew—maybe two years of age; all plump cheeks and bare feet. The sight of them made Malcolm's heart swell painfully, and he soaked up their happiness while he memorized every inch of their perfect likenesses.

Profound relief washed over him, and he felt like he could finally take a whole breath for the first time since that fateful winter night. *This* was what he had been hoping for, a sign that he had made the right choice. His eyes burned with tears of joy, and after he tucked the letter and painting into the breast pocket of his vest, Malcolm gazed south, toward Ghlas Thùr and his witch-bride within.

When he picked his way down the hill for the last time, a small, confident smile tugged at the corner of his mouth. By the time he reached the bottom, the MacKinnon laird decided he didn't want to be married to a stranger any longer.

～ِ

Malcolm rode into the lantern-lit bailey well after dark, his face split into the widest of grins and his chest full to bursting with overwhelming joy. Liberated of his regret and shame, he hadn't felt even the slightest discomfort from the freezing bite of the night's air while he raced back to the keep.

"He made it!" Malcolm crowed and leaped off Ramsey's back to tackle Bram full around the chest as his cousin crossed the courtyard toward the barracks. "The bastard made it!" He shook Bram's shoulders roughly before he thrust the letter he'd found in the cave under his nose.

Bram stared at the white, crisp paper in the torchlight, dumbfounded. "She did it," he whispered, his face full of awe as he read the written words in Colin's hand.

Malcolm's smile wavered. "She?"

"Lady Coira. She hoped that her warding of Ghlas Thùr would ensure Colin's survival."

Malcolm blinked at his cousin and his skin pebbled. He slid his gaze toward the night-darkened walls of the keep, and the runes he knew were etched in neat lines into the stone. Coira had only just completed what he had considered a silly little task the other day.

Bram tapped the letter against Malcolm's chest.

"That's why she did it. To keep him safe. She made me promise I widnae tell ye, just in case it didnae work. She feared it would give ye false hope, but I had faith that she would succeed."

"Thank ye for tellin' me," Malcolm said, his voice gravely with overwhelming emotion. He wanted to laugh. He wanted to cry. He wanted to throw himself at Coira's mercy and beg her forgiveness for being such an arse. But most of all, he wanted *her*. He had wanted her from the very beginning.

Malcolm grinned as he clapped Bram on the back and headed with purpose up the keep's stairs.

"Um, my laird," Bram called to his back.

"What is it Bram?" Impatient to get inside to a hot meal and the company of his wife, Malcolm turned to find the most peculiar look upon his cousin's face. Bright, sea-blue eyes darted between Malcolm and the door before he smiled wide and shook his head.

"Och, 'tis best left a surprise, I believe." And with a chuckle, Bram plucked Ramsey's lead rope from the ground and guided the beast toward the stable with a cheerful whistle.

With Colin's letter tucked safely within the breast of his vest, Malcolm dismissed the odd feeling caused by Bram's statement and pushed through the heavy doors into the candlelit hall. All seemed normal except for the extra men seated at the table with his cousins. No one greeted him, their focus directed at Coira, who was blocked from his view. Malcolm crossed the hall unnoticed and nearly tripped over his own feet when he caught sight of what Bram had been so secretive about.

It appeared his wife was of a mind to seduce him this night.

Reclined comfortably in her chair, Coira smiled openly at Finlay where he lounged beside her. His hands fluttered in the air while he recounted one of his many tales for her amusement. When Malcolm neared the table, Coira's strange, ice-pale eyes snapped to his over the rim of her chalice, and the lovely smile on her ruby-stained lips faltered.

The beast in his chest twitched as he prowled over the stone floor. Flatly ignoring the men that sat at the long table, Malcolm took a long, roving inspection of Coira's body, from the glossy hair on her head down to the gentle swell of her breasts that rose up from her bodice.

My angel is gone. Replaced by a seductress, he thought, unable to look away for even a moment. *She's become the siren I likened her to all those months ago.*

"Hello, wife," he crooned as he took his seat at the head of the table and deftly captured her free hand. Lifting it to his lips, Malcolm placed a kiss upon her open palm and ran his tongue lightly across the center. At his sensual touch, her lips parted, and her fingernails flexed against his unshaven cheek.

'Most dangerous is that temptation that doth goad us on to sin in loving virtue: never could the strumpet, with all her double vigor, art and nature, once stir my temper; but this virtuous maid subdues me quite.' Malcolm silently recited the lines from Shakespeare's *Measure by Measure*, and without breaking her stare, spoke to their audience.

"Leave us."

The command echoed in the hall for only a moment before the groan of heavy chairs being shoved away from the table interrupted the silence. His men departed with raised eyebrows and more than a few knowing looks.

Finlay *wisely* kept his mouth shut.

"They havenae finished eatin' yet," Coira objected and snatched her hand from his, glaring at him through her darkened lashes.

Malcolm shrugged off her protest and bit back a self-satisfied smile when he noticed the way her thumb traced the palm he'd tasted. Starting at her throat, a telling blush crept up to her cheeks.

"They willnae starve," he said and filled his plate.

"It was rude," she snapped.

Still angry with me, Malcolm noted as he filled both their cups with amber-colored ale. *But she's dressed to tempt me. Interesting.*

Malcolm wondered what she would do when she realized he was of a mind to tempt *her*.

Spearing a potato, he decided to go straight for the kill.

"Why did ye ward the grounds, Coira?" He kept his face stoic and watched her lovely mouth pop open in surprise, then snap shut. "Well?"

Coira frowned. "Ye ken why. 'Tis obvious the castle has defensive flaws since a man was free to crawl through my window—"

"Ye began warding before that." Malcolm watched her guarded expression falter and took a long sip of ale before he said, "Ye warded the wall long before that night. I saw ye."

Her large eyes regarded him warily. The kohl Maeve had applied made her irises look like shards of frosted glass that seemed to glow in the candlelight.

"Then why did ye no' say somethin'?"

"Because yer allowed to have yer secrets, and Bram was watchin' over ye the whole time. But now I wish for ye to tell me *why*. Why carve all those runes? It took ye weeks, Coira. And ye ate more than three grown men every day, so I ken they're more than just wee symbols etched into the stone." Malcolm canted over the armrest of his chair, crowding her, causing her to lean back warily. She glanced at the grand stair at his back as though it offered her an escape, and he bit back a smile.

Ye cannae run from me, Angel, he thought. Although he would enjoy it if she tried, and almost hoped she would.

When Coira kept quiet, he broke the silence by saying in a low voice, "I think ye used yer essence on the stone like ye did to revive the rotting crops in the spring. I think ye carved the keep walls with yer magic for a much bigger reason than to keep thieves and murderers out o' yer chamber. There are runes everywhere: in the thresholds, the window casings, the stairwells—in the bloody garderobe too as though someone would be mad enough to crawl up the waste pipe—"

"That *has* happened, ye ken," she quipped, and her face flamed anew.

Malcolm hid his smile at her embarrassment with a swallow of ale. Leaning onto his elbows, he let the full weight of his stare settle on her in the quiet hall.

"Ye huvnea answered my question."

Coira's shoulders slumped, and she studied the grain of the table as she traced a decade old scratch with her fingernail.

"I did it for ye," she breathed, her voice barely a whisper.

Malcolm knocked his heavy chair away from the table, reached for her hand, and tugged: a wordless command for her to stand. She resisted only for a moment and then rose to step between his splayed legs.

"For me? How?" he insisted and looked up at her while she looked everywhere in the hall but at him.

"Because I couldnae bare to see ye suffer in yer worry." Her eyes misted with unshed tears, and he worried she wouldn't elaborate further when she said, "I thought if I could keep yer brother safe, yer thoughts on bein' bound to me widnae be such an awful thing, and maybe ye would let me love ye, even just a little."

Malcolm's heart stuttered painfully at her words, and he closed his eyes. *Thank ye God, for sending her to me*, he prayed silently before he said aloud, "It worked, Angel."

"What?" She gasped and covered her open mouth with her hands, her eyes wide and bright.

Grinning madly, Malcolm reached for her wrists and brought one, then the other, to his mouth so that he could press a reverent kiss over each pulse.

"I went to the caves, like I have a hundred times before. Today… I found a letter. Ye saved him, Angel, and in turn, ye saved me." He stood to pepper featherlight kisses along the soft skin of her collar bone, her neck, the lobe of her ear. "I am in yer debt for life. Ask anythin' of me and I'll give it freely."

His oath purred when her hands circled his shoulders, and she turned her head so he could drag his lips along her neck. Coira's pulse beat wildly under his mouth and her breath caught on a little sigh in his ear.

"Anythin'?" she whispered nervously.

He closed his teeth over her rapid pulse, and she arched her back beneath his hands, thrusting her chest firmly against his own.

"Aye. What would ye like, Angel?" Breaking away from her neck, he looked down upon her and watched a full blush mottle her cheeks before she answered.

"Love me," she breathed, "and allow me to love ye in return. I cannae bear to keep my heart to myself another moment."

Throat tight, Malcolm nodded and tucked an errant strand of hair behind her ear, then swept his thumb over the apple of her cheek.

"Then let me take ye to bed, Angel, for we're wantin' the same thing and I cannae deny myself another moment without ye." And without another word, Malcolm lifted her and headed for the stairs with purpose, her buttocks filling his hands and her legs wrapped tightly around his hips.

With single-minded determination and the corridors blessedly deserted, he made it into their chamber without incident. Placing her on her feet, he threw the bolt on the door and tried his best to calm himself. His body hummed with energy, and the oath prowled with the urgent need to claim the woman standing timidly before him. Swallowing hard, he looked down on Coira to find her slim shoulders stiff while she looked nervously at the bed, softly illuminated by the embers in the hearth. The sight of her had him thickening and straining against the leather of his breeks, and he closed the short distance between them in a few strides.

Coira's breath hitched at the first tug on the silver ribbons that fastened her gown, and she stood patiently while he expertly unlaced the seams. Parting the heavy fabric, it slipped off her shoulders to fall in a heap around her feet and revealed the scarring on her neck and back beneath the wide neck of her sleeveless shift.

"Stop," he murmured gently, and firmly brushed her hand away when she tried to cover the marred skin from his sight. Lowering his mouth to her shoulder, he spoke against her skin, "There's no part of ye that I dinnae wish to see. Why do ye wish to hide from me?"

"Because they're ugly." Her voice was small and unsure, and she fisted her hands in the gossamer fabric of her bodice. With a tiny shiver, she leaned into his touch.

"That's no' true, and I'll prove it to ye."

He spun her around to face him and unbuttoned his vest, drawing her gaze to his chest. After settling it, and the precious letter nestled within its pocket, onto the cedar chest at the foot of the bed, he pulled his shirt over his head and let it fall to the floor beside her gown. Their eyes met, and Malcolm quirked a brow.

"Would ye light a few candles?" he challenged.

Coira blinked at him before she smiled shyly and looked at the candelabra next to the bed. After a few words, whisper-sung in the lyrical language of the Druids, the wicks caught flame and brightened the room. Malcolm softly laughed and shook his head at the sheer convenience of her gift before he sobered and took her hand. When he placed it on his pectoral over a pale, puckered scar five inches long, she immediately traced it with her fore and middle fingers.

"I received this in a skirmish with a foster-brother when I was fifteen. Do ye find it ugly?"

Coira frowned. "No, but—"

"And these,"—he held out his left arm and pointed out several pale striations that ran under the length of his bicep; a few more marred his forearm—"I fell out a tree when I was twelve while I spied on a few lasses bathin' in a stream. The branch I stood on broke." He grinned and waggled his brows. "It was worth it."

She bit her bottom lip to keep from smiling and teasingly pointed to the faint scar on the arch of his brow. "What about that one? A tavern brawl?"

"Och, no, though I wish it was." Malcolm stretched out on the bed and pulled her along with him until she was draped over his chest. He languidly traced his fingers up and down her spine, appreciating all her dips and curves. "I received that little gem the day my Da died."

Coira's face fell, and the corners of her ruby lips turned down sadly.

"'Tis alright, Angel. Now, at least. Nearly seven years ago, I was devastated. A fever had run through the stronghold and took too many lives—old and young. Like many young men, I had expected my father to live 'till he was bowed of back and mad in the head. I wasnae prepared for his death. With his passing, the clan's leadership rested on my shoulders… because o' *fever*, no' battle or age. I was only twenty-five and I had never been so scared or unsure."

Coira nodded sympathetically as her focus roved over his face.

"Ye seem to have managed. They all love ye so verra much."

"And I'm grateful for their love, but that day, I was lost. I hid up in the north tower with a bottle o' my Da's scotch and drowned myself in my sorrow. I felt quite inadequate and unfit, ye see. Angus MacKinnon had been a great man, and I didnae think I could fill his boots. Magnus, the clan's master at arms, he found me the next day in the company o' naught but empty bottles and my misery. I was pissed, fallin' over myself—a total disaster. I barely noted his presence until the bastard dragged me up by the back o' my shirt and walloped me bloody."

Malcolm stared up at the rafters, lost in the blurry memory of Magnus's furious, red face while the world had spun on its axis, and he had gotten the self-pity pummeled right out of him. The soft intake of Coira's breath brought him back to the present.

"Why would he do that?"

"Because, 'tis what my Da would have done. I was laird, the MacKinnon Chieftain for only one day and I had failed them. They didnae *see* my drunken anguish, but 'tis all the same. This scar reminds me to be strong and keep my responsibilities, no matter what life throws at me."

They lay there, both in their own thoughts while he continued to stroke her back.

"I still hate them," she confessed on a whisper and touched the damaged skin under her ear. "They only remind me o' treachery, my father's death, and the absence o' my cousin, Ness."

Malcolm nodded with understanding. "Then there's only one thing for me to do."

"What's that?" she asked curiously.

Malcolm smoothed her hair away and took in the hopeful look on her lovely face.

"Give ye another memory," he said simply as he ran his hands down her back and gathered the soft fabric of her shift in his hands. Drawing the hem up her long, shapely legs, her white, thigh-high stockings were revealed, and he nearly groaned at the sight of them. "Well, I believe *those* can stay, but this will look better on the floor."

With the pesky shift gone and her body beautifully bare, Malcolm's mouth watered at the dramatic dip of her waist and the blonde curls at her apex, where she tightly clamped her thighs together. Her arms, banded across her chest, hid her breasts from his hungry gaze. Stretched out beside her, he allowed Coira her modesty, content to be patient. He was more concerned with teaching her to accept his touch than rushing into what his body greedily demanded. After all, virgin brides were not for rutting.

Malcolm lightly dragged his fingertips down the right side of her face, where smooth skin met textured, before he kissed the shell of her ruined ear. With his main focus on her scars, he held his weight on his elbow and followed the river of marbled skin that spread down her right side. With each kiss and graze of his lips, he committed every whorl, wave, and ripple to memory and watched with delight when her unmarred flesh pebbled, and her breathing grew heavier. Entranced by the way her body responded to his kisses, he reveled in the soft sounds she made as she writhed beneath him. When he reached the end of his journey down the map of her scars, he cast his eyes up the length of her body. With a wicked grin, he kissed his way up and nipped at her flawless hip while he caressed her damaged thigh.

"Let me see all o' ye," he cooed, and nuzzled at her folded arms, willing them to open and reveal her breasts. "I'm dyin' to see what ye look like."

"Ye are?" she asked breathlessly, and bit down on her lower lip.

Malcolm pressed a soft kiss to her lips and smoothed his hand over her disheveled hair and down the rope of her braid, marveling at its silkiness. "Verra much, Angel."

The moment she let her arms fall away, bashful and unsure, he urged her onto her back and closed his mouth over a dusky nipple. A low purr, not entirely human, rumbled up his throat. He rolled his tongue over the tight bud before extending the same attention to the other. Drawing her hard into his mouth, her slight gasp was music to his ears, and his head swam with the primal demands of his body.

With her head thrown back, Coira's fingers speared into his hair and drew its length from its leather wrapping. Rising above her, he took in her nakedness, her rapid breathing, and the lustful look on her face.

So beautiful... and all mine, he thought with triumph, and lowered his lips to hers.

His hair a black veil around them both, his tongue delved into her willing mouth, and he was lost in the taste of her. One of her stockinged legs had wrapped around the back of his thigh and pulled him closer as she made soft moans that fueled his lust to a rolling boil.

Breathless, he tore his mouth away from hers and kissed his way down her stomach to nibble at the soft flesh of her inner thighs where her stockings ended.

"Malcolm," she panted, her breath uneven, and her hands trembling above her stomach. She looked at him with a dark, heavy-lidded stare, her ruby lips slightly parted and wet.

He'd never seen such an alluring sight, and with deliberate slowness, he kept her stare and lowered his head.

At the first lap of his tongue over her glistening slit, she sat straight up with a cry and pushed him away. She looked appalled at what he'd just done to her—what he couldn't wait to do more of—and her slender hands grasped his cheeks. Her unique scent was in his nose—his mind—an essence both vital and lovely. One taste was not enough.

"Wha—what are ye doin'?" she gasped.

Malcolm would have laughed had she not looked so delectable with her swollen, tinted lips and flushed cheeks. He placed his palm between her breasts and firmly urged onto her back with an arched brow.

"What I'm goin' to do is taste ye… down there." When she realized what he meant, her eyes popped open wide, and Malcolm kissed the expanse of flesh below her navel to hide his smile. "Then, after I've had my fill o' ye, I'm gonna make ye mine. Will ye let me do that?"

Coira nodded her head in a flurry of blonde waves and caressed his face with the tips of her fingers. Malcolm leaned into her feather-light touch for a moment before he held her gaze and lowered his mouth to her once more. Her head fell back against the pillows with a strangled sigh, and he hummed his approval against her soft flesh.

Malcolm lost himself in the intimate act, and Coira's singular taste enveloped him while he teased her folds and drew quick circles around her nub with his tongue. Again and again he repeated the sinuous, firm sweeps, and when her legs began to tighten around him, he slowly inserted a finger into her passage. Her excitement and lust made the intrusion slick and smooth, and he groaned at the way her body welcomed him.

Coira's head lashed from side to side on the pillows as she begged him sweetly, *please, please,* the peaks of her breasts pebbled and hard in the candlelight. Her hands clenched and unclenched on her stockinged thighs and her heels dug into the blankets on either side of him.

It was the most beautiful sight he'd ever seen.

"Let go, Angel," he commanded against her core and let loose a fresh assault upon her most sensitive flesh.

Like a mighty wave, Malcolm felt the crest of her release swell within her, and she cried out, her belly and thighs flexing with the onslaught of her pleasure. While Coira rode the tide of passion and Malcolm wrung the last pulses of pleasure from her body, he found the proof of her virginity and applied pressure to painlessly break her maidenhead. Coira let out a contented sigh, and he brushed a kiss along the inside of each of her quivering thighs.

Malcolm left the bed only long enough to shed his boots and breeks before he rejoined her, arranging her back against his front. His arm pillowed her cheek, cradling her, and banded across her chest so that his left hand could freely palm her right breast. With his cock pressed heavy and demanding against her hip, he kissed her neck and ran his palm along her ribs, the dip of her waist, and the slope of her hip.

Over her scarred shoulder, Coira looked at him in wonder, adoration, and complete trust. Malcolm lifted her leg to let it drape over his thigh, and with her core bared and open, he tenderly stroked her in slow, even circles with his thumb. Within moments she soaked his fingers, exciting him nearly to the point of madness, and his oath let loose a deafening roar in his mind to *possess*.

"I cannae wait any longer," he groaned against her parted lips.

At her nod, he brought the broad head of his cock to her opening from behind and rubbed himself back and forth along her slick folds. Gritting his teeth, he primed himself for entry and began the slow process of nudging his way inside her snug, virginal passage.

"Yer so perfect, Angel." Squeezing his eyes shut, he rested his cheek against her hair and rolled her nipple between his middle and forefinger. "Ye cannae ken how good ye feel to me."

Inch by inch, he advanced into her only to retreat, hyper-aware of her inexperience, and repeated his gentle thrusting until he was fully seated. Teeth tightly clenched, he wrestled for control over his body and let her acclimate to his size while he brushed his fingertips over her nub and whispered soothing nothing's into her ear until she relaxed. At the first rock of her hips, he groaned with relief and, with a tight grip on the inside of her thigh, withdrew nearly all the way out before surging back into her heat.

"Ah!" Her head fell back against his shoulder, and he reveled in her surrender with pride and primal need.

"Angel." Malcolm held her firmly against his chest, his arm banded across her breasts, his other hand between her legs. There was not an inch of her he did not want to touch as he pistoned into her body relentlessly, driving her to climax.

Coira cried out, throaty and soft. Her fingernails scored his hip. "Malcolm, I—"

"Again," he commanded as he thrust his body deep into hers and closed his teeth on the soft muscle between her shoulder and neck.

She cried out with overwhelming joy and tightened around him like a vice when her second release seized her body. Delirious with triumph, his movements became frenzied as he chased his pleasure and focused on the connection between his body and hers. Without warning, his climax barreled down his spine, and he spilled himself deep inside her.

"Yer mine now." Voice raw, Malcolm curled against her back and kissed the scarring over her neck and the slightly red mark of his bite. While they caught their breath, Coira sighed contentedly and ran the tips of her fingers over his knuckles.

"I dinnae mind that at all."

The soft pop of embers was the only sound in the room and he held her until he softened and reluctantly slipped from her warmth.

"I'm sorry, Angel," Malcolm murmured as he smoothed her rumpled hair.

Coira fell still, then turned in his arms and brought her chest flush with his. Her brows were furrowed with worry in the faint candlelight.

"Whatever do ye mean?"

Malcolm reveled in the glorious feel of her naked body against his, and promised himself to remember this night forever: the way she looked, the way her nipples brushed against the short hairs on his chest, the taste of her on his lips—all new, yet familiar. Years from now, he wanted to recall the chill of the damp, evening air that crept through the half-open window, the sweat that dried on his skin, and the heat from her body that warmed and cocooned him.

I was indeed a fool to have kept her at arm's length for the past five months, Malcolm thought as he cupped her face with his hands and kissed the fine line that creased the space between her brows.

"I'm sorry for no' insisting we had done that months ago."

CHAPTER EIGHTEEN

COIRA

I had never been as exceptionally contented in all my life as I was that morning, weighted down in bed by my husband's hulking body, his cheek resting heavily between my bare breasts. I listened to his breathing in the grey light of dawn and cataloged the new and welcomed aches of my body.

My bones felt tight and loose and not entirely my own. Between the satisfying soreness at the junction of my thighs and the slight burn around my lips where Malcolm's unshaven face had rubbed against mine, he'd branded me, body and soul. Oh, how I loved each and every ache and all the discomfort caused by his vigorous lovemaking, celebrated them even, for they meant that the act that caused them had truly happened.

Slow and smoothly, I slipped quietly from underneath him and looked down upon his sleep-softened face for a moment before withdrawing to my chamber. After encasing my nakedness within my pine-green dressing gown, I tiptoed down the deserted hallway for a quick trip to the garderobe and found Maeve along the way with her tray of tea and breakfast biscuits. One look upon my face caused her mouth to split into a wide, knowing grin.

"That beet juice works every time," she trilled as she approached me, and her giggle echoed down the quiet hallway.

I blushed a deep red and decided then and there that I would let her believe her meddling was what had brought the laird and I together at last.

"Perhaps a nice hot bath this morn?" she asked.

I thought again of the tenderness between my thighs as I pulled open the heavy garderobe door and nodded enthusiastically. The sooner the soreness went away, the sooner Malcolm could apply his magic to my body again.

Back in my chamber, Maeve and her breakfast tray were nowhere to be seen and I peeked into my husband's chamber to find all five windows along the two outer walls unshuttered to brighten the room, and the tea tray resting upon the chest at the foot of the bed. Malcolm was awake but still snuggled within the blankets like a sleepy bear.

"Good mornin'." Malcolm's baritone greeting caressed my skin as I shyly crawled onto the bed beside him and sat back on my heels.

"A verra good mornin'," I agreed, and worried a loose thread on my dressing gown. I would never understand why I was so timid after all the intimacies we had shared the previous night, but it was hard to face him, and I tried my best to hide the emotions that swirled within my heart.

He patted the space beside him. "Come here."

Before I could make the conscious decision to move, Malcolm reached for me, wrapped his arms around my waist, and brought me firmly against his chest. Arranging me so I lay partially atop him, he peppered my face with soft, slow kisses and fingered the tangles out of my unbound hair. Through the covers, I could feel him hardening against my belly, and an inevitable blush rushed to my face.

"Are ye verra sore?" he whispered against my cheek.

"A little."

A look of regret passed over his features. "I used ye too harshly," he said with a slight frown, and tucked my hair behind my ear.

I pressed my fingertips against his lips. "No. I loved every moment."

Malcolm wrapped his long fingers around my wrist and kissed my palm, much like he had last night in the great hall; it caused a streak of yearning to zip up my arm. His focus fell on my lips, and his brown eyes grew dark and hooded.

"Every moment?"

I opened my mouth to reply when the soft creek of my chamber door opening spoiled the mood, and I shrugged in apology. "Maeve ordered a bath for me."

"Mmm. 'Tis a shame there's no' room for two." Rolling me onto my back, he kissed me twice more before he sat up and poured my tea. Handing it to me with a biscuit placed on a small plate, his fingers brushed mine.

"Enjoy yer soak, Angel."

My bath was glorious, and I nearly purred when the first liquid touch of hot water caressed my sore muscles, and its heat permeated my bones. I felt more like myself after I wiped the last remnants of kohl from my eyes while Maeve sudsed my hair until it squeaked. Once rinsed with spicy, rosemary-scented water, I felt refreshed and deliriously happy.

I dressed myself in what Maeve affectionately called my *"witch garb:"* a faded black frock complete with a stained, white apron I wore for messier tasks such as the one I had planned for today. I needed to gather sap from the young pine to replenish my stores of pine glue. It was an easy enough chore, but one that could potentially ruin one of my nicer gowns.

Late autumn was the best time for harvesting sap, since the cool weather made it easy to chip the sticky gold and amber droplets off the tree in a purer form. I had depleted my stock during the last few months when binding sprained ankles and broken bones with cloth. If anyone were to come to me with so much as a jammed finger, I had nothing to use for adhesive and would need to tie the linen instead; something I thought of as lazy and inefficient, and only to be used as a last resort.

I discovered Malcolm in the library hunched over his desk with a half-empty bowl of porridge pushed to the side, papers strewn about on the surface as well as on the floor. With a few thin tomes open in front of him, he scribbled numbers furiously on a sheet of paper.

"What vexes ye so?" Eager to take full advantage of our newfound intimacy, I ran the heel of my palms up his broad back, squeezed the space between his neck and shoulder, and pushed up my thumbs into his tight muscles to alleviate the tension. "Ye could use some clove oil," I noted as my hands ran over his white shirt.

Malcolm groaned under my touch and bowed his head even lower. "If that oil is the same remedy ye gave to Gunn and Farlan's wives at the Gathering, I'll happily surrender to ye. They raved about it for weeks." He was silent for a time, his white quill loose in his hand while I manipulated his flesh. He finally answered my question with a frustrated growl. "I'm no good with sums. Every month I labor over the keep's accounts, and every month I end up wantin' to gouge my bloody eyes out."

I smiled in sympathy as I ran the length of his bound hair through my fingers, thinking on how wonderfully one night had changed everything. Just days before, had I attempted to touch him in such a way, the laird would have run out of the room as though chased by a swarm of hornets and disappear for hours. At least now I knew it wasn't really *me* he had fled from, but the temptation that came with my presence.

Such an unnecessary self-inflicted punishment, I thought as the dark strands slid through my fingers and wondered if I would have been compelled to ward the castle walls if Malcolm had accepted me with open arms. I hated to think of the danger that could've befallen the keep in the centuries to come without those power-infused runes. And then there was the letter Malcolm read to me late last night. For it to be found mere days after I had finished the warding, I must believe that meant they were working.

Or maybe its timely appearance was just a coincidence…

A coincidence is just fate's way o' screamin' at ye, my mother's words, spoken long ago, echoed in my mind. I blinked back a rush of overwhelming gratitude for all her lessons, however violent and cruel, for she was a wise woman indeed.

"I'm goin' to the village to collect the salt I had ordered, then to harvest sap in the pine grove downriver. Abandon yer work for a time and come with me."

Malcolm turned in his chair and looked at me with regret. "As much as I would like that, I must finish this today. Go to yer errands and we can have the rest o' the afternoon together. Take Farlan with ye though."

I huffed an exasperated breath and yanked the hem of my skirt high enough to flash the dagger tied to my calf.

"I dinnae need a keeper. I ken well enough how to defend myself. Besides, ye didnae care before."

Laird MacKinnon leveled his stare upon me in such a way that I felt as though *he* were the one standing and not the other way around.

"Ye'll take Farlan or ye willnae go, Angel."

I stiffened, ready to snap a retort when his face softened a degree, and he reached out a steadying hand to rest on my hip.

"'Tis more for my peace o' mind, no' that I doubt ye can handle yerself. Ye've become precious to me, and I would feel better if ye were under the protection o' my best man if I cannae be there with ye."

Even while I glared my displeasure at him, my mood lightened at his confession, and he gave me no choice but to forgive him his willfulness. With a huff, I spun around, tossed a flippant "fine" over my shoulder and went in search of my escort.

⁓

"Yer a serious fellow," I mused when Farlan hefted the twenty-pound sack of coarse salt over Una's flank and then helped me upon her back. Farlan's wife, the laundress Bredanna, was bubbly and full of life, so different from the gruff, sullen man that looked up at me with his blue eyes and his brow cocked. She alone seemed to crack his hardened shell, which, I supposed, was as it should be.

"If ye were wantin' entertainment, my lady, ye should have invited Finlay on this wee excursion." With the barest of smiles, he mounted his horse and canted his head for me to follow.

As we rode down the foggy thoroughfare, friendly villagers greeted me with a wave, pleased to see their lady had come for a visit.

I loved it here. No one looked at me oddly or shied away from my presence. I felt I was part of a whole, welcome and needed. The best part was that not a single person crossed themselves at the sight of me and the women of town now sought me out regularly during Sunday suppers and the days in between. They confided their troubles and requested remedies against an unwanted child, a tisane to help conceive, and countless other treatments. I helped each in turn and always refused payment since I no longer needed to scrounge for food or coin to replace the clothes on my back. My herbs didn't cost me, other than the time and sweat it took to grow and gather them. The plot of land Malcolm had gifted me when I arrived was cultivated and, aided with my gifted energy, now stocked with nearly everything I would need. Without my Druid gifts, having such a fruitful garden in its first year would have been impossible.

As we rode past the church in the middle of town, I shied away from the large, red-bricked building and averted my eyes from the stained-glass windows. Just being near it made my skin crawl. But it was not the building and what it stood for that repelled me so much as the man who made it his home.

Father Blount hadn't seen my face since my wedding to the laird, thanks to Malcolm's understanding and foresight to veil me when it came time for church worship. Each time I ventured into the village, I kept a wary eye out for his presence and, so far, was lucky not to encounter him.

We left the church and town behind and journeyed downriver, past the tannery on the other side of the rushing water. Its foul stench chased after us for nearly a quarter mile before we could take a fresh breath again. Mist kissed the air, and bits of fog hung low to the ground when we crossed the water at a wide, shallow area and finally reached the pine grove.

A few weeks ago, I had borrowed a hand saw from the castle's workshop and hacked off the shorter limbs of the trees at eye level and below. Where I'd shorn the limbs from the trunks, rivers of opaque sap had leaked out to protectively cover the exposed wood.

"I'll be quick as I can about this," I promised Farlan while he hobbled our horses.

With a brown glass jar in hand, I brandished the dagger from my calf and began to chip the hardened sap off the first tree.

Farlan snorted from where he stood behind me. "How many other weapons do ye have upon yer person?" he queried.

I looked over my shoulder to find him surveying our misty surroundings, his wrists at rest on the pommel of one of his two swords. "I have just the one," I replied as I peeled off a fat dribble of sap and let it fall with a *plink* into the jar. "Even a woman under guard should have her own protection, dinnae ye agree?"

He shrugged. "I suppose."

"Does Bredanna no' have a dagger to carry when ye cannae be with her?"

Farlan gave me a thoughtful look before he said, "She will now."

A thick, hip-high wall of fog moved in to shroud the outskirts of the grove, giving the trunks of the young trees an eerie impression when they disappeared into the brume. The ground I walked upon, thick with burnt-umber needles and patchy mounds of moss, cushioned my footsteps as I moved from tree to tree.

My fingertips and the sharp edge of my blade were coated with sticky sap by the time we reached the east end of the grove. At its edge, the land opened to a meadow that sloped uphill, covered in brown grass and late blooming heather in shades of mauve and purple. I set my jar full of sap down, breathed deep of the crisp, fragrant air, and ventured out of the shadows, intent on picking a few sweet-smelling bushels of the small, bell-like flowers to take home.

Home.

That's what Ghlas Thùr had become to me. The busy castle full of people was now as much a haven as the quiet cottage I had shared with my mother in the wood. Actually, more so. I hadn't realized how lonely it had been growing up there, especially after Ness's devastating absence. I still missed my mother's solid presence terribly and wished she were still with me, but I now understood why she had bound me to the MacKinnon Laird. I hadn't been living life before Malcolm came—not truly. I wondered if this was why she had felt an attachment to Malcolm since she had delivered him from his mother's womb all those years ago. She hadn't had the gift of Sight, but perhaps she'd felt a premonition, and finally made the connection when she offered Malcolm the blood oath. My lips lifted at that comforting thought, and I crouched down to cut a stalk of heather away from the main bush.

The unexpected swoosh of fletching ripped through the space my head had just occupied, and an arrow lanced with a muffled thump in the ground twenty feet up the rising slope of the meadow. I twisted toward the forest in surprise.

"Get down!" Farlan bellowed from the tree line.

Without hesitation, I flattened myself to the ground between the thick mounds of heather, and pressed my cheek into the damp grass. The musty aroma of vegetation and wet dirt filled my nose, and I couldn't help but wonder if it would be the last thing I would smell. I didn't dare pick my head up, but I could see Farlan crouched low ahead of me, both of his swords drawn as he scanned the interior of the forest. My teeth dug into my bottom lip to keep it from trembling, and I palmed my dagger tightly with one hand, a fist full of twigs and weeds in the other.

Three arrows darted out of the forest in quick succession, one aimed at Farlan, which he barely avoided. The tip slammed into the trunk of a pine just to his left with a loud *thunk*.

The other two flew straight toward me.

My eyes widened when the first arrow pierced the fabric of my cloak and skirt by my hip; the second impaled the soil not three inches from my nose. I watched with terrified fascination when the black-painted shaft vibrated slightly before it fell still.

Farlan lunged back into the mist-veiled forest and his battle cry caused gooseflesh to prick my skin, my stomach plummeting as though it were filled with rocks. The forest was filled with foreboding silence, and I mentally shook myself of my terror. I needed to flee from this place, but I could not go back into the grove.

On shaking limbs, I pushed up into a crouch, and the arrow slid free through the hole it had made in my clothing with little protest. The sharp, unmistakable clang of metal clashing against metal broke the silence, and shouts of frustration drifted toward me through the trees. No matter how hard I tried, I couldn't see through the saplings that lined the outer edge of the pine grove, so like a cornered hare, I crouched, motionless among the heather. Minutes went by, or it could have been less, the clamor within the thicket becoming more frantic with every passing second… until it stopped all at once, and I took a tentative step forward.

"Farlan!" I whisper-shouted, my jaw tight and breath ragged.

I was about to disperse the fog when the rocks in my gut grew heavier, and in an act of pure instinct, I fled uphill to put as much distance as possible between myself and danger. I jammed my toes, tripped on stones hidden beneath the fragrant brush, and fell to my knees, losing precious headway.

Get up! I gripped my dagger tighter, used it to claw myself up from the ground, and pushed onward. *Faster*—I needed to be faster, but with each step, the cumbersome and heavy hem of my gown wicked up more dew from the grass and low-lying branches and flapped around my ankles.

From below, a piercing whistle caused me to pause, and I looked over my shoulder to witness the most frightening man I'd ever seen walk out of the trees and carelessly toss his bow and empty quiver aside. Tall and lithe, he was dressed in black from collar to boot. His scalp, shaved except for a short strip that ran along the top, failed to distract from his face, for he'd painted himself to resemble a corpse. Coal-black rouge stained the skin around his eyes and was smeared down the hollows of his pale cheeks and neck.

It altered his face to look like a bone-picked skull, like a reaper of death brought to life.

To make his intentions clear, a vicious leer distorted his darkened lips and revealed teeth with unnaturally sharp points. My blood ran cold at the sight of those filed tips, and I couldn't keep myself from imagining the damage they could cause. The mere thought of them closing over my throat sent a prickle of terror up my spine, followed by another when he loped toward me with murderous determination.

Run, run, run! My terror commanded me like a beating drum, and I had no other choice but to obey: I turned and ran. My destination, the darker, older forest that loomed ahead, its shadows a welcomed sight.

The air I pulled into my lungs, despite the wet day, was brisk and felt like shards of glass lacerating my throat. I didn't dare look behind me, too fearful that I would stumble and he would catch me. With the possibility of him close at my heels, I surged forward with a burst of speed. Visions of those unnatural teeth sinking into my flesh came unbidden in my mind and a whimper escaped my trembling lips. But no bite came, and at last, I hurtled into the shadows of the forest at the top of the slope.

Beneath the thick canopy, I sobbed a relieved breath to discover tall boulders jutting out of the ground like thick shields, and I wove between them to plunge deeper into the gloom. The stones, white and faintly shimmery, were coated with dark moss on their southern sides. Some rose no higher than my knees; others towered well above my head, and littered the forest, clogging the space between the trees. From the relative safety of one of the stones, I paused to peer through the gaps and saw my stalker prowl into the forest.

Still as a statue, he scanned the stones with the confidence of one who knew he'd find me, and my fear ratcheted to a fever pitch.

"Come out, come out," he crooned, his voice hoarse and coarse.

My pulse pounded like a drum in my ears and throat, and I pressed my back against a moss-covered boulder. I had to be careful. One wrong move—one wrong step—would give my whereabouts away, and he'd pounce.

"I couldnae find a way over that bloody wall without bein' spotted." The volume of his voice ebbed and flowed as he rounded stone after stone. "I've been waitin' a fortnight for ye to show yer face, and I'm no' a patient man."

I barely allowed myself to feel more than a glimmer of satisfaction that the runes I'd etched into the curtain wall worked before I glanced around and winced at the leaves and branches that covered the ground; common enough forest debris, but hardly silent to walk on.

What I needed was a distraction.

With a deep, steadying breath, I reached for my power and tried my best to calm my panting enough to call upon the wind. A feeble bit of magic, but the wind only required a whisper, and I only needed to hide the sounds of my footsteps.

If I timed it right, I would be able to slip past him by using the stones to block my retreat. If I was fast enough, I could make it to Una and ride for the safety of the village; he'd catch me if I attempted anything else. If I continued through the forest, I would run myself to the ground long before I found help.

I grasped what thin wisps of courage I could, embraced my Druid magic, and laced my whispered words with power to bolster the slight breeze that blew from the northeast. As the gale strengthened, I commanded the clouds to darken to the color of slate and shelter me in their shadow. Leaves and branches whipped past me, masking the sound of my whispered song, and I slowly peeked around the edge of my shelter in search of the man in black.

Seven stones were all that separated us. He advanced slowly and leaned into the wind, shielding his wickedly painted face with his forearms from the debris that shot through the gaps between stone and trunk.

Too close, he was too close!

Before I retreated behind the thick trunk to my right, my gaze latched onto the razor sharp daggers he held in his hands, sticky with Farlan's blood. With a sheen of red on the metal, the edges gleamed with threat and promise, and I couldn't help but imagine how easily they would slice into my belly.

Over the gale, I could hear him cursing me. He checked behind each boulder he passed and promised me a gruesome death under his breath. On quaking legs, I moved from one hiding spot to the next while he stalked and taunted me. He knew I was somewhere within the cluster of stones—knew it was only a matter of time before he caught me.

"I'm gonna find ye," he called out, "and when I do yer gonna wish ye stayed behind those walls!"

His threat arrested my breath, and my heartbeat hammered a new staccato. I threw myself behind a squat slab and crawled over the leaf littered ground to keep hidden. From one shelter to the next, I made steady headway to the outer ring of stones. I had started to believe I would make it until the fine hairs on my neck rose when he dragged the tip of a blade along a stone, and I nearly choked on my fear.

"I can smell yer fear," he taunted. "'Tis the most exciting aroma, pungent and bitter." He took a deep inhalation, and I pressed an unstable hand to my mouth to keep silent.

"I cannae wait to bleed ye dry, and bleed ye, I will," he promised.

I willnae make it out alive, I thought.

Terrified, I inched around a thick trunk on the outer edge of the stone grouping and wiped sweat from my brow. I was still too far away from the meadow's edge, and some innate instinct told me he was close, that I was running out of time.

With shaking hands, I pressed the tip of my dagger into the soft spots of my palms and sliced a shallow line. My blood dripped onto the leaves that raced along the ground, and I tucked the blade back into its sheath on my leg before I leaned back against the bark.

I was not naïve enough to think I had any hope of winning a fight against a man skilled enough to kill Farlan… but I could use a weapon he had no defense against.

My blood.

Determined to survive, I rubbed my hands together and coated them front and back until there wasn't an inch that wasn't wet with crimson power. Armed with my only chance at survival, I took a deep breath and commanded the wind to blow harder.

My throat tightened and threatened to suffocate me while the tempest lashed at my hair and ripped at the hem of my dress. It carried with it chunks of earth and branches that slammed into the chest and face of the man in black.

"What is this, magic?" he seethed, and cursed when something hard smacked into him with a thump.

I fought the urge to look around the edge of the tree, the compulsion to look so strong I had to grit my teeth.

"Ye think a bit o' wind can save—" He swore and grunted when a blast battered his face, but I could find no humor in the moment. He roared his frustration. "I'm gonna sink my teeth into ye!"

The tree's thick bark bit into my spine and gave me a strange kind of comfort. I smeared a second coating of blood on my hands and waited… and waited. Each second was like a brand on my nerves. I had one chance—*one chance*—to flick my blood upon his skin. Only then would he be at my mercy.

I waited, listening to his voice as he came ever closer. "Witch!" he yelled out, and spit something onto the ground. "I'll tear yer heart out while it still beats!"

I cupped my hands to catch the blood that flowed from my self-inflicted wounds and looked to my right. I only needed one drop of my blood to touch his skin. Just one drop… I could be faster… my muscles coiled tight, ready to spring to action.

He was close, so close I could hear his feet hitting the ground—

I blinked, momentarily confused by the *thump, thump, thump* of heavy footfalls when the man who stalked me moved so slow.

"What the feck—"

A massive blur of black and white flew past my hiding place, and I cried out when not one but *two* men fell heavily to the ground mere yards from me. Struck speechless, I lost my grip on my magic, and the song that controlled the wind died on my lips.

"Oh my God," I breathed as I watched Malcolm rain blow after blow upon my attacker. His shirt was soaked and ripped down the seam in the back, as well was the sides of his leather breeks, barely containing his enormous, altered body.

The skull-painted man beneath him fought back savagely, his sharpened teeth bared and blackened eyes bloodshot with hate. I screamed a warning just before he sunk one of his daggers into Malcolm's shoulder to the hilt. With an inhuman roar and a spray of blood, Malcolm ripped the weapon from his flesh and slammed it between the ribs of his quarry.

I turned my face away, unable to watch the rest. The begging and pain-filled screams that came from the man in black told me well enough how my husband was killing him. When the cries and whimpers cut off abruptly, and all I could hear was the sound of Malcolm's ragged breathing, I opened my eyes. I found him standing in front of me, his focus on my bloody hands. Once again, his pupilless eyes, illuminated with ethereal light, were harsh and angry. Soaking wet as though he'd torn straight through the river to get to me, his raven hair stuck to the side of his face and neck in wild ropes.

Standing close, he blocked my view of the carnage on the forest floor with his body and spat blood on the moss at his feet. Blood stained his sharp, too-large teeth and ran down his chin to drip onto his barreled chest. Although the sight of him made me shiver, I wordlessly closed the gap between us and pressed my cheek against his pounding heart with relief.

Malcolm's arms, larger and longer than the ones that held me with such passion last night, circled my shoulders and tucked me close. I twisted my fingers into the torn fabric at his back.

"Where's Farlan?" His question made my eyes prick with tears, and I looked up at him, unable to make any words come out of my mouth.

What would I tell his wife? She'd hate me the moment she found out her husband died defending me.

Malcolm tucked my hair behind my ear and nodded slowly as though he knew the painful turn of my thoughts. "Let's go, Angel. Take me to him."

The meadow was no longer a lovely place as I led my husband toward the direction I believed Farlan had made his last stand. Heavy of heart and heedless of the blood that covered us both, we brushed past the purple flowers hand-in-hand. At the edge of the grove, I noted the discarded bow of the man in black as we slipped into the shade.

"This way." My voice sounded small and strangled, and I whispered a few words to dispel the last of the lingering fog and clouds above. Shafts of light speared through the boughs, dappling the amber needles strewn on the floor of the forest.

My heart saddened at the sight of Farlan, where he lay in a pool of golden light just ahead, one of his two swords at his side. It would have been a peaceful sight had it not been for his bloodied shirt and the way his limbs bent at odd angles. Urging Malcolm to go ahead, I stayed back. Guilt twisted my stomach in knots, but I made myself watch Malcolm kneel next to his soldier and rest his hand in the middle of Farlan's chest, the muscles of his back stiff. Head bowed in prayer, he closed his eyes, and I did the same.

Without much practice in the way of prayer, I owed it to the warrior who had given his life for mine to try. Searching for the words in the dark sea of my remorse, I dashed away the lone tear that raced down my cheek.

Please, give me the courage to ask forgiveness o' Farlan's wife, and the strength to—

Malcolm's sharp inhalation of breath drew my attention, and he turned sharply to catch my stare, his eyes nearly manic with an emotion I couldn't name.

"He's alive."

Chapter Nineteen

MALCOLM

"The web of our life is of mingled yarn, good and ill together."
-William Shakespeare, All's Well that Ends Well

"He's alive."

The words were barely out of Malcolm's mouth before Coira lunged into motion and crossed the small, sun-drenched clearing to kneel at Farlan's side. Head lowered, she pressed her ear close to Farlan's face, whimpered with relief, then fumbled under her skirt for her dagger. With the practiced movement of a healer comfortable with a blade, she sliced his shirt and wool vest in two, revealing the extent of Farlan's injuries.

Dear God, he was butchered, Malcolm thought as he stared down in horror at the slices on his friend's chest, arms, legs, and belly. It was as though his opponent had toyed with him and drew out the fight to do as much damage as possible before assuming he was dead. But it was more than just the cuts on his skin. Farlan's left leg was bent oddly at the knee, as well as one of his elbows and several fingers. Malcolm didn't want to know what sort of man could deliver such damage to a trained warrior and not receive so much as a scratch upon himself.

"These trees are too goddamn *small* for this amount of damage," Coira hissed in frustration and clawed at the clotted cut on her left palm with her nails. Coaxing her blood to run freely again, she wiped it on one of the only clear swaths of skin on Farlan's neck and whispered a string of words he didn't understand. Then she looked Malcolm dead in the eye.

Malcolm knew that Coira had many factions of herself. He knew her silent side the best, all watchful and pondering. The magical bit he knew well from those late nights spent healing the land. He'd met her passionate side last night, all soft sighs and exploring hands… but the woman who stared at him over the body of his dying friend was the warrior. The healer. Her countenance was hardened, sharpened, and polished with fearless confidence. He was in awe of her.

"Help me move him," she barked as she dragged Farlan by the arm toward the nearest tree. Between the two of them, it only took a moment, but Farlan's blood began to flow more freely with the movement. Settled between two thin trunks no thicker than his wrists, Coira knelt in the needle bed beside Farlan's chest and, without hesitation, pressed her hand firmly against his open wounds.

"Dinnae touch me, husband. 'Tis best if ye stand over there and dinnae move. There's no time for me to stop."

Malcolm nodded and did as he was told.

She grasped the closest pine and began to sing. Unlike the soft chant she had uttered to make the crops thrive, her song was both deep and pulsing, impossibly layered, and intangible as though she were deep in a cave.

It was the same song her mother had sung in the courtyard the night she died. Where he had been petrified before, this time Malcolm watched in fascination and was not the least bit scared of his wife. Coira's voice washed over him like honey, and he felt that if he lifted his hand, the melody would wrap itself around his fingers like a lover. Knees weak, Malcolm listened to her song and noted the way her beautiful face lifted toward the sun that streamed through the shivering pine boughs.

Fighting the emotions that clogged his throat, he watched the rips in Farlan's skin slowly close while thin, brittle branches showered around them. Coira's song wavered when Farlan's knee slipped back into place with a pop, and the young trunk she grasped turned grey and shimmery. Swiftly, she scurried to Farlan's other side and stretched his arm as far as it would go until she clutched the rough bark of yet another young pine. Her song continued. She did this thrice more as she bounced around Farlan's body, dragging him through the amber needles, and stretched their limbs to the limit.

The quick *pop, pop, pop* of Farlan's fingers straightening sent shivers down Malcolm's spine, and the snap of a broken arm nearly blended in with the crackling of the falling stone branches. When his ribs moved into a more natural position, correcting the shape of his chest, Coira let out a breathy sigh of relief and finally let her song fall silent.

Malcolm felt a fierce pride bloom in his chest. Faint smudges of purple shadowed her eyes as she looked over Farlan's body with a healer's scrutiny. Once satisfied, she blew out a heavy breath.

"Now we just have to wait for him to wake." With a slight wince, Coira reopened the cut on her hand and dabbed her blood against Farlan's wrist. Fascinated, Malcolm crept closer and watched Farlan's sallow skin begin to pinken with the healthy flush of life where it wasn't covered in gore.

"'How far that little candle throws his beams. So shines a good deed in a weary world,'" Malcolm quoted, awe and wonder in his voice. "Ye're my candle, Angel."

Coira huffed a throaty laugh and shook her head. "Is there a moment when ye dinnae think o' Shakespeare?"

The snap of a branch drew his attention before he could answer. "Someone's comin'," Malcolm hissed and snatched Farlan's fallen sword from the ground. Lowered into a defensive stance, he placed himself between the sound of approaching footsteps and Coira, who leaned protectively over Farlan.

"My laird!"

Bram's voice broke the silence a moment before he raced through the low branches; Finlay and a dozen more of the garrison's men followed closely behind. Armed to the teeth, they all had a wild look about them as they stopped and warily looked their laird over.

Malcolm couldn't blame their hesitation. They had all seen him tear out of the south gate—barefoot and eyes aglow—but there had been no time for explanations, or for a request for help. He hadn't even known where he was *going*, only that he had to get there. For a mile and a half, he had rushed headlong through fields and forests with his near invincible body. He had vaulted over fallen trees, boulders, and streams. The obstacles had barely slowed him down.

The river had. He had come upon it at a deep, lazy section, but he was not the best swimmer.

"What the feck happened?" Gavin demanded as he looked around Malcolm's hips toward Farlan's prone body. "Is he dead?"

"No, praise God." Malcolm said a silent prayer of thanks that his body and teeth had receded to their natural state before his men had arrived and pointed to the meadow at his back. "Ye'll find a body just on the other side o' the soldier stones. I want ye to search him. With any luck, we can find out who he was and where he came from."

Finlay rushed forward along with two other men to do his bidding. Bram, however, kept his stare locked with his laird's, and a wordless conversation passed between them.

What the feck.

Now's no' the time.

Ye'll be makin' time later, ye bastard.

Malcolm rolled his eyes.

"He's awake," Coira announced and brushed Farlan's blood-matted hair away from his face.

Farlan blinked in confusion at those who surrounded him and ran his palm along his ribs. He held up the hand that only moments ago had been gnarled with broken fingers and flexed them in the sunlight.

"Did ye do this, my lady?" Awe laced his voice as he looked up at Coira in a daze. At the slight nod of her head, Farlan swallowed and struggled to sit up. He clutched her hand between his, and placed a firm, chaste kiss to her knuckles before touching them to his bowed forehead. "My life is yers, from this day forth. I'll do anythin' ye ask o' me."

"I dinnae want yer life, Farlan. It is yer own to keep," she whispered and stood to help him stand. "I only want ye to live, happy and hale, and I had the means to make it so. Thank ye for protecting me as much as ye could. I'll never forget it."

"I'd do it again. I will, if the need arises," he promised, and Coira squeezed his hand.

A look of bewilderment passed between the newly arrived men, and their brows arched high when Farlan faced them. With his shirt open, his new scars stood out through the drying, sticky blood like beacons on a moonless night. Several men crossed themselves and muttered near-silent prayers of thanks.

Malcolm took his ruined shirt off his body, ripped it into strips, and wrapped the white fabric around Coira's palms before he wiped the dirt and grime from her face. Curiously, his shoulder felt only a little sore, and with a quick inspection, he found the stab wound had already healed as though it had happened weeks ago, not minutes. Malcolm deduced that Vanora had gifted him with rapid healing when needed. As interesting as that was, Malcolm found he would prefer never to test the theory again. The change left him drained and sluggish in his human skin, and even surrounded by his men, he felt vulnerable without the beast's strength coursing through him. Malcolm wanted nothing more than to get Coira behind the thick walls of Ghlas Thùr as soon as possible… and keep her there.

Finlay rejoined the group holding a black bow and quiver in one hand and a pouch of coin in the other. He tossed the leather purse to Malcolm and took a deep breath.

"Well, there wasnae much to find on him, mostly because there wasnae much *left o' him*." Finlay gave Malcolm a queer look before he took a dagger from another soldier. He flipped it once in the air and caught it by the polished, red handle. "Besides the bow, which I stake personal claim to, he had two daggers, nothin' more. Perhaps he has a camp nearby or lodging in the village tavern that can tell us more. Until we find his lair, we ken nothin' else."

"Let us get ye back to the keep, my laird, and we'll comb the hills. I dinnae see a man like that findin' welcome at the tavern or anywhere else in town," Farlan croaked, his voice rough, and held his hand out for his sword. Malcolm gave him a dubious look but relinquished the weapon.

"Ye willnae be joinin' them," Malcolm said sternly. He stepped close to drape his arm over Farlan's shoulders and tugged him through the grove. Coira followed closely behind, flanked between the twins.

"I'm well enough."

"'Tis no' the issue o' bein' well, my friend. 'Tis that ye nearly died, and in service to me. Ye'll be restin' the rest o' the day and the morrow as well."

Farlan argued his case the entire way back to the keep, only to yield completely the moment he caught sight of Bredanna pacing in the shadow of the curtain wall. The blood drained from her face when she saw her husband's bloody shirt and weeping openly, crossed the field that separated them at a run, her dark hair streaming behind her. She threw her arms around Farlan's neck, heedless of the blood he had failed to wash off at the riverbed. Without another word to anyone, Farlan lifted his wife into his arms and carried her into the keep.

Malcolm leaned on his elbows at the head of the table in the great hall, a tumbler of scotch in his hand. After he had ensconced Coira safely in the upper levels of the keep with Maeve, and washed off the gore and filth from his own body, his thoughts revolved around the two attempts on his wife's life.

Since Coira had saved the clan's crops of rot, he'd not felt nor seen even the smallest bit of animosity or hatred toward her from the people of the clan. The women sought her out on a regular basis now, never more than a day or two between someone asking for her. She'd delivered their babies and saved their children from fevers. His people loved her.

He loved her.

Malcolm swirled the amber-colored liquid around in his cup and thought on how the beast's power had ripped through his body, alerting him to danger. He'd been in the library reading over a correspondence when he felt it.

At the first lick of fire in his veins, Malcolm embraced the change like an old friend and vaulted into action. There was a definitive pull in his chest, like a string tied around his spine that reeled him to where he was needed. Surrendering completely to instinct, he'd raced through the keep for the nearest exit.

Malcolm would never forget the looks on his men's faces. No time for a horse or to ask for aid, he sprinted through the southern gatehouse with a speed that rivaled Ramsey. He could hear two of his men attempt to follow, but he was too fast and cleared the field before they crossed a quarter of it. The urge to get to Coira in time overrode his thoughts while he barreled through the woods, any painful stab to his instep from stones or sticks gone a moment later as he pushed himself faster and faster.

The river was an obstacle, though. It dragged at his heavy frame when he plunged in, and its icy grasp knocked the wind from his lungs by the time he crawled out on the eastern bank.

It was the tempest that ripped over a heather-filled meadow and carried the harsh curses of an unknown man toward him that made his blood boil. With a burst of energy, Malcolm's heart pounded within his chest as he surged forward. His powerful legs ate up the distance, and the wind seemed to part for him—

Still armed and in their leathers, Finlay and Bram sat down at the table on either side of their laird and pulled him reluctantly from his brooding. Malcolm rubbed one side of his face harshly and stifled a yawn before he knocked back the rest of the scotch.

"I suppose ye have questions," he drawled as he reclined in his chair and looked between the mirror images that stared back at him.

Bram's brows rose and disappeared into the brown curls that flopped over his forehead as though to say, *Aye, ye daft bastard.*

"I have just the one," Finlay quipped as he hefted a booted foot onto the table and began to clean his nails with his dirk. "Why is there a dead man rottin' in the east wood?"

Malcolm gritted his teeth as he thought of what he'd done to his wife's assailant. When he'd found the man stalking her around the stones, his rage had hit a crescendo at the sight. Surrendering himself to the beast, he'd tackled his target to the ground. Malcolm remembered looking through a thick white haze, aware that he'd loomed over the man whose face was painted as though it lacked skin. He had smelled the man's foul breath and felt the hot rush of blood that coated his hands—his mouth. But something else entirely had made the kill. Something Malcolm did not want to inspect too closely, for he wasn't completely sure it wasn't still him, peeled free of all civility.

"He was goin' to kill my wife," Malcolm explained with a flippant wave of his hand. "I stopped him."

The twins blinked at him.

"Allow me to rephrase the question, my laird, since ye dinnae seem to be keen on divulging yer secrets on yer own." Finlay leaned over the arm of his chair and pegged Malcolm with bright, curious eyes. "How exactly did ye manage to rip off *both* his arms *and* his head with naught but yer bare hands?"

Malcolm frowned and ran his tongue over his teeth as though he expected his canines to grow as he remembered how easily they'd sunk into flesh. At a loss for words, the persistent drum of Bram's fingers on the table drew his attention to the more subdued twin.

"We all saw ye bolt out o' the keep with yer eyes glowin' brighter than Kerr's forge on a winter's night," Bram said, his voice soft. "Ye looked…ye didnae look right, my laird. Ye looked like a goddamn highland berserker. Help us understand."

Finlay sheathed his blade at his hip and folded his arms over his chest. "The men stationed on the wall the night ye threw the vagrant from yer window said there was a moment they saw glowin' white eyes lookin' down on them," he said. "I didnae believe them. Now, I do."

Malcolm heaved a breath and ran his thumb over the side of his empty tumbler as he weighed the merit of sharing with them the basis of his curse. Several moments passed while the twins waited expectantly.

"What ye saw today," Malcolm began in a low voice, "was the price I paid to save my brother—the price I paid so he can reunite with

Meggie again. I swore a blood oath to Coira's mother the night she turned the oak to stone. While our hands were joined, I promised to protect Coira from danger, with my life if need be, and bound my soul with hers. That's how I ken where she is when her life is threatened… and even when it's no'." He patted his chest. "I feel her in here. The thread that connects us."

Malcolm told them everything, beginning with the day he met Coira and how she saved his life after his fall from Ramsey, and ended with her preserving Farlan's life in the pine grove.

"There's somethin' inside me." He rubbed the muscle over where he felt the creature sleeping, and found he no longer despised it. "It comes alive and gives me the strength I need… Och, I didnae ken how it works, only that it alters me so that I am tireless, immensely strong, and savage enough to do what needs to be done." His cousins listened quietly as Malcolm admitted, "But I now fear what the rest o' the clan will do when they find out their laird is no' what he appears to be, now that they ken a monster lurks within. A man can only be so loyal."

Bram scoffed and pointed a rigid finger at Malcolm's chest. "That's nonsense. We'd all follow ye to the ends o' the earth if that's where ye chose to go."

Finlay nodded in agreement. "It little matters to me that yer eyes glow or that ye grow ghastly fangs when yer wife is in peril. I ken a fair amount o' men that would swear away years off their lives for a chance to defend their families in such a way." Sucking on his teeth, Finlay dropped his foot to the floor and shook his head. "No. I dinnae believe ye were so much cursed, as ye were gifted."

Malcolm let loose a relieved chuckle and rubbed his face. "I'm startin' to believe yer right about that."

Finlay grinned and waggled his brows, his chest puffed out with self-importance from his laird's praise.

"O' course I am."

Bram rolled his eyes, beyond sick of his brother, and said to his twin with a deadpan stare, "Yer the biggest pain in the arse."

Malcolm couldn't help the laugh that escaped him.

CHAPTER TWENTY

COIRA

Autumn left the Scottish Lowlands in a flurry of dead leaves and hoarfrost and replaced them with snowdrifts and icicles that hung dangerously from the shingled rooftops of Ghlas Thùr. The once bright, colorful countryside transformed into drab hues of brown, white, black, and the dark evergreen of pine and conifer trees under a perpetually grey sky. Even the loch succumbed to the chilly temperatures and crusted over in a thin layer of ice more days than not.

Without a source of heat, the frigid months of deep winter made work in my tower miserable, and by the start of November, my frozen fingers and toes forced me to abandon it until spring returned. To keep myself busy during the dreary days, I converted one of the lower-level chambers into a type of surgery and a reliable option for those who needed aid. It had come to my attention that the villagers had been in sore need of a proper healer for years. The woman that filled the post was more of a herbalist and tea maker than a healer, and after speaking with her, I found she was relieved the burden would no longer be her own. Word spread quickly through the village and the surrounding land, and by Christmas, it was uncommon for a day or two to pass without someone seeking my help.

Located directly inside the south wing from the great hall, it contained two small beds set to the right of the door and a table that took dominion in the center of the room. Maeve and I swept the floor clean, then scrubbed the stone with lemon-scented soap. Along the back wall between two windows stood a desk and shelving which held my equipment. Several tins of pine tar, linen strips of every size, sage smudges, ginger roots, humble moss, and charcoal were at my disposal. Willow bark, valerian root, and dried juniper berries served as pain relievers, easily brewed into tea with honey. A tall, green-glass cylinder held three leeches I had brought from the loch one day during the summer months. I'd collected them by wading in the murkier north-shore with my skirt cinched high about my waist. Maeve had not been at all amused when I'd walked out of the depths and asked her to gently remove them from the back of my thighs.

While I didn't agree with the term 'leeching', nor using them to remedy fevers or sickness, the slimy little creatures were very useful at alleviating swelling under the skin. Since the day I had stolen them from their muddy homes, they'd tripled in size, staying fat and fed by sucking soft, purple contusions from a well-placed elbow connecting with a poorly-defended eye during training.

Finlay had been the first to receive the attention of my new pets. He'd shown up in my healer's chamber with a splendid purple eyelid protruding two finger-widths from his face. He balked at my suggestion for only a moment before Maeve walked in and fixed him with a hard stare. All bravado promptly disappeared after that. With a grumble, he'd thrown himself down on one of the beds and allowed me to place a leech. An hour later, two bulging black bodies had rolled down his cheek to land with a plop on the pillow, and Finlay found he could open his eye again.

After that, the garrison's men regularly asked for the leech's kiss.

Malcolm had surprised me with a gift of surgeon's instruments from London a few weeks after I had begun offering my services to the people; a ghastly collection of bone saws and chisels that I couldn't imagine using on the flesh outside of a battle site. Most of the tools I'd promptly stored at the bottom of a chest, padded and wrapped within the leather case they had arrived in. I didn't have the heart to tell him they were more along the lines of torture devices than healer's tools.

The *useful* items, like the curved needles, tweezers, and an assortment of shears and razors, I used almost daily. The pliers also came in handy for the common tooth extraction. At some point I would successfully instill the importance of oral hygiene to the common folk, but until that day came, the pliers would stay at the ready.

Malcolm's strict orders of no outsiders employed within the keep walls were followed to the letter, as was the unbendable rule that forbade me to wander outside the walls without an armed guard of not one… but two. He did not receive an argument from me on either decree; with two attempts on my life—attempts that came dangerously close to success—we still hadn't the faintest idea who was behind it.

January and February passed by without another incident, and while those at Ghlas Thùr waited impatiently for the warm breath of soil-scented spring, Malcolm and I preferred to spend lazy days like today lingering in bed until the sun climbed high in the sky. One cold March morning, under the weight of the covers and furs, he'd wrapped his limbs around me like vines, favoring our shared body heat over coaxing a fire from the embers in the hearth.

I didn't mind a bit.

He let out a heavy breath when I ran my fingernails over his nape and shoulders, his face plastered between my bare breasts while he enjoyed my attentions. I smiled to myself; there was not a man on this earth that enjoyed being touched more than he. I took advantage of every occasion and stroked him like I would a fat, lazy kitten, full after a meal of cream.

Our relationship had changed over the last months—wonderfully so. Instead of the shy, hesitant dance of push and pull, it became an explosion of passion and fierce attachment that took my breath away. My trust in him had grown exceedingly, so much I'd stopped feeling the shame and self-pity that had always been present when my scars were uncovered and his to see. By now, there was not an inch of my skin he had not kissed or caressed with love and tenderness. It was the most wonderful, freeing feeling in the world.

He accepted me, flaws and all.

I remembered the moment I first allowed myself to relax. It had happened weeks ago while I sat on Malcolm's lap in bed, late one evening, my bare legs wrapped tightly around his waist as he rocked within me. I had felt the last of my reserve dissolve and, for the first time in over a decade, I was uninhibited by my flawed skin and had shed any lingering doubt that Malcolm saw me as anything other than perfect.

"Are those tears I see?" he asked gently when he stilled within me and thumbed the dampness that had collected on my lashes. "Why do ye cry, Angel?"

I hid my face against his neck and kissed the rapid pulse beneath his skin twice before answering.

"They're happy tears, I assure ye."

"For the pleasure I bring to life inside ye?" I could hear the smile in his voice as he palmed the flesh of my backside and pulled me ever closer to push deeper within me. With a low moan at the feeling of fullness, I wrapped my arms tighter around his shoulders; I couldn't get close enough.

"Och, ye've become a wanton woman after a few months in my bed."

With a gasp, I pulled away to deny it, only to find a wicked grin spread across his handsome face. I pursed my lips to keep them from lifting.

"Beast," I said in mock severity.

With a bark of laughter, he flipped us around effortlessly in one swift movement, and I found my back pressed against the blankets. Malcolm's cock plunged so deep within me I could feel him at the entrance of my womb. Curled around me, he kissed between my brows, the corners of my mouth, and then brushed his lips along the shell of my ear. His whispered breath made my toes curl, and he retreated from my body in one long, drawn-out stroke.

"Witch," he crooned, and then forced a magic of his own upon me.

"What do ye think about, Angel?" Malcolm asked when he turned his face upon my chest and took one of my nipples into his mouth, effectively bringing me back to the present.

I opened my mouth and then snapped it shut, embarrassed at being caught with such personal and lascivious thoughts.

"I—I dinnae wish to say."

"Och, now ye must," he said with a laugh and rolled over to drag me atop his chest. His dark eyes were still heavy with sleep, a lazy grin upon his lips, and he speared his fingers into my wild hair, tangled and knotted from last night's attentions. My eyes fluttered closed at the first delicious tug of his grip at their roots.

"Tell me," he demanded. "What brings that blush upon yer cheeks? I willnae let ye go 'til ye confess."

I believed him; Malcolm didn't make idle threats, especially ones he made in our bed. The night he'd tied my wrists to the bedpost was the night I began to take his warnings seriously.

I licked my lips, unsure how to put my thoughts into words without dying of humility, and rasped, "May I show ye instead?"

"Och, is my Angel shy this morn?" His brown eyes twinkled, but he released his grip in my hair and looked at me expectantly. "Alright then. Show away."

I kept my gaze fixed on his face, and heat bloomed low in my belly when I lowered my lips to the soft smattering of dark hair on the bridge of his chest. As I kissed along his abdomen, the thick chain of muscle clenched beneath my touch, and his hands fell away from my head as I went lower still, past his navel. The amused glint in his eyes turned into something dark and sultry when I let my tongue slip out to taste the enticing V of sinuous muscle between his hips.

"What are ye doin' to me woman?" His voice was rough and rumbled, his heavy-lidded stare locked with mine.

I could feel the curls between my legs dampen at the carnal look on his face—at how heavily he breathed—and I grew bold enough to say, "I want to taste ye, as ye've tasted me. Would ye let me do that?"

Malcolm's pupils dilated, his focus wholly on my mouth now poised over the broad head of his cock. He nodded.

"Och, God yes—"

A strangled moan rumbled from deep in his throat when I brazenly licked him, and his salty, male flavor spread over my tongue. The sight of him, unguarded while I knelt between his long legs, was the most arousing thing I had ever seen. His neck arched to stare at me while his hands twisted tight in the sheets. I could feel the evidence of my lust begin to slide down the inside of one of my thighs, and I pressed them tightly together in an attempt to control my growing need for him.

Until today, I'd never been so bold with him. Until today I'd been content to follow his lead. Ever the subject, never the master.

That would change today.

I took my cues from his reactions and wrapped my hand around his shaft. I stroked him from base to tip once, twice, then took him into my mouth for the first time. His hips jerked forward, surprising me so much I pulled back.

Caressing my jaw in apology, his thumb traced my bottom lip. "Ye have no idea how good that feels or the effect ye have on me. I am completely at yer mercy."

My courage bolstered at that revelation, any reserve I had left effectively destroyed, and I took him into my mouth as deeply as I could. Over and over, I let my tongue slide down the hard length of him, careful to only allow the barest pressure of my teeth to touch him while I stroked him with my mouth.

With a sharp curse, Malcolm sat up and hauled me up his body so that my thighs hedged his hips.

"I willnae last long with that sweet mouth o' yers, and I want to finish inside ye." He ran his hand down along my stomach to cup my core. "My God, yer soakin' wet," he groaned, and his eyelids shuttered. "Ye'll never ken how much I love that."

I settled my palms on the rounded muscles of his shoulders and let my head fall back when he sheathed himself inside me with one powerful thrust. Possessively, he gripped my hips, his fingers denting my flesh, and urged me to move against him.

I needed no other persuasion.

With a roll of my hips, I concentrated on where our bodies were joined as the little pleasure bud he paid so much adoring attention to rubbed against him.

"Faster," he demanded. He released my hips and splayed his hands greedily on the globe of my buttocks. I moaned when his fingers dug deep and forced me to move faster. Within moments my throat became dry, my breath ragged from the pace he set. Lost in a myriad of sensations, I wholeheartedly let myself go to the demands of the man beneath me. My body wound tighter and tighter, and I couldn't have slowed down if I had tried. I gasped for air and chased the release that promised to flay my soul wide open.

With a barked curse, Malcolm trembled between my thighs, and my body exploded in a storm of blissful intensity. It overtook my blood, my nerves, my mind, and ended with a heavy, knocking pulse at the apex of my legs. Still connected, we panted in each other's arms, and Malcolm kissed the column of my neck. I grinned like a fool, delirious from my exertion and the attentions Malcolm had made upon me. My toes curled among the sheets when he placed an open-mouthed kiss along my racing pulse.

"I want every day to begin exactly like that," Malcolm murmured breathlessly against my throat. "When we're eighty, covered in wrinkles, and my bollocks are hangin' on by a thread, promise me we'll do this."

I laughed and caught his face between my hands so that I could kiss the tip of his nose. "I cannae promise ye that, but that was definitely a thing to be repeated."

～

"Excuse me, milady, but I was told ye have someone waitin' for ye in yer healer's chamber."

Malcolm paused his reading of *A Midsummer Night's Dream,* and I turned in the chair I lounged in to find a maid with her arms full of laundry just outside the library doors.

"Do ye ken who it is?" I stretched, sleepy from the comforting heat of the roaring fire in the hearth, the smooth cadence of Malcolm's deep voice, and my belly full of the noon meal we shared.

"No, milady. I was only told to relay the message." She dipped a curtsy and disappeared down the hall.

"Well." I stood up and bent to place a kiss upon Malcolm's lips. "Ye ken I adore the part where Titania wakes and tells her husband all about the strange dream she had about bein' in love with an ass, but duty calls."

He grinned and placed the book on a low table where the gold filigree embossed on the spine reflected the light that shone through the tall windows.

"Ye remind me o' Tatiana before she wakes. Feisty and headstrong. Go, I'm happy to wait and finish when ye get back."

I turned on my heel with a smirk and hurried down the hall, already impatient to be back at my husband's side. Weaving my way down the spiral stair, I hummed a cheerful little tune and passed the maids who worked tirelessly to rid the keep of the musty stench of winter. I pushed through the door to my healer's chamber with a dreamy smile on my face—

And came face-to-face with Father Blount.

"Hello, my dear, Lady MacKinnon," the priest said and lifted his right hand wrapped in a bloody cloth. "I had a bit of a mishap with some broken glass, and I fear the wound is beyond my abilities."

His English inflection, no matter how many times I had heard it during church service, was always a shock to my nerves. I stared at him with only one foot over the threshold, a smile frozen on my face, and gripped the door handle as though it could anchor me in the present. I felt as if I was thirteen again, transported back through time, and I wanted nothing more than to flee. But I was rooted in place by his strangely kind stare, his soft smile a stark comparison to the memory of how he had baited the crowd while my hair had fallen in clumps around me. I remembered his sneer and what it felt like to be tied to the pyre, the stench of rotten food still clinging to my clothing.

Then saw my father the moment he had shut the gate between us, the iron clang a thunderclap of finality in my mind.

I had never been in a position to give aid to someone I would rather see dead ten times over. Thirteen years ago, this man had sold my cousin and ordered me to be burned alive. He was the reason my mother had spent the rest of her life in perpetual heartache. I felt sick just being in the same room as him. How could I bring myself to lay a kind hand upon him when I wanted to tear him to pieces? I wanted to scar his body as he had scarred mine.

Standing beside the table in the middle of the room, Blount looked at me expectantly. I patted my hair to make sure it covered my scars and, with a nervous breath, stepped further into the room, leaving the door open wide behind me. I couldn't rightfully order the priest out of the keep, no matter how terrified I was. No, I needed to see to his needs as I did for everyone else as quickly as possible. The faster I did, the sooner he would leave, and I would be free to breathe easy again.

I cleared my throat. "Glass ye said? Would ye mind if I took a look?"

He held out his hand, palm up. "Not at all, that's why I'm here. You have something of a reputation in the village. They tell me none of the wounds you tend to fester."

"That was kind o' them to say," I said, and barely schooled my features of disgust when I took his hand within my own.

From the corner of my eye, I noticed how he'd aged since that terrible day in Norwich. Nearly bald now, his scalp was marked with spots, his eyes lined with deep wrinkles. His hands, inflamed and gnarled, were bound with arthritis that bent his fingers outward at a painful-looking angle. Clenching my teeth in an effort to keep my touch steady and light, I unwrapped his hand to reveal a nasty slice in the webbing between his thumb and his forefinger.

"That's an impressive wound ye have there. I'm sorry to say it will need stitching," I murmured honestly.

I turned away after directing him to have a seat on one of the stools tucked under the table. With my back to him, I took a steadying breath and gathered supplies off the shelves on the far wall. After placing a pan, a small bottle of scotch, my sewing kit, and a tin of salve between us, I settled onto the stool to his left.

"This is why yer wound willnae fester," I explained, and doused his hand with a liberal amount of scotch over the shallow dish.

I ignored his sharp hiss at the sting and prodded the wound with my thumbs to be certain I wouldn't stitch any shards of glass within.

Satisfied the cut was clean and clear of debris, I dipped my fingertips in the bowl and threaded a curved needle with a boiled horsehair.

A small part of me wished I had the nerve to leave his wound to putrefy and give myself the future satisfaction of sawing off his limb with one of those dreadful inventions Malcolm had gifted me. Unfortunately, the person I was would only allowed me to dream it and be content with the musical notes of his muffled whimpers as I closed the rent in his soft, callous-free palm.

"You have a light touch, my dear," he wheezed unconvincingly, and flashed teeth permanently stained grey from wine. If I weren't so damn tense, I would have snorted at the blatant lie.

My lower back was beginning to ache from holding myself rigid while I worked. Concentrating on the fluid, familiar movements— poke, pull, knot, repeat—I closed his wound in a neat line. It relaxed me ever so slightly, and when he stopped his whimpering halfway through, I pretended as though he were someone else entirely.

When I had completed the last stitch, I smeared a liberal dollop of salve—a mixture of honey, garlic, and clove oil—along the line of knots, padded it with humble moss, and bound his hand with a strip of linen.

Finally, I could make my escape.

"Ye can take the bandage off the day after next and come back in ten to remove the stitches if ye cannae remove them yerself."

Cleaning up after myself, I replaced the tin and my sewing kit on the shelves and turned to find Father Blount seated motionless at the table, his focus fixated on my face. His earlier pleasant demeanor had morphed into something else entirely, and his brows had drawn low in concentration.

He canted his head. "I know you…from before…"

Alarmed by the look in his eyes, my guts knotted painfully when his focus landed on the right side of my face, and his lips mouthed a soundless *impossible*. My hand flew to my hair, and to my horror, I found a few strands had caught on my ear, revealing the ruined parts of my cheek and neck to his hard stare.

Oh no.

I cursed myself and the ease I had become accustomed to within the walls of the keep. I should have known better, and like a fool, I unwittingly let my guard drop around the one person I should have been the most cautious around.

"Where did you get those scars?" His soft words were harsh and slightly demanding, the lighthearted cadence he had arrived with gone entirely.

Father Blount stood and placed himself between me and the door. It didn't matter that he was over twice my age and his back was slightly bowed, I was terrified of him all the same, and because of that, he knew he held power over me.

A response failed to form, my mouth as dry as a desert and my tongue an unmoving stone. I pressed my lower back painfully against the lip of my desk in a bid to put more space between us and desperately grappled for any excuse, however lame, to throw him off the trail of truth. I had known there was a possibility the priest would see me without the veil I wore to the church services, and I should have had an excuse ready. But at that moment, I felt every bit of the paralyzing fear that had overwhelmed me as a young girl, and my mind failed to come up with even a small story.

Rooted in place, I witnessed the moment he had remembered me. When his cynical examination had flitted over my face and pale blonde hair, unchanged since I was a young girl, he remembered who I was. Recognition had flashed over his features, and his upper lip lifted with a sneer of scorn and disgust. It was the same look he'd had when he ordered Ness and I to be taken to the church.

My stomach cramped, my body threatening to toss up my lunch, and I tensed, prepared to flee. I could outrun him. His body was old and frail, mine young and strong, and I would be miles away before he rallied the people to his side.

I managed to take one step toward the door when a deep voice calmed my frayed nerves like a cool breeze on a hot day.

"Hallo there, Father," Malcolm said when he ducked into the chamber. His brown eyes snapped to mine and read the anxiety etched on my face.

Father Blount squared his shoulders as Malcolm strolled confidently through the room and curled a protective arm around my shoulders. The priest's eyes narrowed slightly at the possessive movement.

"Laird MacKinnon. How nice to see you." The priest looked between us as though he wondered how much Malcolm knew about me or if he should be forthright in telling him that he knew his wife to be a witch.

The tension in the room was palpable and I leaned into Malcolm's side while he politely smiled at the man who had his full attention.

"I must say, Father Blount, I believe this is the verra first time ye've visited the keep since ye began yer station, aye? And it only took ye needin' my lovely wife's skill. We're lucky to have a woman with such a vast knowledge in the art o' healin', would ye no' agree?" Malcolm squeezed my shoulder a bit and kissed the crown of my head before he stated, "I'm proud to be married to a woman so *indispensable* to the clan, our own priest's faith in her abilities are proof o' that. I dinnae ken what we'd do without her."

He might as well have bared his teeth and thumped his chest and said, *Threaten her, and forfeit yer life.*

Father Blount examined the wrapping on his hand and said, "Yes, well, these old bones ache in the cold months and makes the trek up here hard on the knees." Looking up, he pegged Malcolm with a hard stare as he backed toward the door. "But I will see you both again during service. Having good *Christian* leaders is important to communities, as you well know."

With one last glare at me, he disappeared toward the great hall. I tightened my grip on the back of Malcolm's shirt to stop him from following the priest, forcing him to stay with me until we heard the heavy door to the keep open and shut with a forceful thud.

"Are ye alright, Angel? What did he say to ye?" Malcolm's hands cradled my jaw, strong and comforting, but their presence did little to calm the turmoil that writhed in my gut.

"No, I'm no' alright. He recognized me. He saw my scars and he *remembered* me. What am I gonna do?" Hot tears of frustration slid down my cheeks. "I cannae go to the church again, Malcolm. He'll tell them all what I am—"

"And what are ye? Who are ye other than *my* wife, *their* lady? Yer the woman who saved them from starvation. The woman who mended their wounds and set their bones, and all the while they came to love ye. Just like I do."

He wiped away my tears and kissed me, his warm lips hard against mine, then rested his chin on the crown of my head. I melted against his chest.

"I will keep ye safe. No' because the oath I swore demands me, but because I cannae imagine my life without ye. No one, no priest, nor pope, will be takin' ye from me."

Another month passed, and spring arrived. Father Blount never returned to have his stitches removed, and I was not forced to endure his presence beyond the hours I spent in the church for Sunday services. I had expected him to berate me publicly, but instead, he studiously ignored me and read from his Bible while I sweated in the front pew.

April in the lowlands, unaffected by a late snow, was a splash of bright green and yellow. After almost a year as the Lady of Ghlas Thùr, I was thoroughly immersed in castle life and no longer felt like a charlatan.

While the castle residents celebrated the long-awaited union between Finlay and Maeve, I settled into my chair and watched the newlyweds through the gaps between dancing couples. Maeve was lovely. Dressed in my dusky-pink gown, temporarily altered to fit her slight curves, she was a vision. Her blonde curls, long and loose, were adorned with a crown of blue and white wildflowers I had woven for her myself.

"Since ye made me the goddess o' spring, I will crown ye it's queen," I had said while I played bridesmaid to her in my chamber earlier today.

Finlay looked dashing in his new snowy-white shirt and black vest, the MacKinnon colors worn proudly around his hips, and his cherubic curls falling into his eyes. But like the scoundrel he was, he hadn't been able to keep his hands off his new wife since he had slipped the dainty silver ring on her finger, not that Maeve minded.

I chuckled to myself at how Finlay's fingers toyed with her hair, and he couldn't let more than a minute go by without kissing her. I figured if I'd had to keep my love from Malcolm secret for years, I'd have had a hard time keeping my hands to myself, too. Now married, they had a chamber on the second floor where they could enjoy endless hours together in private instead of stolen trysts throughout the keep. I just knew they'd be making beautiful babies in no time.

As I watched them giggling at one another, lost in their own little world, I rested my hand on my flat stomach, the slight movement hidden beneath the table. My courses were three days late, but I knew the moment I had conceived. It happened in the middle of the night after Malcolm had made love to me. It was a moment I'd never forget.

A radiating flush infused my body with heat, waking me out of a deep sleep, and I found my skin glowing with a soft golden shimmer that matched Malcolm's as he lay beside me. I had just run my fingertips lightly down the back of his arm, marveling at its glow, when he turned and reached for me, his eyes illuminated with the strange, white light of his beast.

But this time, there was no danger.

"Angel," he murmured. "I need ye."

Still slick from his earlier attentions, Malcolm pulled me astride him and entered me in one powerful surge of his hips. We watched one another while I rode him, and before long the shimmering of our skin faded, and a very different explosion of sparks replaced it.

Wrapped in his arms, with my cheek pillowed on his chest, we waited for our bodies to cool and our ragged breathing to subside. I asked Malcolm to tell me of the blood oath one last time; I needed to hear it word-for-word to affirm my suspicions.

"I've told ye all this before. She cut her palm, and then mine, and when she joined our hands, she asked me to swear to her that I would collect ye before the marsh violet bloomed, which I did… barely." I giggled, earning myself a quick pinch on my ribs when he said, "Brat. Will ye ever let me live that down?"

"Maybe someday," I lied. I actually planned on placing the little purple flower in pots around the keep for him to find each spring.

Malcolm sighed and shook his head with mock remorse, accepting his fate.

"She then asked me to swear to bind my life with yers, which we did in the church when we married, and to keep ye safe until the day I die."

I was quiet for a moment as I listened to the da-dum, da-dum of his heartbeat and the air filling his lungs.

"I dinnae believe the binding meant marriage, Malcolm. I believe we fulfilled that part o' yer oath just this night."

Malcolm's hand stilled from its lazy journey along my hip before he jerked the blankets off of us. Sitting up, he rested one of his hands on my belly. The look on his face in the silvery moonlight was one of awe and tenderness.

"Are ye with child, my love? Is that what she meant?"

I folded my hand over his and blinked away my tears of joy. "Aye, I think it just happened."

Malcolm covered my body with his and hugged me fiercely before kissing my cheeks, my forehead, my neck, and then moved lower so he could press the barest of kisses to the skin below my navel.

I pushed his midnight hair away from his face, and he looked at me with wonder when he said, "If it's a boy, I want to name him Colin."

Swallowing my emotions, I nodded in agreement and lost the battle with my tears. His face blurred, and my voice cracked as I said, "And if it's a girl, I want to name her Vanora."

"What does that look mean, Angel?" Malcolm asked when he claimed his seat beside me and took a swallow of ale. I shook free of my memories and gave him a shy smile.

"I believe I'll have this look upon my face for the next nine months, so ye better get used to it," I whispered. With a tender grin, Malcolm grasped my hand and brought my palm to his lips, a silent promise of love.

My skin still tingled from his kiss when the keep's main doors opened, and with a gust of wet, spring air, a stranger swaggered into the great hall. The music halted, and everyone turned to appraise the newcomer. Several of Malcolm's cousins and closest guards slid their hands over the hilts of their daggers, their previously merry expressions now hard and murderous at the possible threat to their laird.

Tall and lean, the intruder was dressed in black from head to toe, his long legs clad in oiled leather. A three-day growth of beard, a few shades darker than his chocolate brown hair, roughed up his sinfully handsome face and sharp jawline. Keen hazel eyes that seemed familiar snapped toward Malcolm, and he stretched his arms out wide.

"Miss me, Mal?"

"What the bloody hell." Malcolm rocked back in his seat and looked at the newcomer with surprised delight. "Where have ye been, ye sly bastard?" he crowed, and his chair groaned against the stone floor when he pushed away from the table. Malcolm rushed toward the stranger like a charging bull and enveloped him in a rough embrace, like a man would a brother or comrade, clapping him hard on the back.

"Och, ye ken I cannae stay in one place for too long before I feel the need to wander," our visitor answered with a grin and looked over at me with bright curiosity. "I heard ye married and I wished to express my congratulations personally."

The cause of alarm over, Malcolm's men relaxed, and the music started once again. The laird proudly gestured my way and ushered his guest to the empty chair that Farlan had vacated earlier. I watched the man in black curiously as he extended his long legs beneath the table in front of me. He moved with the grace of a dancer, fluid and sinuous, reminding me of clear water flowing over smooth stone.

"Raith Buchannan, allow me to introduce ye to my lovely wife, Coira, Lady of Ghlas Thùr." Malcolm looked at me heatedly with a wink. "I fostered under Raith's father when I was sixteen. He's been a good friend to me ever since."

Raith's intense focus never wavered from mine, familiar and frank. It was as though he already knew who I was, like we'd known one another for years.

"There is no better friend to have than I. I'm glad ye realize it to be so."

Malcolm scoffed into his tankard. "Yer also an arrogant bastard."

The men laughed together, comfortable with one another, as if they had never been apart. It was rare for Malcolm let his guard down and enjoy verbal banter, and as I watched his eyes brighten, I wondered if he had often been like this with his brother.

"Somethin' I ken ye appreciate in someone other than yerself," Raith shot back. He leaned forward to smack Malcolm's shoulder playfully, only to lower his brows and poke the laird's chest in mock severity. "Where'd the stern scholar disappear to? He's been replaced by a warrior! Yer bloody enormous, man."

Bram chuckled from beside me even though he tried to make it appear as though he wasn't eavesdropping.

The laird rolled his eyes and poured ale into the empty tankard in front of his friend. "I assure ye, the scholar is still verra much alive within me. And I'll warn ye now; I no longer care for the heart-racing amusements ye bullied me into all those years ago. I nearly died twice followin' ye around and I'm too old to survive yer antics." Raith held his hands up in surrender, and Malcolm chuckled before asking, "Now tell me, old friend, what trouble have ye been gettin' yerself into these past few years?"

A strange gleam flashed in Raith's eyes. "Funny ye should ask me that."

Quick as an adder, Raith brandished a dagger I hadn't noticed on his person. Before anyone could react, and with a speed I could barely follow, he sunk the tip two inches deep into the thick wood of the table in front of Malcolm with a loud *thunk*.

I cried out in surprise and flung myself against the back of my chair to put as much distance between myself and the madman Malcolm had welcomed into our home. Deathly silence fell over the hall, and the faces of the men surrounding us soured from merriment to fury in the span of a moment. Chaos erupted, and every armed clan member rushed to our aid, knocking over chairs and spilling drinks in their haste.

Women and children cried out in confusion and either fled the hall or huddled against the walls. A few men from the village leaped over their table to get closer to the knave, the tips of their dirks bared and deadly. From his place at my right, Bram, unarmed but undeterred, forced his body between mine and any other threat that may come my way. He shoved me harder against the unforgiving wood of my chair, and I craned my neck to see over his shoulder.

Raith reclined in his seat as though he were sitting upon a throne. With his elegant hands folded over his belt, and not a hair out of place, his gaze flitted over the surrounding weapons. I narrowed my eyes at him, curious to know why he didn't appear the least bit worried that the entirety of the MacKinnon clan stood ready to sever his head from his shoulders.

Instead of wetting himself with fright like any man surrounded by thirty angry, half-drunk warriors would do, Raith's mouth spread into a wicked grin. Farlan grasped the fabric of his jacket in an unbreakable grip and lifted him halfway out of his seat. Raith ignored the hulking warrior and locked his glittering, nearly maniacal focus on my husband as though he waited for something, his excitement plain to see.

Amidst the chaos, Malcolm slowly rose to his feet, his gaze riveted on the table.

"Halt!" Malcolm's voice echoed off the stone walls, and his fist came down upon the table with a meaty thump before Farlan could plunge his blade into Raith's neck.

"I said halt!"

The hall fell silent.

Satisfied no blood would be spilled in the hall, the laird planted his fists firmly on the table and leaned his weight over his knuckles. His upper lip was turned up with a mixture of rage and disbelief as he looked down upon the red-handled dagger that Raith had stuck in the thick wood before him. Malcolm wrapped his hand around the vaguely familiar hilt and wrenched it loose before he turned a murderous eye on his long-time friend. Bram pressed me harder against the backrest, prepared for bloodshed.

"Where did ye get this?" Malcolm asked in an anger-laced whisper. I saw a twitch in his neck and wondered if his beast was fighting to make an appearance.

Raith looked at me, and his eyes softened ever so slightly before he glanced up at my husband.

"We need to talk, Mal."

Chapter Twenty-One

MALCOLM

"Come not between the dragon and his wrath."
-William Shakespeare, King Lear

The polished, red-handled dagger he held gleamed in the candlelight and kindled a fury within Malcolm he hadn't felt in months. Not since the second attempt on Coira's life. The oath dragged phantom claws along Malcolm's insides in a silent request for retribution but otherwise stayed contained, if not content to sit back and wait.

No' yet, Malcolm thought, and cast a glance to his right in time to see Coira shove Bram away and peel herself off the back of her chair. Color made a slow return to her blanched face, but she gave Malcolm a little nod to confirm she was alright. Satisfied she was unharmed and flanked by several warriors, he turned his focus on Raith who shrugged Farlan's hand off his collar and leaned back in his chair as though he hadn't a care in the world.

Arrogant bastard indeed. Not many men would feel the ease he displayed with a swords pointed at the back of his neck and chest, and the wicked little dagger Gavin held ready to plunge between Raith's ribs. The indifference to his surroundings gave Malcolm pause. He sensed no malice or deceit from Raith, which was at odds with the threat he just imposed upon his wife. That—and the fact that a certain toothy beast hadn't taken over his body—was enough to convince himself to hear his old friend out. Trusting his instincts, Malcolm slowly lowered his weight into his chair and inspected the dagger. Turning it over, he found it was the same as the others, alike in every way from pommel to tip.

"That dagger was meant for yer wife's heart," Raith stated and ignored the few muffled gasps that whispered through the hall. "And as ye can see, it missed its mark."

"If that's what ye wish to call it," Farlan grumbled from Malcolm's side. The tip of his short sword rested on Raith's shoulder, ready to strike at the slightest movement.

"I do, my sour-looking friend," Raith said sardonically before he looked back at Malcolm. "I missed in the name o' friendship, regardless o' the reputation I must uphold, which is forever ruined." Malcolm snorted and Raith ran a finger under the flat of Farlan's blade as if it were the throat of his lover. "Ye ken it would be a pity if yer men gutted me now, Mal. Call them off so we may talk as friends."

Malcolm rolled his eyes. "Ye look comfortable as ye are, so I dinnae think I will."

The MacKinnon laird looked upon his friend with a shrewd eye. Dressed in black leather and a thick, sturdy linen jacket with pockets, hidden flaps, straps, sheaths, and the cowl that rested on his back, Raith looked far from his father's heir and more like a scoundrel. Malcolm narrowed his eyes.

The two men had seen one another sporadically throughout the years, mostly during the Gatherings. But Raith had been absent from them the past few years, much to Malcolm's disappointment. As far as he knew, Raith was back at O'ran na Mara living a pampered life, not gallivanting over the land alone, dressed like a reaper.

He looks like an executioner, he thought, and asked aloud, "What exactly is this *reputation* ye've ruined by no' killin' my wife?"

Raith looked around, taking stock of the angry soldiers surrounding them. It would only take be a nod from their laird, and

Raith would resemble a pincushion in a matter of moments. He heaved a heavy sigh and shrugged.

"Can we no' speak in private, auld friend? Ye'll want to hear what I have to say, but what pertains to myself is *my* secret, ye understand. If ye wish me to speak out here, it will only be half-truths."

"After ye just—"

"I ken what yer about to say, Mal, but are ye verra surprised? Ye ken I have a love for all things that make the heart race. I couldnae help myself." He waved a battle-scarred hand gracefully through the air, gesturing at the men around him.

Malcolm pinched the bridge of his nose and huffed a laugh. Memories sprung up within his mind of horseracing in the rain and drunken gambling at the local tavern, followed by half-cocked fist fights when Raith had inevitably been caught cheating.

"I bet yer thinkin' about the time we scaled O'ran na Mara's cliff walls," Raith said with devilish grin Malcolm wasn't immune to. He found himself grinning back.

"Ye mean the time ye broke through yer Da's bedchamber window to steal his good scotch, or the time ye had it in yer mind to scare yer younger brother half to death in the middle o' the night?"

"Either. Those were the days, aye?" Raith snickered as he stood smoothly, heedless of the weapons pointed at him, and looked down on Malcolm expectantly. "Now how about that private audience, Laird MacKinnon?"

Several of his men quickly spoke up with a chorus of *no, my laird* and a few curses which Malcolm ignored.

"Tell me what ye can and I'll make that decision."

"Fine," Raith bemoaned. He leaned slightly over the table, and his face morphed into a mask full of sincerity. "Robena Bothan o' Clan Chattan handed me that dagger two days ago with the explicit instruction to run it through Lady MacKinnon's heart."

Malcolm's blood ran ice-cold as shouts of anger and disbelief echoed the hall.

Laird Bothan widnae dare!

That's cause for a war, I say!

How do we ken he speaks the truth?

Malcolm listened to the arguments echo off the beams high above as rage coiled in his belly, and his oath grew restless. It gnashed its teeth and licked a phantom tongue over razor-sharp claws. A vision of racing through the forests and over the hills flashed through his mind; he could practically feel the cushion of moss and leaves beneath his feet and the cold night air in his lungs. He wouldn't tire, the need for rest unthinkable. He would make it to the Bothan keep by midnight and climb their fortress walls by the light of the moon. They wouldn't see him coming, and they'd die before they sounded any alarm, not that they'd have any hope of stopping *him*. Malcolm's eyes shuttered, and he flexed his hands, imagining how their thick, sticky blood would coat them—

Coira's slim fingers entwined with his, tearing him out of his dark thoughts and grounding him. Malcolm swallowed, pressed his thumb to her palm in thanks, and mentally shook himself from the beast's influence.

"I cannae tell ye any more in such a public setting," Raith murmured in apology, unaware of Malcolm's inner turmoil.

"This could be a trap, my laird," Gavin said as he glared at Raith's back. Malcolm let out a heavy breath.

"I dinnae think so, cousin. If he wanted her dead, he would have done it as soon as he walked through the doors." Helping Coira up from her seat, Malcolm motioned for Raith to follow. "The library. Ye can spill yer secrets there."

After some arguing and Gunn threatening to flay Raith's skin from his ankles up if he so much as looked at his laird the wrong way, they finally agreed upon a compromise. Four fully-armed men would stand sentry in the hallway, with Farlan keeping watch within the library after he swore oaths of secrecy to Raith.

"Tell me, from the verra beginning. I want to hear it all," Malcolm demanded while he plodded in front of the night-darkened windows. Teeth clenched, his pacing was the only thing keeping him from marching to the Bothan keep and razing it to the ground.

"As I said before, a commission had been taken out sometime over the summer for the death o' Lady Coira. It wasnae much coin at first and attracted only the newest members o' the assassin's guild."

"Ye still need to tell me how the hell ye ended up with *that* murderous lot," Malcolm growled.

"Aye, aye, but ye asked to hear *this* tale. We'll save the account o' my soul's downfall for another time, agreed?" Raith rolled his eyes at Malcolm's droll stare. "Och, dinnae roll yer eyes at me, Laird MacKinnon. If ye insist on badgerin' me to death, I willnae speak another word, and then where will ye be?"

Coira suppressed a girlish giggle, something Malcolm rarely heard outside of their chamber. She reached out and lightly touched her fingertips to Raith's shoulder.

"Quit teasing him," she said with mock disapproval.

The dagger planted in the dining table aside, Coira had grown comfortable in Raith's presence in the past half hour. With her legs tucked beneath her in the padded chair near the hearth fire, she looked relaxed and listened intently with her chin perched on her fist.

"As ye wish," Raith said with a smirk and jostled the tankard of ale resting on his knee. "Where was I? The assassin's guild… small commission… ah! The first man to take on the task was a first-year keen on makin' his big debut—which I'm assumin' he failed miserably since Lady MacKinnon still breathes. No' that I'm surprised. I never met the lad, but word has it he was a street-rat and thief before he tried his hand at stealin' lives. If the stories are true, he was one o' the best in all England and Scotia at invading even the most defended fortresses." Raith ran his hand over his stubbled chin in thought. "I did find it interestin' that his demise was kept so quiet there wasnae even a whisper on the wind about it. 'Tis almost as though he'd vanished."

"It was an interestin' night to say the least," Malcolm grumbled as he continued to plod across the room.

Raith looked suspiciously at everyone in turn as though he could figure out what Malcolm wasn't saying and scoffed when he found them all tight-lipped. Realizing any push for more information would be futile, he continued his tale.

"After that failure, Lady Bothan piled on a substantial amount o' coin onto her previous commission, and thus attracted the likes o' *An Diabhal*."

"The Devil," Coira whispered, and curled tighter into her chair. "He certainly resembled one."

Malcolm's steps faltered when he recalled what he had done to the assassin near the sentinel stones. He remembered the blood in his mouth and how easily he'd torn tendon from bone—of soulless black eyes and filed teeth. Those sharp yellow teeth had barely raised a challenge. They'd been nothing compared to the set Malcolm had bared and sunk into the lean muscle between shoulder and neck—

"Piece o' work, isn't he?" Oblivious to Malcolm's thoughts, Raith ran his tongue along his teeth and gave a full-body shudder. "'Tis no' just his terrifyin' appearance that makes my blood run cold. He's the best knife fighter I've ever met. I've seen too many o' his victims sliced up within moments and left for dead." Raith turned to look at Coira with awe. "I dinnae ken how ye survived him, my lady."

"I almost didnae," she breathed, and her wide, cloud-pale eyes focused on Farlan where he stood in silent attention across the room. Raith followed her stare.

"*Ye* fought him?" Disbelief passed over Raith's features as he appraised Farlan from head to toe. "I cannae believe it. Ye should be sliced from ankle to earlobe and cold in the ground, yet here ye stand."

Farlan cast a side-glance at his laird, which Malcolm returned with a slight shake of his head. He trusted Raith, but not with matters of Coira's secrets. Better to keep those not of the MacKinnon clan in the dark when at all possible.

"Now that my brother's no longer with us, Farlan's my best fighter," Malcolm explained, surprised to find the sharp pain that would have once lanced his gut had lessened considerably when he spoke of Colin's absence. With that realization, a strange sense of peace settled over him, and he made a mental note to thank his wife for that serenity later.

Raith shifted in his seat, embarrassed. "I did hear about his death… I'm sorry I didnae express my sadness over his passing sooner, my friend."

Malcolm dipped his chin. "Thank ye. I take solace in the fact that he's on his way to a better place," he said honestly, and caught Coira's small smile from the corner of his eye.

God, he loved that woman.

"The angels will surely greet him in heaven," Riath said, and turned toward Farlan. "I'm glad to see *An Diabhal* met his end to a MacKinnon, though now that I ken who ye've trained with, yer triumph doesnae come as such o' a surprise." Raith tilted his tankard back to catch the last drop of ale and smacked his lips.

"Continue yer story, Raith, and try to stay on topic this time." Malcolm sighed and wrestled with his impatience that Raith was so easily distracted.

"Aye, as I said, when I met with Robena, she didnae recognize me, even though we'd been introduced several times over the years. Ye ken how she is, Mal. Only the power o' titles interest her. Her eyes had always passed right over me, bein' the spare to the heir and all." Raith rolled his eyes again before falling serious. "She told me from her own lips she wanted me to kill yer wife and make it hurt. She didnae ken that we're friends or that no amount o' coin could convince me to betray ye. So here I am, riskin' my reputation with the guild so ye can have yer vengeance."

Malcolm stopped pacing and rested his lower back against the sill while he mentally raced through all his options. His pride told him to march southeast that night and demand retribution; his fury told him to send Raith back to return Robena's dagger to *her own* heart. His brain…

Malcolm tilted his head in thought. "Where was Laird Bothan when this meeting took place?" he asked.

Raith shrugged. "I didnae see him. Robena met me outside the cookhouse."

"Ye spoke only to Lady Bothan? No' the steward, no' the guards?"

"No one else. The instructions said to be outside the cookhouse doors at midnight on a full or half-moon. I was there. Only she came out. No one else."

Malcolm closed his eyes in relief. "Farlan."

"Aye, my laird."

"Have ten men prepare to leave at dawn tomorrow. We ride to the Bothan keep."

Farlan hesitated at the door. "Only ten? Are ye certain?"

Malcolm met Coira's bright eyes from across the room. "Aye. There willnae be a battle. We'll camp on the road tomorrow night and ride to the castle at first light."

Farlan nodded and left the room.

"I'll come with ye," Raith said, and stood to offer his arm.

Malcolm pushed away from the window and clasped his hand tightly around his friend's forearm, shaking his head. "I have a more important task for ye, my friend. Stay here and protect my wife while I'm gone."

Raith blinked at him, shocked. "I—I will. With my life, have no doubt about that."

"The Sunday supper is tomorrow. Ye cannae wait until after?" Coira asked anxiously from where she leaned forward in her chair.

"No, Angel, we cannae wait even a day. Besides, our people dinnae need me here when they have ye to hear their worries."

His praise didn't have the effect he'd hoped for, and he watched the worried expression on her face grow grimmer when she pressed the palm of her hand protectively against her abdomen. Just the sight of that motherly gesture warmed his heart, and he brushed past Raith to kneel on the fur-covered floor at her feet.

"Are yer guest quarters still in the north wing?"

Malcolm looked over his shoulder to find Raith backing out of the room, a roguish smirk on his face. He had always known when to make his exit.

"Aye. Second floor, but dinnae take the one next to Finlay's or ye willnae get any sleep this night. That was his weddin' feast ye interrupted."

"Ah. Noted. Good night, Lady MacKinnon." And with a short bow, Raith swaggered down the shadowed hallway to find his bed.

"I dinnae want ye to go," Coira whispered as soon as Raith was gone, her focus on her lap.

"Nothin' will happen to me, Angel. I promise ye."

Her mouth turned down in an adorable pout and she shook her blonde head stubbornly. "Ye cannae promise me that. Ye dinnae ken what will happen a year from now, let alone a day. No one does."

Malcolm took her face within his sword-calloused palms, brushed a featherlight kiss to her lips, and touched his forehead to hers.

"I do. I also ken that if I dinnae go, there will be further attempts on yer life. Ye heard what Raith said, the bounty is raised with each failure. I cannae allow anyone to take ye from me. And 'tis no just ye anymore." Malcolm looked meaningfully at her flat belly and the precious life within. "Raith will be here to protect ye while I'm gone, and even though I could happily strangle him for that stunt in the hall, I trust him." He tucked an errant lock of her hair behind her ear and kissed her nose. "Chattan Keep is a full day's travel on horseback, but I dinnae want to spend more time than necessary in their company. As soon as we're done, we'll ride straight back. Alright?"

Coira straightened her shoulders and nodded. "Then take me to bed. I dinnae want to spend another moment talkin'."

Malcolm laughed softly, stood, and lifted her into his arms with little effort.

"Aye, my lady."

Neither of them spoke another word for the rest of the night.

Chapter Twenty-Two

COIRA

Dressed before dawn and with Maeve at my side, I watched from the steps of Ghlas Thùr as Malcolm and ten of his men rode through the main gatehouse, the warm caress of his kiss still fresh on my lips.

"I cannae believe Finlay left ye less than a turn o' the sun after ye wed," I murmured as our husbands disappeared through the fog-shrouded field beyond the curtain wall. Maeve waved a hand between us.

"Och, he would have stayed had I asked, but I ken he wanted to be with our laird." She paused and bumped her hip against mine. "Although if last night will be any indication on how our lives will be if I give the man free reign, I say it to ye now, I will *always* let him go."

I grinned at the telling blush that spread up her neck.

"Maeve!" I laughed as she fanned her cheeks and comically puffed out a breath of air.

"Och, like ye dinnae ken what I'm talkin' about." She stuck her tongue out at me and giggled as she disappeared into the keep, probably to catch up on lost sleep if she felt anything like I did.

Malcolm's attentions the previous night had been…ravenous to say the least. He left not an inch of my skin untouched by his hands or mouth, and had moved above and within me as though he wanted the impression of his body to remain during his absence.

'Tis only two days, what are ye moonin' over? I chastised myself. There had been times I'd spend weeks alone in the cottage in the wood—looked forward to them even. Those nights when I could spread out on the bed alone were coveted.

I imagined that would not be the case anymore.

The sun limped along the cloud-spotted sky as if it was chained to a mountain, and each minute behaved as though they aspired to be hours.

The highlight of my day had been stitching the eyebrow of one of the green-boys as well as binding a jammed finger. I tried to busy myself with going through my medicinal supplies and made a mental note of what I needed to order from the apothecary. Caring for the entire clan of people, I had used an alarming amount of linen bandages and willow bark. Not that I minded.

Seated at my desk, my head pillowed on my arm, I listened to the bustle of moving furniture in the great hall and idly tapped on the green-glass cylinder that held my leeches. Through heavy lids, I watched them, mesmerized as they fluttered together in their watery dance.

"May I escort ye to supper?"

The sound of a male voice at my back startled me and my eyes snapped open in drowsy alarm. I spun in my chair to find Raith leaning against my surgery door; candlelight from the great hall illuminated the left side of his face and crisp white shirt. His tartan, woven with the Buchannan colors of red and black—a stark comparison to the MacKinnon green and blue—wrapped around his hips. Without all the leather he'd arrived in, he looked less the rogue and more like a nobleman, especially with the pair of gilded dirks strapped at his waist.

I blinked at the darkened windows, surprised to find I'd slept most of the afternoon away, and discreetly wiped at the corner of my mouth before I rubbed some life back into my cheeks.

"Please do."

"I had to take a wee nap myself," Raith explained as he held his arm out for me to take and together we walked the short distance into the hall. "Bram, kind man that he is, made sure I found a guest chamber *'befitting my station.'*"

"If he did so, why were ye so tired?" I wondered out loud.

Raith shook his head and chuckled humorlessly. We wove through the gathering clan folk toward the laird's table where I settled into my usual seat. Raith, being Malcolm's envoy until he returned, claimed the large carved armchair at the head.

"Because Bram's a feckin' liar, that's why. I didnae realize he'd ushered me to the chamber beside his twin until the sound o' the newlyweds consummatin' their marriage woke me from a dead sleep." He heaved a deep sigh and ran a hand through his dark brown hair. "By then, it was too late to find another bed."

I sucked my lower lip between my teeth to keep from laughing and thought of what Maeve had said to me earlier. It was little wonder Raith had been in need of a nap.

"The man has stamina that cannae be natural," Raith muttered as he plucked a grainy brown roll off a platter and scanned the room until his attention landed on one of the kitchen maids. She gave him a sweet, sultry smile when she set a dish of roasted venison down on our table and headed back to the kitchen with an added swing to her hips. Raith waggled his brows at me as though to say, *did ye see that invitation,* then piled his plate with meat and roasted turnips.

"I dinnae think her da would be keen on havin' an assassin for a son-in-law," I chastised.

"Och, who said anythin' about marriage?"

A derisive snort escaped before I could reign in my judgment. "I suppose a second son *would* lack the pressures of marriage."

Raith frowned, his fork halfway to his mouth, when he said, "I may be a second son, but with the death o' my eldest brother, I am now my father's heir."

My cheeks heated with shame. "Forgive me."

Raith nodded his acceptance of my apology and rolled his shoulder, saying, "Happened two years ago. He died o' the same affliction that now plagues my mother. It was a long, drawn-out death with nearly a year o' bedridden pain. Some days were terrible, others he'd behave as though nothin' was amiss."

My brows lowered as I tried to think of what ailment would cause those kinds of symptoms and came up empty.

"And yer mother?"

Raith stabbed at his food as though the turnips were the cause of his mother's sickness. "She's frail and takes to her bed for days at a time before she recovers. Sometimes she's good for a day, sometimes a wee bit longer, but the illness always returns." He cleared his throat of the emotion that had crept into his words and flashed a smile that failed to reach his eyes. "An assassin I may be, Lady MacKinnon, but I am truly a coward when it comes to her pain."

I understood all too well what it was like to witness a loved one's agony. For me, it was not an illness, but my mother's heartbreak. I was born with the ability to bring a man back from the cusp of death, yet I was completely powerless to heal her heart. Some days I hadn't been able look at her; to do so would have been like witnessing my father's end all over again, and that day haunted me plenty.

A very large part of me wished I could heal with abandon and travel from town to town to cure the infirm and diseased of their ailments. Tales like Raith's were hard to ignore, and I knew the pain in his voice would fail to leave my mind any time soon.

With no advice or knowledge of a cure for his mother's unfamiliar malady I said, "Go home, Raith. Ye may no' enjoy her last moments on this earth, but ye willnae regret the time ye spent with her after she's gone."

Raith's jaw tightened. "Maybe I'll do just that after my next commission."

My brows shot high at the casual way he spoke of his next murder. "Ye murder so often ye have a waitin' list?"

His bark of laughter startled me, and I looked around nervously to make sure I hadn't been overheard by those at our table.

"No' all o' my appointments involve death, Lady MacKinnon. In fact, this next task is a bit more like kidnapping." He waved his hand in a cutting motion between us and shook his head when I opened my mouth. "Again, 'tis no' what ye assume. Think o' my next appointment as a recovery o' sorts."

I wasn't sure if I liked the sound of that any better but managed to withhold my judgment. "Where?" I asked.

"Carlisle."

"Yer guild reaches England?" Intrigued, I ran the tip of my middle finger along the rim of my chalice.

"Och, we are but a small faction o' no more than thirty or so men at a time. We were once divided by country, but after the Skeleton King took over the guild, we became blended, English and Scot alike."

"Skeleton King?"

"Aye." He cleared his throat and averted his eyes. "In fact, the commission is bein' paid by another man o' the guild. Apparently, he has a family member wrongfully held by a man in Carslile."

I frowned, wanting to hear more about this Skeleton King, but didn't pry.

"Why does he need ye?"

"Because he's too fat to scale the wall o' the fortress himself." He chuckled and shoveled a portion of turnips into his mouth before he said, "Truth is, I'm mighty excited. I've never broken anyone out o' prison before. That is where I'll go when yer husband returns."

"Ye lead a verra interestin' life," I mused, and he waggled his brows at me.

"That I do," he boasted, and dug into his meal.

Like every Sunday supper, the people heartily devoured their meal and quickly cleared the floor of tables and benches to make room for dancing. In addition to the minstrel, a few of the villagers pounded drums, and a spirited fiddle shook the MacKinnon clan into a frenzy of twirling skirts, stomping feet, and wide, uninhibited laughter.

"Would ye care to dance, Lady MacKinnon?" Raith asked me when he stood from the table and tugged down the hem of his vest.

I shook my head. "I believe I see a more willing dance partner for ye."

I cast a meaningful look past his shoulder toward the scullery maid who was all fluttering lashes and pink cheeks. With a rakish smirk and a quick bow, Raith strode confidently toward her and bent to whisper something in her ear. Over the pounding of the drums, I watched the girl blush and nod eagerly before he grabbed her waist and spun her around the dancing circle amidst the other couples.

Alone at the laird's table, I traced my fingertip over the new gouge in the wood as though I could smooth it away and didn't notice I was no longer alone until it was too late.

"*Lady* MacKinnon."

My blood froze in my veins and worms writhed in my gut at the condescending tone that layered Father Blount's voice.

I turned to find the priest perched on the arm of the empty chair to my right, his hands folded in his lap. As close as he was to me, the golden cross that hung from his neck seemed to mock me at eye level, and his black robes reminded me of death.

My teeth closed down on my bottom lip to keep it from quivering. All these weeks I'd thought myself safe, and all the while the priest had bided his time to confront me the day the laird ventured away from the keep. I had underestimated him. I should have seen this coming; I shouldn't have allowed my growing love for Malcolm to blind me to all else.

Father Blount stared boldly down at me, his sharp gaze intent on the right side of my face and the mottled skin barely covered by my hair. Under his harsh examination, my hands began to shake, and I clasped them in my lap to hide my fear.

"I must say, I'm surprised you're still here," he said candidly. "You must be quite confident in your dark hold over the laird. How *did* you manage to weasel your way into his life?"

My tongue peeled from the roof of my dry mouth, and I rasped, "I have no hold over him."

"You're a witch, of course you do," he spat, the music and laughter loud enough that no one heard him. "Why else would he have married you? You've bewitched him, don't deny it."

I flinched as though he'd slapped me, his words a mite too close to the truth. Malcolm *was* bound to me through magic and he *had* been bewitched.

Just not by me.

The priest pinched his cross between the knuckle of his crooked forefinger and his thumb. "I made a vow to God to set him free," he sneered. "And like He has so many times before, God has delivered me to where I am needed."

I trembled under his hateful scrutiny and scanned the hall for an ally. But to my dismay, no one paid attention to me or the priest while he spewed his justification for wanting me dead. The last thing I wanted was to call out for help and present Father Blount the opportunity to accuse me of witchcraft and seal my fate. Malcolm was a day's ride away; he would never make it back in time if the priest turned the clan against me. And turn against me they would. I was not naïve to assume the people loved me enough to speak against their man of God. If I had learned anything in my twenty-six years, it was that fear was enough to make fools of even the smartest men.

"I'll tell you what, witch," Blount said, his voice low and menacing, "as much as I find making a deal with the Devil distasteful, I will risk it this once and tell you this; leave tonight and never return. I remember that day in Norwich as though it were yesterday. I *know* what you're capable of, and I don't want to see any of my flock hurt when your serpent tongue calls the heavens down upon them. You don't belong here in this seat of power. As far as I'm concerned you belong under the dirt."

My shoulders curled inward when he leaned forward, and I looked up at him in alarm. I could smell fermented wine on his breath and see the grey teeth that peeked out from thin lips as he hissed his hatred at me.

"I watched you summon a demon from the depths of Hell in my courtyard to help you escape. Do you have any idea how many God-fearing men that beast slaughtered after you disappeared? *Twenty!* And seven more were left with the loss of a limb."

My honor urged me to speak up, to tell him the demon he'd seen from wherever he'd cowered was my father come to rescue me. I wanted to tell him those men deserved to die for what they had done on his orders—that I wished he had also been amongst the dead. But the words would not form. I blinked away the tears that welled at the memory of my father's inhuman roars and how they'd chased after my mother and me as we had run for our lives.

"You're the Devil's spawn, and I will not allow you to stay and taint my parish any longer. I want you to leave. *Tonight.* Do this, and I will spare the other half of your body from the pyre because rest assured, *witch*… I will not allow you to escape the flames again."

The priest's rheumy eyes passed from the top of my head to the bodice of my gown and left behind an impression of oil and grime on my skin. Satisfied I understood his threat, he stood, and his features slipped into a mask of false courtesy.

As though he hadn't just threatened my life, he bent his waist slightly and nodded once in mock respect before he shuffled away. Sickened, I watched him stop to say a kind word to a few villagers or laid a gentle hand upon their shoulders.

He blessed them.

He smiled at them.

He playfully pinched the cheek of a little girl.

The villagers and castle folk did not see that gnarled hand for what it was. Not like I did, for his arthritic knuckles were as warped as his soul. I was still watching when he reached the threshold of the keep, and looked over his shoulder to stare at me boldly. He knew I hadn't been able to take my eyes off him, and I hated him for that.

Like a viper ready to strike, Father Blount let the weight of one last silent threat settle between us, his dark expression full of promise. Then he turned away. Within moments, the evening's shadows swallowed him up, and he was gone.

The backs of my eyes grew hot with unshed tears. I wanted nothing more than to flee from the hall but noticed Maeve approaching me. Her sleepy eyes were smudged with lavender, and she lacked the usual bounce in her step.

"I'm exhausted milady, can we—whatever is wrong?" She searched my face, and she ran her fingers down the back of my arm. Eager to leave the hall, I forced a reassuring smile and stood on quaking legs.

"I'm a bit tired, is all. Shall we?"

Maeve didn't look convinced but dutifully followed me up to the third floor of the keep. Only when I shut the heavy door to my chamber did I begin to relax.

"Just unlace me and go find yer bed. I can handle the rest just fine."

"Are ye sure?" Maeve asked as she stifled a yawn with the back of her hand. She looked as though she'd be asleep as soon as her head hit the pillow.

I nodded. "Verra sure."

As soon as she left, I rushed to the chest that held my traveling costumes and quickly switched my gown for a riding habit of heavy brown wool that buttoned up the front and a matching cloak. After pocketing a flint and the coins that some of the villagers insisted on paying for curing their ailments, I retrieved my dagger from under the pillow and strapped it to my calf.

Eager to be on my way, I pulled the wide hood of my cloak over my hair and yanked open my chamber door to find a Maeve, her hand raised as though she were about to knock. Shocked, her gaze traveled down my body as she took in my attire.

"What's goin' on?" Her voice, layered with hurt, broke my heart. I grabbed her wrist and pulled her within my chamber.

"'Tis no' what ye think," I explained in hushed tones. "Somethin' happened tonight, and I need to go. I dinnae have a choice."

Maeve's lips thinned with defiance as she leaned against the door in her dressing robe. "I kenned there was somethin' wrong with ye. That's why I'm up here instead o' divin' face first into the pillows like

I wanted to. What happened?" I must have looked apprehensive because she clasped my hands with her own and said, "Have I no' been loyal to ye? Let me help."

Maeve was right, she had been loyal to me, but never had I been totally forthcoming about my magic. I knew she was aware of some of my abilities since I healed the crops last year, but I had never divulged the extent of my power to her. The thought of doing so was too frightening, too damning. I'd only ever shown her the medicinal side of my knowledge because I couldn't bear to have her wary of me like she had been when I first arrived at Ghlas Thùr. But I could not stay here, and therefore had no choice but to trust her completely.

"Ye saw me talkin' with Father Blount in the hall?" When she nodded, I looked down at our entwined fingers and prayed she would listen to my words and not her fear. "When I was a young lass, I visited England…"

Maeve stood stock-still as she listened intently; her eyes never left mine. When I was done recounting how I received my scars and the conversation with the priest in the hall, Maeve pulled me into a firm embrace. Her slim arms wrapped around my back like bands of iron, and my chest squeezed with painful relief.

"So ye understand why I must go," I whispered through my tight throat.

"O' course ye must," she said and held me at arm's length. "And I'll be comin' with ye."

I blinked at her twice before her words penetrated my mind and I vehemently shook my head. "No, Maeve. Finlay would have my head—"

"I will," she snapped, and her fingers dug into the back of my shoulders. "Ye cannae go by yerself, milady. Maybe we can talk to Buchannan. The laird trusts him—"

"But what if Raith's faith is stronger than his friendship with my husband and gives me up to the priest?" Maeve loosened her grip on me and her brows furrowed with worry at the possibility. "I cannae trust him, even if I want to. The only person who can keep me safe is Malcolm."

Maeve looked at me long and hard before she said, "Alright. But I'm still goin' with ye. And if ye even think about usin' yer magic to keep me here, I'll never forgive ye. Where ye go, I go."

After much arguing, Maeve bullied me into agreeing and instructed me to sneak down to my surgery while she gathered the supplies we'd need. Reluctantly, I followed her order since I didn't want her to snitch on me if I left without her. I had to admit allowing her to accompany me would make my journey easier. With her unhindered run of the castle, she could pack away blankets and enough food to last us several days without attracting attention. So, in the surgery, I waited.

"How do ye expect us to leave the keep without bein' spotted?" Maeve whispered when she crept into the night-darkened surgery with a pack strapped to her back stuffed with supplies. "Ye ken the men have this place locked down tighter than a frog's arsehole, and 'tis even worse with the laird gone."

I bit my lower lip to keep from laughing at the look on Maeve's face. The excitement suited her; her eyes were bright with mischief, and there wasn't a trace of the weariness so prominent earlier. It was as though the promise of adventure had chased her exhaustion away and renewed her with a store of restless energy.

"I hauvnae thought that far ahead, unfortunately. Until ye caught me I had planned to sneak out with the villagers." I shrugged. "They're all gone by now."

Maeve blew a lock of her hair from her face. "Damn. And Buchannan is still in the great hall with his face is fused to the lips o' that silly lass from the village who works in the cookery. I doubt he'd notice if we waltzed right past him, but I widnae chance it."

"Even if we got past him, there's still the night sentry."

Like a couple of owls, we peered out the window and watched the guard on the wall make his slow journey back and forth, his focus directed to the fields beyond. It was well after midnight, but a few men still lingered in the bailey and would certainly foil any attempt at walking out the main gate. Two women about at night was suspicious enough, but there was no way they'd allow the Lady of Ghlas Thùr to leave the keep without alerting Raith.

Maeve huffed an aggravated breath. "Can ye no' use a wee bit o' magic as a distraction?"

I turned toward her in surprise, shocked that she would urge me to do so. But it was dark out, and I could use the shadows to our advantage.

"That's actually a verra good idea, Maeve."

I led the way, and steering clear of the great hall, we navigated the deserted main level toward the west bailey. Smaller, and generally quieter compared to the courtyard on the eastern side of the castle, it had a downward sloping yard with patches of grass. Only one man stood on the wall that overlooked the loch below.

The night was clear and still, the sky full of stars and a brilliant, nearly full moon high in the sky. The loch resembled glass, reflecting the heavens above, not even a ripple to be seen.

Perfect for the theatrics I had in mind.

Grateful for dark cloaks and well-oiled hinges, we silently exited the keep, and I herded Maeve into a corner next to an outcropped window where the shadows were thickest. I tapped my finger to her lips for silence before I pressed my back against her front, all but squashing her into the grey stone.

Satisfied with our hiding spot, I directed my attention to the shore that I could just see over the lip of the wall. I reached deep into my soul, where my Druid magic swirled like a fathomless pool, and wove power around my whispered words; a demand for darkness and shadow. I gathered it around us like a shroud, wrapping it tighter and tighter, until we *became* the shadows and night. Confident we wouldn't be discovered if someone should walk by, I changed my tune. Low and deep, I serenaded the earth and water while the shadows muffled my song and kept my secrets.

I knew the moment the guard noticed my distraction. His back snapped ramrod stiff, and he reached into his quiver for an arrow as he watched the shore. Power swelled inside me as I commanded the waves, stones, and bracken beneath the surface to cluster and writhe until they converged and resembled a massive beast prowling in the shallows.

Maeve's fingers tightened into the fabric at my waist when she peered over my shoulder and witnessed the monster I had conjured from the depths. I felt badly for it, for I knew this man wouldn't swim in that water for years to come, but it couldn't be helped.

The guard called out a frightened shout for help as he ran down the length of the wall, and almost fell off twice as he tried to keep his sight on the loch. I pressed Maeve harder into the corner and strengthened my demands upon the stones. I guided them to roll beneath the surface, causing the water to foam and splash. Within moments, armed men tore around the north and south ends of the keep, and a minute later, Raith Buchannan exited the door to our right, flanked by an entourage of men still in their sleeping shirts.

His face a mask of calm fury despite his kiss-swollen lips, the assassin barked orders to hold positions while he formed a plan to investigate the creature in the loch.

My shadows kept us concealed, and they passed by us without a glance. Once their attention was fixated to the west, I gripped Maeve's hand and dragged her toward the south gate, my shadows keeping us covered all the while. As I'd hoped, the boy stationed at the south gatehouse had been too curious to stay at his post. Unnoticed and unchallenged, we slipped beneath the arches and fled the lantern-light into the night-darkened fields.

Despite my flagging energy, I didn't release my hold on my loch monster until we had reached the edge of the forest. Only then did I let the stones settle where they were and took a deep, steadying breath. The shore would look different come the dawn.

"I… I ken it wasnae real, but *Iosa Crìosd,* it looked *alive,*" Maeve wheezed when we slowed our mad dash through the forest and walked at a more leisurely pace toward the village.

"I may have gotten a wee bit carried away," I squeaked, and held my hand tightly under my ribs where a cramp had formed.

"A wee bit?" Maeve burst into anxious laughter, then slapped her hand over her mouth and shot a nervous look behind us. "Milady, ye scared the shite out o' hardened warriors with naught but rocks and waterlogged branches. They're gonna think the worst when they find us missin'."

I frowned. She was probably right, but I pushed away the niggling sensation of guilt. Their concern over our absence was better than my fiery death.

"Nothin' to be done for it now. We'll be back in a couple o' days if all goes to plan."

"Och, this *plan* o' yers. How is it yer so sure the laird will find us? Did ye send a messenger I dinnae ken about?"

I held a leafy branch out of the way as she walked past.

"No. My mother bound him to me. I can only feel our connection, but he can sense where I am," I explained, and paused when we came to the edge of the wood, only the spread of a silvery wheat field separating us from the sleeping village.

"No matter where ye go?" she asked skeptically as she came to stand by my side.

I nodded. "Aye. No matter where I go."

I kept the hood of my cloak pulled low over my brow while Maeve argued with the boy in the stables over the price of a horse. With her hands curled into claws in front of her chest, she looked moments away from completely losing her temper.

"Ye cannae expect me to pay ye thrice the amount o' coin just because 'tis after dark, ye wee bawbag!"

"O' course I can!" he hissed as he stood on his tiptoes and tried to appear bigger than she. "Me da always said that anyone needin' anythin' in the middle o' the night is desperate enough to pay triple."

Maeve spoke through her teeth, "And yer da would want ye takin' advantage o' two women?"

With a smug smirk, the boy shrugged and yawned dramatically. "Way I see it, ye need a horse. I have one. Now do ye want it or did ye wake me for nothin'?"

Maeve's nostrils flared. "Ye *s an Iar-Dheas*—"

"Maeve." Moving deeper into the barn, I pushed the hood off my head and pegged the 'cheeky brat,' as Maeve had most eloquently called him, with my most intimidating glare.

Stunned, he paled and blinked up at me. Maeve made a satisfied grunt and crossed her arms over her chest.

"Ye'll have a fair price for the horse now because that's all we have. In a week's time, ye may come to the keep for the rest—"

"Milady!" Maeve squawked, and I silenced her with a look.

"—as payment for yer discretion."

The stable boy's brows furrowed with confusion as he took in Maeve's bulky supply sack and our dark traveling clothes. His shoulders drooped, and all his bravado vanished, revealing his youth.

"Are ye leavin' for good? Cause ye cannae do that to us. Ye cannae do that to my laird." The betrayal in his voice cut me to the quick.

"No. I'll never abandon him," I promised as I grabbed his boney shoulders and bent slightly until we were eye level. "I'm just in a wee bit o' trouble, and ye cannae tell anyone ye saw me leave."

A few minutes later, and a pouch of coin lighter, we left the village on the back of a chestnut mare and ambled down the east road beneath the fading stars. We had perhaps an hour until sunrise.

"He'll have told everyone ye left by first light, ye ken," Maeve grumbled in my ear from where she rode pillion.

I looked back at the few glowing windows in the distance and the dark impression of the church in the middle of the village.

"I'm countin' on it."

Chapter Twenty-Three

COIRA

My back ached from Maeve's weight pushing against me while she slumbered, and I fought the urge to stretch. Our mount carried us along the road toward a small camp with a low burning fire. Seeing it, I shifted my grip on the reins, elbowed Maeve, and settled deeper within the hood of my cloak.

"What's goin' on?" she murmured groggily, having fallen asleep as soon as we lost sight of the village.

"Road travelers ahead," I whispered. "Let's hope they're still asleep."

But luck was not on our side. Lounging against the rough bark of a tall Scots pine on the right, a dark-haired man with a thick mustache sucked on a foul-smelling pipe, the tip flaring a brilliant amber in the pre-dawn light. His black jacket and white neckcloth looked a bit travel-worn, but he held himself straight and proud despite his appearance. The glow of the fire revealed a second figure bundled under blankets, and a snore emanated from within.

Dawn rapidly approached, lightening our surroundings by the second, and I spied two horses hobbled not far from the camp.

"Hello there," the Englishman drawled, and blew a thick plume of smoke toward us.

The back of my neck tightened in warning; at the same time, Maeve's arms slipped around my waist and locked tight just below my ribs.

"My, my…" With a lazy lurch away from the tree, he sauntered into the middle of the narrow road to intercept us. With one hand shoved into his pocket, he peered at me to muse aloud, "What are two women doing out here all alone, I wonder, and on such a cold night? Come. Warm yourselves by our fire."

I clenched my teeth and nudged my horse to sidestep him. The thorny blackberry canes that grew wild and high along the north side of the road prevented us from getting far. They snagged my stocking-covered ankles and nipped at my mount's legs, causing her to prance with agitation.

"I'm afraid we must decline yer kind offer, our group is just up ahead," I lied and tapped the ribs of my horse.

His jovial look vanished, and he reached out, snatching at the reins. "I insist!" he snapped.

I yanked back to keep control, and with an equine shriek, our horse reared and would have dumped us off her back if it wasn't for the death grip I had on her mane. Maeve's frightened cry made my ears ring, and she clung to me so tightly I swore I could feel her heart pounding against my back through our clothing.

Ripping hard on the reins, I swung our mount around and violently dragged the highwayman into the wall of thorns. Caught within their barbed hold, he released the reins with a curse and yelled for his companion. The man leaped up from his pallet and raced toward us with a single-minded determination that hinted he'd been awake all that time.

"Hold on!" I barked at Maeve and kicked hard.

Ears flattened to her head, our horse shot forward, and I corrected her path before she ran us straight into the second man. Bent over the mare's powerful neck, I hugged her ribs with my thighs as I guided her over the wagon-rutted road and berated myself. I should have stayed off the roads and left Maeve at the castle, where she would have been safe. I had put her in danger, and I *knew* better.

"Oh my God," Maeve whimpered and shook my arm. "They're chasin' after us."

The wind ripped my hood off my head, and I glanced over my shoulder to find both men mounted and closing fast on our lead in the grey morning light. On either side of the road, I could see fog rising from the earth, blanketing the wet grass and squat bushes that lined our path.

"They'll catch us!" Maeve's panic rallied my need to protect her. I drove our horse faster, frantically looking for an opportunity to hide… but there was nothing; nothing but open fields and small clusters of pine and birch.

And so, with no other options, I began to sing.

Power infused my veins as I called the clouds from the sky and vapor from the earth. I guided it to billow behind us like a cape while we raced along the curves of the road. My voice wove with the staccato of pounding hooves, and I gave in to the rhythm of our flight. Thicker and thicker, the fog condensed until it was a swirling wall of white, and I could barely see more than a few feet behind us.

I felt my forbidden side unfold and purr as I reticulated my song. It seduced me to delve ever deeper—to *become* the mist and the fog. That ancient magic invited me to wrap invisible hands around the necks of those who threatened me and mine. To squeeze their throats until no air could get past. I would count their last heartbeats—

"I cannae see them anymore," Maeve whispered. "I think it worked."

The relief in her voice, so close to my ear, drew me out of the vortex, and I took a deep, tremulous breath to ground myself.

Gooseflesh spread over every inch of my unscarred skin. I had not felt the enamoring pull of the full force of forbidden magic since the day in Norwich, and I had forgotten. Forgotten how truly devastating my power could be.

How devastating *I* could be.

With my grip firm around the thick veil of conjured brume, I wrenched us south, off the road, and through a field covered by tall green grass and white and blue wildflowers. I could tell our horse was tiring, her breathing labored as she struggled to keep up with my demands. With a gentle nudge, I pushed what energy I could spare into her fatigued body, and her speed increased.

Just a wee bit farther, I silently promised, and gave her neck a firm pat.

At the edge of a boggy forest, I reined her to a sharp halt and tumbled from her back. My knees hit the soggy peat with a wet squelch, but I barely noticed the water that crept into my slippers. I thrust my hands out before me, held my breath, and strained my ears for a hint of our pursuers through the ground cloud. I would open the very earth beneath their feet and bury them alive before I would allow them to touch us. A small part of me wished they would try.

Minutes passed while I stared into the silvery wall of vapor, ready and waiting to unleash my magic upon them. But to my relief, the muffled shouts of their voices in the distance faded to silence and eventually turned into cheerful birdsong.

"What do we do now?" Maeve asked as she soothed the horse, calming her heavy breathing with long strokes along her neck.

I spun around, plucked the reins from the ground, and clicked my tongue for the mare to follow.

"Now? Now we stay off the bloody road."

It took most of the day, slogging through forests and bogs, but by the time the sun neared the horizon, the moss-covered cottage came into view. Upon seeing it, my eyes became blurry with emotion. When Malcolm had taken me away a year ago, I never thought I'd see it again. But in the last couple of months, I found I'd stopped wanting to.

Besides the wind-strewn leaves piled up on the small porch and a cracked window, it looked the same as it had when I left. The same pines towered above the mossy roof; the same ferns huddled next to its foundations. The steep hill behind the cottage hadn't swallowed it any further. Everything was the same…

Except me, for there could be no denying I was a profoundly different woman today.

After turning the mare out into the grassy meadow to enjoy a much-deserved rest, I helped Maeve bring our supplies into the cold interior of the cabin and brushed the dust off the worn table. It felt wet and musty, and in sore need of a good drying out. With the absence of a daily cooking fire, the dark green moss that covered most of the stone wall abutting the hill was dewy and vibrant with health.

"Ye grew up here?" Maeve took in the single room and climbed a few rungs of the ladder to peek into the loft. "No wonder ye were so wary and quiet when ye arrived at the keep. Ye were so secluded here."

My brows furrowed and I looked up at her curiously. "My seclusion wasnae why I was so wary, Maeve."

Looking down on me, she followed the path of my hand as I traced the scars on my face. She tilted her head and leaned heavily against the ladder.

"Ah. I honestly forget about them most times," she said with a soft smile. "I dinnae see them anymore when I look at ye. Neither does anyone else."

My heart constricted, and I blinked up at her, wishing I could say the same. "Thank ye for that, Maeve."

Hours later, after we'd filled our bellies with a hearty vegetable and barley soup before the cheerful hearth fire, we climbed to the loft and slipped beneath the worn, heavy blankets in the bed I had once shared with my mother. It smelled different than I remembered; the scent of her skin long gone.

But her presence wasn't.

I felt her in the corners of the room, and when I closed my eyes, I could imagine how she had moved as she hung bushels of herbs to dry in front of the window. I remembered how the light would catch her profile as she turned to smile at me. I felt the comforting touch of her hand on my shoulder when she would pass me by and the warm press of her lips on the crown of my head. I could hear her faint humming while she rooted the vegetables, and I could see the white chunk of hair that fell from her part to frame her face, signifying her endless mourning of my father.

Maeve's even breath was a comfort while she dreamed beside me, the sound a strange sort of lullaby. After arranging the blankets up to my chin, I stared at the vaulted ceiling above me and watched shadows made by the flames in the hearth below dance along the beams.

I'd changed so much since I last slept in this bed. Friendless and motherless, I'd felt like my heart had been sliced in half with loss while Malcolm—then a stranger, now a lover—slept on the floor below. That night and many months after, I could not fathom why she had chosen to bind me to a stranger and save the life of a man she didn't know at the price of her own.

Now, I understood.

She had traded her life for the one she wanted for me; a chance at a life surrounded by people. With no possibility of finding a match for me within the Druid community, and after years hiding away in the secluded forest, constantly afraid of discovery, she had taken a gamble. She had known how much the last spell to save Malcolm's brother would cost her, but she had wanted me to have chance at love. So, she purchased as much as she could, and she did it with only love in her heart. I understood that now.

Because of that same love, my mother had allowed my father to swear a blood vow. Even though they both knew the cost, knew he would probably die trying to save me, the price had been worth it. They had done it because they loved me… and that was why she'd traded the rest of her years for what would be my only chance at security. My only chance at finding love because if she hadn't forced me to truly live my life, I had no doubt I would have died an old woman, alone and miserable.

I ran my palms over the soft curve of my abdomen, the precious being that grew within my womb, and knew I would do *anything* to protect it. I would give anything, take anything, steal, lie, and barter… I'd even walk through the fire that haunted my dreams. I would suffer *anything…*

I understood now.

Thank ye, mother. I sent my thoughts out to the heavens, where I knew she was with my father, and let my heavy lids slide closed.

〜

Coira.

Coira, wake up.

The echo of my mother's throaty voice, so close yet so very far away, roused me from a dreamless sleep, and I opened my eyes to find the loft brimming with smoke. Dark, hazy tendrils caressed my face and stuffed themselves up my nose, burning my eyes, conjuring memories I had fought so hard to forget. Fear raced up my thighs and back, lifting every hair upon my head. With a gasp, I sat up only to choke on the dense, acrid air.

My first thought was that the hearth-fire had thrown an ember, and the floor had caught ablaze…but then I heard the laughter, and I realized we were no longer alone in the wood.

"Maeve!" I threw myself across the bed and shook her awake. "Maeve!"

Her eyes and mouth flew open in surprise, and she gagged on the smoke that pressed down on us where it gathered thick among the rafters.

"Come on!" Half blind, I rubbed at my burning eyes, and clumsily slid down the rungs of the ladder to smack hard on the floor. A moment later, Maeve tumbled down after me, her blonde curls a wild halo around her face.

BOOM, *crack*!

BOOM, *crash*!

Glass shattered, and something whizzed past my head to punch into a cupboard door. The impact left a splintered hole in the wood. Maeve screamed in panic and curled up on the floor, her arms wrapped protectively around her head. The shrill sounds that came from her mouth made me cringe, and I shook her a bit to stop her terrified cries.

"Dinnae get up from the floor, do ye understand? Stay low." After she jerked her chin and pressed her cheek to the floor, I crawled to the window and chanced a peek out into the night. What I found made my blood run cold with dread.

Twenty men, torches in hand, gathered in a loose semi-circle around the cottage. I recognized one of them—the highwayman that had accosted us earlier that morning. Their faces held a wide range of manic emotions—from anger, to excitement, to murderous madness. A few held muskets; others looped rope.

"Come on out, witch!" a man with a thick, brown beard bellowed as he raised his musket to fire on the cottage. The sound of powder igniting was deafening, and his shot collided with the stone between the windows.

I coughed anew as grey-green smoke forced its way through the windowpanes where the piles of leaves smoldered. I felt a tiny bit of relief that the cottage was too damp to catch fire, but the smoke would only get worse.

With my back pressed against the stone wall, I tightened my fragile hold over my fear and chanced one more glance at the witch hunters. The man from the road took a few lazy steps forward, a torch in one hand and a bottle of amber liquid in the other.

"Blount was right about this witch," he called out with a dark chuckle.

It was that moment I realized Father Blount must have summoned them to hunt me down. He had done his part well by sowing seeds of doubt in my mind and made me question my safety enough that I had fled from my home. I felt like twice the fool for running straight into his trap. He must have planned, having these men wait and watch for a woman who looked like me… *And I had made it worse by calling upon the fog,* I realized, for now these men—these witch hunters—were in a frenzy.

There would be no doubt of my guilt after that.

No trial.

No witnesses.

No evidence.

And Maeve stuck in the middle, destined to suffer the same fate they had planned for me.

"Your tracks were too easy to follow, witch," he yelled, "God surely wants your death, and we plan to deliver." The rest of the men behind him crowed with bitter delight, urging him on.

Five more steps brought him closer to the cottage, and with a dangerous gleam in his eye he took a long pull from the bell-shaped bottle, raised the torch, and blew the liquid above the flame. His fiery breath took on a low roar, and sent a billowing spray of yellow and orange toward the roof.

The damp thatch dried quick, and when the flames touched the thick moss and straw on the roof, the ceiling lit up in brilliant yellow and orange.

I shouted in alarm and crawled back to Maeve. Through the window I saw the madman blow fire onto the porch, and within seconds I could no longer see him through the smoke and flame.

"*Burn! Burn! Burn!*" they chanted, their laughter a hateful madness that beat on my fraying nerves.

"Die in there or out here, witch. Makes no difference to us how the Devil takes you!" another shouted.

Maeve sobbed, and I struggled to control my voice enough to sing for rain, to bring a deluge massive enough to drown the fire that rapidly spread out of control. But my fear was too great, my voice too hoarse from the smoke, and I failed to grasp the Druid cadence.

Embers from the burning roof fell around us like luminescent snowflakes, and I retched when I smelled the stench of singed hair and fabric.

I grasped Maeve's hand, and she looked up at me with large, terrified eyes. Tears paved rivers down the apples of her sooty cheeks, and I noticed tiny spots of broken red around her pupils from her coughing.

"We're gonna die in here," she wheezed. "I dinnae want to die. No' this way."

Over her shoulder, the little hearth at the far side of the room pulsed gently. The logs that had burned so brightly while we ate dinner were now grey and black with cracks of orange-red. But they breathed.

They beckoned me and begged me to remember.

Remember.

Remember.

A coincidence is just fate's way o' screamin' at ye. My mother's words, spoken long ago, echoed in the recess of my mind.

At the sight of those crooked stones at the back of the hearth, I didn't know whether to laugh or cry.

Maeve huddled in my arms while black smoke filled the cottage, bearing down on us. The massive beams that held the thatching groaned under the stress and mingled with the witch hunter's muffled celebrations and bellowing.

I ignored it all, smoothed away the soot-stained curls that plastered to Maeve's forehead…

And smiled.

CHAPTER TWENTY-FOUR

MALCOLM

Knock at his study, where they say he keeps
To ruminate strange plots of dire revenge;
Tell him Revenge is come to join with him,
And work confusion on his enemies.
-William Shakespeare, "Merchant of Venice"

With the morning sun warming his back, Malcolm guided his horse leisurely to the main door of the Bothan keep and dismounted. He had not been the least bit surprised that they were welcomed with open arms as soon as their party had been spotted in the small village at the bottom of the hill, or that the laird of the castle now stood in the doorway with a confused but friendly smile upon his fleshy face.

"MacKinnon. Forgive me, I wasnae expecting ye. Did ye send a message I had no' received?" His round belly bounced in front of him as he descended the stairs and clasped his hand to Malcolm's forearm.

"I didnae, my apologies. It was a thought in the moment, this visit. Are we interruptin' breakfast?"

"No' at all, man. Come in, come in." Bothan put a hand on Malcolm's shoulder to guide him into the keep and barked at a boy standing just inside the door. "Dalton, send for some more boiled sausages and bread. Enough for... eleven it seems."

Malcolm took in the great hall of the Chattan keep and forced himself to look relaxed when he caught sight of Robena Bothan and her daughter Edeen sitting at her side.

Edeen's brown eyes widened when she noticed him, and her cheeks flushed a deep pink that Malcolm had once thought charming.

"Laird MacKinnon, I… hello," she said breathlessly. Her avid gaze roved from the crown of his head to the toes of his boots while she smoothed her long brown hair. "The past year has been most kind to ye."

Malcolm sat down in the chair opposite of Lady Bothan and gave the women a roguish smile. Both women beamed back at him and began whispering to one another, their hands clasped together.

Laird Bothan squeezed into his chair at the head of the table to Malcolm's right and speared a link of greasy sausage with his two-pronged fork. "So, MacKinnon, what has brought ye all this way that a letter couldnae achieve?"

Funny ye should ask, he thought sardonically as he imagined impaling one of the red-handled daggers into Bothan's pudgy neck instead of into the table like Raith had. Shoving that highly undiplomatic thought away, Malcolm crooked a finger at Farlan who wordlessly set a shallow wooden box down on the table and then resumed his post behind his laird. Malcolm placed his hands on the lid.

"This does," Malcolm said, his voice low and soft as he outlined the polished corners with the tips of his fingers and studied the man at his side. "But to be honest, I dinnae think ye have the faintest idea about what is in here."

From the corner of his eye, he saw Robena's shoulders stiffen and her smile falter, solidifying Malcolm's suspicions.

Confused and slightly aggravated, Laird Bothan wiped at the grease from his chin with the back of his hand and pointed at the box. "Unless ye show me what the bloody hell yer talkin' about, MacKinnon, I willnae be able to confirm or deny, so stop with the fargin' mystery and open the damn box," he snapped.

Malcolm let his pleasant mask slip into one of ire and flipped the case open, revealing three red-handled daggers nestled within a lining of blue velvet.

His stomach digging into the edge of the table, Laird Bothan grunted and reached over his plate to pluck one up.

"Yer right, MacKinnon. I dinnae—" His bewilderment morphed into recognition as he turned the blade in his hands. "Where did ye get these? They're part o' my daughter's dowry. Ye shouldnae have possession o' them," Bothan sputtered.

Malcolm turned his attention to the two very white-faced, very *guilty* women on the other side of the table.

"Yer right, I shouldnae be in possession o' them." Malcolm lifted the other two from the case and slid their edges against one another. The high-pitched *shiiiing* of blade scraping against blade set his teeth on edge. He held Robena's stare and said darkly, "Would ye care to tell yer husband why I'm here today, or shall I?"

Bothan shifted his perplexed gaze back and forth between Malcolm and his stone-faced wife before he threw his pudgy hands in the air with exasperation. "Why would she ken why ye're here if *I* dinnae even ken why ye're here?"

Malcolm's vision blurred around the edges as he pointed the tip of one dagger at Lady Bothan. "I'm here because Lady Bothan hired *assassins* to kill my wife. Three to be precise."

Shocked and at a loss for words, Laird Bothan's mouth opened and shut a few times before he turned to his wife and stared at her as if she had sprouted an extra head. Seconds passed before his face turned beet red, and he hissed, "Did ye risk startin' a bloody war between our two clans to satisfy yer displeasure, woman? I kenned ye were angry, but this… this—I ought to take it out o' yer hide!"

"But Da—"

Laird Bothan gasped and blinked at his daughter. "Dinnae tell me *ye* were part of her scheme, too?"

"He was supposed to marry *me*!" Edeen shouted, her face twisted into an ugly mask of hatred when she turned her glare upon Malcolm.

"Ye were betrothed to *me*. I promised myself to ye and ye just tossed me aside for a common-blood whore—"

The sound of a blade being lifted from its scabbard and Farlan's deep, menacing voice silenced the young woman Malcolm had thankfully escaped marrying.

"Ye willnae speak about my lady in such a way again, or so help me God, I will tear out that barbed tongue o' yers with my bare hands and damn the consequences."

Without having to look, Malcolm knew his friend's features held murderous promise by the way Edeen trembled.

"Da, did ye hear what he just said to me? Ye cannae allow—"

Laird Bothan smacked the table and pegged Farlan with a beady glower. "Ye're in no position to make such threats to my, daughter," he said gruffly before he leaned back in his chair and pinched the bridge of his nose. His cheeks were ruddy with displeasure, and he turned his angry glare on his daughter. "But ye'd certainly deserve it. Ye plotted his wife's death, Edeen!" Bothan turned to Robena and pounded his meaty fist on the table so hard the remaining sausage rolled off his plate and fell to the floor with a splat in the silent hall. "Ye plotted against our ally! *My* ally! And for what? What did ye think was goin' to happen?" Laird Bothan's face flushed to near purple with rage.

Edeen looked guiltily at Malcolm and tightened her lips into a thin line.

"Ye thought I would come for ye," Malcolm guessed. "That's what ye assumed had happened just a few moments ago, was it no'? Ye assumed the third assassin had finished the job, and before my wife's body would have been in the ground a day, I came here to take ye for a replacement. Is that right?"

Edeen clenched her teeth and looked away, but her surly silence was just as loud as if she'd said *aye*.

"Dinnae play games with me, Edeen. Ye willnae win," Malcolm promised when he stood and dropped the two daggers back in the box. He nodded toward the knife Laird Bothan held. "I have no need o' the third, but these two… they'll be comin' back with me." He held Robena's stare, and then Edeen's, before he said, "Listen to me well, for I'll swear this right now. If ye even so much as send an ill-wish in the direction o' Lady MacKinnon, I'll come back and plunge these into yer black hearts myself." Malcolm closed the wooden case with a sharp snap and nearly grinned at the comical way they jumped in their seats.

Sidestepping his chair, he turned on his heel and found his men staring viciously at the Bothan women, silently promising them worse, and headed for the door.

"MacKinnon." Laird Bothan's tired voice chased after him, and Malcolm glanced over his shoulder to find the man at a loss for words, his hand open and held out in front of him as though asking forgiveness. Malcolm knew Bothan did not want a clan war over this.

"Dinnae allow anything like this to happen again, Bothan, and we can keep our alliance. I only say this because I ken ye truly had no idea about yer wife's wretchedness, or yer daughter's betrayal. But ken this truce is only as strong as yer hold over *them*, aye?"

Jaw set, Bothan gave him a jerky nod that sent his jowls jiggling, and Malcolm left the stuffy keep just as the page returned with a platter piled with grey sausage and bread.

"Feckin' harpies," Bram muttered as they approached their horses. Malcolm grunted in agreement and contemplated the odd mix of relief and unease he felt.

"I'll forever remember the look on that shrew's face when ye threatened to cut out her tongue," Finlay said to Farlan, his puckish face split into a wide grin.

"I was serious," Farlan grumbled as he mounted his horse.

Malcolm slapped Farlan's thigh as he walked past and said, "I didnae doubt it for a moment."

～

An hour's ride from the Bothan keep, the slight tingling of unease grew to agitation, and Malcolm slowed Ramsay to a halt. He rubbed his chest and looked out toward the northern hills.

"What is it, my laird?" Gavin whispered as he followed Malcolm's gaze and notched an arrow into his bow, searching for a threat.

Brows drawn low, Malcolm glanced in the direction of Ghlas Thùr.

She's no' there. Why would she leave? he wondered.

"How about an excursion today, lads?" Malcolm called out to his men. He tapped Ramsey's flanks and looked at Bram and Finlay meaningfully when his mount stepped off the road and into a long, rolling field. The trepidation that tightened his gut magnified with every beat of Ramsey's hooves.

"Why are we headed north? I thought we were goin' straight back to the keep?" Finlay asked in a low voice.

"Because yer lady is no' *at* the bloody keep," Malcolm growled.

Realization passed over the more serious twin's face, and Bram barked orders at the few men lagging behind. Urging Ramsey into a brisk gait, Malcolm found he didn't much care if they caught up or not. He was heading north with or without them.

"Where is she, my laird?" Bram asked as they cantered side by side through the field.

"I dinnae ken, but she's that way and headin' east."

Malcolm looked up to judge the arc of the sun and determined it was just past mid-day. They probably had miles and miles to travel until they caught up with Coira and wherever the hell she thought she was running to. With each hour, unpleasant thoughts infested Malcolm's mind, each speculation worse than the last. Mostly he worried that he'd judged Raith's integrity false when he'd left the man to look after his wife. Had he planned to kill Coira anyway and only feigned friendship to add to the thrill? The creature in his chest moved restlessly within, causing Malcolm's own unrest to intensify.

As sun made its slow descent toward the horizon, their party passed grazing sheep and navigated through thick forests and rocky moors. When they reached a ravine too steep to guide their horses down and a river too swift and deep to cross, Malcolm cursed the extra distance they had to ride out of their way until they found a safe place to ford.

The MacKinnon laird drove his men on and refused to rest for any longer than it took to water their beasts. They had even stopped asking for explanations and resolved to dutifully follow on Malcolm's unknown quest while they ate their rations on horseback.

Long after the sun had set and plunged the countryside into darkness, Malcolm tried to find relief knowing Coira had reached her destination hours ago and had been stationary ever since.

"We're pretty far out. Do ye ken any reason why she'd leave the safety o' the keep?" Finlay asked with a gravelly voice. He'd passed the day telling stories and kept everyone more or less entertained, but his efforts had left him hoarse.

Malcolm shook his head. "I cannae help but think the worst, but I didnae ken. I just feel… I feel desperate to find her, like the tether between us has stretched. This bond… 'tis like a homing pigeon, and she's home, no matter where she goes. I tracked her once before, when she tried to slip away last spring. I found her runnin' as though the Devil himself snapped at her heels." Suppressing a grin, he turned to Finlay and said, "She nearly beat the breath right out o' my lungs when I caught up to her."

In the light of the moon, Malcolm watched Finlay's carefree smile sink and the blood drain from his face.

"*Iosa, Màiri, agus Iòsaph.* Yer feckin' eyes are glowin'," Finlay whispered just as heat suffused Malcolm's skin and an arc of lightning burned a jagged path from his heart to the tips of his fingers and toes.

"Dear God," he heard Farlan echo from his left as his horse pranced away with a nervous knicker.

In the middle of the field, alarm blared like trumpets in Malcolm's mind when his body shifted and grew, one bone, tendon, and muscle at a time. Wide-eyed with fear and concern, the rest of his men murmured prayers of protection, and more than a few kicked their horses into action in a desperate need to put more space between them and their laird.

"Dinnae fear me—"

The sharp crack of musket fire echoed off the hills, and Malcolm abandoned any attempt to reassure his clansman. He gave in to the demands of his oath with an inhuman roar. Arms spread wide, he welcomed the power that suffused his veins and pumped an unmatched strength into his muscles. He felt his chest expand nearly twice its size; his jacket split the seams at his shoulders and the buttons popped away from his shirt and vest. His feet filled up every bit of his soft leather boots.

Beneath him, Ramsey's legs buckled from the unexpected weight of Malcolm's altered body and kicked out toward Finlay's horse. Malcolm felt his incisors punch through his gums as he slipped from Ramsay's back and took off with single-minded determination once his feet hit solid ground.

"He's still yer laird!" Farlan bellowed when some of his men shouted their surprise, but Malcolm did not care. Come with him or not, he could not afford to tarry.

Malcolm's powerful thighs ate up the ground, his stride now three times that of a normal man, and he rushed headlong into the night. Change complete, he stretched his new, reinforced body, and used every bit of it to his advantage.

The soft, white glow from his eyes illuminated the terrain, ensuring he did not misstep or falter. His speed, faster than any horse he had ever ridden, was resolute; rocks did not slow him, nor did the roots that jutted out of the forest floor. His balance was perfection as he vaulted over fallen trees and moss-covered stones. He did not tire, his body a perfect instrument of speed, strength, and endurance.

The ear-splitting blast of another musket seized his lungs with dread as he hurtled through a familiar spread of land overgrown with saplings. Thin, willowy branches tipped with soft leaves whipped at his face and neck. He shot past the spot he'd fallen off his horse and nearly died…and looked ahead to see the pulsing glow of a massive fire.

When he broke through the glen, the horrible things Malcolm had imagined didn't compare to what lay before him. Twenty men stood in front of the cottage that burned like an inferno, the rumble of flames nearly deafening but not loud enough to drown out the screams of a terrified woman from within.

Rage—overwhelming, dark, and suffocating—consumed Malcolm's thoughts when he realized Coira was trapped within that unholy blaze, trapped in a cage made of the fire she so feared. His oath pushed him toward the group of men, and through the red haze of his wrath, he focused on the one with a musket aimed at the cottage. Malcolm plowed his shoulder below the man's neck so hard he felt the audible crunch of severed vertebrae.

His victim crumpled dead on the ground, and with Malcolm's next step, he unsheathed his sword and swung it in a wide, practiced arc. At one with his weapon from the last year of hard training, he took the head off one villain in a spray of blood and embedded his crimson blade in the thick neck of a second. With the element of surprise gone, the remaining blackguards rushed him with daggers and rapiers. With his newly heightened senses, Malcolm could smell the scotch on their breath and the underlying stench of fear lacing their sweat when they surrounded him, effectively cutting him off from the cottage.

"What the hell are you?" one of the men—an *Englishman*—spat, his bloodshot eyes wild, uncertain if he wanted to fight or flee.

"Blount tried to warn us the witch could summon demons!" another yelled.

Blount! *I'll kill him myself and enjoy the way his blood coats my hands,* Malcolm seethed, and revealed his sharp, gleaming teeth. One by one, he'd tear them apart, but he was running out of time.

Malcolm lunged at the men separating him from the cottage just as Farlan and Bram tore through the forest on horseback, the rest of the MacKinnon's close behind.

In the confusion, Malcolm snatched at the nearest marauder and pulled him close. He caught the terrified features of his victim a moment before his oath overtook his instincts. His vision sharpened, and Malcolm noted an inhuman rumble of satisfaction that crawled up his throat when the creature tore open the man's throat with his teeth. A gurgle bubbled out of the gaping wound, and Malcolm dropped the dying body to bleed out at his feet. He took a step, then another, toward the blaze—

The sharp sting of pain in his chest caused him to spin defensively to his left, and he looked down with annoyance at the dagger hilt sticking out of his pectoral.

"Die demon!" spat the one who had stabbed him, and then screamed, high-pitched and full of fright, when Malcolm picked him up and tossed him over the heads of his comrades to the encroaching tree line.

Terror consumed the remaining fifteen, an chaos and madness erupted when Malcolm ripped the dagger from his body and slaughtered the eight men closest to him. He slashed, stabbed, and ripped into their bodies until he stood in a field of carnage. Innards spilled from bellies. Throats, sliced open like grotesque apertures, gurgled before falling silent. The ground appeared pockmarked, riddled with pools of thick, black liquid in the firelight. The ones that fled from his reach were picked off by Malcolm's men one by one.

None were left alive.

Entranced and blood-drunk, Malcolm turned toward the snap of a mighty beam and watched in horror as the cottage roof shifted and sent a thick spray of embers up to the blue-black sky.

"Coira!" Malcolm's throat felt like it was being ripped from within with the force of his panic, and he lunged toward the overwhelming heat of the blaze when someone gripped his wrist.

Leave me be, Malcolm thought as he shook them off and strode forward, ready to brave the flames and his own death to get to her.

Arms wrapped his arms around Malcolm's ribs and wrenched him back.

"No, my laird!" Bram's voice rasped in his ear.

"Let go," Malcolm growled, enraged that the beast had encouraged him to waste so much time killing when he should have run straight into the cottage, blaze be damned. "I have to find her."

"No, we willnae allow ye to sacrifice yourself!" Finlay's determined face appeared in front of him, a bit lower than usual.

Bram tightened his hold around his laird's waist, and Finlay defiantly placed himself between Malcolm and the burning cottage. Amazingly undeterred by the tattered jacket and the blood that soaked

Malcolm's mouth, chin, neck, and, his cousin leaned against him with all his might to keep his laird from taking another step.

CRACK, SNAP!

Another beam broke, and Malcolm's eyes widened with fear as he watched the roof collapse into the cottage with an earth-trembling crash. The fire guttered for the span of a breath before it rallied and raged even brighter than before.

Och, no. No one could survive that. His throat closed painfully at the devastating thought, and he barely heard Bram yelling for help over the howl of flames.

With his superior strength, Malcolm pushed forward despite the two men that held him and hissed when several others joined in. Their battle-hardened hands gripped his arms and wrists tight; another two wedged their shoulders against his knees.

Malcolm blinked into the flames, and his tears dried up from the heat before they even had a chance to spill. His wife was dead, along with the child they'd made.

The purest part of themselves he'd never get a chance to meet.

Oh God, this hurts, he thought, and prayed his death could come swiftly. He didn't want to live without them—without his Angel—and eagerly awaited the end of his torment.

"Ye dinnae understand," Malcolm croaked, his words barely pushing past the agony that clogged his throat. "I'm dead anyway. I failed to save her and now she's gone. I have no choice but to follow. That was the oath I made."

"To *die?*" someone asked, as though they thought it impossible.

Malcolm ignored them and pushed forward another foot, eager to put an end to his heartache.

Finlay looked up at him in confusion and gripped the lapels of Malcolm's ruined jacket. He shook him, a silent demand for his laird's attention.

"If that's true, then *why aren't ye?* Why have ye no' dropped dead at my feet?"

Malcolm's eyes burned as he stared into the all-brilliant orange and yellow translucent whips and waves of heat that lashed out with ravenous need. It would be a quick death, to enter within that blaze. A mercy even, for the kiss of those flames would be gentle compared to the grief that lashed barbed whips upon his heart.

He was a fool indeed to yearn for love, for to lose the object of that love was the worst sort of pain. That kind of pain lurked under the skin to haunt a person's every thought, every memory, every hope and dream. It was a constant reminder of loss.

He'd never again feel Coira's light touch, never hear her laughter. Never again draw a lock of her silky, wheat-blonde hair between his fingers while he read to her, or smell the clean, floral scent of her skin.

There would be no more joy for him, for she was the light in his days. And now that light was forever snuffed…

Better to die, than endure the dark.

Chapter Twenty-Five

COIRA

Ten Years Ago

Sprawled out alone in the middle of the little meadow in front of our cottage, I looked up at the grey morning sky and twisted a pale lock of hair around my finger. I frowned at the clouds. After three years, my hair still wasn't long enough to decently plait, but at least there was finally enough to hide the ruined side of my face.

We'd just come back from the Highlands the day before last. Since the death of my father and after we had fled England, my mother had been reluctant to return to our empty cottage. Instead, she took us north to the Druid settlement near Inverness.

I had thought she wanted to be near our family, but I'd been wrong. The moment we arrived, she turned me over to our kin and disappeared into the open hills on foot. I had expected her to come back that night, and when she didn't, I looked for her with the rise of the morning sun and again when it disappeared over the craggy hills. When she hadn't returned by the end of the month, I stopped looking altogether.

When we'd reached the little village of cottages and mud and stone huts scattered in the hills surrounding it, they had welcomed us with open arms. That was until they'd realized what had been done to me. After that, they treated me a with detached difference I hated, and without my mother to console and defend me, I had fast become an outcast. Upon seeing my scars, the girls I had once played with shied away from me. And when they talked to me, they couldn't seem to take their eyes off the proof of my shame, as though they feared my marbled skin would leap off my face and attach to theirs.

The boys were worse.

Since my blonde hair was only a wisp of fuzz on my head—singed and crackling from where the heat of the fire licked the ends that hadn't been shorn down to my scalp—they would run past me and pull and tug on the fragile ends until they broke off.

"Ye look like a true witch now," one boy said to me when he poked me in the ribs with a stick. A group of three others jeered him on.

"She's ugly," another hissed.

"Yer mam should have just let ye burn. Everyone will ken what ye are now and it will only be a matter o' time before they catch ye again."

Their words followed me long after I ran out of the village until I arrived at the base of a foggy moor covered with wide patches of yellow gorse. It was a beautiful place, with a burbling stream that ended in a pond, but the flowers sweet scent and cheery color nauseated me.

I looked in the reflection of the pond and ran my hands over my rough hair. There were strands as long as four inches, the rest just a clumping of strange-feeling knots close to my scalp. A tear fell slowly down my cheek as I brandished the small knife I always kept tied to my ankle, and brought the sharp edge to my hairline.

When I returned to the village, I no longer had anything left to grab. With my nose in the air, I walked past the children I had once played with and ignored their laughter.

The rest of autumn had been lonely. I spent my days working with the older women, distilling oils and foraging for herbs. I did my part, as was expected of everyone, but I refused to practice my magic and preferred solitude over being gawked at. And worse, I heard the whispered lectures of mothers to their daughters warning them that the same would happen to them if they were reckless like me.

I wanted to scream at them, to tell them that I didn't care what had happened to my body. I only cared that I lost my father and my beloved Ness. I wanted to say I would have gladly born more if it meant they would still be with me… but I kept quiet, raged silently within my memories, and let them believe what they wanted.

They'd never understand. I had lost more than my hair. I'd lost my father, my sister, and my future. Nothing they could say or do would be worse than the pain of those losses.

Mother returned the day the first snow of winter fell. She never told me where she went, but when she changed for bed that night in the small one-room hut we always used on our visits, I noticed the thick red scores of self-inflicted injuries on her forearms. The sight of them lashed at my conscience with guilt and remorse.

"I'm sorry," I choked, my gaze locked on those thick red lines. "I'm so sorry, Mother. I didnae want him to die."

She looked at me, her face haunted and gaunt from so many months surviving alone in the highlands. She looked like a skeleton, and I gasped when she gathered me into her arms. I could feel each of her ribs and the knots along her spine.

"I dinnae blame ye." She ran her hand ran over my short hair. "I just… I hurt, Coira."

She told me then, as we huddled under the blankets of the bed together, of how she had tied her soul with my father's on the day they married.

"Binding yer soul with another's is the ultimate act of love, Coira. We do it to ensure that when a bound soul comes back to the earth, the soul's mate will also be sent. That way, we always have a chance o' findin' one another in the next life." Her breath hitched, and she dashed away a silent tear. "But until that happens, the one who's left behind feels the loss o' the other until their own death. Ye see, daughter, I will never remarry nor take another lover. I will just… exist… until it is my time. Only then will I see him again."

"Do ye… do ye want to be dead, Mother?" I ran my fingers over the raised marks on her arms so that she would know exactly what I was asking.

"No," she said fiercely. She kissed my cheeks before pulling me into a fervent hug. "No, I dinnae want to be dead, but I needed to feel somethin' else. My heart needed a distraction. It was the only thing I could think to do."

I nodded against her breast—I understood. My anger and self-loathing felt like shaken bottles of ale, their corks only so tight and ready to explode in a spray of foam at any moment. Her grief must feel a thousand times worse.

"I cannae lose ye, too," I whispered.

She squeezed me again and said, "Ye willnae lose me. No' yet."

We stayed in the highlands for three years, tucked in that little valley. During that time, my body shed the last of my adolescence and softened with the new curves of a young woman. I watched, ever feeling like an outsider, while the young women my age were courted. I witnessed chaste kisses and the timid handholding of my peers. Jealousy burned in my breast with the need to taste what I would have experienced if my body had not been burned. I yearned and hungered for the touch—the feel—of another.

"No one will ever want ye, Coira," a boy had said to me once when he caught me watching a young couple during one of our spring festivals. "No man would ever willingly bind themselves to a woman who'll attract the witch hunters. Ye'll be alone *forever*. Get used to the idea."

As much as I hated him for saying that, he was right. There wasn't a single interested suitor that held my stare once he saw my scars, and each rejection felt like a slap to the face.

After three years of feeling like a leper, I nearly wept in relief the day my mother told me we were to journey home. I looked forward to the seclusion of our little corner of the forest, where I could go about my duties without feeling the need to hide my face. Besides, if I was destined to journey through life alone, what better place to be?

Memories of that terrible day in Norwich still haunted me as though they'd happened yesterday. I woke up nightly with the smell of burnt hair in my nose and phantom pain where the flames had scorched my skin. In my dreams, I never escaped, and the fire always engulfed me, melting my skin while I cried out for mercy.

As I had every morning for the last three years, I woke drenched in sweat and a soundless scream stuck in my throat; a call for my father he'd never hear. Last night was particularly bad. Like every night in my dreams, I watched him from within a ring of fire as he battled his way toward me, never reaching me before the flames overwhelmed my body. But last night my dream was different.

Last night he didn't even try.

"Coira wake up. Yer safe, my love. Yer safe," Mother crooned as she wiped my hair off my sweaty cheeks and kissed my damp forehead. "Yer safe."

Breathless, with my heart hammering in my chest, I looked up at her face, ghostly in the faint light of pre-dawn. At the sight of her, hot tears collected on my lashes before they slipped past my temples and into my hair. As always, after my nightmares, I fought the urge to check the rest of my skin for more damage. With one foot still in my dreams, my mind wouldn't allow me my voice just yet. I could only cry as the vision of my father being swallowed up by the crowd played over and over in my head.

"This one was different, was it?" Mother asked.

I didn't know how she knew, but I nodded and blew out a heavy breath. With a sigh, she lay back onto the pillows and pulled me against her, my cheek rested against the top of her soft breast.

"Tell me."

Words failed to form, and I was quiet for several heavy moments until I confessed, "He smiled at me."

Mother knew of who I spoke, and paused the soothing stroke down my arm.

"Go on," she urged.

I stared at the space between us and the wall, then said, "Every night Da pushes through the crowd to reach me. Every night he cries out for me, and even though he never reaches me in time, I dinnae feel so alone when I start to burn—" I choked on a sob and turned my face into her chest, seeking comfort. I hated to tell her about my dreams. They hurt her as much as they hurt me, but she always insisted

I get them out in the air. She said they hurt less when I exposed them and didn't allow them to fester within my soul.

"And he didnae do so last night?"

"No. He just stared at me from the middle of the crowd as they cheered for my death, and then he smiled at me. It was the saddest smile I'd ever seen… and then… then he walked away."

In the meadow, I shook myself from the memory. The snap and rip of thick tree trunks and limbs filled the quiet, and I felt the groan of the earth beneath my thighs. Spinning around, I gasped as I beheld my mother standing in front of the cottage. Her arms were raised at her sides while the trees on the steep hill flanking the cottage swayed as though caught in a fierce wind.

Cautiously, I crept closer until I could hear her song and the words she wove together to move earth and water. Her arms shook with exertion as she sang louder, her voice layered: old and young, harsh and soft.

The voice of a Druid.

I hadn't touched that space within my soul in three years. Not since that terrible day in Norwich, when I tried to call forth the sea. I didn't want to chance losing control, too terrified to touch that dark pool of power within me.

I watched my mother standing barefoot in her thin, white shift, her skin luminescent in the weak sunlight. The air around her shimmered, and the wind danced about her body. It tugged at the hem of her nightgown and violently raked invisible fingers through her unbound hair.

Even with my view of her back, she looked majestic, otherworldly, and fearsome, and I had never been more in awe. I'd always known she was powerful. I'd seen her call storms, direct floods, and heal men within an inch of death… but I'd never seen her as she was now.

Her fingers curled into claws, her muscles strained, and her song became labored as she pulled at the earth. The trees on the hill continued their dance, limbs clacking into one other. Birds took flight, and creatures scurried from the underbrush. The ground moaned under the strain of her demands.

I could tell she was tiring, but she refused to let go.

Terrified her magic would consume her, I rushed to grasp her bare shoulders. Without hesitation I poured my energy into her, and breathed a sigh of relief when she straightened her back, renewed her song…

And moved the whole goddamn hill behind the cottage.

Like water parting around a stone, the ground split around our home. The pine trees that grew behind it only moments ago, now resided on either side like tall, looming sentinels. The earth whispered and groaned as the soil flowed, and she didn't slow her song until the whole rear-half of the cottage was swallowed by the steep incline, from floor to roof.

Satisfied, she released her hold on her magic and teetered on her feet. I slipped her arm over my shoulders and looked up at her in wonderment.

"Thank ye for that, daughter," she said, her voice scratchy and dry.

"Ye moved the hill. Why?"

But she only smiled tiredly and told me to fetch some water from the well so she could make our supper.

The next morning, I woke alone in the bed to the sound of grinding stone and falling rock, and clambered down the ladder to find the floor of our cottage covered in dirt, mud, and displaced stone. I called out for my mother and breathed a sigh of relief when I spotted her crouched within the cold hearth covered from head to toe in dirt.

"Are ye mad, woman?" I squawked as she came to stand beside me.

She brushed off her filthy clothing, dust puffing out around her. I then noticed she'd removed all the stones at the back of the fireplace. Her laugh at my confusion, was the first I'd heard from her in years.

Hearing it made me want to cry.

"Do I look mad?" she asked.

"A bit," I admitted, and peered into the darkness behind her. "What are ye doin'?"

Her gaze turned heavy as she gripped my hand within hers. I could feel the dust and every kernel of sand that clung to her fingers.

"Givin' us a way out, should we ever need one."

Later that evening, covered in dirt from the top of my head to my bare toes, I realized I hadn't been woken up by a nightmare. For years I'd been plagued by them, terrorized, and haunted… every night the same save one.

As I fit another stone into the wall behind the hearth, I reflected on the difference in my latest dream and wondered if maybe my father hadn't actually abandoned me when I watched him walk away. Maybe it was his way of saying goodbye instead.

And then I wondered if maybe my mother had had a dream of her own.

CHAPTER TWENTY-SIX

MALCOLM

"I love you with so much of my heart that none is left to protest."
-William Shakespeare, Much Ado About Nothing

Malcolm stared in horror at the blazing inferno. His exposed skin tightened from the deadly heat, and he staggered back when his men collectively heaved his bulk away from the flames. The two pines that stood on either side of the cottage were ablaze. Like spires straight from hell itself, they rained embers from their needles upon them.

Finlay's questions rang in his head as loud as a church bell.

"Why aren't ye? Why hauvnae ye dropped dead at my feet?"

Why indeed? he wondered as he searched the flames that seemed to reach toward him, ever hungry for more flesh.

The oath he swore to Vanora had been specific… or had he been mistaken? Because of the way his oath had attacked him last spring, had he only *assumed* he would die if he failed to keep Coira alive? He acutely remembered the phantom claws that seized his heart when he had waited too long to collect her.

Malcolm sifted through his memories of the night he had sworn the oath and came up wanting. His oath should have killed him by then, and anger at having that swift end taken from him raced like a herd of wild highland ponies through his veins.

He hissed in pain when his hands burned. His fingertips grew heavy, and when he lifted his hands up against the orange glow, Malcolm gasped in horror at the black claws that had punched out of his flesh. Thick, hard talons meant for tearing and ripping; they glistened in the firelight as though they were made of obsidian. The skin of his palms tingled and grew tough with unforgiving callouses, like the thick footpad of a badger.

"That's new," Finlay muttered, his lip turned up in partial disgust and more than a little fear. Malcolm nodded in agreement before icy fingertips seemed to walk up his back, and his skin erupted in gooseflesh.

Then he felt the tug.

"I can still feel her," he breathed.

He tore his attention away from his modified hands and the burning cottage. Without explanation, Malcolm shrugged off his men like they were young children and hurtled away from the blaze to run along the base of the hill that edged the cottage. With single-minded determination, Malcolm followed the invisible tether, his heart hammering in his chest.

Where are you? I can feel you!

Malcolm's newfound hope plummeted when he skidded to a halt and blinked at the face of the steep slope, overgrown with brush and vines.

"My laird—"

Malcolm interrupted Farlan's worried voice with a feral roar of frustration, and on pure instinct, slashed at the foliage with his newfound claws. He could feel his men gathered behind him, unsure of what to do—too terrified to come any closer.

Rock, roots, leaves, and dirt came away with little resistance against his claws as he ripped at the earth like a man possessed. The muscles of his back strained as he scooped away dirt and stone…

To reveal a door.

The soft glow emanating from his eyes illuminated the thin, boxy outline, and Malcolm's chest tightened as he swiped the rest of the dirt away. Thick, half-rotted planks and wood casings marked a tunnel entrance, wrapped in rusted iron and sealed tight with tar. But years of neglect made it impossible to pry open.

With a growl of frustration, Malcolm stepped back and kicked out at the door, the heel of his too-tight boot connecting with a harsh thud. Again and again, he kicked until the thick planks loosened and a ribbon of black smoke crept from between the slats to disappear into the pre-dawn air.

A faint, distinctly female cough, muffled and weak, bolstered Malcolm's need for entry.

"Coira!" Malcolm bellowed as he ripped at the door with his sharp talons. With a final grunt, he tore the whole bloody thing off its rusted hinges and hurled it away, the splintered wood and sharp scrape of rusted metal barely felt through his padded callouses. The mangled door narrowly missed some of his men as it flew past them, and they watched as it bounced once to land in the grass thirty feet away.

Without wasting another moment, Malcolm stuffed his enormous body within the narrow, pitch-black passageway and ignored the sharp stones and roots that scratched at his shoulders and the top of his head. As he pushed his way deeper, his teeth receded, his black claws dropped to the ground, and the glow from his eyes faded to nothing, leaving him in the dark without their guide. By the time his body returned to normal, his outstretched hand connected with someone soft and warm leaning against the side of the tunnel. A relieved sob escaped his chest, and when Malcolm reached down to wrap his arms around his wife, he realized there was not one, but *two* women huddled together within the tunnel.

"Angel," he barked as his clawless fingers traced over Coira's slack face, then shook her shoulders. "Angel. Answer me."

Only silence.

Choking on the smoke that clogged the pitch-black shaft, and reluctant to leave the other woman behind, Malcolm gathered the two limp bodies against his chest and dragged them backward toward the egress.

"Ye have her?" Farlan called out when Malcolm neared the opening, and gasped when he beheld the second woman in Malcolm's arms.

"Maeve!" Finlay's voice pierced the shocked silence, and he shoved through the circle of concerned warriors to get to his wife.

Malcolm collapsed in a fit of hacking coughs and handed Maeve over to her husband. Finlay drew Maeve into his lap and rocked her in his arms, his eyes wide and full of worry as he ran a trembling hand down her arm.

Neither woman stirred.

"What do I do? *What do I do?*" Malcolm yelled as he rolled Coira onto her back. He cupped her limp neck with one hand and lightly slapped her cheek with the other. "Wake up and tell me what to do!"

Malcolm's head felt light with panic, and he checked her body for damage. He found nothing but countless singed holes in her soot-smudged shift, and angry, blackened burns on the soles of her bare feet.

At the sound of pounding footsteps, Malcolm looked up to see Bram running at full tilt with a bucket full of sloshing water. He skidded to a halt at his laird's side.

"She's no' gonna be happy about this," he warned breathlessly a moment before he dumped the entire contents onto Coira's chest.

As soon as the frigid water touched her, saturating the fabric of her thin nightgown, Coira's quick intake of breath, followed by violent coughing, caused a cheer to echo off the hills. Pale irises, framed by black grit collected in the fine lines around her eyes, focused on Malcolm's face for only a moment before she pitched away. On shaking arms, she held herself above the ground while she wretched into the wet grass.

"I'll get some more water," Bram told his twin, and tore off for the well on the other side of the raging fire as though he had wings.

Malcolm braced his hands on either side of Coira's ribs, supporting her while she coughed and retched all over the trampled grass. Beneath his palms, he could feel the way her lungs fought for each hoarse inhalation. It terrified him.

"Tree," she wheezed, her voice just a wisp of crackling air. "I need… Hurry."

Recollection of her mother using the enormous ancient oak to save his brother, and Coira's use of the several small pines to heal Farlan, had him scanning the far side of the field in the pre-dawn light. Panicked, Malcolm scooped her up in his arms and ran across the field, past the younger trees that lined the western side, and toward the dark silhouette of a knotty elm; the trunk thick, bulbus, blemished with warts, and half covered by vines.

He could only pray it was big enough.

Breathless, Malcolm sat her down among its roots and made to kneel at her side when she feebly pushed him away. "Ye cannae touch me," she wheezed through blue-tinged lips.

"I willnae, I promise," Malcolm swore, and made no move to leave her.

She shook her head weakly and dug her nails into his forearm. "Ye *will*. Now go. Keep the others from fallin' under my spell." Her voice was barely a whisper, and Malcolm's brows furrowed when he noticed the tear that rolled down her cheek as she lowered herself within the maze of roots. "No matter what, ye cannae touch me, or ye'll feel it, too."

He shook his head in confusion. "Feel what, Angel?"

Coira's lower lip trembled, and another tear raced along her temple; its thin track shimmered in the faint light. Her right hand cupped her lower abdomen where their child grew, and he could plainly see her despair and apprehension in the set of her mouth.

"The pain," she said.

Malcolm's jaw went slack when the enormity of her words sunk in and he realized what she meant. To heal herself, she'd have to endure without the aid of a sleeping spell. Coira nodded and squeezed his arm once before she gathered the wet, nearly translucent bodice of her shift into her mouth.

"Go, please," she croaked around the fabric, and then sucked hard to wick the moisture into her mouth. She narrowed her eyes at him. *"Go, Malcolm."*

His stomach taut with dread and brow slicked with sweat, Malcolm slowly rose to his feet. Clumsily, and with his focus never leaving her ghostly form cradled within the roots of the elm, he rushed back to the other side of the meadow.

"What's she doin'?" Farlan asked when Malcolm reached the group of men, their focus intent across the field.

The fire that continued to eat up the cottage casted a hazy orange glow on the flattened grass. Malcolm noticed the thick line of pale grey in the east that preceded the fast-approaching sun was now thick and smudged with pink. He cleared his throat to answer, but the words caught in his throat when Coira's voice, feeble and weak, drifted across the field and caressed an ethereal hand over his nerves.

He knew the rest of his men heard her as well when they shifted on their feet, and their murmurings and questions fell silent. Even Finlay ceased his soft chatter to Maeve, who was still unconscious in his arms.

The lyrical, soothing tones he'd heard the day she had healed Farlan were absent. Instead, they gave the impression of a flute stuffed with dirt, and the violent twist of dry reeds. But even her ruined voice failed to diminish the power of the Druid words she sang. He could feel their weight, their allure. They beckoned his men like a siren's song, and Malcolm snatched Gavin by the collar when he made to cross the meadow in a dreamlike state.

"Hold yer wits about ye, lads, and stay where ye are," Malcolm warned. He gritted his teeth when Coira's voice grew stronger and then pained. At her first high-pitched wail of agony, Malcolm's oath woke with a blaze of fury, and he grunted against the onslaught to his senses.

His men swore and backed away, their attention half on him and half on their lady where she writhed among the roots across open grassland. The sky continued to brighten, and Malcolm closed his eyes as he fought for control of his body.

Phantom talons raked his ribs in a bid to escape, and he felt each scrape like a sharp stick being dragged along a garden fence. With a pinch, his vision altered to a back-lit glow; his mouth ached to make room for the beast's incisors. Enraged, it thrashed within the cage of Malcolm's body, delirious to escape and protect—to destroy whatever caused Coira pain.

It just didn't understand that the person it wanted to destroy was *her*.

I cannae allow it, Malcolm thought as he curled his fists tight and braced his legs wide.

Beneath the pink and periwinkle sky of dawn, Coira's song grew to a crescendo, her suffering interwoven with the musical language of her people. The ground trembled and the elm shivered above her when her voice morphed into an ear-splitting scream that echoed throughout the shallow valley.

Malcolm's hold over the beast broke.

In an agonizing moment, his body exploded in a rush of strength and size, and his men shouted their confusion and surprise as they watched Malcolm's muscles stretch, ripple, and grow.

No!

Malcolm fought against the tidal wave of animalistic instinct and rage that beat against his sense of self… and failed when fangs ripped through his gums.

Freed from its tether, the beast lunged forward, determined and fraught with urgency. At the bidding of another, the muscles of Malcolm's thighs bunched and flexed, and propelled him across the meadow at a frantic pace.

Closer.

Closer.

Coira's song rang like a death knell in his ears, and he vaguely made note of the branches falling to the ground around her—branches now made of stone. They clacked against the roots, snapped and shattered to pieces.

Malcolm wrestled for control over his body, silently pleaded within the confines of his mind for control, but the beast snapped its teeth and roared in argument.

Look.

The word rang out in Malcolm's mind, the tone as resonant and sharp as thunder during a rare winter storm, deep and unfathomable.

Ancient. Older than the hills and the ocean. Older than the stars.

So, Malcolm looked.

He saw Coira laying within the maze of roots, her back arched and chin thrust into the air while she sang through her clenched teeth. Under the lightening sky and through his superior sight, he noticed the blisters on her bare feet fading by the second. Then she coughed— once, twice—and black, wet soot sprayed from her lips when she purged the smoke from her lungs.

LOOK.

The deep voice howled in his ears, and to his surprise, Malcolm felt himself veer off the path that would take him to his wife. Through eyes he had no control over, he spied movement in the forest that ringed the field.

There wasn't time to feel guilt or regret over his attempt to keep the beast at bay. Malcolm gave himself over in a burst of gratitude, and as he pounded closer toward the man who crept between the trees, he felt himself become one with the beast he both feared and loved.

I will fight ye no longer, Malcolm promised.

Heat and bright, golden light flooded his mind and body as his consciousness melded with the beast's, and power like he'd never experienced pulsed like lightning through his veins. His attention split: he watched Coira as her voice faded, and the last branch cracked off the elm; at the same time, his focus zeroed in on a man with a thick, black mustache rounding a boulder.

His neckcloth stained red, his suit ripped and grimy with blood and dirt, Malcolm vaguely recognized him as the man he'd thrown toward the tree line. His blood ran cold at the sight of the flintlock he held. Dark, hazy eyes, like that of a sleepwalker, gazed at Coira as he stumbled forward and lifted the pistol with purpose.

Blinding rage, and the overwhelming need to protect, burned through Malcolm's self-preservation, and he let loose a bellow of warning so forceful and loud his throat bled.

As Coira's song fell silent, he calculated the distance and growled low in his throat.

We willnae make it, he thought.

Malcolm watched his target shake his head as though casting off a veil and took notice of the massive being headed straight for him.

The beast sighed in relief when the man swung his pistol away from his original target…

And aimed it right at Malcolm's chest.

Chapter Twenty-Seven

COIRA

Black mist erupted from my lungs in a thick spray, and gritty liquid ran down the corners of my mouth. I panted through the pain while my body knitted itself together, layer by agonizing layer.

My injuries, substantial and deep, took every bit of life from the elm Malcolm had carried me to. Nearly all the skin on my feet had been either blistered or severely burned down to the bone from kicking the back of the hot hearth stones away in the cottage. The smoke had been so bad that I wasn't able to vocalize the words to sing them away and instead resorted to standing in the embers and coals, removing them by force. All the while, memories of my time on the pyre haunted me, for I could smell my skin cooking away while I cried and coughed through the pain.

By the time I had cleared the passageway, Maeve was an unconscious heap on the floor. Embers had rained down around her and burned tiny holes in her white shift. How I'd found the strength to carry her, I'd never know, but the need to get into the tunnel before the roof collapsed drove me. With her limp arms clasped over my chest and small body draped over my back like a heavy cloak, the tips of her toes barely scraped the coals as I stooped beneath the mantle and we disappeared into the pitch-black tunnel that burrowed under the hill.

Blindly, I carried her and felt my way along the wood planks my mother had used to reinforce the tunnel all those years ago. The smoke followed us into the hole, and my head pounded from lack of air. I collapsed before I ever reached the door to safety and…I awakened to a deluge of icy water that felt like a thousand needles on my breasts.

Now fully healed, I severed the connection to the elm and took my first deep breath, free of the smoke that had clogged my airway. I looked up at the brightening sky—one I'd never expected to see again, and opened my mouth to call out for Malcolm. The steady thump of a great weight pounding the earth drew my attention, and I looked to my left just in time to see Malcolm's enormous, oath-altered body career by from where I sat huddled among the roots.

Golden light—not the white I was accustomed to seeing—pulsed from his eyes, and his skin shimmered with glittering, gold-and-black shadows. I blinked in wonder as I watched his mouth open, his beast's teeth on display, and clapped my hands over my ears when he roared at some unknown threat.

I was not prepared for the flash of unnatural light or the sharp pain that followed. I gasped at the feeling of my heart being ripped in two. The string—the one that connected my soul to Malcolm's—drew tight and threatened to fray. Air whooshed from my newly healed lungs, and I sat up among the stone roots to watch Malcolm fall to the ground. His speed caused him to roll, a vortex of moss, twigs, and dirt until he finally stopped. His hand rested over his heart, and I choked when an impossible amount of blood welled between his still fingers.

Malcolm did not rise.

"Demon my arse," an English voice muttered, and I looked beyond Malcolm's motionless form to see the man from the road—the one who spewed fire from his mouth onto the roof of my childhood home—throw down a still-smoking pistol. Our eyes locked, and he rushed at me with arms outstretched, his crooked teeth bared beneath his thick mustache. He pounced upon me and wrapped his hands tightly around my neck.

Still weak from my use of healing magic and the echo of self-inflicted pain, I struggled beneath his weight and clawed at his wrists, trying to free myself, all the while fighting for breath. The sensation of the connection between me and Malcolm fraying bit by bit maddened me, and my vision became focused, my awareness heightened. I ignored the sight of Malcolm's men, who began to sprint across the field. I knew they wouldn't get a quarter of the way before the witch hunter snuffed out my life.

"You're harder to kill than the rest of Blount's witches," the Englishman said as he leaned closer to me and tightened his grimy grip on my soft skin.

Black spots swam between us, and I dug my heels into the ground and bucked, trying to throw him off. He smiled cruelly at the failed attempt and quickly glanced behind him before saying, "I don't care if those bastards run me through." He looked down on me with a hard gleam in his eye, lifted me just enough for my shoulders to leave the ground, and spoke through gritted teeth, "As long as there's one less witch in the world, my death will not be in vain."

With a sharp shove, he slammed me to the ground, and the back of my head cracked against a thick stone root. My eyes rolled from the pain, and for a moment, I was back in Norwich, reliving the moment my father had crumpled to the ground. I felt the ghosts of unfamiliar hands on my legs while I had been carted away to the church… and I remembered. I remembered the moment I discovered that vast expanse of power that dwelled in my soul—how that black lake of molten force felt: seductive, demanding and *necessary*.

It had *beckoned* me, not unlike a lover, and promised me great and terrible things.

I never fully touched it that day. I only danced along its black-pebbled shore, too young and petrified to allow myself to dive headlong into that promising darkness. Because I knew—I *knew* I would become something there would be no return from.

But for my husband, I would. For the babe I nurtured within my womb, I would risk *anything*.

Even the purity of my soul.

The suffocating grip tightened further around my neck, and tears brimmed my eyes to race down my temples. My sight blurred, the edges blackening.

Before I lost consciousness, I allowed myself to dive headfirst into the fathomless pool of darkness and power. I clawed my way deeper, *deeper*, and a voice I'd never heard before whispered in my ear. With an alluring, flawless tone and pitch, the voice seduced me, called me to join her in the depths of my soul where she'd been all along.

And that was when I realized… that darkness wasn't entirely *me*.

Immersed within the forbidden part of my soul—that place I had feared to explore for the past thirteen years—ice crackled in my veins and a surge of power pulsed through my body like the strong beat of a drum. My sight sharpened to that of a predator, illuminating the shadows around me and highlighting every blade of grass and fissure of bark. I felt my nails grow long and sharp, and something else— something ancient, terrible, and vengeful—stepped into my body.

Cold, inky magic forced its way into my mouth, down my throat, and into my eyes, blinding me—*binding me!*

No, no, no!

A binding spell!

I thrashed against the inevitable, helpless against the onslaught of magic far beyond my understanding. No Druid possessed the knowledge to bind another. It was not in our teachings, the act forbidden to even attempt.

Dragged deeper into the depths of that dark magic, I realized who had awaited me… and as the last pinprick of light was snuffed out, I hoped with all hope that she did not destroy everything in her path. Then everything faded to black—

—*Where am I?* Tlachtga wondered when she opened her eyes for the first time in ages and noticed an uncomfortable squeeze of her throat.

"What—" The man above her hesitated, and his eyes flared with uncertainty when they locked with hers.

He trembled, his pupils widening with fear. His punishing grip fell from her neck, but he could not break her gaze, no matter how much he desired to look elsewhere. He was the moth, she the flame.

I'll burn him alive, she thought.

The first breath of unhindered air rushed through her nose, over the back of her tongue, and left traces of soil, soot, and blood on her sensitive palette. With a soft sigh, she slid her palms up the lapels of his dark jacket like a lover, took note of the tightly-woven texture, and then caressed his unshaven cheeks with unfamiliar hands. Tlachtga pulled him closer, and she caught sight of herself in the dark reflection of his eyes. She grinned ferally at what she saw.

Magnificent, she thought.

She was beauty incarnate, and she preened beneath him, basking in the way her irises shone with a ring of ethereal, swirling silver. Her lips, lined and blackened from soot, twisted into a savage leer, and she dug her nails deep into the soft flesh behind the human's ears. His yelp of terror-filled pain excited her, and she tightened her grip to keep him still so she could look her fill.

"*Mortal*," she purred in a throaty voice not her own. "I have ye now. There is no escaping me."

His bottom lip quivered. "P-please…"

"Silence! Did ye think ye could abuse my body? Did ye think I would allow that to happen *again*?" She sneered at the pathetic wretch caught in her snare and rose steadily to her bare feet. He made room for her graceful movements but stayed on his knees, his eyes beseeching and wide with fear as she rose above him.

He should *fear me*, Tlachtga thought.

As a full-blooded Druid, she could control the earth and the wind. She could command the water in the oceans to recede or pummel the shores, and the molten rock oozing far beneath the surface to rise with naught but a thought. Nothing and no one could stop her.

Movement drew her gaze to the right, and she snarled at the band of men who dared approach her, their weapons drawn but held loosely as they beheld her glory. A fire raged behind them, the greedy flames slowly eating their way up a hill beyond. Black smoke clogged the early morning sky, tainting the air with ash and embers. Two men at the rear skidded to a halt when they found themselves the objects of her attention and turned to leave. By far the smartest of their group if they preferred their chances with the fire than with her. She may let them live. The rest—

"My lady, let us help ye," one said as he took a tentative step closer. His bright blue eyes and brown curls were strangely familiar, and she tilted her head. He took another step and reached toward her, his palm open. "Let me help him—"

Her brows pulled down low and she bared her teeth. Fools. She did not need aid from *humans*, let alone their *men*. They were nothing but distrustful, raping filth.

"No," she hissed, and with a swipe of her blood-tipped, moon-white hand, she reached for the essence of earth and wrapped it within her grasp like ribbons. Those invisible strands sparkled with energy, and she wove the power through her fingers, looped the invisible threads around her wrist, and *yanked*. She needed no words to direct her will of silent fury, for the song of the elements was contained within her mind.

At her whim, rock and roots and dirt speared from the surface in front of the line of men in a spray of dust, and her captive cried out anew when the ground rumbled beneath them. She laughed, dark and menacing, as the steep wall grew higher and higher. Until it stood forty feet from the ground, topped with spears of sharp slate.

Satisfied with the barrier, Tlachtga looked down on her prey, caught a rivulet of blood on his neck with the pad of her forefinger, and brought it to her lips. She sighed the moment the sweet nectar of life touched her tongue, and she tipped her chin to the sky in ecstasy.

"I have no' tasted the blood o' man in *centuries*," she crooned, the pitch of her voice different than she remembered, and swayed on her feet. "I have slumbered for too long."

Drunk on the metallic tang, she ignored the human's feeble whimpers and focused on her connection to the tiny creatures under the earth's surface, the feathered souls in the trees, and the furry beasts who slept, safe in their burrows. Each creature sang a different song in her ear, a never-ending lullaby of harmony. But there was one—one soul that stood out and could not be ignored. It demanded her attention. It was… attached to her. Strange, but not interesting enough to distract her from sliding the flat of her tongue along the human's neck for another taste.

"So sweet."

She moved to lap at his skin again when her gaze snagged on the prone form of a man not fifteen paces away. He was still, but it was not the stillness of death, no. Death was close, but it had not claimed him yet, for his soul was still affixed to…

Mine? she pondered. How curious.

Memories of events she had not lived bombarded her mind. There were visions of earthy brown eyes and soft lips, a low voice reciting poetry within a sun-lit room, and lazy mornings wrapped in blankets. She recalled the naked flesh of another pressed against hers and the way this man would coax her body to shattering heights with his fingers and tongue. She saw that very mouth pressing a reverent kiss on her abdomen over the new life they'd made together.

Malcolm.

Is that his name? she asked herself.

She could feel the string that connected them fray—so thin now, nearly a wisp of spider's silk—and focused on the red swath of blood saturating that thick chest. A vision of how he became injured flashed in her mind, how he'd put himself in harm's way to protect…

Me, she thought, and more memories she had never experienced flooded her mind with urgency. She could feel his arms around her waist while they rode on horseback. Remembered how he'd carried her through sodden fields by moonlight. She could hear his beast dismembering a man with a painted face before he found where she had hidden.

She blinked at a memory not her own of a man—of Malcolm— sliding a faceted ring upon her finger. Then she saw the way his body had convulsed as though someone had run him through, not with a sword, but with the strange contraption now half-hidden among the leaves by his side.

Confused by the unfamiliar memories she hadn't lived, they warred with the rage that boiled in her veins because she *felt* them. She felt… was that love? Not the kind of love a parent feels for a child. She would recognize that love because a mother's heart is torn open wide for her children, even if they were conceived through actions of hate.

No, this was a Druid mating love: incomplete but still sacred and pure.

She turned her attention to the sniveling mortal in her clutches, the one responsible for destroying such a rare bond.

"*Ye* did that." Tlachtga repositioned her hands, and her nails sunk into the back of his neck while she hissed her hatred at him.

Still on his knees, the mortal struggled to break free from her grasp, and thrust his palms against her hipbones as he tried to push her away. But he was no match for her strength. Even a dragon of old could not outmatch her.

The earth heard her rage and sent the wind to writhe around her. Faster and faster, it circled her feet, her calves, her torso, and lifted her hair off her neck. This human would pay. She'd punish him for daring to harm the soul's connection and tether attached to this body, which was still mortal and capable of feeling such emotions as love.

Her fingers flexed and his flesh tore, sending her nails deeper into the muscle while he struggled. The wind tore his cries of pain from his throat.

The scent of his blood grew stronger, but it was no longer his *blood* she wanted. Now, she wanted his life.

All of it.

Her lips curled into a sinister grin, and she whispered the word *death*. Such a bitterly sweet word, death. It tasted of lemons, honey, and rue. Pliable and warm, like dripping sap on a hot summer day, it slid out of her mouth with finality and dropped into his like a stone in a well.

She knew the moment he felt his doom, for he tried in vain to pry her fingers from his flesh and begged and pleaded for mercy. But he was no match for her god-like strength, and she was incapable of forgiveness.

He could only scream, and she laughed while she memorized the sensation of his life fading from his body—reveled in the way it traveled through her fingertips, up her arms, and absorbed into her essence. She celebrated the sight of his skin growing old and dry and spotted with age by the second. His eyes became milky and sunk into his skull. The dark whiskers on his face grew thin and white, and what little hair he had left scattered from his scalp like dandelion fluff in the swirling wind.

She stole his years, his decades. And when all that was left was a husk of bones and skin with only minutes of life remaining, she disengaged her nails from his flesh and let him fall to a heap on the ground.

Tlachtga breathed deeply and sent the wind away with the flick of her wrist. Her body thrummed with the stolen life, and the need to absorb *more* made her spine itch. She wanted to suck the life out of the men she could hear climbing the wall made of dirt and rock—the temptation was too great to ignore.

She took a step, then another, prepared to trap the first human-fool to peek over the edge, when that strange tether to her soul unraveled more. The pain took her breath away, and she bowed over with her hand clutched over her heart.

So thin. So fragile. It threatened to dissolve into nothingness.

Fists battered the back door of her mind, and she looked over her shoulder at the prone form that lay so still. Death was close. Minutes away. *Seconds.*

A persistent thought nagged, annoying and loud.

Go to him.

Save him.

Love him.

She knew that voice. It was hers… but… not.

Her feet were moving, hurrying across the cool grass, and she fell to her knees beside the dying man. The coppery stench of his blood stuffed itself up her nose, sickening her and confusing her nature. With a hiss, she ripped the offending blood-riddled fabric away with a swipe of her nails.

"What is this?" she asked when she spied the tiny hole in his chest so very close to his heart. "What is in here?"

Those phantom fists hammered harder.

Save him.

Save him.

Save him.

I could, she mused as she peered into the wound. It would be so very easy. She could sense the unnatural, earthen object wedged against his spine. She knew exactly where it was.

The string stretched taut, making her gasp, and she knew a part of her body would die with him once it snapped. With no other choice, she twirled her finger above that wound, not unlike stirring water in a cup. Inch by inch, she guided a little metallic sphere and a strange golden mist through the hole until it escaped his chest with a sucking *pop.*

Captivated by this human beneath her, with whom she shared that strange soul-bond, she lowered her lips to his and dropped the word *life* between his bloodied ones.

Death's mortal opposite tasted strangely of peppers, spice, and charred meat, and left her tongue tingling even after it left her mouth.

The ground beneath them shuddered, and the trees above vibrated with energy. She poured those stolen decades into his mouth, and the string that connected them strengthened until it became a brilliant wire of gold entwined with silver. His wounds closed before her eyes.

Spell complete, she hovered over him and waited for him to wake, her pale hair a veil on the right side of her face. She was eager to have him look upon her like he did in her memories, wishing to fully experience the warmth his touch had brought to her skin.

She didn't have to wait long.

Thick black lashes fluttered open to reveal the warm brown irises she recognized from her memories, and she found herself transfixed. He swallowed, the reflex slow and almost nervous when he lifted a hand and carded his fingers into the hair close to her scalp. She purred at the gentle touch, the first she'd experienced in so very long. His gaze roved over her face, at her glowing, silver eyes and pale, iridescent skin.

"Angel," he breathed, and urged her head down to receive his kiss.

Angel?

At the first touch of his lips, phantom hands grasped her shoulders, and she plunged back into the darkness—

—My lungs felt like they were filled with water, and I clawed up from the depths of that magical lake, the light from above my guide.

Angel. That's me, I cried out, but the words were silent and naught but bubbles and foam.

I kicked for the surface.

Angel.

I was not Tlachtga. I was good; I was gentle and kind, honest and true. I was not the monstrous, other-worldly being who had taken over my body. I fought back for control, determined to win.

I am good, I reminded myself.

I kicked with all my might and strength, repeating that mantra in my head over and over as I fought for the surface. I could feel a powerful *something* behind me; a hand tipped with claws and sharpened teeth.

I would not let her catch me again.

Desperate, I focused on the fortified bond that was the bridge between souls and grasped it with everything I was, everything I could be. I climbed it like a ladder, hand over hand, and hauled myself up. The surface grew closer and closer, and I fought harder with every inch gained until my face broke the surface—

I opened my eyes to find Malcolm's questioning look. I knew my irises had just lost their glow, and I watched the skin of my forearms and hands return to its normal hue. My dark nails turned to smoke and drifted away on a breeze.

"Have ye come back to me?" Malcolm whispered as he ran his fingertips lightly down my cheek.

I nodded. "I almost lost ye." My voice broke, and I lightly dragged my finger over the new scar on his chest, a perfect circle of pale pink. My vision blurred at the sight of it. "I didnae ken what else to do. I… I almost lost myself to the darkness."

Malcolm frowned and urged me to look at him again with a firm touch beneath my chin.

"Ye're too strong to be lost, Angel."

At his praise, my eyes filled with tears and my throat closed off any response. I cupped the sharp angles of his jaw, rested my forehead against his, and cried.

Chapter Twenty-Eight

COIRA

"Will ye tell me what happened?" Malcolm murmured in my ear, his breath a puff of warm air. His question was vague, but I knew of what he asked.

He'd seen my face while Tlachtga wore my skin.

I shivered in his arms and focused on Ramsey's lulling gait as we reached the road and headed west. Wrapped in Bram's heavy coat and my husband's arms, I tried my best not to think of the power still swirling inside me. Even now it beckoned me to return.

I would not. Ever again.

I cleared my throat and looked up at him from where I sat sideways in his lap. My bare feet bounced against his calf. "Do ye remember the day I told ye about my people's history? When we sat by the loch and I made the water dance in yer palms?" He nodded. "Do ye remember the story about my ancestor, the immortal Druid who bore children conceived from rape?"

"Aye."

"That was her ye saw in my face." I barely heard my own words, afraid if I spoke them too loudly, they might summon her back and I'd be lost forever.

Malcolm's brows drew low in confusion. "But she's been dead for hundreds o' years."

"Tlachtga and her father were the last o' the immortal Druids. There is a legend that tells o' her last spell. She wanted to keep her immortality but live no longer in her own body, so she fused her soul with her great-granddaughter's. People have speculated why she didnae want to live forever… but I ken why, now. 'Tis because she *hates*. I felt it, before she left me alone in the depths o' my soul and stepped into my body. She still hates the men who violated her and left their children in her belly."

I traced the spread of skin beneath my sternum and imagined it swollen with babies conceived in such a way. I looked out at the hills we slowly passed by. "I dinnae ken if she meant for it to happen, but she lives in me. 'Tis no' life, no' really. 'Tis just a bit o' her soul fused with my power. Terrible, deadly, all-consuming power."

Malcolm's arm tightened around me, and folded his other hand over mine, twining our fingers together over my heart. "Ye're no' terrible. Nor are ye deadly." He kissed the top of my head. "Ye're wonderful," he murmured into my hair.

My throat closed painfully at his words, and hot tears flooded my eyes to the brim before cascading down my cheeks.

"That's what freed me. At first, I thought I'd be imprisoned there forever, but while I was in the dark, I still felt ye dyin'. I felt that bond between us stretch itself until there was nearly nothin' left. I was goin' mad—mad at my inability to break free." I looked up at him, and he wiped the wetness from my cheeks. "So, I did the only thing I could. I pushed my memories *out*. I forced her to see. I thought about all my favorite moments between us—and demanded she save ye. I needed her to see that no' all men are monsters." My voice cracked, and I caught a twitch of Malcolm's lower lip before he pressed a fierce kiss to my forehead.

"Ye looked like a demon, with yer black lips and eyes glowin' like a silver flame. I realized right away it wasnae really ye."

"Ye called me Angel. I heard ye." For a moment I was back in the black depths, fighting for the surface. "It was what gave me the strength to escape. She did no' want me to."

"I would have fought for ye," he said, and I believed him, but we both knew he would have died trying. The beast was gone. She'd taken it from him when she took the small ball of lead from his body.

I took a steadying breath and squeezed his hand. "I ken ye would."

We stopped along the river leading to our little village late that afternoon, and while I dozed beneath the dancing branches of a birch tree, Maeve settled down by my side with a wreath of buttercups and puffy pink thrift in her hands. She looked much like me, wrapped in a man's coat to hide her soot-stained nightgown, her blonde hair left wild to curl around her face.

"Ye've been avoidin' me," she scolded and arched an accusatory brow. The sun caught the rosiness of her cheeks, her smooth skin fresh and clean, lacking even the barest trace of soot. So very different from the grey pallor of death that tainted her skin only a few hours ago.

At the sight of her healthy blush, I could not help but to think of the moments that followed after I re-entered my own body.

"My laird!" Farlan's voice rang out. I looked from where I lay draped over Malcolm's chest to see Bram tumble down a peaked embankment made from loose oil and rock in the middle of the field.

He landed hard at its base in a cloud of dust and scrambled to his feet a few strides away, only to jump back from a heap of oddly bunched clothing. Eyes wide, he murmured a prayer of protection and even crossed himself before he approached us.

"I'm alright," Malcolm called and sat up, his body healed of any wound despite being covered in blood from chin to navel. His brows lowered at the sight of the thin, damp fabric covering my body. "Bram, give over yer jacket."

I didn't move from where I knelt on the grass. I could only stare, transfixed by the sheer size of the wall, for it didn't stop at the edge of the meadow. It speared right through the sapling forest and beyond, curving around us like a crescent moon. I spun around and saw that it went just as far in the other direction as Bram settled his warm jacket upon my shoulders.

Gavin and Farlan slid down the incline with more grace, their eyes wild and wary when they took me in. The rest of the men popped their heads above the crest a moment later but did not make a move to come down.

Dinnae be afraid o' me, I wanted to say, and huddled deeper into Bram's jacket, in part to hide my exposed, scarred skin seen through the sleeveless shift, and to hide from their judgment. I could not look them in the eye, too afraid of what I may find. I'd worked so hard for their acceptance, and all that hard work could be gone in a matter of moments. The thought of becoming the outsider again was deeply depressing, but when I watched Malcolm stand, I knew I'd gladly start from the beginning if given the choice. Maeve would help me. She'd win anyone—

"Maeve." The moment her name left my lips, I caught Bram's anguished look and refused to believe the worst. "Step back!" I ordered, and with my next breath, I harnessed my birthright and tore down the middle of that forsaken wall.

With a grumble, earth and stone parted and rolled away at my whim, and I rushed through a moment later with four men at my heels. I ignored the inferno that raged in place of my mother's cottage, my destination straight ahead. My stomach soured as I ran across the field, each step an eternity.

I came to a halt a few paces away from Maeve's bare feet. Finlay held her where he leaned back against the base of the steep hill, her limp body tucked between his legs. He ran his hand over her wet hair, turned his dead, bloodshot eyes up at me, and said, "The water didnae work on her."

Realizing someone must have tried to revive her with a bucket of water, I crouched to inspect her. Finlay hissed at me, his lower lip quivering, and pulled Maeve's limp body tighter against his chest. I'd never seen anyone look at me with such venom-laced blame.

"Dinnae touch her or I'll kill ye where—"

"Finlay!" Malcolm's sharp voice cut Finlay's threat off. "Ye will allow her attend to Maeve."

My cheeks heated at the truth in Finlay's stare, and I tried not to squirm as the rest of Malcolm's men milled behind me. Watching. Waiting. This was my fault. I had brought Maeve here; if she had stayed at the keep, she would be fine. But she was not fine, and if she had any life left in her body, I could save her.

"I understand yer anger, Finlay, I do," I said softly as I stretched my hand out and inched closer, desperate to touch her skin and know if what he believed was true. "Let me, please."

Finlay glared at me, his cheek pressed hard against the top of Maeve's head, and didn't bother to wipe away the tears that fell into her hair. Her skin was a sickly color, not even a hint of pink, and I knew that if I had been anyone else, I would have assumed her dead.

Good thing I knew better.

Finlay held my stare and curled his lip into a sneer when I wrapped my hand around Maeve's ankle. I closed my eyes and used my Druid senses to find the very faint beat of her heart, and I gasped at the steady but faint flutter beneath my fingertips.

I spun around to face my husband and said, "She lives. I need a blade." Malcolm unstrapped his dagger and handed it to me.

Finlay's voice rang out, "Ye lie! I willnae let ye touch her with yer evil magic. I've seen what ye can do, what ye became. I forbid it!"

A clump of wet soil hit the back of my head. I turned back to him and smacked away another uprooted fern aimed for my face, my mouth slack in disbelief.

"Ye'd rather her die than let me save her life?" I cried out and watched him attempt to tug a half-buried stone from the ground.

"She's already dead," Finlay roared, and abandoned the rock to hurl a handful of wet leaves that landed with an awkward plop at my feet. "I willnae allow ye to desecrate her body."

I held my arm out to stop Malcolm from his angry advance and pegged Finlay with a harsh stare. "Finlay, she's alive. I can heal her."

He shook his head. "She doesnae breathe!"

"She does, but it's faint! Ye cannae feel it because ye willnae stop fightin' me."

Finlay stilled, but only for a moment. "Ye'll bring her back a soulless monster."

I sputtered in disbelief. "I cannae bring anyone back from the dead, Finlay. No one can."

"I dinnae believe ye."

Anger and exasperation heated my face, and I gripped the hilt of Malcolm's dagger so hard the knuckle of my middle finger popped.

"Ye stubborn bawbag!" I snapped, using Maeve's insult toward the stable boy the night before. "She doesnae have time for this." And before he could get another word out, I scored the palm of my left hand and flung my blood on them both. Red

droplets, imbued with my power, peppered his neck and her forehead, and I whispered the word for sleep.

"Wha—what are ye doin'?" Bram squawked from behind me when Finlay's arms went slack, his head falling back into the waiting arms of a soft fern.

"What needs to be done," I answered, ignoring the pain. "Malcolm, carry Maeve. We need to hurry."

It took three young oaks to heal the damage, for it wasn't just the smoke in her lungs that was killing her but the stress on her heart and other organs from lack of air. Once I was done, I ordered Farlan and Bram to carry Finlay to Maeve's side and asked Gavin to bring me a bucket of water and a spare cloth to clean them.

Reluctant to be anywhere near Maeve, not wanting to see the same look her husband had given me, I left them to wake and turned my attention on the burning hillside. I could barely make out the square foundation of the cottage, now just a heap of charred beams and a collapsed chimney. The fire continued to devour the trees and underbrush up the hill, and smoke billowed up to sully the blue morning sky.

With a few lyrical measures, I snuffed it out—

Maeve cleared her throat, dragging me from my thoughts. She sat at my side with an expectant look on her sun-kissed face and said, "Well?"

I lifted my left shoulder. "I widnae say I'm avoiding ye," I grumbled, and sat up to hug my knees to my chest. "'Tis more a self-isolation."

She snorted. "Same thing."

"No' really," I mumbled, unable to look at her. Instead, I watched the river snake lazily around the bend. The southern side, where we took our rest, was pebbled and sandy, the other side a hedge of densely packed ash trees. It would be a beautiful sight come the fall, a brilliant line of gold mirrored on the calm water.

"I've wanted to thank ye all mornin'," she said, and leaned forward to draw my attention. "Will ye no' look at me, Coira?"

Hearing her say my name for the first time—not *my lady*—was a beautiful sound. It shredded the wall I'd hastily erected around my heart and clogged my throat with broken glass. I swallowed thickly.

"I dinnae deserve ye, Maeve."

She shifted beside me, and I thought she was going to leave when she settled right in front of me and gripped my upper arms.

"Why ever would ye say that?"

My brows shot to my hairline, and I gaped at her. "Ye nearly died, Maeve. Ye were moments away from death because o' *me*."

She wrinkled her nose, her grey eyes mere slits as she scowled at me. "Did ye happen to invite those men to burn the cottage around us while we slept?"

What? "No."

"And didnae ye tell me to stay at the keep?"

I paused.

"And did ye or did ye no' carry me out o' danger through a bloody hidden tunnel under the hill—ye *must* explain that to me someday soon, by the way."

With my slight nod she continued.

"Good. I'm glad we cleared that up." She looked down at my toes where they peeked out from under the charred hem of my shift. "The men told me yer feet were so badly burned they could see the bone at yer heel."

"I—I had to carry ye out. The passage entrance was behind the hearth."

Her face blanched. "Ye carried me over the coals?"

I nodded, and my vision blurred for a moment before my tears escaped my lashes. I could not speak, even though I wanted to tell her I would have carried her over far worse.

Maeve took my bandaged left hand in hers and turned it over to kiss my palm. "And did ye no' use yer magic to incapacitate my foolish husband to save my life?"

I barked a watery laugh and wiped at my cheeks. "Aye. I called him a bawbag, too."

She grinned and blinked her tears away. What she said next shocked me to my core.

"Then I am lucky to call ye friend, Coira." A sob broke free from my feeble hold on my emotions, and I willingly surrendered to her embrace when she said, "Ye absolutely deserve me."

As she soothed me, rubbing her hands up and down my back, I cried for so long on her shoulder that I thought my knees would be permanently dented from the sharp pebbles within the sand.

"Thank ye," I whispered, and pulled away to find her eyes red too.

She smiled shyly and plucked the yellow and pink garland of flowers from the ground at her side. "I brought ye a little somethin'."

"A crown?"

She grinned. "Well, it starts out that way. My mother taught me when I was but a wee lass. She said, 'to make a circle o' friendship, ye must first start with one, for only one can become two.' Or somethin' like that."

I watched as she untangled the weave in two places and fashioned two smaller circlets, handing one to me. She blushed and slipped the garland onto my right wrist, then held out her hand for me to adorn with the other.

"It's silly, I ken, but I wanted to make one for us."

"I love it," I said as I traced the delicate yellow petals of the buttercup.

A *friend.*

For years I'd lived my life alone, barely tolerated by my own people. Now, there was someone who wanted to be my companion. She had chosen me because she enjoyed my company and was not bound to me by familial ties or a wedding vow. I'd never had that before. I could not count my cousin Ness, who was family, or Malcolm, my husband, lover, and soul-mate. My heart squeezed with glee at the sight of our matching bracelets, and I wished I could keep them fresh and vibrant for the rest of my life.

Maeve's grin grew somber, and she bit her lip before she said, "Finlay told me what he said to ye. He didnae really mean it. He was just scared."

I shrugged, reluctant to tell her that a part of me still agreed with him, whether it was said in duress or not. I was spared by a sharp whistle that drew our attention upstream. It was time to go, and we would have to hurry if we were to make it back to Ghlas Thùr by sundown.

Malcolm's voice carried toward us as Maeve and I walked arm in arm. "We'll break from the road two miles from the village and approach the keep through the wood." He held out his hand to me, and I wordlessly let him draw me forward while he spoke to his men. "I dinnae want the villagers to ken we're back, so once we arrive at the keep, I want the gates barred. No one in, no one out."

"For how long?" a man named William asked.

A shadow passed over Malcolm's eyes as he said, "With luck, just the night."

⌒⌒

"Where the hell have ye been?" Raith bellowed at me from atop the wall. His dark hair was in disarray as though he'd run his fingers through it a thousand times since the previous night.

Malcolm patted my thigh before helping me from Ramsay's back outside the south gate where our group dismounted. We'd made good time and arrived at the keep just as the belly of the sun touched the horizon.

"He's no' verra happy with me," I muttered, and cast a nervous glance up at the assassin before he turned on his heel and vanished over the side.

"O' course he isn't. I put him in charge o' yer safety, and ye gave him the slip the first chance ye got. If ye weren't my wife, he'd probably take ye over his knee." My eyes widened, and Malcolm chuckled. "'Tis a good thing for ye, that ye are, aye?"

Indeed, I thought, and fought against the urge to cross my hands protectively over my backside.

"Although, the thought is mighty appealin'," Malcolm muttered to himself as he strode away to intercept Raith when he appeared at the gate.

"Ye widnae dare," I whispered challengingly at his back. He shot me a roguish grin over his shoulder—a promise—before he grasped Raith's arm and steered him toward the keep.

Reluctant to be the recipient of Raith Buchannan's ire, I wrapped my arms protectively around my middle and followed them both to a quiet place near a herb garden beneath the library windows.

Farlan barked orders to bar the main gate, his voice bouncing off the grey stone. The rest of our group quickly disbanded, either heading straight to the kitchen for a hot meal or their bed.

"Where's she been, Mal?" Raith seethed and pointed an accusing finger at me. "I thought the worst. This whole bloody time I thought that—that *thing* in the loch had gobbled her up!"

Malcolm's head rocked back on his shoulders, and he looked at his friend in confusion. "What thing—"

I cleared my throat and waved Malcolm off. I'd explain *that* little bit of the story to him later. "As ye can see, I am hale and whole," I explained flippantly and lifted my hands, palms up, at my side. "I—I simply ran into a problem."

"A problem," Raith muttered. His dark brows hiked high in mock disbelief. "And what, Lady MacKinnon, was so *pressing* that had ye hie yerself across the countryside in the middle o' the night with naught but a handmaid to guard ye?"

I shifted on my feet and anxiously glanced up at Malcolm for help, to which he responded with a look that seemed to say, *Ye dug this hole, ye can climb out on yer own.*

Bastard.

I rolled my eyes. "Fine," I groaned, and tucked my hair behind my imperfectly shaped ear to expose the scars that bordered my cheek and snaked down my back. "Do ye see these?"

Raith crossed his arms over his chest. "I noticed them before, aye."

I swallowed thickly when Malcolm's arm circled my shoulders, and I cast a grateful glance at him before I said, "I received them when I was but thirteen, in England when a priest accused me o' witchcraft."

Raith's hazel eyes softened from their accusatory glower, and his arms loosened a degree. "Bloody hell. Mal, did ye ken about that?"

"I did." Malcolm's gave my arm a comforting squeeze to continue.

"I escaped, and never thought I'd see the priest again… and I didnae. No' until I came here."

I knew the moment the assassin put the pieces together.

"I saw ye talkin' to a priest yester eve. Ye left for yer chamber shortly after. Was *he* the one who did that to ye?"

Malcolm must have taken pity on me, for he said, "Coira told me on our wedding night, and from that day on we hid her identity with heavy lace veils. She wore them when we went to worship and completely avoided him whenever she went to town."

"Then how did he find out?"

"A few weeks ago, he came in with an injury that needed stitching. I was careless while I worked and gave him an unhindered view o' my face. He figured it out then, but he didnae confront me until Sunday."

"He must have caught word that I had left the keep and, for the first time since he began his tenure here, he made the trek up for supper." Malcolm flexed his jaw. "If I had been here, none o' this would have happened."

"None o' this is yer fault," I whispered and frowned at the guilty set of his mouth.

Malcolm shook his head in disagreement.

"But I dinnae understand," Raith looked down on me with disappointment. "Why could ye no' tell me that? I would have protected ye."

I shrugged. "I was scared, Raith. He told me I had to leave that night or he'd turn the clan against me. Ye dinnae ken what it was like for me. I still dream o' that day. I still wake up some mornings with the smell o' my burnin' skin in my nose."

"*Iosa Crìosd*, alright, alright." Raith dragged his hands through his hair and paced in the shadows.

"That doesnae matter. What does matter is Blount had highway men on the road, and they tracked me to my family cottage. They tried to burn Maeve and me while we slept."

The assassin halted mid-step, his features morphed from worried compassion to a deathly calm. "He what?"

"Malcolm arrived in time," I explained hastily.

Raith narrowed his eyes at both of us with suspicion. "How did Mal ken where to find ye? There was no way for ye to send a messenger."

"Yer too clever for yer own good, my friend," Malcolm said with a chuckle, and looked down at me. He tipped his head toward his friend. "Ye can trust him, Angel. He's never gonna leave us alone until ye tell him anyway."

"I give ye my word that ye have my confidence." Raith bowed slightly at the waist.

I scoffed and lifted a brow. "An assassin's word?"

He grinned, slow and sultry. "Would ye rather a blood vow?"

Malcolm shivered beside me, and I bit my lower lip to hide my grin.

"Please no. If Malcolm trusts ye, I should too." I took a deep breath to steady my nerves and stooped to snap a sprig of rosemary from the herb garden. Once I was sure no one loitered around us, I held the fragrant stem with its sticky needles in the fading light.

"What are ye doin'?" the assassin asked. Though he looked skeptical, he moved closer for a better look.

I didn't answer. Instead, I sang, soft and slow, and willed my energy into the stem. The sprig trembled, and in the faint orange light of the fast-setting sun, lavender flowers sprouted between the bladed fronds.

Raith's hazel eyes widened with excited disbelief. When I cut off the flow of magic and offered it to him, he took it from me as though it were made of glass.

"How—this cannae be possible." His voice was as thin as a wisp of smoke, and he traced the lip of the uppermost flower with his fingertip.

"Blount wasnae entirely wrong about me," I admitted. "He thinks I'm a danger even though I've never used my abilities for ill."

"She's saved my life with her powers, and my clan from starvation." Malcolm ran his hand down my unbound hair and looked deep into my eyes.

With tears clouding my sight, I broke my husband's stare to look at Raith.

"I'm a healer. That's all. I'm no'—I'm no' evil."

Raith tucked the rosemary into his breast pocket and nodded. "I willnae tell a soul, Lady MacKinnon. Although I wish ye had trusted me sooner, I understand now why ye chose to leave rather than chance my reaction." He looked at Malcolm. "What are ye goin' to do about yer priest?"

The last light faded with the setting sun, and the shadows in the courtyard thickened. I pulled the lapels of Bram's jacket tighter around me and flexed my toes against the compact dirt.

Malcolm glowered. "He sent twenty witch hunters after her, Raith. He wanted her dead that badly." A dark look passed between the two men, a secret understanding.

Raith stepped in close, his movements sinuous and deliberate. Like a predator stalking its prey.

Like an assassin.

"Ye left me in charge o' yer wife's safety, Mal. I failed. It seems I owe ye a debt."

The corner of Malcolm's lips lifted into a smile that didn't reach his eyes, and he glanced my way when he said, "Then I will call upon that debt tonight. Coira is owed her vengeance."

Chapter Twenty-Nine

FATHER BLOUNT

Henry Giles Blount, Englishman, and man of God, celebrated the death of yet another witch in the silent sanctum of his church. Alone, he pranced around the pulpit with only a single candle flame to see by and laughed out loud. Clumsy with drink but light on his feet, he loosened the collar of his black robes.

When the townspeople stopped buying his ale, he had wandered from the village tavern a half hour ago and wandered back to the church. Reluctant to spend his own money, he pilfered the cellar beneath the pews instead. And why shouldn't he? He'd spent the last ten miserable years of his life, day in and day out, in service to the Scottish heathens. He deserved a bottle or cask for himself. Yes, indeed.

Over the last few years, Scotland's air had begun to suffocate him. Most days, Blount could barely keep a smile on his face and longed for the day his exile would be over. One more year of forced faux pleasantries, and he could leave this damn hellhole behind to return to England—to civilization! He had tired of country living, where the inhabitants were mundane and simple, and the roads were naught but rutted dirt riddled with goose shit.

Blount's upper lip lifted in disgust. Why shouldn't he enjoy the parish's spirits? He deserved all of it, and more, for he had singlehandedly rid the Christian world of another witch.

"*I did!*" He swirled the wine around in his cup and breathed deeply of the fragrant vintage. Blount barked another hoarse laugh, choked on his spit, and laughed again. Oh, how his luck had turned!

Thirteen years—*thirteen years* had passed since he'd witnessed a young witch summon a demon from shadow. In all his years as a Hunter, he'd never seen anything quite so terrifying. His faction never told him such a thing could be possible; there wasn't even a hint in the archives. It was little wonder they hadn't believed him even though the beastly creature had left a pile of broken bodies in the courtyard.

"*Where's the demon?*" they had asked, but the monstrous beast had reverted to the body of a man the moment it died. Since Blount had been the sole witness, having watched from the shadows while the creature tore arms from soldiers and ripped their throats open with elongated teeth, no one truly believed him.

To prove to the faction he'd not been mad, a few months after that young witch had turned the midday sky black, he had caught another witch and attempted to provoke her into summoning a demon of the same ilk. Unfortunately for him, that day had also been his downfall.

Exiled for fifteen years, all because of a little *misunderstanding*.

Blount grunted into his cup. That day was all *her* fault, not his. She should have told him her familial name before he began his forceful persuasion. If she had, neither of them would be where they are now. If she had been forthcoming, he'd still be in his parish in Norwich, and she'd still be alive. He would have never killed her—let alone *tortured* her—if he'd known she was the great-niece of a fellow Hunter.

No matter. She may not have been a witch since she had failed to summon the demon he demanded. But the girl *had* been filled to the brim with evil. The foul things that spewed from her mouth before she'd died still made him cringe. No God-fearing woman would have said such things to *him*, a man of God.

When his faction found out what he'd done, they hadn't listened to him—*again*. It wasn't enough that he'd been the church's most active enthusiast against the growing population of witches. It hadn't mattered that he alone was solely responsible for rooting out thirty-seven witches in his lifetime. None of it mattered. They exiled him to Scotland anyway, to the frigid highlands in the dead of winter.

Thirty-seven. All of them touched with unfathomable beauty, a gift from the Devil himself to ensnare God-fearing men. Blount remembered every single one of them. But his first…oh, he'd never forget his first. Many years had passed since then, but if he closed his eyes he could see her clear as day. He'd been sixteen, and she nearly twenty. He had just left his first Hunter meeting when he spotted her outside St. Paul's Cathedral.

Completely captivated and full of excited energy, he decided to follow her down Cheapside and through the market. She'd been a slight thing, willowy and delicate, her nearly-black hair in a loose plait bouncing against her spine. She'd carried a basket of flowers in the crook of her right arm and fanned the skirt of her grey dress invitingly while she called out to potential patrons.

"Penny for a posy!" she called out in a come-hither sort of way that caused Henry's blood to heat and his cheeks to redden.

"A penny for a posy and a shilling for even more." She winked at an older gentleman as he walked by, but the man only smiled and kept walking.

Henry grew bolder the longer he followed, and he found himself wanting her to notice him, for he noticed everything about her. He'd memorized the way the sun glinted off her dark hair and kissed her cheekbones as though it paid homage to her beauty. He knew the small, dark mark on her cheek that got lost in a dimple when she smiled and the seductive shape of her hips.

Enamored, he hurried to close the space between them and edged along the side of a brick building when she ducked into an alleyway. He didn't want to lose sight of her—

"Hello."

Henry skidded to a halt, his eyes wide when he found her waiting for him in the narrow pathway, her crossed arms beneath her breasts. Forced up high, her breasts were like milky pillows. He gaped at them a moment, and he nearly bolted when she reached out a hand and ran a perfectly tapered finger down his forearm. Henry's body jolted at the touch. He felt as though he were caught in a snare, and if she ever decided to cut him free, he'd stay as her captive of his own volition.

"Have you been following me?" she asked, and bit down on her full, inviting lip. She dragged that lip through her teeth. "Don't lie. I'll smell it if you do."

Henry tilted his head, his attention fixated on the way her lips glistened where she's just bitten them. "You can smell lies?" he asked.

The girl threw her head back and laughed before she plucked a long-stemmed flower from her basket and dragged the velvety petal along his jaw. He shivered, and his belly clenched down low.

She tilted her head to the side and swiped the cool, silken petals over the tip of his nose before she turned the flower upon herself. "What do you want, lad?"

"Um." Henry swallowed and wondered how she expect him to answer while she dragged the flower over the swell of her left breast, then her right.

"You're fascinated," she whispered, and dropped her basket so she could entwine her hands behind his neck. "Tell me, do you like my charms?"

Bells rang in Henry's head. His priest had warned him about women who could cast spells and trap a man. Was this what she was doing? Had she lured him into this ally? Were none of his thoughts his own?

Sweat bloomed on his forehead. "Ch-charms?"

She lightly scratched the nape of his neck, sending chills down his spine, and his trousers grew tight beneath his belt.

"Oh, don't play coy. I see that you do," she purred and wedged her thigh between his. She rubbed herself against him and grinned wickedly. "You're an easy mark."

I knew it! *Henry thought. She* had *cast a spell on him.*

"Come with me, lad. I'm going to make you see stars, and you'll never get me out of your mind for as long as you live." She took his clammy hand and led him between the buildings, deeper into the shadows. Deep enough, no one would see them if they weren't looking.

Henry's breathing became erratic and his hands shook with anticipation.

This must be God's first test for me, *he thought. To leave his first Hunter meeting and stumble upon a witch outside the society's doors? It was Holy Fate, he was sure of it, and he would not turn his back on his calling.*

The witch looked over her slim shoulder. "I must be your first," she cooed. "You'll never forget your first—wait!" Henry pounced, and with the power of God on his side, among the refuse and litter of the dark alleyway, the witch succumbed to her fate. Killing her hadn't been hard. She'd admitted she bewitched him, and everyone knew the only way to break a witch's spell was to kill the one who cast it.

He brought the flowers back with him to the little room he lived in beneath the church and placed a bloom between the pages of his Bible—

The creak of floorboards drew Blount's attention to the heavily shadowed rear of the sanctuary, and he squinted into the gloom.

"Who's there?" he called out.

When only silence answered, he turned his wine-muddled focus to the task at hand and refilled his cup.

"Must have been the wind—oh!" Dark red wine spilled over the goblet's rim and splashed onto the two-step stool that led to the pulpit. The liquid pooled on the waxed wood into a shape that looked curiously like a cross before it ran over the edge and dripped onto the polished floor.

Another sign that God is on my side, he mused. "I'll call you the spoils of war." He snickered at the spilled wine and slurped at the rim of the over-filled cup. "And war—*hic*—there will always be war between angels and demons—"

"Ye're the demon," a female voice whispered from the darkened corner under the large stained glass window.

Blount spun toward the voice at his back, flinging the contents of his cup in a wide arc. The wine splattered on the floor, glistening stark and dark on the golden planks in the candle light.

"Who's there?" he called out, his voice hollow and his breath ragged. He took a step forward, his hand gripped around his now empty chalice, and raised it over his head to strike down whoever hid in the gloom. The single candle on the pulpit did little to chase away the shadows that collected at the room's edges, and when Blount reached the night-dulled window, he found nothing but a straight-backed chair.

His shoulders sagged in relief. He was alone, just as he thought.

"My mind is playing tricks on me," he said to the chair, and swayed on his feet, making his way back to the bottle he'd left on the stool. *Just one more drink and I'll find my bed,* he promised himself. He had a big day ahead of him. A day of praying for the laird's wife with the villagers. They'd know she was missing by then, and they would look to him for spiritual guidance.

And when word arrived that she was dead, which she would surely be by the end of the day, he would be there to console them. And his poor flock, they'd be none the wiser they'd had a witch for a lady. She truly had them wrapped in her evil snare. And Laird MacKinnon? He'd be free from her spell, too.

Blount still ridiculed himself for not recognizing her sooner, but on the day of her wedding to the laird, she'd kept her head bowed, her hair like a veil. She hadn't even looked at him. After that, she'd worn dark lace draped over her head like a pious, devote believer, and had dutifully sat with her gloved hands in her lap while he preached the word of God.

She had deceived him for a year. A whole year of Sunday's a witch had sat right under his nose and laughed at him from behind her lace shroud.

Blount squeezed the empty chalice and ground his teeth when he remembered praying over her bowed head after she'd played midwife to a villager. There was no doubt in his mind that she had placed a hex on each new soul she helped bring forth before he was able to introduce them to God. He could only pray that her black stain had not had time to sink too deep, and only an extra prayer or two would be all that was needed to bring the children to the right side once again. If they proved to be evil later on in life, well… children suffered accidents all the time.

Father Blount still couldn't believe his luck finding her in *his* parish after all those years. The villagers had told him many stories of how talented a healer their lady was, and how lucky they were to have her. He now knew it was a sign from God when he'd cut his palm and been forced to seek aid at Ghlas Thùr.

The moment he'd caught sight of those disgusting marks on her face, he had known exactly who she was. He knew every inch of flesh the fire had tasted. He'd fanaticized about that day enough—even had a lock of her hair wedged in his Bible. It didn't matter that she was older and not screaming for mercy, or that her hair was on her head and not in a shorn heap at his feet. He knew.

Then Laird MacKinnon had shown up as though she'd summoned him to her aid, and Blount realized just how deep her evil influence went. If she had the chieftain bewitched, there was no way Blount could sway the rest of the clan, to open their eyes to her sins.

That very same day, he'd sent word to his contacts in Glasgow demanding the society send him a number of Hunters straight away. He told them a witch had enthralled the MacKinnon laird and was too powerful for him to handle on his own. Then he reminded them of the demon she summoned when she was young. Blount couldn't imagine what she'd be capable of after thirteen years of honing her skills, and he knew their only chance of defeating her would be to get her out of the keep and alone.

A few days after his Hunters had arrived, Blount nearly wept when God granted him a gift; the laird had left for a neighboring clan and the witch was unprotected at the keep.

It was a simple thing to station his Hunters along the roads and even simpler to scare her away. He saw the dread in her eyes when he confronted her in the great hall. He didn't miss the beads of sweat on her brow or the way her pulse hammered in her neck. Two hours after dawn the next day, a Hunter stationed on the east road had arrived on a breathless horse. He told of how the witch had escaped by calling on a fog so thick he could barely see the ears of his mount and was forced to return for the rest of his cadre. Within an hour, the Hunters had assembled, and they raced east in search of her trail.

Blount grinned and picked up the bottle. He expected them back with news of her demise by tea time.

"Damnit to hell." His mood soured when he found the bottle empty but of one sip. "I want to *drink*, not my tongue wet."

Bound for the cellar, Blount traded the empty bottle for the candlestick. He shuffled beneath a stone arch, down a hallway, and into his humble chamber. He ignored his lumpy bed, intent on the open trap door that led to the cellar. His mouth watered, and his stomach clenched at the prospect of more wine.

Just one more, he promised himself.

The candle flame flickered in the musty air that wafted up from the cellar, causing his shadow to dance madly on the whitewashed walls. Blount lifted the hem of his robe, and on shaky legs, descended the creaking stairs. He hummed a nameless tune as he chose his footing, and when he reached the hardpacked dirt, he turned for the casks in the far corner.

His smile faltered and the hairs on his neck prickled. He was not alone.

"Hallo, Father Blount," a female voice purred from the shadows.

Blount's heart hammered in his chest. "Show yourself," he demanded and thrust the candlestick forward with a shaky hand.

The flame on the wax stick flared to that of a torch, and Blount yelped when molten wax fell onto his wrist. Stunned, he dropped the candlestick, and it bounced once at his feet before the wick was snuffed out in the dirt.

His breath sounded harsh in the dark, and he blinked blindly into the black.

"So clumsy," the voice said, soft and smooth.

Along the wall to his right, a line of candles flared to life of their own accord, and Blount gasped when he beheld none other than the witch perched upon a barrel.

"Surprised to see me?" she asked with a slight curve to her lips. When he could only gape at her in silence, she ran her graceful hands over the lap of her dark blue gown and picked at a piece of lint. "I can only imagine how confused ye may be." She flicked the lint to the side and looked at him levelly with her strange, ice-colored eyes. "Especially considering ye tried to have me murdered… again."

Blount gripped the thick beam at the base of the stairs and contemplated fleeing. When she hummed low in her throat, the ground beneath him trembled, and his feet sank below the surface of the dirt. Before his wine-altered mind could react, his balance teetered, and he pinwheeled his arms to stay erect when his calves disappeared into the cool ground followed by his thighs.

"Help me!" he cried, and the ground solidified, his black robes bunched around his hips.

The witch smoothly vacated her seat as though the earth hadn't just half-swallowed him. "Yer witch hunters set my home ablaze while I slept in the dead o' night." She glided toward him and gestured to her body. "As ye can see, they failed, and I dinnae have a scratch to show for it. Do ye ken why ye failed, Father? Do ye ken why *all* yer witch hunters died doin' yer bidding?"

Blount's eyes widened. All of them dead? The realization that his entire faction of Hunters had perished in their quest sickened him, but he refused to believe God had forsaken them entirely.

He tipped his chin up to sneer at her and snatched the candlestick from the ground. He swiped through the air between them to keep her from coming closer. He hated the confidence in her voice, despised the way she looked down upon him as though he were a spider beneath her shoe. *She* was the insect, not him!

"Because you're a child of the Devil, and God's mortal angels were not strong enough to fight you. Ahh!—"

A lyrical whisper echoed off the walls, and Blount's hand burned as though he handled the end of a torch. With a hiss, he dropped the candlestick for the second time, and the red-hot metal pulsed as though it had just come from a forge. The pain in his hand ate away at the last of his wine-induced haze, and he looked at his palm.

The angry blisters that rose on his skin formed the shape of a cross. His hand shook all the more because for the first time, Blount was unsure of what that sacred symbol meant, and the sight of it did not fill him with its usual warmth.

The witch dropped to her haunches in front of him; her forearms braced on her thighs. "No," she said with a shake of her head. "They died because they were bad men on an evil mission." She unfurled her fists to display her empty palms to him. "These hands have never caused another harm. They have never maimed nor killed. They have only ever preserved life and fought for the side o' good, always."

He struggled to free himself from the dirt's tight grip. "Every word from your honeyed mouth is a lie," Blount spat. He remembered the demon that ravaged the church courtyard in Norwich. "You killed my Hunters. You've ensnared the laird and the people of this village, but you cannot bewitch me. I know you for what you are!"

Her lips pulled down in a frown and she took a deep breath, revealing her frustration. "Who did ye sell my sister to?"

The abrupt question gave Blount pause. "What?"

The witch's pale irises flashed with anger, and she stood with her hands curled into fists at her side. "Ye sold the younger lass who was with me that day in Norwich. *Who did ye sell her to?*" Her words came out with such force his ears hollowed and rang. He almost cowered at the power he felt in her presence.

Almost.

"You'll never find her, if she's not dead already," he said with a hateful smirk and enjoyed the sight of her cheeks darkening; celebrated the sheen of tears in her eyes. Blount twisted his verbal knife deeper and leaned forward. "I would have preferred to see her tied and on the pyre with you, but he seemed to know her for the witch she was, and the gentleman made me an offer I couldn't refuse. I didn't know what he wanted with her. I didn't care… but I imagine it's the same as what all men want when they seek possession of a young girl."

Disgust distorted her lips. "Where did he take her?"

Blount glared up at her. "I didn't care enough to ask."

The witch spun on her heel, turning her back to him, her shoulders and spine stiff.

Blount yelled at her back, "I am a man of the cloth! Release me now, for you know you cannot kill me without drawing attention to yourself."

"I should kill ye," she murmured. "I should pelt ye with rotten food while screaming my hate at ye. I should shear the hair from yer head." She looked over her shoulder and arched a brow. "Not that ye have much left."

"To be bald is easier to receive the Lord's kiss," he shot back. Her responding smile, small and pitying, made his blood boil.

She began to pace the small room, the hem of her gown making soft swishing sounds as it dragged on the hard-packed dirt. "I should still rip the remaining hairs from yer head, if only to hear yer whimpers. I should smile when I light the kindling beneath yer feet." She wagged a chiding forefinger at him. "Just on one side o' yer body, o' course. Widnae want yer death to be quick."

The witch stopped her pacing to look upon him. Talking so candidly about the horrible death she planned for him, he was unable to break her stare.

"I should watch while the flames devour yer skin inch by inch and applaud when it climbs up yer legs and chars yer manhood until it crisps." Blount trembled and refrained from cupping himself with sheer will alone. "I should laugh when yer eyes burst from the heat, and when ye're blind and the pain brought on by flames have stolen yer will to beg me to end yer pitiful life… I promise ye right now, I widnae."

When she lifted her hand to caress the underside of his chin, Blount could only stare at her in terror when she said, "I would sooner bring forth the rain to douse the flames, for I would rather prolong yer agony than hurry yer death."

She let her hand fall away, and a short, high-pitched whine escaped Blount's throat. Such torture would be unthinkable! Surely God would not allow His faithful servant to perish in such a way. Had he not served Him well?

The witch continued, "I should do all those things to ye and more, for I have no doubt ye have tortured many other women because o' yer belief that we are evil." She stooped, lifted the hem of her dark gown, and revealed a short-bladed dagger strapped to her calf. She slid it from its sheath and held it loosely in her hand. "But I'll do none o' those things."

Oh, thank God, he prayed. The relief of not being burned alive coursed through Blount's body and made him want to weep, but the blade that glinted in the candlelight held his attention.

"Y-you say you've never killed, yet here you stand, and my hunters do not. And now, you point your dagger at me," Blount said with a slight tremor.

Her blonde brows lifted, and she whispered a word that was beyond his comprehension. The dark mass of shadows behind her right shoulder fell away like a shroud of black silk, and the MacKinnon laird stepped out of the gloom.

"I didnae kill them," she said with a slight shake of her head. "'Tis no' in my nature. I fear if I ended yer life, yer blood on my hands would change me too greatly."

The laird stood by her side, his glower menacing and full of promise. Blount knew *he* would not hesitate to plunge a blade into his heart, bewitched as he was.

"You would make him kill me instead," Blount guessed. "An order upon another makes you just as guilty."

The corner of the laird's mouth lifted. "She widnae need to order me," he replied.

The witch cast a grateful glance at her husband before said, "I'll make ye a deal, priest."

He dared to scoff. "I do not make deals with the Devil."

She tilted her head. "Ye did the other day, when ye told me to leave my home."

Blount frowned and narrowed his eyes. Perhaps a small deal would be forgivable in the eyes of the Lord if it would save his life. "What deal?" he asked.

The witch touched the tip of her dagger to her forefinger. "Much the same deal ye gave me, but I promise there willnae be anyone waitin' to accost ye on the road." When Blunt remained silent, she continued, "If ye give me yer word, promised upon yer Bible, that ye willnae come after me again—that you will give up yer hunt for *all* witches—I will let ye go."

The MacKinnon laird brought Blount's worn Bible he had left on his nightstand from behind his back and held it out.

Blount looked between the two of them, convinced of trickery, but took the Bible with trembling hands. He pressed it hard against his chest as though it were a shield.

"I promise this, and you'll let me go?"

The witch flashed a close-lipped smile, and Blount almost cringed at her beauty. The way the candlelight illuminated the untouched side of her face and the pale gold of her hair, he would have thought her a heavenly being. But he knew better.

Lucifer was a fallen angel, the most beautiful of all, he reminded himself.

"I only require honesty and truth," the witch said softly. "Give me that, and ye can leave tonight."

Blount nodded eagerly, and struggled anew in the dirt. "I promise—" His words died on his tongue and he fell still when she held out her hand.

"Hold my hand while ye make yer vow so I ken ye speak the truth."

Blount stared at her perfectly formed fingers, hesitant to willingly touch a being born of Satan's loins. His skin crawled, and he barely schooled his features before he lightly grasped her first two knuckles.

"I promise to leave you in peace." He bit the inside of his cheek while he said silently in his mind, *Until I can rally new hunters. Then I'll be back for your head.*

The witch looked hopeful. "And?" she prompted.

"I will give up my hunt for witches." His lips formed the words as easily as any other, and he didn't feel the least bit bad for their deceit.

The witch sung a phrase that sounded like windchimes and the whistling of long grass. The dirt around his legs loosened just enough to allow him to wiggle free. She kept her grip upon him, and God forgive him, he let her help him up out of the loosened soil.

"That wasn't so hard, was it?" she asked.

Blount wanted to step away, yearned to rip his hand from her grasp, but a glance at the laird's dark, watchful eyes stopped him. "I endeavor to always speak the truth," he muttered, and tucked his Bible tight against his sternum. He couldn't wait to get out of there and ride straight for London to report to the society of what had happened.

Surely, they would act swiftly and send the full weight of the Church crashing down upon her head. The thought made him nearly giddy with anticipation.

"As I expected." The witch's pleasant smile faltered, and before he could react, she turned his palm up, and drove her dagger into the meat of his flesh.

Blount's breath escaped him in a strangled cry at the unexpected pain, and he pulled hard on his hand. She let him go, and he stumbled backward, over the loose dirt, past the stairs, and bumped into something both hard and soft.

"Easy there, Father. Widnae want ye to take a spill," an unfamiliar voice drawled, and Blount spun around to gape at the menacing presence. Dressed all in black, the unknown man wore a cowl that obscured all but the harsh slash of his mouth and stubbled chin.

"Who—who are you?" Blount wheezed, his breath thick in his lungs. A cold sweat trickled down his spine, and his stomach quaked.

"I'm yer executioner," the hooded man said, his voice dripping with arrogance.

"No man is my judge," Blount seethed through his fear, and shook his Bible between them. "Only God is my judge!"

The stranger canted his head. "Wrong. Ye *have* been judged. And that is why I am here." Blount's eyes widened, and he wiped at the sweat that beaded upon his brow with the back of his blistered hand. The man in black took a step closer. "God is yer judge when ye die, auld man. But until then, yer fate lies in *her* hands." He reached out with gloved hands and spun Blount around until he faced the witch once again.

Blount struggled, and his worry was burned away by his rage. How dare she!

"You would dare order the death of a man of the cloth? That is what you're here to do, isn't it?" Spittle flew from his mouth with every seething word until he remembered her offer, and he glanced hopefully from the witch to the laird. "You—you said I could leave if I promised—" The witch clicked her tongue twice and directed the glistening tip of her blade in the direction of his Bible.

"No," the witch said, her voice hard and sharp as flint. "I said ye could go if ye spoke the *truth*."

And then, to the priest's horror, she dragged the tip of the blood-glazed dagger across the flat of her tongue. He wanted to retch at the sight.

"I can taste yer lies, priest. They're bitter, just like ye," she said, her voice whisper-soft. She spat on the dirt, a look of disgust on her face. "Ye willnae stop, will ye? It widnae matter what I did or said, ye willnae change, just as I expected."

Blount could only glare at her in anger.

The witch looked up at her husband, and a wordless conversation passed between them. He nodded and pressed a kiss to her forehead, then turned his stone-faced expression toward the priest.

A slimy stone landed in Blount's gut, and he felt his face pale under scrutiny.

"God will not forgive you, my son," the priest reminded him. "Murder is a sin against Him—"

The laird bared his teeth and clenched his fists, silencing him. "Yer death willnae come from my hand, but from my assassin," The laird growled.

Blount's back prickled with a flush of clammy heat with the newfound knowledge of who stood behind him. A trickle of sweat slithered down his spine, and it was an effort not to look over his shoulder at the hooded man who held his arms.

The MacKinnon laird glowered at him. "Ye deserve worse than the fate ye'll get. If it were up to me, I'd tie ye to the willow outside and lite ye aflame, but I willnae allow ye to be a martyr." He poked a stiffened finger against the Bible with a thump. "Ye will die down here, surrounded by the wine ye covet and steal, and I will sleep better this night with the knowledge that ye willnae be able to do to another woman what ye did to my wife." And with a final glance at the man in black—at the assassin—the laird gathered the witch against his side and guided her up the rickety stairs.

"Witch!" Blount called out. "You insist on my death, yet you don't stay to watch?"

The witch halted in the heavy shadows and looked over her shoulder, her face a mask of indifference. "No. And I willnae think about ye even a moment longer than it will take me to leave this church." She then linked her fingers with her husband's, and they continued up the stairs. "Burn in Hell, *Father*," she called back, and Blount jumped within the assassin's grasp when the trap door fell closed with shuddering finality.

The low-burning candles flickered in the displaced air, mimicking his own trembling, then fell still on their wicks. He stared in shock at the darkness above and listened to the retreating footsteps, one heavy, the other light, until all that was left was his own ragged breathing.

"God does not want me dead," he said, more to himself than the stranger at his back.

A dark chuckle tickled the back of his neck with claw-tipped fingers, promising pain and unforetold tortures.

"He doesnae?" A sharp kick connected with the back of Blount's knees. His Bible flew out of his hands, and he crumpled to the floor with a whimper. The man loomed above him, his face fully obscured by shadow. "I dinnae hear anyone comin' to yer rescue."

Blount shimmied on his back in a last-ditch effort to escape and barked a curse when a booted foot came down upon his knee.

"Arh!" Spittle flew from his lips, and he looked up in terror at the man who now held a bottle of wine in his hand. The assassin unstopped the cork with his teeth and then held his hand to his ear.

"Do ye hear that, priest?" His leather clad calf grazed Blount's ruined knee, and it was everything he could do not to cry out. "'Tis the sound o' silence, because there is no rescue from yer fate." A set of straight, white teeth flashed in the faint candle light before Blount's vision was obscured by a deluge of wine.

The rancid reek of bad wine soaked into his robes, and he choked on the liquid that ran into his nose and down his throat.

"W-why?" Blount sputtered, and wiped his eyes.

The assassin tossed the empty bottle into a corner, and the glass shattered before he replied flippantly, "Because ye took a drunken fall down the stairs, o' course. An unfortunate accident. Ye broke several bones on the way down."

Blount didn't have time to be confused before the man stomped on his ankle, then his shin. The crack of his bones echoed off the walls a moment before the resulting agony flooded his mind in bursts of blinding white. Blount screamed, shrill and hoarse until no sound came out, and he writhed in the dirt at the base of the stairs.

The assassin brought his leg up again, aiming for Blount's chest when his focus snagged on the Bible open on the ground.

"Stay there," he said with a chuckle, and stepped over Blount instead of on his ribs. With his back turned to the priest, he picked up the open Bible and flipped through the pages. "What is this?" he asked when he slipped a thin braid of golden hair from between the pages. Blount pursed his lips.

The assassin turned, and the flickering light illuminated a darkly handsome face before his hood obscured his features once more. He turned another page, and a tattered blue ribbon an inch in length fluttered to the ground followed by a lock of amber hair tied with string. "What the feck," the assassin said, his words barely a breath of air in the near silent cellar.

While he was busy inspecting the small bits of torn fabric, locks of hair in six different shades, ribbons, and finally the dry stem of a once lush, red rose, Blount dragged his body up the stairs. With his heart pounding within his chest, he kept his sight on the trap door above and counted each step as he clumsily shifted his broken bones higher and higher. His fingertips had just brushed the underside of the door when a crunching grip encircled his damaged ankle, and he was wrenched forcefully back down the stairs.

Pain bloomed in his jaw as it slammed into each step on the way down. He felt one of his front teeth chip, and he bit through his tongue. He heard the cracks of small bones breaking in his hands, his wrist, a rib.

The assassin followed him to the floor, flipped him over, and landed upon his chest with the weight of a charging bull. Blount's vision swam in circles when a gloved hand wrapped tight into the wine-sodden fabric of his robes and lifted him an inch from the ground. A garbled cry leaked from the priest's throat, and he tried his best to clear his mouth of blood. It dribbled along his cheeks and collected in the creases of his neck. Pooled into the hull of his ear.

Blount couldn't see the assassins face within his cowl, but he could *feel* the fury radiating from his body. It pulsed from him in waves like the rays of a black sun.

"Is this hers?" The assassin held the pale braid between their faces, and Blount trembled when he bellowed, "Is this Lady MacKinnon's hair?"

A whimper crawled up Blount's throat from both his fear and the unbearable agony that wracked his body. When he tried to push the heavier man away, pain shot from the broken bones in his hand, and his back hit the ground when he was released. The assassin reared up, planted a knee upon the priest's chest to hold him still, and raised the Bible above Blount's face.

The thin pages fluttered and flapped, and all thirty-seven tokens, stolen from each witch he'd had killed, fell upon him in a grotesque shower of hair, cotton, and lace scraps. They caressed his cheek before they landed on the floor, his lip lifted in disgust at the tufts that clung to the blood on his face.

"Th-they had evil souls," Blount wheezed, and whined at the pain in his hand when he wiped at the hairs.

"Ye repulse me," the assassin muttered. He tossed the Bible to the side and palmed Blount's chin with one of his broad hands before wrapping the other around the back of his head.

Blount choked on the blood in his mouth and pawed uselessly at the assassins corded arms. "God guides my path," he gritted through his teeth and bruised lips. "He led me to them so I could dispatch them back to Hell, which is where you will go when you meet your death, *assassin.*"

The hood bobbed in agreement. "I have no doubt I'll see ye there, Father, but ye'll be waitin' a long time before I join ye."

The grip on his jaw tightened, and the priest looked at the reaper looming above him. His vision blurred.

"P-please don't," Father Blount whimpered.

In the darkened wine cellar beneath the church, the last thing Father Blount heard was the snap of his neck.

CHAPTER THIRTY

MALCOLM

"I love thee, I love thee with a love that shall not die.
Till the sun grows cold and the stars grow old."
-William Shakespeare

Beneath the dappled shade of a birch, Coira ran her fingers through Ma lcolm's unbound hair and tipped her face up to the summer sun.

His wife had wanted a picnic lunch down by the loch, close to her mother's resting place. She'd taken to visiting the grove often, especially when something troubled her, and always returned to the keep lighter in spirit.

They lay sprawled upon a woolen blanket, his head cradled in her lap and her growing belly brushing against his ear. He nearly purred at her attentions and was reminded for the thousandth time that his beast was gone.

He still felt the golden string that tethered his soul to Coira's, knew he would still be able to find her anywhere, but the beast was no longer a part of him. Coira told him Tlachtga had taken it from him when she drew the lead shot from his chest. She assumed it was because his oath was attempting to heal him and had wrapped its essence around the object.

Many times over the last few months, Malcolm wondered if his beast hadn't sacrificed itself. During that last run, when he gave himself over and embraced the beast with love and gratitude, he wondered if maybe it hadn't saved *his* life, too.

He found he missed its presence terribly. Its movements within his chest had become a comfort and as familiar as the beat of his heart. The absence was akin to a missing limb, a hole that couldn't be filled.

"Angel," he said, and pouted when her fingers fell still on his scalp. "Mmm?"

He sat up and brought her hand to his lips to place a whisper of a kiss to her palm. "Ye said once that ye didnae ken how Vanora commanded that blood vow I made to her. Is that still true?"

She frowned and shielded her eyes from the sun. "I think I ken how she did it… and how she did all those things that no one else can do."

"Oh?"

Coira pulled away and sat back on her heels with her hands loosely cradling the small bump between her hips. She glanced over his shoulder in the direction of Vanora's grave and shrugged.

"When that man shot ye and I saw ye fall to the ground… I tunneled into my power, deeper than I've ever ventured before." She swallowed and shivered as though the mere memory of that night caused her pain. "I had stood on its shoreline once when I was young— the day I gained my scars and lost my father and Ness. That shoreline is but a small taste of intense power, a prelude to the precipice o' madness, and where I unknowingly invited Tlachtga into my body."

"But ye went deeper, and I almost lost ye."

Coira bit her lip and nodded guiltily.

"What if I asked ye to touch this shoreline o' yers again?"

Her grey-rimmed eyes grew wide and she shook her head. "Yer mad. Why would ye want me to take such a risk?"

"Are ye no' still in control? Ye said yerself that's how yer mother made the more powerful magics. Nothin' ever took over her mind."

"Why do ye ask this?" A pale brow lifted in expectation, and Malcolm suddenly felt nervous she would say no to his request.

"'Tis been a couple months since Father Blount took that *fatal fall* down the stairs," he began, "and I've received two letters from Laird Bothan assuring me his scheming wife and daughter willnae be sendin' any more assassins our way—"

"Nothin's goin' to happen to me, Malcolm."

He held her gaze and shook his head slowly. "We dinnae ken that for sure," he said, his voice barely louder than the rustling leaves of the trees.

"No one does. That is life." She tilted her head to the side and caressed his cheek. "We need to live it as though each day is our last."

Malcolm dragged her across the blanket and kissed her. God, how he loved his woman.

"But what if I dinnae want to?" Slowly, leisurely, Malcolm ran his hand from her waist down her thigh, and when he got to the hem of her gown, he lifted the fabric to bare her calf. "I had a feelin' ye'd be armed, Lady MicKinnon," he teased, and unsheathed the dagger she'd tied below her knee.

Her brows furrowed, and she gasped when he slid the sharpened edge directly over the faint white scar in the middle of his hand.

"Malcolm," she chastised, "That will need stitchin'."

"No, it willnae," he said, and reached for her opposite hand. "I need ye to do somethin' for me, Angel." She fell still and blinked at the blade poised over her flesh before she looked up at him. Her eyes filled with tears. "I think ye ken what I want."

She swallowed and dashed away the silvery damp tracks from her cheeks. "Ye want to swear an oath to me?"

"Aye."

"Why?"

Malcolm looked down at where his blood welled and dripped onto the knee of her gown.

"I want it back," he admitted. "I want the beast back… but no' just for *yer* protection this time. So, can ye no' try for me? Just this once."

Coira's ethereal eyes burned into his, her beautiful face unreadable before she said, "Alright."

She lifted her palm to meet the tip of the blade. Malcolm winced at the pain he caused her, and nearly apologized until she clasped their palms together with surprising strength. He felt a jolt of energy course through his veins and the fine hairs on his back stood at attention.

"Malcolm MacKinnon," Coira's voice, layered, terrible, and wonderfully musical, washed over his body, and he sagged with relief. He could feel the power that flowed beneath her skin, but one glance at her face was enough for him to know she kept complete control over her mind. "Do ye swear to protect me with yer life, and to protect our children in the coming years?"

Malcolm squeezed her hand and smiled wide. "I had a little somethin' else in mind."

There, in the shade of the birch trees, next to the sun washed loch, Malcolm shared with Coira his oath of choice.

"Is that alright?"

Fresh tears fell over her cheeks and she laughed, the throaty sound of her Druid voice laced with plucked harp strings and the deepest beat of a drum.

"More than alright," she breathed, and grinned through her tears.

The sheer happiness he felt, brighter than the sun, nearly blinded him when he looked at her. She was everything he'd ever wanted, all he'd ever dared to dream.

And after today, I'll never live another moment without her, he thought. He walked on his knees until they touched hers.

"I'm ready."

The breeze kicked up from the loch and dragged invisible fingers through Coira's loosely bound hair. Her dewy lashes fluttered, and she took a deep, steadying breath.

"Malcolm MacKinnon, do ye swear to protect me and our children from harm?" Her musical voice faltered, and her lower lip trembled with the same emotion that beat in his own heart. He knew what she'd say next.

"Do ye swear to love me forever as I swear to love ye… until the last breath leaves our lips? And if I should die before ye, do ye swear to follow me into the next life… and all the ones' thereafter?"

Malcolm's vision swirled and blurred, and he blinked it back into focus. She'd changed the vow to include her own love and swore an oath to him in return. He swallowed a thick lump that lodged in his throat.

"Nothin' would make me happier."

A flash of brilliant, golden light flared between their clasped hands, illuminating the bones within, and before he could even inspect the closed wounds of their palms, Coira launched herself into his arms.

"I love ye," she murmured against the skin of his neck. Malcolm laughed and fell back on the blanket. He kissed her forehead, her nose, her mouth—

Then he felt it… the strange but not unfamiliar feeling of something rooting beneath his skin. It traveled up his arm, over the globe of his shoulder, and settled within the hollow of his chest. A deep, thrumming purr crawled up his throat, and Coira looked at his sternum a moment before she pressed a reverent kiss over his heart.

"Yer beast is back," she whispered against his skin. "And now yer mine forever."

He could hear the smile in her voice, and she laid her ear atop his chest to listen to the drumming beat of his heart.

Malcolm closed his eyes, rubbed a lock of her hair between his fingers, and savored the fact that no matter what happened in their future, everything was going to be alright.

EPILOGUE

THE SLAVE

For thirteen long years, Lord Rothland has kept me Prisoner. Thirteen years I've been surrounded by death and despair, and now, I'm numb to it. The taint of my sinful deeds collected on my skin like layers of dirt fail to slough off my conscience when I wash my hands. And I *always* needed to wash my hands after a session with Lord Rothland.

"I'm tired, Fox," I mumbled as I picked underneath my nails with a tiny sliver of bone and scraped away the last of the blood. Disgusted, I flicked it onto the smooth floor of my cell.

Fox lifted his furry golden head from his place at my feet. He peered at me from over the lip of my bed pad and cocked his head.

My only companion for the last three years, Fox knew me better than I knew myself, and looked at me as though to say, *You just need a nap*, before he settled his blocky head on his paws and heaved a heavy sigh.

"Maybe I do," I grumbled and fell back on my bed. The ropes beneath the padding creaked, and even the brandy that sloshed through my veins wasn't strong enough to make my sleeping arrangements comfortable.

Even though I knew it was a wasted effort, I flayed around my bed on the off chance my movements would beat the lumps smooth. And just like always, I failed.

Drunk, and irritable, I bellowed at the rafters above until I ran out of breath. Seconds later I heard the metallic *snip* of the little peephole flip open and two beady eyes peered through the slat.

"What are ye lookin' at ye bumblin' half-wit?" I raged and lobbed the empty brandy bottle at the reinforced door. It shattered into a thousand pieces to rain down in a storm of anger and regret.

Disembodied laughter drifted through the thick door of my cell.

"Clean that up girl, or your pup will tear his pads," the guard said. I scowled at the door and the sound of his fading laughter.

On unsteady legs, I crossed the floor in seconds. I was so angry I barely felt the glass slice deep into the soles of my feet, and I slapped my hand upon the slat.

"My name is Ness, ye feckin' coward!" I yelled against the door.

I stood there waiting for a reply, my pulse hammering in my ears and my vision blurry, but none came. I slammed the meat of my fist against the door twice more. I should have known he wouldn't have risen to the bait. He'd said more than I've ever heard come out of a guard's mouth in the last three years, for there was one supreme rule in the prison, and the guards learned the hard way to follow it to the letter.

No one was allowed to talk to Lord Rothland's slave.

The End

Thank you for reading *The Oath*
The Assassin and the Slave will be the next installment of *The Grey Tower Chronicles*
Please consider leaving a review to help this story's success. It doesn't have to be long to make a difference, and they mean the world to an author.
Especially this one.

Acknowledgements

To my husband Josh, who is my muse and the source of unending support, I love you with all that I am, and all that I will become. Thank you for loving me the way you do and for giving me—however begrudgingly—our two beautiful little boys.

To Candice, who I know will cry as soon as she reads this, thank you for loving my writing. I'll never be able to convey what it means to me to have someone feel so strongly about something I've created. You make my heart warm, and I hope we meet someday soon.

To Christine—my PA and Alpha Bitch Supreme, without you my life would not be so organized! You are the thread to my fabric, and the conductor to my orchestra. Cheers to many more years together.

To my family, thank you for always supporting me.

To my Beta readers Geraldine and Amanda, thank you for all the helpful feedback!

To Jennilynn Wyer, who spent hours and hours combing through this book. You have helped me so much in the last two years, and I am so grateful for your keen eye and your ability to see what I cannot. You helped me make this book perfect.

To Coco, who brought my characters to life on this cover. I am in awe of you and your talent, and I can't wait to work with you in the years to come.

To Franzi, you designed the most beautiful lettering and naked cover. I bow to your talent!

To my wonderful editor, Patience Voight, thank you for taking me on as a client. I just know we're going to become great friends.

To Janet, thank you for proofreading for me and for always offering sage advice.

To Jessica—my work-wife and bestie, I just love you.

To Ashley and Danielle, though our lives are different, and we can go months without speaking, please know that I think of you often, if not daily. I love you both very much.

And a special thank you to the Bookstagram community. I have never felt more welcomed by a group of strangers, or so uplifted. @alexbetweenthepages @vanbuurenlibary @thebookwormadventures @thehsmatthews @alexinaribooks @old.enough.for.fairytales @tata.lifepages @literaryfaery @ve_xo @heartof.tati @_mkarys @_ckarys @bewareofthereader @anxioustatooedandbookish @author_l.c.son @canxdancexreads @all_book_great_and_small @bookqueenhm @mollys.must.books @listenbithbritt @book.reviewsbyjess @amajesticread @crosstitchandstories @mayaseranawriter @thebookishcamper @readit.with.red @ohyouread @obsessive.book.lover @nishireads @scotlandandbookobsessedmom @akindleincolorado @wendyhewlett_author @3starsandup @michaelwebbnovels @lisavalentine_89 @victoriabooklover

ABOUT THE AUTHOR

Jillian Bondarchuk lives in Charlotte, North Carolina where she is living her own happily ever after with her husband and two young children. When she is not writing, you can find her elbow-deep in hair color, murdering her houseplants, or with her nose in a book. Jillian loves to hear from her readers and makes the time to respond.

You can also subscribe to her newsletter for sneak peeks into upcoming works, access to bonus chapters, character interviews, and much more.

Scan the QR code for access to Jillian's social media, newsletter, and website information.